NEVER WALK
ALONE

NEVER WALK ALONE

Paula Detmer Riggs

AN ONYX BOOK

ONYX
Published by New American Library, a division of
Penguin Group (USA) Inc., 375 Hudson Street,
New York, New York 10014, U.S.A.
Penguin Books Ltd, 80 Strand,
London WC2R 0RL, England
Penguin Books Australia Ltd, 250 Camberwell Road,
Camberwell, Victoria 3124, Australia
Penguin Books Canada Ltd, 10 Alcorn Avenue,
Toronto, Ontario, Canada M4V 3B2
Penguin Books (N.Z.) Ltd. Cnr Rosedale and Airborne Roads,
Albany, Auckland 1310, New Zealand

Penguin Books Ltd, Registered Offices:
80 Strand, London WCLR 0RL, England

First published by Onyx, an imprint of New American Library,
a division of Penguin Group (USA) Inc.

ISBN:0-7394-3628-7

ACKNOWLEDGMENTS

Many thanks to Tom and Sandra Osborn for "lending" me their awesome midnight blue Kenworth rig—and for opening a whole new world to me in the process. Any errors in translation from the real world of long-haul trucking to the one I created for Rhys Hazard are mine.

Equal thanks to David Lindenauer for sharing his considerable knowledge of classic Corvettes. Again, any errors are mine.

This book has traveled a long road and a winding one. My formidable—and most patient—agent, Nancy Yost, has been at my side the entire way. Without her, I'd still be in a lonely ditch, trying to dig myself out.

And to the great editor at the end of that long road, Ellen Edwards, my most sincere appreciation.

Finally, as always, and forever, to Carl, my rock and my dearest love, thank you.

Chapter 1

Michael Rhys Hazard would rather take a beating than atted a
cocktail party.n

Alone in the private bathroom off his penthouse office, he
lifted his freshly shaved chin and studied his latest attempt to
wrestle a slippery black bow tie into submission. Six tries and
the frigging silk tie still looked like roadkill plastered against
his starched collar.

Even in a hand-tailored pleated shirt and antique onyx
studs, he was a blue-collar guy more at home in the cab of an
eighteen-wheeler than hanging around the ballroom of the Ritz
Carlton, where tonight's charity gala to benefit the Second
Chance Foundation was being held.

Fifteen years ago, when he'd started the Second Chance,
he'd had to beg for donations. There hadn't been any black-tie
bashes at five thousand dollars a ticket, no pictures in the society page of the *Arizona Republic,* no bragging rights at the
country clubs. More often than not his requests for money had
landed him back on the sidewalk, empty-handed and furious.

*Help ex-cons score jobs? Are you nuts, buddy? Let the mis-
erable assholes starve.*

He nearly had. When freight-hauling jobs had been scarce,
he'd lived on peanut butter and day-old bread. Sometimes
he'd gone hungry for a couple of days before he'd managed to
score a contract. He'd lived from job to job then, sometimes

bedding down in the cab of his rig in order to save enough on rent to buy fuel for the next run.

At the time, North Star Trucking had consisted of one third-hand long-haul Kenworth rig instead of the five hundred or more he owned these days. Before his company got too big for him to manage from that same cab, he hadn't owned a pair of pants and jacket that matched. The tuxedo he was wearing now, even one custom-tailored to accommodate his wider than average shoulders, made him feel trapped.

It had been more than ten years since he'd driven long-haul on a regular basis. These days he ran his company from the penthouse suite of the often photographed ten-story, glass and steel North Star Tower in downtown Phoenix. When he wasn't chairing a meeting of his board of directors or meeting one-on-one with high-end customers, he preferred well-worn Wranglers and comfortable work shirts.

Attending social functions was his executive VP Hank Dunnigan's responsibility. Networking with the money players, Hank called it. Making personal contact with other CEOs and executive VPs who were in a position to steer lucrative freight-hauling contracts in North Star's direction.

A dead bore was more like it. Lying about golf scores and exchanging stock tips weren't even blips on Rhys' personal radar screen. Why should they be? He couldn't play more than a couple of holes of golf before his bad hip started screaming. As for the stock market, forget it. Damn near every cent of his own money was tied up in shares of the company he'd single-handedly built into one of the largest freight-hauling businesses in the Western U.S.

Dunnigan had originally promised to represent North Star at this thing tonight, his last official act before assuming the position of chief operating officer of the new regional depot in central Washington. So where was the disloyal SOB now? On his way north, that's where. Claimed he needed to be settled in and up to speed when North Star Northwest officially opened in two days. Settled in, hell. The man just wanted to see what his new Jag would do on those long stretches of freeway between Phoenix and central Washington.

"Rhys, are you ready, sugar? Max is downstairs with the motor running, hyperventilating 'cause the traffic's already a mess." The voice was a low, sultry purr, the kind of voice another man might dream about in the loneliest hours of the night, but in this case, Ms. Odella Campbell-Browne was his adopted kid sister, not his lover. She was also his best friend—and one of the few people who knew he'd done hard time—and why.

"Della, get your world-class ass in here and fix this damn tie!" he bellowed.

Taking her sweet time the way he knew she would, the cheeky female finally sashayed into the room, a smug grin on her exotic café-au-lait face. Her dress was long, shimmering and the color of sunshine gilding a calm lake, and when she moved, it rippled over the curves of her body like a liquid flame. Her fanny-length ebony hair had been crimped into what she called a "Diana Ross in-your-face style," and the air seemed to crackle around her when she strutted on heels as high as stilts.

"My world-class *African* ass to you, boy," she chided with a sassy grin. "And don't go using that boardroom voice on me, you hear?"

"How about my 'I'm the boss and you're my dutiful assistant' voice?" he threatened.

Stunningly beautiful, Della had a face fashioned by benevolent angels. Rhys' seemed to have been thrown together out of leftover parts by a drunken demon. Her eyes were amber ringed with ebony and fringed with thick black lashes. His were the color of concrete, his short, dense lashes and brows bleached a couple of shades lighter than his hair. Her chin was rounded; his was square and gashed by a thin white scar. Her cheekbones were the stuff would-be models dream about. One of his had been smashed by a vicious left hook he hadn't seen coming and was a little lower than the other, giving his face a look Del called "outlaw sexy."

An unlikely pair for sure. Yet for the last thirteen years they'd made themselves into a family that was more satisfying than the dysfunctional units they'd each endured as kids. Now, as her golden eyes part teasing, part affectionate, twinkled back at him, he felt a lump form in his throat. Damn, but he was going to miss her daily nagging.

"I'm an exec-u-tive now, remember?" Glossy lips the color of ripe plums parted in a mischievous grin. "Director of Human Resources for North Star Northwest. Gonna have me a *fine* office right down the hall from Hank's, and my own assistant—as soon as I hire one." Her eyes laughed. "Mmm, mmm, I sure am looking forward to having some prime young stud prancing around my office. One with world-class buns. Now, turn around, hotshot, and let Odella tidy you up."

Rhys felt the corner of his mouth twitch. "That's *Mr.* Hotshot to you," he grumbled, glaring at her.

She chuckled and whacked him hard between the shoulder blades. Obediently, he turned to face her.

"Now that I'm not going to be around to nag you into taking care of yourself, you'd best be thinking about getting yourself a wife." Della leaned back slightly, her hands busy under his chin.

"I can take care of myself."

She snorted, concentrating on her task. Even when she was teasing, Del had a way of looking into a man's soul that was damn intimidating, especially to a guy who'd been hiding his feelings for more than half his life. "Man gets set in his ways without a good woman to love him into relaxing."

"I relax just fine."

"Uh-huh. Between the hours of midnight and five a.m. and only on the nights when your wonky hip isn't giving you fits, which isn't all that often." She leaned back to give him one of those measuring looks he hated. "And before you make one of your nasty remarks about love, it *does* exist."

"Sure it does, just like Bigfoot and honest politicians."

She tugged on the knot, all but shutting off his air. "One of these days, Rhys, you're going to turn a blind corner and there she'll be, that sweet, special lady your soul's been waiting to find."

Not a chance. Rhys was born alone and would die alone. "Bastards don't have souls."

Her frown said she pitied him. His gut knotted around a sudden flare of anger. He wanted pity about as much as he wanted what passed for love in this messed-up world. "Back off, Del. I asked you to fix the freaking tie, not play street corner shrink."

"And if I don't?"

"Then I'll toss you out on that fine African ass you're so proud of."

The woman had the nerve to laugh in his face. "Give it up, sugar. Last time you scared me was the first night we met, and that didn't last much past that glass of warm milk you all but forced down my throat."

Rhys felt his face soften. The woman sure knew how to work him. "I thought you were going to dump it over my head," he admitted.

Her laughter was rich with affection that touched him more than he wanted her to know. "I thought about it, but then you gave me that sweet smile you try so hard to hide, and I figured I could bully you real well after all."

"Yeah, well, don't let my drivers know what a wimp I am," he muttered, shifting more of his weight onto his good leg.

It'd been a long day, and he'd been on his feet too long. All but pulverized when he'd been seventeen, his pelvis and hip joint had been patched together in a series of operations that had enabled him to walk with the assistance of a sturdy cane— though not without considerable discomfort. Even when he wasn't on his feet, the ache was always there—sometimes dull, sometimes slicing white-hot through muscle and bone, especially when he moved too fast.

Tonight it was somewhere in between. By the time the evening wound down, however, it was a good bet his thigh muscles would be twisted into an angry, throbbing knot.

"By the way, you look . . . nice," he muttered when Del was finally finished.

"Well, shoot, sugar, I was aiming for knock-their-eyeballs-out sexy," she groused as she helped him into his tux jacket.

"Yeah, well, that, too." Too damn sexy by his reckoning. His protective instinct flared hot before he remembered she was nearly thirty and able to take care of herself. "The way that dress moves is definitely X-rated. Maybe I should ask Max to play bodyguard."

She shot him one of those indulgent looks that always made him feel like an overprotective ass. "Not to worry, big brother, I can handle these tame corporate wolves just fine." Mouth softening, she leaned up to kiss his chin. "But thanks for worrying about me."

"Part of a big brother's job description." He felt an ache in his chest. If things had been different, he might have married and had a daughter a lot like Del.

In the last six years since she'd come to work for him after earning her MBA at Arizona State, a lot of local studs had tried to seduce Ms. Campbell-Browne, but the lady was picky. Claimed she was holding out for her soul mate—whatever the hell that was. Him, he had resigned himself to occasional affairs with women who were looking for affection and regular sex with a guy whose blood was virus free if not purebred.

Suddenly tired, he flexed his shoulders in the confining tuxedo jacket and reached for the hickory cane propped against the cabinet. "Make a note to dun Hank for an extra thou as penance for dumping this on me," he ordered.

Della grinned as she flipped off the light and followed him

into the office. Beyond the windows the city was spread out like a mystical fairyland. Over the years he'd come to love this place. It was as raw and hungry as he'd been when he'd arrived eighteen years earlier, with the prison stench still clinging to his skin and everything he owned stuffed into a secondhand backpack.

"I'm going to miss this place," Della murmured as she draped an embroidered silk shawl over her shoulders.

"You'll be back too often to miss it." As he retrieved his wallet from his desk drawer and tucked it into the inside pocket of the tux, Rhys fought a sudden need to pull her into his arms and keep her close. Hell of a thing, feeling like he was being abandoned when he was the one who'd convinced her she was ready to handle an executive position.

"Maybe I'll . . . I'll learn to ski." She offered him a smile that was a little too bright. Though she lowered her lashes, he saw that her eyes were suspiciously damp. "So I can impress you when you come up to visit—"

"No visits, Del," he declared with enough of an edge in his voice to make the point nonnegotiable.

Her smile faded. "Rhys, it's been over twenty years since . . . well, *since*. Like you told me once, a person isn't her past. Or *his*."

"Leave it be." He retrieved his keys and the battered notebook he'd started carrying to keep track of his expenses when he was on the road.

"But, Rhys, Osuma was your home. You grew up there. Once the people who, well, who hated you find out—"

"They won't." He slammed the desk drawer shut. "If you're ready, we'd best—"

The phone rang, interrupting them. A quick look told him it was his private line. Only his senior executives knew that number. "Probably Hank wanting to give me a list of people to suck up to," he muttered as he grabbed the receiver. "Hazard here."

The voice on the other end was a clear tenor flavored with a slight accent Rhys couldn't place. "Mr. Hazard, this is Dr. Limchee at San Francisco General Hospital."

Rhys felt a cold hand squeeze his chest. Hank had planned to stop off in the Bay Area to take care of some personal business before driving north. Before he could snap out the questions rocketing around in his head, the doctor went on. "Your name is listed as next of kin for one of my patients, a Mr. Henry Cruz Dunnigan."

Rhys felt the blood drain from his face. What breath he managed to suck in froze in his throat. "Sweet Jesus," he managed on a thin trickle of air. "Hank's . . . been killed?"

"Oh no, please, *no,*" Della cried softly, hurrying to his side.

"No, no, I'm sorry, that was tactless of me," the doctor went on quickly, his tone staccato with embarrassment. "Mr. Dunnigan was involved in a multicar pileup on the Bayshore Freeway late this afternoon. According to the CHP, a delivery van in the lane next to Mr. Dunnigan blew a tire and swerved into his lane. In trying to avoid a collision, he hit a guardrail. He is severely injured, yes, but he's expected to survive."

Weak with relief, Rhys fumbled for his chair and sat down heavily. Della clutched his shoulder and he lifted a hand to press hers. "How bad are his injuries?"

"Severe concussion, two crushed vertebrae, a shattered knee and a ruptured spleen, which I've removed. He's in recovery now."

"He . . ." Rhys paused to clear his throat. "His back, will he be . . . paralyzed?"

The pause that followed had his stomach filling with acid. "His spinal cord is badly bruised, but intact." The doctor's voice was carefully without inflection. "Nevertheless, it's too soon to tell how much permanent damage has been done—if any."

"Man's tough. He'll handle it." Rhys squeezed Della's hand, and she murmured a soft prayer of thanks. He closed his eyes and added a silent amen before taking a shaky breath. "Tell him . . ." He had to stop when his throat seized tight. "Tell him his friends will be there as soon as my pilot can get the plane in the air."

Dawn was still hours away when the midnight blue Gulfstream IV with the silver shooting star on the tail lifted off the runway with North Star's chief pilot, Skip Tanner, at the controls. Though the jet's plush blue-and-silver interior could accommodate twelve, Rhys and Della were the only passengers. A white-knuckle flyer who swallowed airsick pills like candy, Del fell asleep almost instantly, curled into the corner of one of the cushy, butt-pampering couches.

Too wired to close his eyes, Rhys reached for the phone built into the bulkhead. Though it was well past midnight, his senior executives were used to receiving middle-of-the-night calls from their insomniac boss. Since he paid them extremely well for the privilege, none complained—at least not in his hearing.

His first call was to Joan Majenek, the blunt-spoken, fortyish former schoolteacher who had taken Del's place as his executive assistant.

Forty-five minutes later, he'd updated the handful of people who needed to know about Hank's condition, made several time-sensitive business decisions and rearranged his schedule. He rose stiffly and sought out a Mountain Dew in the galley kitchen's compact fridge. He'd downed the drink by the gallons when he'd been driving.

Rhys rarely drank the hard stuff. He'd tried that a few times in the early days when he'd still been full of bitterness. After waking up with a head the size of a flathead V-8 and a full-on hurricane raging in his gut, he'd decided the few hours of numbness he managed to achieve weren't worth the price. Besides, no matter how drunk he got, the images in his head never went away.

Soda in hand, he settled into a thickly padded armchair by the oversized windows. Beyond the panes was an ink black night, with only the stars and the strobe on the upturned wingtips cutting the darkness. Bone tired, he rested the soda can on the chair arm, his eyes heavy-lidded and stinging. He could hardly believe how much had changed in the last few hours. It had taken months of planning and work to put this deal together, months during which he'd been reminded on a daily basis of memories he'd fought hard to suppress.

It had been the first week in September last year when he'd flipped on CNN in the middle of a restless night and seen the stark images of flooding in the Osuma Valley in central Washington. All the towns in the area had been affected, but the worst hit had been the town where he grew up.

His grandfather Dubois had taught him to fish for salmon in the Columbia and trout in the Wenatchee, both of which had overflowed their banks. A few miles before the Wenatchee spilled into the Columbia, the smaller river made a wide, sweeping circle around the town where a pretty little island provided sanctuary for countless waterfowl. Years earlier the Army Corps of Engineers had constructed dikes to contain the spring runoff from the slopes. Usually the dikes worked just fine.

This year, however, warm spring rains had hastened the thaw, resulting in the worst flood in more than a century. Like a wild beast slamming against the bars of a too small cage, the river had finally burst free, surging over the battered dikes in a seething rush. Snuggled tidily into a picturesque bowl formed by the Cascade Range, the village of Osuma had struggled to withstand the pounding of silt-heavy torrents tearing through the streets.

One by one the gaily painted chalets with their fringe of bright gingerbread had been swallowed by the churning brown water until all but the higher sections of the town were underwater. Outside the city limits, where thousands of acres of rich

bottomland produced the pears and apples that provided virtually half the jobs in the valley, the devastation had been even
worse. To his surprise, it had torn him up inside when he'd
seen the muddy water splintering trees that he himself had
helped plant.

As soon as the waters had receded, he'd sent Hank north to
check out the situation. Damage in the valley itself had ranged
from slight to severe. In the town proper only the houses on
the ridges and a small enclave of historic homes on the northern edge of the business district had escaped with minimal
damage.

In contrast, the town's central district had been decimated,
the old buildings filled with silt, the contents ruined. Motels,
restaurants and shops had been forced to close for repairs and
renovations. According to even the most optimistic projections, Osuma was facing years of rebuilding before the econ-
omy could be restored to anything approaching its former
prosperity.

Surprisingly, however, Sullivan and Son's huge fruit-packing
warehouse located six miles to the northwest of town had survived virtually unscathed, largely due to the cement slab floor
and reinforced concrete block walls. The outbuildings had
been hit harder but were still structurally sound. Without fruit
to pick, however, the shed had been forced to close.

As soon as Hank had told him the facility was for sale at a
price far below preflood value, Rhys had given serious
thought to snapping it up. The grounds were big enough for a
hundred trucks, and the maintenance bays were already
equipped to handle heavy diesels. Though in need of modern-
ization, the facility even had a fuel depot. Bottom line, with
only a minimal outlay of cash, the warehouse could be turned
into a freight depot.

Though he hadn't planned to expand into the fast-growing
Northwestern U.S.–Canadian market for another year or two,
Rhys had run the numbers with his chief financial officer, then

called in his lawyers. After his financial people had torn through Sullivan's books, Rhys had sent Hank north with an opening bid.

J. T. Sullivan had proved to be a tough negotiator, which Rhys had expected. What he hadn't expected were some of the terms the big Irishman had demanded—an executive position for his son, John Thomas Junior, who'd been Sullivan's director of sales and marketing, and an ironclad guarantee of jobs for any of his former warehouse employees who applied.

Hank had strongly advised against hiring Junior, who'd done squat to build the business, even with the explosion of demand in the Pacific Rim countries for premium fruit. *The old man looks tough as hell, but he's got his balls to the wall. He's got to cave to save his financial ass,* Hank had argued. However, J. T. had held firm.

Because Rhys had wanted the deal, he'd accepted the man's terms, with two provisos. Sullivan employees were to be subjected to the same drug screening and polygraph testing as any new hires. Once on the payroll, they were guaranteed employment for a maximum of twelve months only—as long as no company policies were violated. After that, they would rise or fall on their own merits. That had been *his* bottom line. Non-negotiable. He figured Junior would step on his own dick eventually and Hank would be justified in cutting him loose.

Three months ago today he'd signed the papers transferring ownership of J. T. Sullivan's pride and joy to North Star Trucking, Inc. He had leveraged himself way too thin personally to make the deal happen so quickly, but in the end he'd had no choice. Smiling grimly, he lifted his can of Mountain Dew in a symbolic salute to the burly redheaded Irishman he'd once worshipped.

"Here's to family loyalty, Pop," he said in a low, deadly tone he'd developed in prison to keep the predators at bay. "I hope you choked on those damn escrow papers."

Chapter 2

Despite the two alarm clocks she'd set the night before, Brina Sullivan overslept. It was, she knew, a serious violation of the *The Successful Innkeeper's Guide to Gracious Hospitality*. Rule Six, in fact. *The Successful Innkeeper never keeps a guest waiting for even the most minor service.*

She had a long way to go before she lived up to that standard, something she'd learned during what she'd come to call her shakedown period, when she'd been trying to make the transition from stay-at-home mom to savvy, organized businesswoman.

You're going to run a bed-and-breakfast? her ex-husband John had sneered after she'd laid out a large chunk of her divorce settlement for a sadly neglected three-story, twenty-room inn in Osuma's historic district. Built in 1890—and once the most famous bawdy house in the Northwest—the turreted, multigabled Victorian mansion had been in desperate need of tender loving care—in other words, major refurbishing.

Brina had accepted her first guest two years ago July 3 and had been well on her way to making Nightingale House a success when the flood had torn off the front porch and deposited an inch of silt in the first-floor rooms.

Like just about everyone else's in the area, her insurance hadn't covered acts of nature—or God, depending on one's point of view. Either way, she'd been facing bankruptcy when

Henry Dunnigan had come riding to her rescue in a rented red Lexus. The option he'd taken on four of the inn's nine rooms—including board—for a minimum of three months, prepaid, allowed her to catch up on her payments to the bank with enough left over to repair the porch and muck out the silt. The rest of the scouring and painting and refinishing she'd done herself.

After a marathon work session ending at exactly 2:45 this morning, she'd finished the last of her pre–North Star's arrival projects—putting up a Victorian-era light fixture in Mr. Dunnigan's room. She took a moment to bask in the glow of her accomplishments, then steeled herself and tossed off the covers.

Once the living quarters for the servants who'd kept the elegant brothel running smoothly for more than thirty years, the four rooms and a bath on the third floor now served as a private apartment for Brina and her two kids. Who, because it was Saturday, were still blissfully snoozing.

Still groggy, her curly dark brown hair in its usual hideous bird's nest tangle, Brina dressed in a button-down oxford cloth shirt, hand-knitted sweater and her last pair of clean jeans. After slipping her feet into her favorite slides, she hurried across the narrow landing sandwiched between the front and back stairs to the bathroom. Ten minutes later, her face scrubbed clean, her hair anchored haphazardly atop her head with antique chopsticks, and her eyes still slightly unfocused, she clattered down two flights to the kitchen.

By the time she'd rustled up a full gourmet breakfast for her two permanent guests, it was a few minutes before 8:00, the precise time when she was due downtown for a meeting of the Welcome North Star committee. Fortunately, her boarders were dear souls—more like family, really.

"You run ahead, dear," Miss Ernestine Winkle urged with her usual sweet humor. "Colonel Fitz and I can clean up after ourselves." They would, too—and then make sure Marcy and Jay ate a good breakfast when they finally surfaced.

After jamming her arms into her old yellow slicker, Brina tucked her meeting notes into a folder and raced through the driving rain to the twelve-year-old van they'd bought when Jay had been born. After an awful moment when the hit-or-miss starter turned obstinate, the engine choked to life.

To make up time she shot down the alley behind the inn, then detoured through the parking lot of the Presbyterian church to Elm. Noticing that the barrier was finally down on Maple, where rushing water had undercut the foundations on several old homes, she braked hard, then took the corner on two wheels.

Before the flood, this first weekend in May had been one of the most profitable of the entire year. Tourists had booked months and sometimes years ahead for Osuma's famous Maifest. In the recent past, several movie companies had incorporated the colorful Maypole dance in their films. The six square blocks of shops, restaurants and beer gardens that made up Osuma's city center would have been thronged with visitors from early morning until late at night. Now the streets were virtually deserted.

Wanda's Waffle Haus was on Alpine just three blocks from the recently reconstructed band shell. After parking as close to the entrance as possible, Brina sprinted to the door. Dripping raindrops, she entered to a steamy wall of noise, heat and the mouthwatering smells of bacon and fresh-brewed coffee.

Built originally to house a saloon in the heyday of the post–World War I logging boom, the long, narrow building had whitewashed brick walls and exposed, rough-cut beams. The main dining room was decorated with mismatched oaken tables and chairs, the tablecloths a homey blue-and-white check.

Two women chatting near the hostess station looked up as she let the door slam behind her. Wanda Kemperer, in a pink waitress uniform, had big hair, perfect teeth and a size two figure Brina had always coveted.

The other woman, Lucy Steinberg, was tall and bony with
piercing bottle-green eyes that seemed to bore through pretense like lasers, and an imperious nose just shy of hawklike.
An unabashed spinster at sixty-four, she was first cousin to
Brina's late mother-in-law, Marceline Dubois Sullivan—and
about a million times more likable.

As was her habit, Lucy wore baggy pants, an ivory fisherman's sweater that she herself had knitted (badly), and Birkenstocks with argyle socks. Her iron gray hair had recently been
shorn ruthlessly short, revealing a surprisingly graceful neck.
Emerald studs the size of peas glittered in her earlobes. The
town's only graduate horticulturist, she owned and operated
Lucy's Garden Shop and Nursery, which had recently reopened after extensive renovations.

"Hey, there she is now!" Wanda exclaimed as Brina did her
best to drip on the rubber mat instead of the pine plank flooring. "Lucy was getting worried."

Lucy studied Brina with critical eyes. "You look peckish,
girl. Have you been dieting again?"

When wasn't she dieting? "I'm not peckish; I'm sleepy. I
was finishing a project until the wee hours and slept through
both alarms."

"I thought you planned to use some of the advance from
North Star to hire those things done," Wanda said.

Because she was with friends, Brina allowed herself the
luxury of complaining. "That was before John missed three
support payments."

"Again?"

"Apparently it came down to a choice between supporting
his children or taking the spandex slut to Vegas for two
weeks."

"What does John's father have to say about that?" Lucy
asked as Brina handed Wanda her folder so that she could

hang her slicker on one of the old-fashioned brass hooks lining the entrance.

"I'm not sure J. T. knows that John's been missing payments," she hedged because she found it hard to criticize a man who was a softhearted darling despite his rough edges.

Lucy's eyes flashed. "Then tell him! It's time he faced up to the mistakes he made with that boy."

Brina pushed back a lock of hair that was threatening to topple. "It's too late for that, Luce. John stopped caring what his father thinks of him a long time ago."

Lucy gave her a sour look that acknowledged the skewed dynamics between father and son. Marceline Sullivan had doted on her younger son and spoiled him rotten. The world had always revolved around Johnny as a child. As an adult he saw no reason to change that. Whatever influence J. T. had had with his patrician wife had been lost years ago, and nothing had changed in that regard since her death last year.

"I'll have Shirl bring coffee to the back room right away," Wanda said, returning the folder before moving to the cash register to ring up a bill.

At the same time, the door suddenly swung open, and J. T. himself was all but blown inside. Big, bluff and imposing, he wore a red-and-black flannel work shirt and faded black cords that hugged long, muscle-thick thighs and sturdy calves. For a man who had just turned sixty-nine, he seemed remarkably fit physically.

Beneath the brim of his faded red Sullivan and Son ball cap, his pale blue eyes lit up at the sight of Brina. "Well now, this is an unexpected pleasure on a gray day," he said before bending to kiss her cheek. She caught a whiff of rain and Old Spice along with the distinctive smell of wet flannel.

"You're looking good, J. T."

"Nice of you to say so, darlin' girl. You look ravishing as always." His gaze shifted, then locked on Lucy's unsmiling face. "Top o' the morning, Miss Lucy."

She inclined her head in a regal nod. Her voice was cool, her expression severe. "J. T."

His eyes narrowed before he turned his attention back to Brina. "So, tell me, lass, how are my grandbabies?"

"Marcy's bubbling over about the cap and gown she gets to wear for her graduation from kindergarten next month, and Jay thinks everything and everyone, especially his mother, is either 'gross' or 'bogus.'"

J. T. chuckled. Someone at one of the tables near the entrance called a greeting his way and he returned a wave before asking, "You ladies comin' or goin'?"

"Coming," Brina explained. "I'm here for a meeting of the parade committee." She shot Lucy a teasing look before adding, "The chairman's a real taskmaster, you know. Rules us with an iron hand."

His gaze drifted to Lucy once more. An expression Brina could only call wistful flitted over his weathered features before he looked her way again. "Goin' to be a real wingding of a party, I hear."

Wanda asked a passing waitress to take the coffeepot around, then greeted J. T. "Don't know if I mentioned it before, but Jackson and I are right sorry you had to sell out."

He acknowledged that with a genial smile that didn't quite reach his eyes. "Not any more sorry than I am. But it's done."

"Both my brothers hired on with Sullivan's right out of high school. They were goin' to have to relocate until you finessed that deal with North Star. Just got letters from a Ms. Campbell-Browne, both of them, setting up interviews for the week after next."

J. T. lifted a hand to the back of his neck. "Glad to hear it. It was a concern."

"For all of us, too," Wanda said, "especially my sis-in-law Becky—you remember her, Brin? She was a cheerleader with you your senior year."

"Sure. Her Mason and my Jay are in the same homeroom at Valley Middle School."

Wanda frowned at a busboy who wasn't moving fast enough, before rushing on. "Well, anyway, Becky nearly had herself a nervous breakdown at the thought of leaving her mom and dad. She said it was the worst thing she could imagine, being forced to leave the only home you've ever known."

"Especially if you were told you could never come back again—not even if you wanted to," Lucy interjected, her piercing gaze fixed on J. T.'s face. "Right, John Thomas?"

A dull red tinge bled upward from the V of his shirt collar to darken his cheeks. "I never said he couldn't come back eventually," he said in a tight voice so unlike J. T.'s normally upbeat tone that Brina found herself staring.

"Didn't you?" Lucy shot back. "Funny, I doubt your son would agree." Before he could answer, she turned her attention Brina's way and snapped out brusquely, "If you're ready, we have work to do." Without waiting for an answer Lucy marched off toward the private dining room in the rear.

Wanda and Brina exchanged puzzled looks before Brina turned to J. T. to ask, "What's Lucy talking about, J. T.?"

His jaw flexed. "She was talking about Michael," he replied, his voice strained.

Brina felt a hole open in the bottom of her stomach. For years she couldn't think about John's older brother without experiencing a sickening rush of bitter hatred. From the look of revulsion on Wanda's face, Brina was pretty sure she shared the town's deep-seated anger against J. T.'s elder son.

"Is that why Michael didn't come home after he got out of prison?" Brina asked, her voice thin. "Because you wouldn't let him?"

"Ask Lucille," he grated with what sounded like bitter frustration. "She's the one who has all the answers."

*   *   *

Ninety minutes later Lucy wound up the meeting with a reminder that they would get together again next Saturday same place, same time. As was her custom, Lucy remained behind to collect her thoughts and make final notes. Brina lingered over her coffee, waiting until Lucy finished writing.

"Is it true J. T. refused to let Michael come home?" Brina asked, her tone low and terse.

Lucy was silent for a long moment, her green eyes troubled. Finally she shook her head. "I'm sorry, Brina. It's not my story to tell."

Much as she would like to, Brina didn't push. Experience had taught her that Lucy was unmovable when she stood on principle. Still, she couldn't help saying, "I was a part of the Sullivan family for eleven years, and this is the first time anyone ever mentioned Michael's name in my presence."

It was as though the entire Sullivan family had decided to pretend he'd never existed. In fact, her two children didn't even realize their dad had a brother. Or that their father had been the star witness against him at the trial that had resulted in a four-year prison sentence.

"Come to think of it, I don't recall seeing a picture of Michael in the photo albums Marceline kept so carefully. Not even in the family groups."

"You wouldn't," Lucy said as she shoved her notes into her well-worn briefcase. "If Marceline could have had Mick's birth certificate canceled, she would have."

Something in her tone sharpened Brina's attention. "You don't like talking about him either, do you?"

Lucy compressed her lips in a thoughtful frown before sighing heavily. "Michael—Mickey—is my godson, Brina. I loved him dearly when he lived here, and I love him now."

"I'm not sure I would be as generous if I were in your place," Brina admitted in a tight voice.

Lucy smiled briefly. "I've never denied that Mick made a

terrible mistake, but he paid an equally terrible price. Worse, I think, than we can know or perhaps even imagine."

Suddenly, Brina felt all the old anger surging up from a dark, angry place deep inside her. "What about the price I paid?" she asked, her voice lashing out with enough force to make Lucy wince. "Or the Schotts? Or Mr. Gregory's wife and *five* children? Our lives were changed forever because of Michael Sullivan."

"I can't deny that, Brina. Nor, I suspect, would he—if he'd had the chance."

"What you're saying is that J. T. was afraid to give him that chance. Isn't that it? Afraid folks here would make good on some of the threats going around during the trial?"

When Lucy remained stubbornly silent, Brina drained her cup, then pushed it away. "I don't know why I'm even talking about this," she said as she dug into her purse for her wallet. "To tell you the truth, I couldn't care less what happened to Michael Sullivan once the marshals took him away." She picked up her check and her notes before rising. "But whatever it was, it couldn't be horrible enough to make up for what he did. Nothing can ever do that."

Sorrow darkened Lucy's eyes. "It's not like you to be so unforgiving, Brin."

Brina sucked in a harsh breath. "In case you've forgotten, Michael Sullivan killed my brother. How can I possibly forgive that?"

The private hospital room had soft blue walls and the latest in monitoring equipment built into a console behind the bed. Two well-worn armchairs had been jammed into a space big enough for one. Rhys was slouched in the nearer of the two, the sleeves of his shirt rolled to his biceps, his bad leg propped up on the bottom rail of the bed.

"You still here?" Hank Dunnigan asked, his voice thick with sleep and slightly slurred.

Rhys glanced up from the financial report he was reading. "Seem to be, yeah. How are you feeling?"

"Better. At least it doesn't hurt to blink my eyes."

The voice of the paging operator told Hank that the shift had changed. After two—or was it three?—days, he was becoming used to the routine. "What is today, Sunday?"

"Last I checked it was Monday, May 3." Rhys' thick sunbleached eyebrows rose above the thin gold rims of the reading glasses he'd recently acquired. "Why? You got a hot date?"

"Hardly." Hank hadn't dated in a long time. "Is Del grabbing coffee downstairs?"

Rhys shook his head before pushing his glasses to the top of his head. "She kept falling asleep in the middle of a sentence, so I sent her back to the Fairmont to get some sleep. She'll be back in time to feed you more of that white junk for supper."

Hank studied the hard knot between his friend's aggressive eyebrows. Rhys almost always played his cards close, even in minor matters. Hank suspected it came from clawing his way up alone for so many high-pressured years. Somehow he'd retained his decency and compassion, both rare qualities in the trucking industry—and in life.

"What time does Del's plane leave tomorrow?"

"First thing tomorrow morning. Seems she couldn't wrangle a seat on the commuter from Seattle to Wenatchee until the end of the week, so Tanner's flying her up. Plan is for him to do a quick turnaround so I can be in Phoenix for the board meeting Wednesday afternoon."

Hank had forgotten about the board meeting. Several of the members—all major stockholders—had begun grumbling about the flat line in the company's profits because of the huge and unanticipated start-up costs for the Northwest division.

To assuage their fears Rhys had ordered his chief financial officer to work up profit projections for North Star Northwest that were intended to offset the poor showing for the parent company this quarter. Provided NSN started bringing in revenue within two months as Hank had planned.

"Looks like I really fouled up your schedule," he said.

Rhys shrugged. "Can't be helped. Besides, Limchee's call came just in time to save me from that damn fool charity thing." His grin flashed, the too rare, surprisingly mischievous one that never failed to both amaze and sadden Hank. Buried somewhere inside the hard, cynical man he knew as M. Rhys Hazard was a little towheaded boy known as Michael Rhys Sullivan who, Hank suspected, had once laughed a lot.

"CHP couldn't find my briefcase or laptop at the scene of the accident, but Elena has copies of my disks," Hank said. "Franklyn and Scruggs are due in on . . . uh, Wednesday."

Rhys leaned forward to tug a small wallet-sized leather notebook from the back pocket of his Wranglers. Using the stub of a pencil tucked inside, he made a note before glancing up again. His eyes were heavy-lidded and deep-set, giving him a sleepy look that was deceptive. It hadn't taken Hank long to figure out that Rhys' agile mind was always alert. Especially when he seemed half asleep, in fact. Like a big cat luring his prey into a false sense of security.

"When is Elena due to arrive in Osuma?" Rhys asked.

As Hank answered that and a long list of questions from Rhys, his brain began to grow fuzzy, the effect of the painkillers kicking in. It became more of a struggle to reply.

"Anything else I should know?" Rhys asked finally.

An image of a woman with big brown eyes and a mess of corkscrew curls piled in a crazy knot atop her head shimmered just beyond Hank's haze.

"Nightingale House," he thought aloud. "Junior's ex. 'Member, I told you she ran the B and B where we're staying?"

Rhys' expression turned glacial. "And I told *you* I'm not interested in hearing anything even remotely related to that son of a bitch, John Sullivan," he said, returning the notebook to his pocket.

"Ex-wife's not bad, though. Matter of fact, she's damn easy to like." Hank searched for a name to go with the dark-eyed gypsy who'd made his weeklong stay so pleasant. "Has a coupla sweet kids. Little girl as cute as a button and a half-grown boy who feels too much and is terrified someone will find out."

"Is there a point to this, Dunnigan, or are you taking a side trip for your own amusement?" Rhys' voice was as frigid as his eyes.

"Point I was making, Ms. Sullivan expected Del and me to check in today. Don't want her to think we're reneging on our agreement."

"Del took care of it. Said the two of you had been unavoidably delayed. Thought that was best until we knew for sure what was happening."

Hank took a moment to process that. "You have a reason for not being more specific?"

Rhys rubbed absently at a spot just below his sternum with a large, scarred hand. "Truth is, I'm not real eager to see North Star stock take another major hit, which would be pretty much a given if the word got out that the new division is without a COO before it's even opened its doors."

"So you do realize you're going to have to handle this yourself, don't you?" Hank asked.

Awkwardly, Rhys struggled up from the chair and, without meeting Hank's eye, grabbed his cane and went to the window. Keeping his back to the bed, he slid his free hand into the back pocket of his jeans and stared out at the fog-shrouded city.

Hank waited, accustomed to Rhys' occasional black moods. "I was homesick for years before I managed to convince myself I was well shut of that frigging town," Rhys said after a long moment. "I'd be crazy to go back to a place that hates my guts." The words were clipped and cold.

"You'd know that better than me, of course." Hank waited a beat, then took a chance. "You could always turn things over to your little brother until I'm up to speed."

Rhys whipped his head around. "Don't push it, Dunnigan. I'm not in the mood."

Hank steadied his gaze on those haunted gray eyes. "Go back, Rhys. Make peace with the past that's been eating you up inside for more than half your life."

Rhys stared, then frowned. The anger faded from his eyes, replaced by a bleak look. "How does a man make peace with what I did?" he asked in a voice that was barely above a whisper.

Hank's smile was gently chiding. "I'm no expert, but you might start with forgiving yourself for being alive."

Chapter 3

Even before Hank had laid the painful truth on him, Rhys had known he would be heading to Osuma before the week was out. Expansion was always a risk, but this one was especially vulnerable since he knew just how close the new depot came to being underfinanced. Knowing that Hank would fight hard to make it work had been one of the factors that had encouraged him to take a calculated risk.

Maybe with a few weeks' lead time he could have found and trained the right person to put in Hank's place. Problem was, he needed someone he could trust not to screw it up, and that list was damn short. Four, maybe five people, tops. Key people in Phoenix who would be equally difficult to replace. Handling it himself was the only logical choice. Much as he hated the very idea of walking into that damn warehouse again, he hated the idea of maybe screwing up North Star's bottom line even more.

Short on sleep and even shorter on patience, he chafed when fog delayed their takeoff from San Francisco, then fought an acute attack of claustrophobia for three hours when they were forced to fly through that same thick cloud cover all the way to Washington.

It was spitting rain when Tanner landed at Wenatchee's Pangborn Memorial Airport a few minutes before nine a.m. Though the overcast had thinned, the air below was still dank and cool, seeping deep into Rhys' bones as he limped from the plane to the squat redbrick terminal. Because he'd had a gut feeling he just might be heading north before the week was out, he'd called his driver, Max Stillwell, on Sunday and ordered him to drive up to Osuma, just in case.

Having arrived late Monday, Max was waiting at the airport with the Mercedes S600 that Rhys found more comfortable than a limo. Still half asleep from the airsick pills, Del curled into one corner of the backseat while Rhys settled into the other.

The heavy sedan rocked gently as Max slammed down the trunk. An ex–professional boxer who outweighed Rhys by a good seventy pounds, most of it in his rock-hard biceps and bull neck, Stillwell had served eight years for involuntary manslaughter. The man he'd killed had been his brother-in-law—and a wife beater. When his sister ended up in the hospital one too many times, Max had decided to teach the mean bruiser a lesson. One of his body blows had ruptured the man's aorta.

Hooked up with Second Chance by his parole officer, Max had applied to North Star as a short-haul relief driver. Ben Jacobs in personnel had liked the man's blunt honesty and had mentioned him to Rhys one day after a staff meeting. After a week's tryout, Rhys had offered him the chauffeuring job. They'd been together five years now, an association that pleased them both.

"There's a bridge out on Route 2," Max said as he slid behind the wheel. "Had to take a detour through hell and gone to get to the airport," he added as he snapped the belt in place. "Reminded me of one of them cheesy disaster movies."

Damn appropriate, Rhys decided as as Max started the car.

"You want music, boss?" he asked, watching Rhys in the rearview.

"Please."

As Mozart drifted through the speakers, mellow and smooth,

Rhys leaned back and stared at the glowering clouds. The Mercedes glided through the streets of Wenatchee and over the bridge spanning the mighty Columbia River, which swallowed the much smaller Wenatchee a few miles downstream. Wide awake now, Della glued her nose to the window and sucked up the ambiance. A native Californian who'd never been to the Northwest, she was fascinated by the wide rivers and tree-covered hills. As they headed south, the evidence of the flood's cruelty grew more pronounced.

"It's a lot like pictures I've seen of Hiroshima after the bomb," she observed as they passed yet another patch of barren, water-scoured earth where prime Bosc and Bartlett pear trees had once flourished. "It's hard to imagine those raw fields covered with trees."

Rhys flicked a reluctant glance at the passing landscape. This was Sullivan land, had been for the past mile or so. "Place used to look like a blizzard in the spring when the petals dropped," he remembered aloud as Max slowed for a corkscrew curve. The entire valley had smelled of pear blossoms for weeks.

"Looks like they've replanted some," Max commented, accelerating again. "Be a while before them little bitty trees bring on fruit, though."

"Six years," Rhys told him, picturing the seedlings growing sturdy. Bloody hard work, grubbing out stumps, even with the orchard's monster Cat. No doubt the bloody stubborn Irish SOB, J. T. Sullivan, had done most of the grunt work himself.

"Is that the Wenatchee River down there on the flat?" Del asked after a moment's silence.

"Yeah, that's the sucker that did all the damage." Ahead, the jagged peaks of the Cascades were lost in the low-lying cloud cover while below, splintered trees that had stood for decades offered stark evidence of the flood's savagery.

They drove in silence for several minutes before Max said,

"Intersection comin' up, boss. Don't see no detour sign point-ing the way, though."

Rhys directed a quick look ahead. When he realized where they were, it sucked the air out of his lungs and ground rocks in his belly. Whoever said God didn't have a mean streak was dead wrong. "Make a left onto Old Orchard Road, then pull to the shoulder and stop."

Precise as always, Max signaled the turn, then pulled to the berm, letting the big engine idle while he waited for further in-structions. Curious, Del cast a quick look around before fas-tening her attention on a four-foot-tall slab of rough granite standing a dozen or so feet from the pavement.

"Is this where it happened?" she asked quietly.

He nodded, his throat constricting.

"Do you want me to come with you?"

He shook his head. "Stay inside where it's dry. This won't take long."

Max shut off the engine and pushed back the seat. Gritting his teeth, Rhys climbed out, then reached back for his cane. Outside the sheltering warmth of the car, rain pelted his shoul-ders and tore at the Stetson he'd pulled low over his forehead as he crossed the rain-slick pavement.

The skid marks from his pickup were long gone, as were the gouges made in the graveled shoulder where the school bus had come to a metal-splintering stop. No sign remained of the blood or mangled wreckage.

The memorial stone hadn't been here twenty-two years ago when he'd been driven past this same spot in a prison van on his way to McNeil Island Corrections Center on the Seattle side of the Cascades. Three names were carved on the smooth face. Theodore Paul Eiler Jr. and Stefan Peter Schott were classmates at Osuma High. A couple of fourteen-year-old kids who'd had the back luck to sit on the wrong side of the bus that afternoon. The third name was that of the driver, Anson Richard Gregory.

Rhys' eyes stung as he stared at the lonely expanse of road winding upward at a steep angle. He remembered hurtling down Old Orchard Road, his eyes burning with tears and sobs shaking his chest. He'd seen the school bus heading along the intersecting highway, seen the light ahead of him turning green, seen a flash of yellow as the bus kept coming.

At the moment of impact he'd gone through the windshield, catapulted like a sack of grain onto the pavement. He remembered the crunch of his pelvic bones as he landed and the searing agony as iced-over ruts as sharp as razors sliced his back to ribbons.

The wind had been brutal that day in December, freezing tears he hadn't known he'd shed to his cheeks and eyelashes. With every breath, he'd drawn in the stink of diesel fuel—along with the coppery smell of blood. He had no idea how long he'd lain in the snow helpless and in agony before someone had stopped. Someone else had called the paramedics.

Later in ICU, swathed in bandages and plaster, he'd been bewildered to find himself shackled to the bed. The hard-faced cop summoned by the doctor told him that the bus driver and two boys sitting behind him had died.

You killed three people, you worthless piece of shit. To prove it, the cop had brought pictures, holding them so that Rhys could see the twisted, bloody bodies.

The boy who'd been Mick Sullivan had broken down, sobbing so violently they'd had to sedate him. As the drug had taken him down, the cop had raked him with unforgiving eyes before walking away, leaving him cuffed to the bed.

Bowing his head, he closed his eyes and rested his fist on the rough granite. He'd thought prison was the worst of it. Now he knew better.

This was his true penance, returning to this place, facing the people who had erected this monument. Compared with the way he felt at this moment—and the way he expected to feel for a lot of moments from here on out—prison seemed like a four-star resort.

. . . you might start with forgiving yourself for being alive.

Not a chance in hell, he thought as he turned back to the car.

Merribelle Nightingale would be pleased, Brina decided as she cast a critical eye around the octagonal room she'd assigned to Mr. Dunnigan. Once the madam's own bedroom, the President's Room was as large as the first-floor sitting room directly below, with the same polished cherry floors and a carved ceiling imported from San Francisco. Situated in the northwest corner of the huge Victorian mansion, it offered guests a spectacular view of the sun setting over the western peaks.

Originally, the walls had been lined with pale gold watered silk, which Brina had replicated with paint because she liked the idea of bringing the sun indoors when the weather turned winter gloomy. To coax more light into the room she'd painted the ceiling and woodwork a rich off-white that always made her think of vanilla ice cream.

In Ma's day the ceiling fixture had been an Austrian crystal chandelier, long gone now, although there was a picture of it in Brina's small but precious collection of photographs of the house in its heyday. Someday, when she could afford it, she hoped to have a copy of the chandelier made. Still, the glass and brass replacement served the purpose well enough.

The furnishings were mostly genuine antiques, with a few reproductions including the massive nine-foot oak armoire. The cherrywood rocker with the curved arms and thick, comfy cushions had once belonged to her grandmother Eiler.

Humming to herself, Brina whisked the feather duster over the rocker's intricately carved backrest, then sank into the seat and gave the chair a couple of celebratory rocks. Bliss was having five full minutes with absolutely nothing to do.

The kids were in school and Ernie was at the library, where

she worked in the research department. Colonel FitzHugh had gone out a little past nine, and the house had a hushed, expectant feel to it. According to the message taken yesterday morning by Cindy Tsung, her part-time maid–desk clerk, the first contingent of North Star people would be arriving sometime today.

Her thoughts froze when the telltale jangle of temple bells attached to the front door heralded the entry of . . . someone. It couldn't be Dunnigan, she thought as she darted an anguished look at her work grubbies. The first scheduled flight from Seattle wouldn't land for another twenty minutes.

Probably a walk-in, she assured herself as she jumped up.

When greeting guests for the first time, the Successful Innkeeper must always appear serene, competent and professional. Rule Seven.

"Anybody here?" It was a man's voice calling from downstairs, as deep as Mr. Dunnigan's, but with a gritty quality that his had lacked. A frown tugged at her lips as she tried to put a face to the distinctive voice, but she came up blank. Whoever her visitor was, one thing was certain. He did *not* sound like the patient sort.

Chapter 4

As soon as she made the turn at the landing, Brina saw him at the bottom of the stairs. Standing with legs spread, he leaned on a sturdy, dark-colored cane, studying a full-length portrait of Merribelle Nightingale in an ornate gilt frame.

Early to mid-forties, he was taller than average with a sinewy, athletic build and the broadest shoulders she'd ever seen. Beneath a worn leather vest, he wore a pale blue Western-style shirt with the cuffs rolled back against thick forearms. His butt-hugging Wranglers had the familiar worn white look at the seams and knees that could only come from frequent wear. Beneath the frayed hems, scuffed brown cowboy boots had the same worn-in look.

Though the brim of a well-seasoned fawn-colored Stetson hid most of his face, she caught a glimpse of bronzed skin stretched taut over a square jaw and starkly defined cheekbones. What she saw of the thick blond hair curling against the strong column of his neck suggested that it was carelessly styled and would most likely be soft to the touch.

Just her bad luck she'd always had a thing for cowboys. When she realized she was staring—and, okay, mentally stripping that big, sinewy body bare—she took herself firmly in hand.

"Good morning, I'm sorry to keep you waiting," she said in her most congenial innkeeper voice. "My maid called in sick and I'm doing double duty this morning."

His eyes were the color of smoke, deep-set in a tough, seasoned face with a stern mouth. An angry scar shaped like a comma rode just above a suggestion of a cleft in that square chin, adding a dash of danger to his face.

Her stomach did that dreaded falling-elevator thing she hated. Worse, the libido she'd been convinced had died along with her marriage suddenly came roaring back to life.

Because she knew he would tower over her on the flat, she stopped on the second step from the bottom, giving *her* the advantage. Well, an inch or two, anyway. Instinct told her she would need more than a temporary height advantage to hold her own against this man.

"As far I've been able to discover, that was the last portrait of Merribelle Nightingale ever painted," she said. "Apparently she used to greet her guests in just that spot."

Something like curiosity broke the smooth surface of those gray eyes. *Familiar* gray eyes, she realized. But where had she seen them before?

"Merribelle is the inn's original owner, I take it?"

She nodded. "Of course, it was known as Mrs. Nightingale's Sporting Palace when she owned it. According to the advertisements of the day, Ma and her many 'daughters' provided 'refreshments and entertainment for gentlemen of refinement and discrimination.'"

"Yeah?" His gaze made a quick circuit of the entry before returning to her face. "Pretty fancy for a brothel."

"The best in the West," she said brightly.

Instead of responding with a smile as she expected, he held her gaze for a couple of mesmerizing beats before he shifted his attention to the painting again. With a deliberation that was apparently as much a part of him as that aura of command, he stood utterly still, his head cocked to one side. Finally, he turned her way again. Even though his gaze was impersonal, even cool, she had a sudden—and intense—urge to cross her arms over her full breasts.

"You look like her, but I imagine you've heard that before."
His voice had a raspy Southwestern drawl that evoked images
of star-bright desert nights and tangled sheets. She reminded
herself that she was thirty-four, not thirteen and giddy.

"There's a rumor that my great-grandfather had been Ma's
lover during the twenties and that my grandmother was really
Ma's love child."

"Yeah? What do you think?"

"It's certainly possible," she admitted. "One of my permanent guests, Ernestine Winkle, is a research librarian. She did
some checking and came up with some pretty convincing evidence that my grandmother was adopted when she was only a
few weeks old. According to newspaper accounts of the day,
Ma had been traveling in Europe during the critical months
before Gran's birth. When she was young, Gran did look a little like Merribelle. My mother could have been Ma's twin."
She fought a familiar feeling of loss. Her mother had been
dead for twenty-five years and she still missed her. "At least in
the pictures I've seen," she added softly. "She died when I was
nine."

"Sorry, that must have been rough," he said in an abrupt
way that suggested he, too, had suffered a similar loss.

Over the years she'd learned to size up a guest quickly and
for the most part accurately. Before her welcoming smile had a
chance to fade, she usually knew if a prospective guest would
be demanding or easygoing, safe or dangerous, reliable or
flaky. She almost always sensed if she needed to warn Cindy
to avoid a particular male guest who might have more than
extra towels on his mind. She also had the kids to think about;
she had never hesitated to refuse a room to someone she didn't
feel she could trust.

The sharp bones of this man's face, the unyielding line of
his mouth, his blatantly masculine stance—and especially the
guarded look in those oddly familiar eyes—suggested a man
with no inner warmth. Paradoxically—and surprisingly—her

instinct told her that he presented no danger. His affect on her libido was another story, one she wasn't prepared to explore.

Swiftly, she slipped into innkeeper mode. "I'm sorry. I don't usually rattle on like this," she said. "Are you with North Star?"

"Yes. Dunnigan didn't mention a check-in time. If we're early, we can wait." His gaze shifted toward the large parlor to the left of the entrance. Clearly a man who was used to setting his own rules, she decided.

"Check-in is listed as two p.m. in our brochure," she said, "but your rooms have been ready since Sunday so there's no problem."

"Fine."

Clearly a man of few words, she thought, opening a mental file. *Doesn't like chitchat.* He didn't seem to care all that much for her either, if the wintry look in his eyes was an accurate gauge.

"Did Mr. Dunnigan accompany you, or will he and Ms. Campbell-Browne be arriving later?" she asked.

"Dunnigan's Jag tangled with a UPS truck on Friday. The Jag lost."

She sucked in a shocked breath while her stomach took a quick trip to the floor. "Please tell me he's not . . . I mean, was he badly hurt?"

"Bad enough to keep him tied to a bed for a few weeks. I'll be taking his place until he's up to speed again." A subtle tightening of his jaw told her he wasn't as unaffected as he sounded.

"Oh, I am so sorry! When Ms. Campbell-Browne called on Sunday, she simply said that she and Mr. Dunnigan had been delayed." She conjured up Dunnigan's pleasantly homely face in her mind and then visualized healing energy surrounding him, before adding with a smile, "Please give him my best wishes when you speak with him again."

His face softened noticeably. "Might help if he had a name to go with those wishes."

"Oh, right. I'm the chief cook, bottle washer and concierge. Brina Sullivan."

The change in him was subtle, a taut muscle along his jaw, the flicker of those thick eyelashes. She noticed because she'd trained herself to notice. Her curiosity sharpened.

"Sounds like you don't have a lot of time for hobbies," he said.

"My kids are my hobby. Along with plumbing, of course. My heart goes pitty-pat when I get a chance to get out my trusty plunger and go three rounds with a plugged-up john."

"Don't take this wrong, Ms. Sullivan, but could be you need to get out more often."

So he did have a sense of humor, she thought, laughing. "Brina, please. Things are pretty informal up here in the Northwest." She smiled expectantly.

"Name's Hazard. Most people call me Rhys." His gaze held steady, his face utterly still, as though he was waiting to see how she responded. Had they met? she wondered again, then rejected the idea. Any woman who'd spent more than a few seconds with this man would never forget him.

"A pleasure, Rhys." She extended her hand. After a brief hesitation he stepped forward to take it, and she caught a faint whiff of leather, rain and soap. His grip was firm, with only a hint of the strength suggested by his wide, callused palm and thick, sinewy wrist.

The jolting sexual tug she felt as his hand slid from hers rocked her back. The last man to make her go shaky and sweaty inside had ended up breaking her heart. Somewhere between sobbing her eyes bleary and threatening to take a chef's knife to the part of her weasel husband's anatomy that she'd been unknowingly sharing with the Bimbo Without a Brain, she had discovered a basic truth. She might have blown the top off her SAT scores and made Phi Beta Kappa at the

University of Washington, but when it came to men, she was a total doofus.

How long had she known John Sullivan before she'd married him at twenty-one? Fourteen years, that's how long. During all those years, had she spotted even a glimmer of the bottomless weasel potential behind the good-looking face and Irish charm? No, she had not. Ergo, she planned to be very, very careful before allowing a man she found even remotely attractive into her life again.

"If you'll follow me to the office, we can take care of the paperwork my accountant insists on, and then I'll show you to your room," she said briskly.

Politely, Mr. Hazard stepped back to allow her to precede him. As she led the way, she realized he walked with a limp, and slowed her steps to match his. "I'm afraid I don't have anyone in the house right now to take care of your luggage, but we have a bellman's trolley you can use."

He caught the look she slanted toward his cane, and his eyes turned to brittle ice. Careful, Brina, she told herself as her intuition warned her to tread softly around this man's pride.

"Luggage won't be a problem," he declared.

Perhaps not, but walking clearly was, she thought with a pang of sympathy she took care to hide. A fall from a horse? she wondered, her mind busy conjuring up a picture of that lean, hard body atop a wild-eyed stallion.

Like all the other rooms on the first and second floors, Brina's office had a high ceiling framed by heavy crown molding, elaborate woodwork and two large double-hung windows overlooking the newly replanted rose garden.

The large oak desk with a deep kneehole had been one of the few things she'd kept when she'd sold her dad's auto repair shop after his death four years ago. Refinished now, it served as a perfect platform for her computer and printer. At present, however, it was piled high with three days of junk mail, a rough draft of the "Osuma Welcomes North Star" program, and a half-eaten poppy seed muffin.

She found the folder with the North Star paperwork in the slot where it was supposed to be and allowed herself a moment of self-congratulation. "Mr. Dunnigan's assistant faxed the final list early last month. Four rooms, including meals, at the corporate rate, prepaid. I'll just need the license number of your car for the records."

"No problem. We'll need one more room for my driver if you have one available," he said as she opened the folder.

She felt her pulse leap at the unexpected increase in her bottom line. "As a matter of fact I do have a vacancy. It's one of the smaller rooms on this floor, but it has a private bath and lots of light. I'm sure he'll find it comfortable." She took out two registration cards before sifting through the papers on her desk, searching for the pen she'd laid there earlier. Somewhere. "Uh, his name?" she asked, stalling.

"Max Stillwell." A large, sinewy hand holding a black fountain pen appeared in her line of vision. It was a beautiful hand. Deeply tanned, with prominent veins and clean short nails. A plain gold watch with a brown leather band circled his wrist. He wasn't wearing a wedding ring. Not that she meant to look.

"I'm usually more organized," she muttered as she uncapped his pen and printed Stillwell's name on one of the cards. The other she put in front of him, then handed him the pen.

While he wrote, she surreptitiously dropped the half-eaten muffin into the wastebasket. She was hastily brushing crumbs into the palm of her hand when he glanced up.

"Midmorning snack?" he asked with a hint of teasing.

"Breakfast, actually. It's been a busy week."

"Sorry about the mix-up in plans," he said as he tucked his pen away again.

"Please don't apologize. I understand completely." She cleared her throat and tried to forget she was wearing jeans that her malevolent dryer had shrunk a good two sizes since she'd bought them, and a faded Grateful Dead sweatshirt that had actually been loose when she'd bought it twenty years and two babies ago. "I hope you know how happy we are to have you here."

He studied her for a moment. There was a stillness about him, even when he was moving, that made her very nervous. "Are you?" he asked finally.

"Of course. North Star gave this town a precious gift, something the flood took away."

"Yeah, what's that?"

She let him see the gratitude in her eyes. "Hope."

Something changed in his face, made it more cynical somehow. "It was a business decision, nothing more."

What has hurt you so terribly that you need to push people away with both of those big powerful hands? she wanted to ask. Instead, she said pleasantly, "In case Mr. Dunnigan failed to mention it, we're having a huge celebration in North Star's honor on the fifteenth, with a parade and a cocktail party hosted by the governor that night. Mr. Dunnigan agreed to give a brief speech at a ceremony before the parade. Since you're taking his place—"

"Public relations are Hank's thing, not mine."

She narrowed her gaze at him. "I beg your pardon?"

"Parties. Speeches." His voice took on a hard edge that seemed out of character with the empathy she'd glimpsed earlier. "Dunnigan's paid to do those things. I'm not."

Offended on behalf of the dozens of people who were working so hard to make the celebration special, she deliberately chilled her voice to the same cool tone. "What exactly is it you're paid to do for North Star, then, Mr. Hazard?"

"Whatever's necessary, Ms. Sullivan."

"And you don't consider accepting a friendly gesture necessary?"

"A property tax break for a year or two would be a lot more useful."

Brina caught herself before she actually scowled at the man. He was, after all, *a paying guest.* "You'll have to take that up with Mayor Kurtz. He'll be on the platform on the fifteenth." She drenched her smile in saccharine. "I'll be happy to introduce you."

"Don't bother. I'm here to do a job, and that's what I intend to do."

Her face turned hot. "Well, *pardon me* for thinking you might actually *appreciate* all the trouble the town has gone to, to make North Star feel welcome!"

It infuriated her when his mouth twitched. "Anyone ever tell you it's not a good idea to tick off a paying guest?"

"I . . . you . . ." She opened her mouth, then shut it again. It took effort, but she managed to talk herself out of plowing her fist into that annoyingly flat belly.

"It's damn infuriating, isn't it?" he said in a soft tone. "Having to swallow all that righteous indignation in the interest of your bottom line when what you really want to do is take my head off?"

"I was planning to aim a little lower, actually."

He dropped his gaze, not to his belly but to his crotch. Of course, just like a man, she thought, as his gaze meshed with hers again.

"Are you always so combative, Ms. Sullivan?"

"Are you always so aggravating, Mr. Hazard?"

"Always." His smile was fleeting and just a little crooked, revealing white, straight teeth and a hint of a crease in one hard cheek.

Despite her pique, it came again, that miserable I'd-like-to-strip-you-naked-and-lick-every-part-of-you feeling she hated. When she realized she was rubbing her palm against the side seams of her jeans, she took herself in hand. So what if she'd taken a quick detour into erotic fantasyland? It was only natural for a woman in her sexual prime to experience an occasional hormonal surge, especially after a long period of celibacy. Now that she'd had her own up-close-and-personal moment of lust, she could move on to more important innkeeping things.

"Would dinner at seven thirty be convenient, or would you prefer eight? I usually serve cocktails and hors d'oeuvres in the main parlor first."

"Don't bother. We'll eat out tonight."

"It's no trouble, really. Besides, the only place in town that's open for dinner is Wanda's Waffle Haus."

"Is that a warning?"

"No, of course not. It just seems silly to pay for dinner twice." She had a sudden thought and added, "Or maybe you didn't realize North Star is paying for board as well as lodging?"

"Don't worry. We won't ask for a refund."

"Good, because you wouldn't get it," she shot back before she remembered that a Successful Innkeeper never snaps at a guest. "Truly, I don't mind serving tonight."

"Tomorrow, when things settle down."

He glanced away, his chest rising and falling slowly, as though he was having trouble getting enough air into his lungs. When he lifted his gaze again, his jaw was taut and his eyes held a bleak cast that shook her. "Brina, there's something you should know, something I . . ." He paused to clear his throat.

Curiosity gave way to a skitter of apprehension. "Yes?"

He tensed, then squared those enormous shoulders, causing the vest to fall open and the shirt beneath to stretch taut over the hard-packed muscles of his chest. "Look, there's no easy way to say this. I should have told you up front, but—"

"Now, this is my idea of a great house!"

A blur of vivid color from across the room caught Brina's eye and she glanced up to find a stunningly exotic woman standing in the doorway, an oxblood briefcase slung over one shoulder and a look of eager anticipation on the most gorgeous face Brina had ever seen. The epitome of understated elegance in mauve silk and tasteful gold accessories, she looked to be a few inches taller than Brina's five feet four, and far more slender. Size four, Brina decided, fighting an unbecoming pang of envy. A *perfect* size four.

Brina wanted to hate her, but the woman had such energy it was impossible. She was also incredibly beautiful. A Nubian princess come to life with flawless skin the color of rare cognac. Her eyes were a clear, shimmering amber outlined with long feathery lashes. This is the woman who should have played Cleopatra, Brina thought as they exchanged smiles.

"Ms. Campbell-Browne?" she guessed.

The woman nodded, coming forward to extend a slender, beautifully manicured hand. Brina sighed when she saw the flecks of dried paint firmly lodged under her own blunt nails.

"Please call me Della. That way I can call you . . . ?" She lifted an inquiring brow, queen to servant, and yet she did it with such a nice smile that Brina was more charmed than offended.

"I'm Brina. Brina Sullivan."

Her sooty lashes flickered slightly. "Sullivan? Any relation to the man who owned the warehouse?"

"I was married to J. T.'s son John for eleven years. We've been divorced for nearly two." She managed a smile. "John will be working with you at North Star, but then I imagine you know that already."

"Actually, I just last week sent him a benefits packet."

Brina caught the quick look the woman sent Hazard's way and glanced at him as well, only to find that those compelling eyes had gone cold and remote. "Which room is mine?" he asked.

"Number 4, top of the main stairs. The key is in the lock."

"Is there an adjoining room?"

"Why, yes, Number 5."

"Give that one to Della." He smiled briefly before turning to leave.

Twenty minutes later, Rhys stood in front of the dormer window, watching Max unload the bags from the trunk onto the brass trolley. The rain had slacked off, but heavily pregnant rain clouds lingered overhead. Water dripped from the gnarled branches of a horse chestnut tree that dominated the inn's large front yard, and glistened like a sheen of sweat on the recently paved street.

Nice neighborhood, he thought, as he swept his gaze up and down the wide street. A good place for kids and dogs and families. He'd rarely visited this section of Osuma as a kid.

Most of the houses here appeared to have survived the flood with far less damage than those in the lower areas. Still, signs of the rushing water were obvious, especially along the fringes of the street where the trees sported gouges from debris crashing into them.

If the signs of the repair work were any indication, the house across the street appeared to have been especially hard hit. Had this one suffered damage as well? he wondered as he heard a quiet knock on the door between his room and Della's.

"Are you decent, sugar?" she called.

"It's open."

He heard the latch click open, then shut. An instant later Del came to stand next to him. "I liked her," Del said quietly. "Brina Sullivan, I mean."

So had he. Too much. "It's her job to make you like her." He kept his voice cool and hoped Della would drop this line of thought.

"It's more than that," she mused, and he bit off a sigh. "She has a sensitive face and very kind eyes."

Big brown eyes with silky lashes. When she'd cried on the

witness stand, they stuck together in dark spikes. "I didn't notice."

Del clucked her tongue. "You *lie.* Ain't a man alive who wouldn't notice a figure like hers, sugar. Girl's got her some kind of curves, you know what I'm saying?"

Oh yeah, he knew. Ripe, womanly curves that tempted a man to sink in and forget his problems—or his past. Scowling, he shifted his weight. It didn't help. His hip ached like the very devil. Worse, the rest of him felt hot-wired and antsy.

"She's attracted to you," Della persisted. "Although I think she doesn't want to be. And you, big bad brother, had the look of a man who'd just been hit with a club, right smack in a spot where a man just naturally pays attention." Her grin grew gleeful. "Sugar, I got me the *strongest* feeling you just turned that blind corner and met your match. Yes sir, I'm thinking this is gonna be a *real* interesting few weeks."

He felt heat climbing his neck. "You're reaching, Del," he warned.

"Huh-uh. I don't think so."

"Think what you want. You always do. Me, I'm just here to do a job." He crossed the room to the bed, which was damn near as big as the converted toolshed where he'd lived his first six months in Phoenix. There his bed had been an army surplus sleeping bag spread on the oil-stained floor. This monstrosity was covered by some kind of fancy spread with a whole rainbow of colors in a complex pattern that should have been fussy, but wasn't. Like the woman with the dizzy hair and made-for-sin hips downstairs, it drew him in and made him wish he could reach out and wipe the slate clean.

Putting aside his cane, he reached down to jerk the coverlet from the mattress. It was soft against his rough hands as he wadded it into a ball. His mother, Marceline Sullivan, had been partial to delicate things like this, cobwebby shawls and pretty pillows covered with lace that always made him feel out of place and awkward. No matter how hard he tried, he'd always ended up messing up anything precious.

"Here, this looks like it belongs on a lady's bed," he muttered, thrusting the coverlet into Della's arms.

She frowned and narrowed her eyes. "Something tells me Brina embroidered this herself."

"So?"

"You'll hurt her feelings if you get rid of it."

There was a band of hot tension across his shoulder blades and a knot in his gut. He'd known that coming to this place again would cost him. He'd thought he'd prepared himself to meet the people who'd known him before. Who had every right to despise him.

He'd been wrong. Nothing could prepare a man for that.

"Remember the girl I told you about who tried to dig her brother out of the wreckage with her bare hands?"

Della clutched the coverlet tight against her breasts, a stunned look on her face. "The one whose brother died in her arms? That was Brina?"

"Yeah, Brina Eiler. She was just a skinny thing then with a mouth full of metal and this wild mane of hair down to her butt. Had the jury in tears, talking about how she'd held her brother's head while the medics worked on him." He felt a sharp, insistent ache of regret in his chest. "The hell of it was, her father was damn near the only person in town who didn't want to lynch me."

"Did you know she owned this place before we arrived?"

"I knew it belonged to John's ex-wife. I didn't know he'd married Brina Eiler."

"She didn't recognize you?"

He glanced up to find Della's eyes dark with understanding. "I doubt it, since she didn't slap me or spit in my face."

"Why didn't you tell her who you really are?"

"Hell if I know."

A shadow dimmed her eyes. "She has to know, Rhys."

"Trust me, she'll know soon enough. They all will."

"Better you tell her yourself." Her voice was quiet, but firm.

"You're right. I need to tell her." He'd tried. He'd also been grateful when Del had interrupted him.

"Shit, I have to get out of here," he muttered. "I'll tell her the truth when I get back. Right now I need some open space around me."

He had his hand on the doorknob when Della's anxious voice stopped him. "I know housing's tight here because of the flood, but I could try to find us another place if you think that would be best."

God, *yes!* Anyplace but here where he didn't have to face her—and the emotions she aroused in him—every damned day. No one would blame him—except the merciless bastard who lived in his skin.

"Once she realizes who it is she's welcomed to her bed and board, it may not be our call. But if it is, we'll stay." He dropped his gaze to the spread still clutched in her arms. "Just in case, you'd better put the damn spread back on the bed. I have enough to answer for without adding one more sin to the list."

Chapter 5

It was just past eleven when Brina rapped on the door of Number 5. Marcy's morning kindergarten class was due to let out at noon, and she had this one last thing to do before she left to fetch her.

"Sorry, I was on the phone to Phoenix," Della said as she swung the door wide. "Ooh, daffodils! I love them." Her eyes sparkled behind huge red-rimmed glasses. "And where did you ever get that gorgeous vase?"

Brina grinned as Della traced a vein of gold in the shimmering blue glass. "It was my mother's. She collected carnival glass."

Della took the vase from her, holding it with the greatest care. "The question now is where to put it so I can enjoy it best." She seemed to float as she circled the room, finally settling on the small piecrust table next to one of the dormer windows. "What do you think?" she asked finally, lifting her gaze to Brina's.

"Perfect," Brina agreed with a warm glow of satisfaction. Nothing pleased her more than making her guest's day a little brighter. "I didn't get a chance to tell you earlier, but you're welcome to use the parlor and the library whenever you like. My office has a fax machine you can use as well. Oh, and the kitchen, too, if you feel the need to fix yourself a midnight snack." She smiled at the thought of Del rummaging in the fridge wearing a French silk negligee and mules. "Only, I should warn you, don't touch the peppermint candy ice cream in the freezer. That belongs to Colonel FitzHugh. He's one of my two permanent guests—and he's had combat training."

Del laughed. "So have I, of sorts, but thanks for the warning."

"After the flood, we had very few guests for weeks on end, and my children got used to the run of the house. In fact, they've come to consider Ernie—Miss Ernestine Winkle—and the colonel as surrogate grandparents, which means they're constantly in and out of the guest floors as well as the family quarters."

"You have children?" Della's eyes glowed with what appeared to be genuine delight.

"Two. Jay's twelve and Marcy's five, going on a hundred and twenty." Brina took a deep breath, her gaze instinctively shifting to the open door between the two adjoining rooms. Twin leather suitcases sat at the foot of Ma Nightingale's bed, waiting to be unpacked. She remembered seeing the bald-headed bruiser named Max carrying in a matching garment bag and a briefcase with bulging sides as well.

She'd been taking linen to the driver's room when Hazard had passed her on his way out, his face set in grim, angry lines. Trailing a few steps behind him, the chauffeur with no neck had actually glared at her as he'd passed.

"What I'm trying to say with an embarrassing lack of finesse is just this, Della. I would appreciate it if you and Mr. Hazard would be discreet about your sleeping arrangements."

Della's face went blank and then dissolved into a delightful grin. "Oh Lordy, Brina, Rhys and I aren't lovers, although I do love him dearly." Amusement fading, she touched one of the daffodils with a shiny fingernail, then drew her hand back and crossed her arms as though touched by a sudden chill.

"I met Rhys when I was a sixteen-year-old with a crack head for a mother and God only knows what for a father. At the time, I was a high school dropout, trying to survive any way I could, which was mostly turning tricks in truck stops between Phoenix and Flagstaff." She lifted her chin and regarded Brina with eyes that were suddenly as guarded as Hazard's had been earlier. "Does that shock you?"

Brina took a careful breath and considered. "It does, yes," she admitted because she respected Della's willingness to be honest with her.

"Does that mean you would prefer I stay away from your children?"

"Of course not!"

Her mouth tightened. "Sugar, there's no 'of course not' to it. Some folks would hold my past against me forever."

Brina thought about the portrait over the fireplace in the adjoining room. "Merribelle Nightingale was a prostitute before she became one of the most respected businesswomen in the state. It wasn't her choice either, but when she found herself an eighteen-year-old widow with two half-grown stepdaughters to support and no real skills to do it with, she did what women had been doing for generations in order to survive. So did you."

"I almost didn't actually. If it hadn't been for Rhys, I'd simply be another forgotten statistic."

Brina cocked a brow. Had he been one of her customers? she wondered. "You met at one of those truck stops?" she asked, reluctantly settling for tact over what she realized was a sharp curiosity about the man behind the shuttered gray eyes.

Della nodded. "The moon was full, which is always a scary night for workin' girls 'cause that's when the crazies come out. This night was especially bad. Turned down more dates than I accepted. Long about two a.m., I was really feeling the pinch so I took a chance on this guy who said he was from Kansas or Colorado, one of the those square states folks have to fly over to get from coast to coast."

Brina laughed, easing the tension. "Where they grow all that corn."

"Exactly. Anyway this john and I were behind the building, negotiating, when all of a sudden he took it into his head to rape me. I fought, but he outweighed me by a hundred pounds easy. The next thing I knew the guy was crumpled up against the side of the building, looking like he'd just been run over by a tank. Only it was Rhys who'd flattened him." She grinned. "What that man can do when he's riled would purely send chills racing down your spine."

Brina felt a few of those chills now as she imagined the damage those big hands could cause. "He didn't die, did he? The . . . john?"

"Nope, but ain't a doubt in my mind he walked crooked for a lot of months afterward."

"Serves him right," Brina declared.

"That's true enough." Della's eyes took on distant look. "I was bleeding and dizzy when Rhys bundled me into the cab of his rig. A crowd had gathered, and someone said the truck stop manager was threatening to call the cops, so even though I knew better, I went with Rhys so I wouldn't get busted. I figured he would want a freebie as payback, but he was about as interested as a monk. Stopped at the next motel on the interstate, he did, then ran me a bath and waited outside the door until I'd scrubbed away the blood and the shakes." Her eyes softened at the memory. "I came out of that bathroom wrapped in a towel, ready to pay him back. Instead, he gave me a clean T-shirt to sleep in and then bandaged my cuts and got me some ice for my bruised face. The room only had one bed, and the next thing I know I'm in it, alone." Her lips curved. "He slept on the floor, which I found out later played hell with his bad hip." She drew in a slow breath as though to settle her emotions.

"Anyway, three days later I'm living with friends of his in Phoenix—Tex and Belinda Muleshoe—going to high school and feeling safe for the first time in my life. Rhys paid for it all—room and board, tutors to help me catch up, my clothes and medical bills, even braces for my teeth. After I graduated college and went to work for North Star, I tried to pay him back. He wouldn't take a penny, just told me to find another lost girl who could use a friend and help her." Her smile was sad. "There are more and more of those girls selling their souls on the streets every year. We're throwing away an entire generation of our children and no one seems to care."

"Except you," Brina said softly.

"And Rhys."

"Yes," Brina said thoughtfully. "And Rhys."

She saw it all. The seedy streets, a frightened, outwardly cocky girl-child trolling for rent money—and a big-shouldered man with a hard face and dangerous eyes hauling her out of harm's way. It was an image she suspected would stay with her a while. She took a breath and went with the curiosity prodding her. "Something tells me you had a reason for telling me this now."

Surprise rippled over Della's exotic features. "One thing about hookers, sugar, they learn to size up folks real quick. Kinda like lady innkeepers, I suspect."

Brina acknowledged that with a rueful smile. "It gets to be a habit, I admit."

"The man who used his fists on me the night Rhys and I met, I knew he was a bad one. I needed the money, so I took a chance. I was bleeding pretty good and hazy around the edges, and Rhys can come on right dangerous when he sets his mind to it. Soon as I got a good look at the gentleness hidden in those streetwise eyes, though, I knew I was safe."

Brina understood the feeling all too well. It had shaken her even more than the unexpected jolt of sexual heat that was still simmering like a low-grade fever in her blood. "I think you were very lucky," she said quietly. "And I'm glad."

"Me, too." Della glanced toward the adjoining room, her brow furrowing beneath the riot of soft corkscrew curls. "Rhys will likely chew me out for talking about him to you, but the moment we met, I knew you were someone I would very much like for a friend. Since he's my friend, too, I . . ." She made a helpless gesture. "I saw how you looked at him when he walked out of your office, and I just wanted you to know he's not always so . . . prickly."

"To tell you the truth, I had the feeling I had offended him."

"It wasn't you. It's, well, circumstances, I guess. He's going through a . . . difficult time now."

"Because of Mr. Dunnigan's accident?"

"That's part of it, yes. Hank is the closest thing he has to a real brother, and seeing him so beat up and in pain was stressful for Rhys. For me, too, of course, but I had Rhys to lean on. Rhys himself, he doesn't have anyone. Hasn't had anyone for a very long time." She hesitated, then added softly, "He's been on his own since he was a teenager, and his life hasn't been easy. He doesn't let many people get close."

"I'm sorry; I didn't realize." She took a deep breath and wished there were a pill she could take that would give her the tact she so obviously lacked. "Does he—Mr. Hazard—work for Mr. Dunnigan?"

"No, Rhys works alone. He always has." Della averted her gaze, looking out the window for a long moment. "He's not only the strongest man I've ever known, but also the kindest and most decent as well. A better man than he's willing to believe." The plea in Della's eyes stunned Brina. "He doesn't believe he deserves to be happy, but I do, and so do a lot of people he's helped over the years. I just wanted you to know that."

Even at a distance, Rhys could see that the old warehouse glistened with a coat of fresh white paint, but the roof was the same dull gray he remembered. The big metal SULLIVAN AND SON sign with its bright emerald letters on a gold background was gone. *Destroy the frigging thing* had been the only order Rhys had given Hank when he'd turned the Northwest project

over to him. He'd wanted it shoved it up Junior's ass, letter by
letter, but he figured Hank had had it hauled off to a recycling
center.

The new sign bore the trademark logo he'd drawn on a napkin in a New Mexico truck stop. A silver shooting star on a
midnight blue sky. Not fancy, maybe, but it had suited his vision for his company. The first time he'd seen the logo on the
side of a North Star trailer, he'd damn near burst into tears.

"Place is as big as an airplane hangar," Max commented as
he drew the big car to a stop in front of the closed gates of the
main entrance.

The guardhouse and the six-foot Cyclone fence with its
deadly collar of razor wire were new. So was the hulking
armed guard, hired through Pinkerton's security by Hank the
day the property had closed escrow. Though the rent-a-cop
was young, not more than late twenties would be Rhys' best
guess, he had the look of a man willing and able to use the
Glock .45 strapped to his hip. Ex-military, Rhys decided as the
guard moved toward them. Just the type Rhys himself would
have chosen to protect the valuable rigs and cargo that would
soon be rolling in and out of these same gates.

"Afternoon, sir," the guard said, bending low to lean a
khaki-clad forearm on the window Max had slid down. He had
suspicious eyes and a crisp voice. "Something I can do for you
gentlemen?"

"This is Mr. Hazard and this is his company you're workin'
for," Max growled at him. "He'd like to go inside his facility."

The guard's gaze slid past Max, his expression unreadable.
"May I see some identification, sir?" His tone was respectful
but firm.

Rhys liked the kid's style. "Sure thing, son."

Leaning forward, he pulled his wallet from his back pocket
and extracted his North Star ID card. It was identical to the
ones all his employees wore in plain sight. Company rules.
Their insurance carrier gave a discount for tight security,

which pleased his CFO. Keeping a tight lid on who came in and out was also one way of making sure no one stashed contraband in one of his rigs. The last thing he needed was a squadron of DEA agents crawling all over his facilities and stopping his rigs in transit, especially now when they had an excellent shot at landing MemoryData's business.

Max waited until the guard disappeared into the shack again before snorting. "Kid thinks he's freaking Rambo."

"Be nice, Max. He's just doing his job. I respect that."

The guard returned a moment later, carrying a clipboard. After making note of the Arizona tags, he walked to Rhys' side of the car and waited for him to open the window. He returned the ID, then passed over the clipboard. "If you would sign next to your name and ID number, sir."

Rhys scrawled his name, then handed back the clipboard.

The guard thanked him. "I'll get the gate."

"You want I should park or just circle the building?" Max asked as he drove through the opening.

"Park, please."

The parking lot had been newly refinished, and the stripes marking the parking spaces gleamed white beneath the rain slick. Max pulled dead center into the slot with Hank's name stenciled on the concrete tire barrier. "Want I should come inside with you?"

"No, wait here, please. I won't be long."

Max nodded. During their first few weeks together, he'd been determined to open the door for Rhys every time he got in or out. Like Rhys was some kind of cripple, which he wasn't, even if he looked like it sometimes. *Part of the freaking job,* Max had insisted. Rhys had threatened to dock his pay if he didn't cut it out. After a couple more bouts of heated—and mostly profane—verbal sparring, they'd settled on a compromise. When anyone but Del or Hank was in the car with him, Max would be allowed to open doors and "yes, sir" and "no, sir" him to his heart's content. Otherwise, he'd drop the courtesies and just be one friend driving another.

The warehouse door was unlocked. According to the schedule Hank had roughed out, the depot would run only one shift for the first two or three months while Del and the other department heads conducted interviews and trained new employees. After the rigs started hauling cargo on a regular basis, they would add the swing and graveyard shifts as needed.

With only a row of eight windows cut into the upper third of the eastward facing wall as the source of natural light, the cavernous interior was a gloomy place of shifting shadows and dark corners. Rhys thought about flipping on the lights, then decided he liked the blurred edges better.

The first thing that struck him as he crossed the threshold was the quiet. No matter what the season or the time of day, the warehouse he remembered had been a noisy place, with packers shouting to one another over the din of the conveyor belts and the high-pitched whine of forklifts shifting bins. Even in high summer, it had always been cool inside to protect the fruit.

In the rear, the storage rooms had been hermetically sealed and the oxygen replaced by CO_2 to preserve the freshness. One of his earliest memories was J. T.'s telling him never, under any circumstances, to go into any room with a skull and crossbones on the door. That he would die because he couldn't breathe. At the time he had thought J. T. really cared.

The signs that had warned the unwary not to enter were gone now—along with the conveyor belts and bins. The forklifts were still there, neatly lined up against one of the walls. North Star's property now.

Rhys walked slowly along the wide yellow strip newly painted on the floor, pointing visitors to the metal stairway leading up to the office loft. Because there was no one watching, he took the stairs slowly, one halting step at a time. At the top, he paused.

The smell of fresh paint was still strong, making him want to sneeze. There were hints of other scents, too—pine cleaner and floor wax and stale air. Prison smells, he realized as his chest knotted, a mixture that had burned into his memory so deep he'd never been able to get it out.

The loft, with its large bank of windows designed to provide light and air, had been expanded and remodeled. Where there had been six offices before, there were now eight, the largest occupying the southwest corner.

Every last sign of the man who'd inhabited this office had been stripped away. Even the mission oak desk where J. T. Sullivan had propped his big feet had disappeared, replaced by a state-of-the-art oak work center, complete with the elaborate computer setup Hank favored. The numbered lithographs and carefully chosen paintings that had hung in Hank's office in the Tower were still in their shipping crates, stacked against one newly painted wall. They would stay there until Hank was able to tell maintenance where to hang them. In the meantime, Rhys would make this office his own.

He'd paid enough for the privilege, hadn't he? he thought grimly as he crossed the newly varnished plank flooring to the trio of double-hung windows overlooking the undulating hills beyond. His heart slamming, he trailed his gaze upward along one of the replanted slopes. Halfway to the top, a jagged line of green lawn and trees marked the flood's crest. In the center of the green belt sat a white two-story frame farmhouse. Nestled in a grove of mature maples that turned a brilliant red in autumn, it had two full stories wrapped on three sides by a deep porch, and a dark red metal roof with an arrow-sharp peak to keep the snow from piling high and heavy.

Damn house looked exactly the same, he realized, then snorted a bitter laugh. What the hell had he expected? That the place would implode without him in it? No doubt Marceline had washed the place down with Lysol to get rid of every last sign that Michael Sullivan had ever existed.

Rhys' hand went to the pocket of his vest before he remembered he'd quit smoking years ago. Old tapes, he thought, shifting his gaze toward a spot at the edge of the main lot where a large shed had once housed the warehouse trucks and tractors—and, for a while, the stuff of his teenage dreams.

He'd turned fifteen that summer when his mother's father, Granville Rhys Dubois IV came up from San Francisco for a visit. A good head shorter than J. T., the man everyone called Rhys was tennis trim and silver-haired, with the remnants of a Boston Brahman accent and twinkling eyes. *A blue blood to be sure, your grandda, but a decent man for all his fancy ways,* J. T. had told him once.

After retiring from the Bank of America, where he'd been the head of the trust department for many years, he'd devoted most of his time to searching out and restoring vintage cars. This time he'd arrived in the most recent addition to his collection, a black-as-sin 1963 split-window Corvette coupe in cherry condition. The first Sting Ray. A collector's dream.

As sexy as any woman, with graceful lines and a lean and hungry fuel-injected V-8 under the hood, the 'Vette was the most beautiful thing Mick had ever seen. One look and he'd fallen head over heels in love. During his grandfather's visit, the two of them had spent hours in the vehicle maintenance bay, going over every inch of the classic sports car. The old man knew engines and cars even better than some of J. T.'s senior tool pushers—and almost as well as Wayne Makepeace at Eiler's Automotive, who was universally accepted as the best mechanic in the valley.

Runs as smooth as the day she left Detroit, Wayne pronounced when Mick had talked his grandfather into taking it in to show the uncommunicative mechanic who they called Spider Man because of his long arms and legs and skinny torso. Mick didn't care about ol' Wayne's looks. He liked him because he'd taken time to answer a little boy's questions.

That weekend Marceline had been furious when Mick had

shown up for a formal Sunday dinner with grease under his fingernails. Her father had laughed, then stunned Michael by making him a proposition. On the day he brought home a report card with all A's on it, the 'Vette was his free and clear. Sell it, drive it, take it apart—it would be his call. As a token of his faith in him, his granddad had left the Sting Ray behind when he returned to the Bay Area.

Though Mick hated school and had never studied a minute longer than it took to keep his athletic eligibility, he'd made himself hit the books. Rhys Dubois died that winter, and Mick grieved. Though he longed to drive the sweet machine and the keys were readily available, he made himself wait until it was truly his.

The last day of school before Christmas break his junior year he sweet-talked the school secretary into checking the grades that had been mailed out the day before. Mrs. Tolliver grinned from ear to ear when she dropped the news on him. Five subjects, five A's! Damned if he wasn't proud of himself.

Johnny's door was open, his room empty as Mick walked past. His brother's bus was late again, which was just as well. When Johnny was around, Mick might as well be invisible, for all the attention he got.

Downstairs, a Christmas carol spilled from the den at the end of the hall. The house was decorated like a scene from a magazine, and he was careful not to bang into anything fragile.

His father was fixing himself a drink at the wet bar built into one corner of the den when Mick entered. Instead of looking relaxed, however, the old man looked aggravated, the way he always did when he and Mother were wrangling.

Not tonight, please! Mick thought, darting a wary look toward his mom. Done up in green slacks and a fussy red-and-green Christmas sweater he'd never seen before, she sat in her favorite wing chair facing the fireplace, an all too familiar sour-lemon look on her face. A bottle of the fancy French wine

she favored sat in a silver ice bucket on the spindly-legged antique table by her elbow.

All too aware of the pecking order, he greeted his mother
first, then his dad.

"You're lookin' pretty spiffy, boyo," his dad said. "Plannin'
on goin' somewhere special after dinner?"

"He most certainly is not," his mom declared before Mick
could unlock his jaw. "He's still on restriction for coming in
late last weekend."

Fifteen frigging minutes, and only because the battery in his
ten-year-old pickup had given out while he'd been inside the
bowling alley.

"Now, darlin', he's seventeen," Pop chided with a placating
smile. "Boys his age need to blow off steam." Pop caught his
eye and winked before lifting his glass to his lips. "Just keep it
within bounds, son, okay?" he said after swallowing a good
third of the tumbler's contents.

"Yeah, sure, only I'm not going anywhere." Mick realized
he was nervous. A good kind of nervous, the kind that felt like
a thousand bubbles in his chest. It was the same feeling he
used to get as a kid right before he raced down the stairs on
Christmas morning.

"Actually, I had something I wanted to, uh, show you
guys," he said, turning to look at his mother again. After all
the crap he'd taken about his lazy study habits and rotten attitude, he wanted to see the surprise bloom in her eyes when he
sprang the good news. "Guess what, Mother, I—"

"Why haven't you gotten a haircut the way you promised?"
she interrupted in that strident voice he'd learned to hate. "I'm
warning you right now, Michael Rhys Sullivan, I will not have
you going to mass on Christmas Eve looking unkempt."

"Jesus had long hair," he shot back before he could stop
himself. *Big mistake, Sullivan,* he thought, catching his dad's
quick frown. "Sorry, that just slipped out," he mumbled, hoping he could skate out of one of his mother's scathing lectures.

"Another remark like that, young man, and you will spend your Christmas vacation in your room," she said.

"Yes, ma'am."

"And another thing, Lupe said you tracked slush all over her freshly waxed floor when you came home earlier."

"Sorry," he mumbled again. He looked down at the envelope in his hand, his elation slipping away. "If you want, I'll scrub the floor again after dinner." Hell, he'd lick the damn thing clean if that would make her ease up on him.

"There now, darlin', the boy's trying to make amends for his mistake, and isn't that what we've always taught him? Admit the wrong, and do your best to make it right again?"

"Fine, take his side." His mother's mouth snapped shut.

Pop let out a noisy sigh. The cubes in his glass tinkled as he took a quick sip. "Marceline, it's been a bloody awful day, and I'm after needing some peace tonight so I'd take it as a great favor if you'd accept the boy's apology and let it go at that."

"Oh, all right," she grumbled, shooting Mick a look that said he'd only been granted a reprieve. Later, when Pop wasn't around, she'd flay him alive with that razor she had for a tongue.

"What was it you wanted to tell us, son?" Pop asked after taking another healthy slug.

Mick got up to hand his father the envelope. "Grades came today."

"That a fact?" Pop studied him intently before setting his drink on the bar. His eyes twinkled as he took the envelope. "Guess you have a reason for wanting us to see this now?"

Mick shifted his feet, working to rein in his impatience while his dad swept his gaze over the neat columns. "Well, I'll be damned. Nothin' but A's." His dad stuck out his hand. "Congratulations on a job well done," he said as they shook. "Your grandda would be proud."

"Thanks." Mick took back the flimsy copy and ran his gaze over the neat letters before carefully refolding the paper and putting it in his pocket. Uncool or not, he broke into a goofy grin. "Uh, I thought if it was okay with you, I'd take the 'Vette over to Eiler's garage tomorrow, have Wayne check it over before I drive it to the DMV to have the title transferred."

His dad started to answer, only to have his mom beat him to it. "You'll do no such thing, young man! Father's car stays in the shed until your brother is old enough to drive."

"No way!" Mick blurted. "Granddad gave the 'Vette to me, not Junior."

His mother's eyes flashed. "He most certainly did not!"

Mick opened his mouth to protest when he caught the quick look his dad shot him. He felt a rush of relief when he realized Pop wasn't going to let him twist in the wind the way he usually did. "Now darlin', it was always Rhys' intention that Mick have the car, but he wanted the boy to earn it. Now that he has, it's his."

"Father never said that to me," she declared flatly.

Something like panic shot to Mick's brain, then spread to his gut, where it coiled like an icy rope. "Yes, he did, Mother," he protested more impatiently than he'd intended. "Don't you remember? It was the summer after he had it restored and he drove it up here to show us. You said I wasn't smart enough to make all A's, but Granddad said it was just because I didn't apply myself, and—"

"Don't you dare to call me a liar, Michael Sullivan!" Her nostrils flared as she took a quick gulp of wine. A few drops spilled onto the front of her sweater and quivered there as her chest heaved.

"Mom, I swear to God I didn't—"

"Watch your mouth, young man! You will not take the Lord's name in vain in this house."

"He's just excited, darlin'," his dad jumped in. "He didn't mean to offend."

The message came through loud and clear. Though he nearly choked on his own rising anger, he forced himself to apologize again. It was like she hadn't heard him, he realized when he saw her face flush red.

"You've been nothing but trouble since we brought you home from the hospital. I told your father we should send you to military school, but would he listen to me? No, of course not." She drained her glass, then reached into the silver bucket for the bottle. Mick prayed it was empty, but he should have known better. His prayers were rarely answered.

"The boy was merely attempting to jog your memory," Pop jumped in with a placating smile as she slopped white wine into her glass.

"I don't need my memory jogged, J. T.," she snapped before stabbing the bottle back into the bucket with a crunch of ice. "I know what I heard—and what I didn't hear. Father did not promise that car to Michael."

"Now, Marceline—"

"Legally, as Father's only heir, it belongs to me." A look of triumph distorted her face which Mick had once thought the most beautiful he'd ever seen. "And I say Johnny has more of a right to it than Michael. He's always gotten good grades."

Mick felt the blood race to his face. "That's fucking bull-shit!"

"That's enough, son!" Steel clashed in his father's voice now.

Rage bloomed hot in his head. "What about her?" He was shouting now, too angry to care. What was supposed to be the best day of his life was ruined and it was her fault. "Christ, she treats me like dog shit no matter what I do, and you let her!"

His mom gasped. "Did you hear that, J. T.?" she cried again, even more shrilly. "I warned you this would happen, but you were so sure genetics didn't matter. So what if he didn't carry our blood? you said. He would still be as much a Sullivan as the baby we lost. Well, you were wrong, weren't you? Gutter genes are gutter genes."

Mick froze before he slowly turned to look at his father. "W-what . . . what's she talking about?"

His father dropped his head, then rubbed at the bridge of his nose with his thumb and forefinger. When he looked up again, the man who'd seemed invincible to Mick looked old and sick. "It's a fact you're not our biological child, Mick, but make no mistake, you're as much our son as your brother."

Mick's chest heaved, but he couldn't seem to get enough air into his chest. "I'm . . . adopted?"

Pop nodded. No, not Pop, he thought. Not his anyway. "The child your mother . . . that is, the child we were expecting died at birth."

His knees threatened to buckle. "Why didn't you tell me?"

When J. T. remained silent, he shifted his gaze to Marceline, who countered with a sleepy-eyed look of satisfaction. It made sense now. Why she never hugged and kissed him the way she had before his brother was born. All the hits he'd taken for no reason. The look in her eyes, as though he was some kind of mangy stray that had dared to cross her path.

"My real mother, who . . . who was she?" he made himself ask.

J. T. looked as uncomfortable as Mick had ever seen him. "A sweet lass from Seattle who had her baby the same day as ours. Being only sixteen and alone, she loved you enough to give you a good home."

Marceline snorted, and her eyes took on an ugly glitter. "She did no such thing and you know it."

"Enough!" Pop ordered, his voice harsh.

She ignored him. "Garbage, that's what she was. A hard-eyed little slut who sold us her mongrel bastard for ten thousand dollars."

"No, it's not true!" Mick turned to his father. "She's lying, right?" he begged, tripping over his words in his eagerness to get them out. "Tell me you didn't buy me the way she says."

J. T. shot Marceline a condemning look before answering.

When he did, his voice had a rough edge that scraped Mick raw. "We gave her money, yes, but only to help her get a new start."

Mick couldn't seem to get his mind around it all. "So . . . so I'm a bastard, right?"

"Technically, yes, but—"

He'd bolted, Rhys remembered now.

An hour later he'd been bleeding into the snow, his mother's vicious words still echoing in his head. Mick Sullivan should have been driving the 'Vette that day instead of his pickup, Rhys thought with a hard twist of his mouth as he turned away from the window. The fiberglass body would have shattered like an eggshell against the bus and only he would have died.

Chapter 6

Brina had just paid Angelo Stefanelli, her once-a-week gardener—who was also an old and dear friend—and was about to go back inside when she caught sight of Johnny's Corvette pulling into the lot. As he climbed out, he exchanged nods with the old man he'd known since childhood, then hailed her with his usual flashing grin.

To her surprise, he was dressed in a suit and tie. Although he had just turned thirty-seven, he was in better shape than when she'd married him. Not surprising, since he'd had the benefit of private lessons from his very own personal aerobics instructor for the last two—no, *three* years. The same one she herself had introduced him to after class one day. Little did she know her lawfully wedded *husband* and her good *friend*, Sherri McFee, would soon be getting sweaty together.

"Hey babe, lookin' good today," Johnny called, sidestepping the puddles on the walk as he strode toward her. "But then you always do."

Her heart sank. Johnny never complimented her unless he wanted something—or intended to be late with the child support. Probably the latter, she decided grimly.

"Nice tan," she commented sarcastically. "Makes you look almost young enough to be what's-her-name's daddy."

His friendly expression slipped long enough for her to feel a wicked satisfaction. "Cute, Brin. Real cute."

"Your *other* daughter is in the kitchen having her lunch," she said sweetly. "I'll tell her you're here."

"Wait," he said, his voice sharper. "I want to talk to you first."

Resigned to yet another battle over money, she leaned down to pluck a peony blossom from the bush next to the porch steps as Angelo's truck rumbled to life, spewing exhaust into the damp air.

"I don't know why you're still using Stefanelli to do your yard work," John grumbled as Angelo backed out. "The old geezer's so crippled with arthritis he's all but worthless."

Angelo waved as he drove off, and Brina lifted a hand in return. "He's just slow, that's all, and no one is better with roses than he is. Besides, I can't resist the clam sauce he gives me every Christmas."

John's gaze dropped to her hips. "Yeah, I can see that."

She felt the snide remark settle like lead in her stomach. *Remember, Brin, he can't make you feel bad about yourself. Only you can do that.* "Still the charmer, I see."

"Still the sarcastic bitch."

She inhaled swiftly, catching a whiff of his designer cologne. It was suffocatingly heavy. Sherri's choice, no doubt. "If you've come to give me another hard luck story about why the check will be late again, don't bother. The second installment on Jay's braces is due this month and you're already three payments behind."

His eyes narrowed, giving his face a sullen look. He'd been nearly insufferable since becoming one of the first locals hired by North Star after the buyout. He'd bragged all over town, hinting that his salary was only slightly smaller than Mr. Dunnigan's. As if he knew what Dunnigan earned! But when Brina had pressed him to contribute more to the children's support, he'd turned poor mouth again.

"I've explained about my financial responsibilities, Brina.

In two weeks, when my salary from North Star kicks in, I'll cut you a check."

"Like you did when your dad sold to North Star and you got a share of the profit?"

He had the grace to look mildly uncomfortable, which for Johnny was remarkable. "I realize this is a tough concept for someone with your limited common sense, but I was burned out. I needed that break in Vegas."

"I'll tell that to Jay's orthodontist. I'm sure he'll understand."

"Back off, Brin. I have an important job coming up. Once those trucks start rolling in I'll be living in a pressure cooker again, something someone like you can't begin to understand."

"I *understand* that your children need new clothes and an annual physical and the security of knowing their home won't be taken away because their father cares more about his stress level than their welfare."

"That's bullshit and you know it."

"Is it? What about that trip to Disneyland you've been promising them for the past three years?"

"Don't put that on me, Brina. I had it all arranged. You're the one who quashed the trip."

"Because *you* refused to leave your mistress at home."

"Sherri is my fiancée, and the kids aren't stupid. They know Sherri and I sleep together."

"Yes, but they shouldn't have to be in the same room when you're doing it!"

"Oh, for Christ's sake, Brina, give me some credit here. I—"

"Forget it, John. I don't have time to hassle with you now. Just send the check. In full. Otherwise, I swear I'll take you back to court."

Something ugly surfaced in his eyes. "Look, I didn't come here to swap threats with you," he said.

"Then why did you come, John?"

"This morning on her way to the gym Sherri stopped to fill

up at Dutch's Texaco and happened to see a top-of-the-line Mercedes with NORTH STAR 1 plates pulling out. As soon as her first class was over, she called to let me know. I figured it had to be Dunnigan, so I decided to come by and welcome him personally."

"Now, there's a new concept, the golden boy having to suck up to the boss." As soon as the words were out, Brina was ashamed of herself. "I'm sorry, John, " she said quietly, laying a hand on the arm that jerked under her touch. With an inner sigh, she withdrew her hand. "I know losing Sullivan and Son was almost as rough on you as it was on J. T."

"At least Dad kept the orchards and the home place."

With the yellow house that Brina spent years remodeling swallowed by the river, Johnny and Sherri had been forced to move in with J. T. temporarily. Brina had been surprised—and, though it pained her to admit it, deeply hurt—that J. T. had welcomed John's mistress into his home. She told herself it was because he was lonely, rattling around in that big house.

"Have you been to the warehouse since the contractor finished with the changes?"

John opened his mouth to reply when the smooth purring of a powerful well-tuned engine drew his quick gaze toward the lot. "Hell of a car," he said, his gaze greedy as he took in the sleek lines of the dark blue luxury sedan. "Must have cost a good hundred fifty grand easy. Probably more."

Brina had never been impressed with wealth. Johnny had had to order her to buy the designer clothes and flashy jewelry he'd considered a social necessity for the wife of a man in his position. After he'd started missing support payments, she'd been forced to sell off most of the jewelry to keep from losing the inn.

Johnny flicked her an annoyed look. "It wouldn't have hurt you to fix yourself up a little, Brin. Present a more sophisticated image to the paying guests."

She glanced down at the new jeans and loose fitting shirt

she had put on to replace her grubbies. "I'm the daughter of a home economics teacher and a mechanic, Johnny. I don't do sophisticated."

"Fake it, then. Like I told you more than once, I'm in a position now to recommend your inn to visiting customer reps, but I won't do that if you continue to look like the frigging maid instead of the owner."

She stifled the caustic remark that came to mind and instead leaned closer to say quietly, "Johnny, about Mr. Dunnigan—"

"Yo, who's the big guy with the cane?" he interrupted, his voice pitched too low to carry.

She shifted her attention to the lot where Rhys Hazard was climbing out of the car, his movements stiff as he favored his left hip. Sympathy ran through her as she watched him lean heavily on his cane, as though waiting out a stab of pain.

Though he still wore the sexy vest and jeans, he'd abandoned the hat. As he lifted his head, the wind tore at his thick sun-streaked hair, tossing it over his wide forehead. Robert Redford as the Sundance Kid, only taller and tougher, she decided as he lifted an impatient hand to brush it back. As he did, he gave the black Corvette a hard look before turning to say something to his driver, who'd just emerged.

"Jesus, who is that?" Johnny muttered, his tone derisive.

"Mr. Hazard's driver," she said, preparing to enjoy the meeting between her glib-talking ex and the rough-edged cowboy now heading their way.

Johnny jerked his gaze to her face. "The gimp with the cane, that's M. R. Hazard?"

Brina frowned at him. "He registered as Rhys Hazard."

"That's the guy."

The excitement in his voice surprised her. "How do you know him?" she asked. "Did Mr. Dunnigan mention him?"

"Oh yeah, he mentioned him, all right!" John shot his cuffs and straightened his tie. Amazing, she thought, the way he could turn it on. One minute he was in weasel mode; the next he was the suave corporate player working an angle. "Where is Dunnigan, anyway?" he muttered, as the rear doors to the Mercedes remained closed.

"That's what I started to tell you, John. Mr. Dunnigan had an auto accident on the way here. Mr. Hazard is going to take his place until he's recovered. I think he's some kind of troubleshooter for North Star."

He snorted, but his gaze remained on Hazard. "Troubleshooter? Jeez, Brin, how dumb can you get? The man *owns* the fucking company. Has his own high-rise in Phoenix. Had it designed by some famous Chink architect."

"He didn't *say* he owned the company, so how was I to know?"

"John Sullivan, this is your lucky day," John said under his breath before striding confidently down the walk, a well-manicured hand outstretched. Glaring after him, she wondered what the penalty was for breaking an ex-husband's nose.

Hazard stopped halfway to the porch, letting Johnny come to him. A grim look darkened the driver's face as he stepped forward. From his manner Brina had to wonder if Mr. Stillwell doubled as Hazard's bodyguard. For sure he had the build for it, not to mention the intimidating manner, although the tailored gray slacks, crisp white shirt and silk tie under a navy blazer seemed more appropriate for an executive than a thug. After a quiet word from his boss, he nodded—reluctantly, it seemed to her—then headed for the house.

Reminding herself that this particular thug was a guest, she managed a smile as he approached. "Your room is ready, Mr. Stillwell. Number 3. It's on the first floor, first hallway past the stairs. The key is in the lock. I've put extra towels in the bathroom, but if you need anything else, please don't hesitate to ask."

"Appreciate it, ma'am," he muttered in a rich tenor before climbing past her. Conscious of all she still had to do today,

Brina knew she should follow, but John had reached Hazard and she found herself lingering.

"Mr. Hazard, it's a great pleasure to meet you, sir," Johnny effused over the sound of the driver's heavy tread on the porch. "I'm John Sullivan Jr., your new director of sales and marketing."

Mr. Hazard made no move to accept the hand Johnny offered. He stood there for a long moment, his eyes turning colder and colder. "I know who—and what—you are, Junior," he said finally.

Johnny's brilliant smile faltered, and his jaw turned to chalk. "Holy Mother of God. I can't believe it! *Mick?*"

Brina's hand crept to her throat, and her heart started to pound. She took an involuntary step backward, her gaze riveted on the tanned face with the slashing cheekbones and square jaw. The Michael Sullivan she remembered had been a rawboned teenager, his face still showing hints of a young boy's innocence. There had been no cynical lines gouged next to his mouth, no hard-bitten anger in the thickly fringed eyes. No steely aura of power.

During the trial he'd been on crutches, his pelvis encased in plaster. Every time he moved, his face turned white from the effort. Brina had felt sorry for him, then hated herself for it. *Serves him right if he never walks again,* Stevie Schott's mother had said loud enough for the entire courtroom to hear. Michael Sullivan's broad shoulders had jerked, but he'd continued to stare straight ahead, his jaw rigid, his mouth set.

Seeing it again in her mind's eye, Brina had enough maturity now to recognize a scared boy's attempt to hang on to his dignity in the face of overwhelming hostility. It had taken courage to keep his head high and his shoulders back, especially when the judge had handed down his sentence.

Took his punishment like a man, her father had repeated over and over, as though he'd needed to reassure himself as well as her. Punishment aside, it didn't seem fair that Michael

Sullivan, now Rhys Hazard, was so successful while her brother and Stevie Schott had tasted only a few years of life. And that Mr. Gregory never got to watch his five children grow up. *Doesn't it haunt you to know what you did?* she wanted to shout.

"Jesus, Mick, does Pop know you own North Star?" John asked a little too loudly.

Hazard's wintry eyes narrowed. "I have no idea." Like a scorpion's tail, his quiet voice had a lethal sting. John visibly recoiled, but true to his weasel nature, he recovered quickly.

As though sensing her gaze on him, Michael shifted his attention her way. His mouth quirked as though he wanted to say something. Instead, he set that granite jaw and waited.

"My brother was one of your victims," she said in a wooden voice. "Teddy. Teddy Eiler. Or have you forgotten the names of the people you killed?"

"No, I haven't forgotten." His words had an edge, and there was a bottomless sadness in his eyes.

Now it made sense, the urgency in Ms. Campbell-Browne's voice, the plea in her eyes. She *knew,* Brina realized with a jolt of anger. "This morning, you let me think you were a stranger, Mr. *Hazard.*"

"I *am* a stranger."

"Is that why you took a new name? So no one would know who and what you really are?"

"My reasons are my own." His mouth flattened. "For what it's worth, I'm not any happier to be here than you are to have me, but with Hank laid up, I didn't have much choice."

"Don't mind Brin, Mick," John jumped in quickly, his smile ingratiating. "She's just a typical female. Everything's a big deal with her."

"We both know she has right to feel the way she does." Apology shimmered in Michael's eyes long enough for her to take a breath before his gaze turned dark with anguish. He lifted a hand to rake back his wind-tossed hair once again before glancing toward the street. When he looked back, his expression was once again guarded. "Look, I figure to be here for only a few months, less if I can work it out. Say the word and I'll bunk someplace else."

"Hell, no, a deal's a deal," John answered before Brina had a chance to unlock her clenched jaw. "Besides, Brina needs the bucks, don't you, babe?"

The lethal look Hazard sent Johnny's way had her ex's mouth snapping shut. "North Star will honor the contract as it stands whether I sleep here or not," Hazard said.

Surprised, she took a moment to consider. Could she really extend the hospitality of her house to her brother's killer? Cross paths with him every day, change his sheets, clean his bathroom with his belongings all around her? And what about Jay and Marcy? Michael Sullivan was their uncle, one they didn't know existed, to be sure, but still a blood relative. Family was sacred, her father had always said. A bond created by God that must be honored.

But he wasn't *her* family. Her kids were her only family now.

She could hear the questions now—and not just from the kids. Even though an entire generation had grown up since the accident, it hadn't been forgotten—and not just because of the monument either. Both the Schotts and the Gregorys had large, extended families that still lived in the area. Their lives had never been the same because of this man. How would they react to his reappearance?

She glanced down at the fluffy white flower still clutched in her hand. Without North Star's money, she almost certainly would be packing up to move out of the house she'd come to love. Money she'd already spent. Money she intended to *earn*. God, she hated these moral dilemmas and she hated Michael Sullivan. But Rhys Hazard? Did she hate him, too?

He's not only the strongest man I've ever known, but the

kindest and most decent, Della had said. *A better man than he's willing to believe.*

Even Brina's father had urged everyone to forgive and forget. *He's just a lad, scarcely older than you, darling girl. Our lives will never be the same, but neither will his. We've lost Teddy, but he's lost his entire family, at least for the years he has to spend locked up in that prison. We would all do well to remember that.*

She took a breath and lifted her head. Her father was the wisest, most decent man *she'd* ever known. She had no doubt he would have welcomed Teddy's killer into his home without reservation. How could she do less and still honor his memory?

"I'll stand by the contract as signed, Mr. Hazard," she said coolly, but firmly. "But I will ask that you not tell my children of your . . . relationship to them until I have a chance to prepare them."

Surprise crossed his face, followed by a look that seemed to hold a wary admiration. "Done," he said quietly before shifting his gaze to Johnny. "Be in my office nine o'clock Monday morning with a detailed outline of your marketing plan."

Johnny looked startled. "Jeez, Mick, what with me just getting back from Vegas yesterday, that doesn't give me much time."

"Then you'd better get started." The look he gave John warned against further protest. After waiting a beat to make sure his message had sunk in, he started forward, his pace deliberate, his features cast in impenetrable stone. For the briefest of moments, however, she'd glimpsed something white-hot and lethal beneath that stone.

She felt a chill, which turned to an actual shiver as he drew nearer. "It's not too late to change your mind," he said in a low voice. "Say the word and I'm out of here."

Oh, she was tempted. But she'd given her word. Besides, she abhorred cowardice, and that's what it would be if she sent him away simply because his presence would cause her pain. "There are twenty rooms in this house. I imagine we can manage to stay out of each other's way for a few weeks."

"I imagine we can."

Pausing at the top step, he turned to pin John with another icy look. "One more thing, Junior. My senior executives call me Rhys."

Johnny winked. "Sure, in the office, but we're family, you and me. It's hard to think of you as anything but Mick."

"We're not family, John," he said coldly. "We never were—and if you call me Mick one more time, you're fired."

The 'Vette's monster engine screamed as John rocketed along the narrow road bordering the river. Hands clenched around the wheel, he scarcely slowed for the twisting curves and bends he knew like the back of his hand.

As he drove, fury pounded in his head and poured acid into his belly. *No one* got away with treating John Sullivan Jr. like a half-wit flunky—especially not some fucking no-name mongrel son of a whore.

Hatred as deep as the flood waters at their zenith rose in his throat like bile, forcing him to swallow several times. Arrogant bastard had deliberately set out to humiliate him in front of his ex-wife. And the bitch had loved it, hadn't she? Smirking like she was getting off on Mick cutting him off at the knees.

Don't call him Mick? The very name was a foul taste in his mouth. His fury increased until it was a red haze between him and the road ahead. If it was the last thing he ever did, he would make *Mick* pay for what he'd done today. No, not just pay. He'd hold his head down in the muck and stomp on it. He'd make him *grovel*—and then he would ruin him!

It started drizzling again a few minutes before Brina collected Jay and his two classmates who made up her car pool. By the time she'd dropped off Eric Marsfelder and delivered

Petey West to his place near the Sullivan orchard, drops the size of quarters were battering the van's roof.

Every time she drove the boys' car pool she had to pass the intersection where Teddy had died. Sometimes she stopped at the memorial for a few minutes to remember the brother whose face was recalled only from photos now.

As she approached this time, the light ahead turned red, and Brina braked to a stop.

It had been below zero that awful December afternoon, the last day of school before Christmas vacation. She and Teddy had been talking across the aisle about what to buy their dad when their aunt took them shopping in Seattle the next day. She'd just suggested an insulated flannel shirt when Mr. Gregory jammed on the brakes and called out a violent curse. An instant later something slammed into the bus, sending it careening into the ditch.

Sometimes in the half-remembered nightmares that plagued her still, she could see Teddy's eyes filling with shock as the bus lurched sideways. He and Stevie Schott had been pinned in their seats when the side of the bus had crumpled inward. Teddy had screamed before losing consciousness. It was the last memory she had of her brother alive.

Pain ran through her. Damn Rhys Hazard, she thought, tightening her jaw. Just when she thought she'd made peace with the survivor's guilt that had been with her for years, he'd raked it all up again. Not just for her, but for all the families that had been affected. Now, Jay and Marcy were being pulled into the mess.

Lucy had been beside herself with joy when Brina had called to break the news. At least someone was pleased, she thought, glancing at Jay. This was as good a time as any to tell them what was happening, she decided. With a hard thud of pain, she realized that this was the perfect place. A not-so-subtle nudge from the universe, she decided.

When the light turned, she pulled across the intersection

into the paved turnout while her stomach did sick flip-flops. "Are we going to say hello to Uncle Teddy?" Marcy asked, craning her neck to peer through the windshield.

"I have something to tell you both, something important," Brina explained, letting the motor idle because the starter was still iffy.

"If it's about Dad and Sherri getting married on the Fourth of July, we already know," Jay said. "He told us before they left for Las Vegas."

"Actually, it's sort of about Daddy, but not about getting married." She realized she was stalling and took herself in hand. "When Daddy was growing up, he had a brother named Michael. He's three years older than Daddy. We haven't seen him for a very long time. Since way before Daddy and I were married, in fact."

Jay shot her a startled look before twisting to look at the memorial. He *knew,* she realized with a jolt. But how?

"How come me and Jay haven't ever seen Daddy's brother?" Marcy asked, sounding puzzled. Brina twisted around to smile at her daughter, who sat in her car seat like a princess on a throne. Beneath the hood of her red slicker, a riot of auburn curls framed a small, heart-shaped face. As dainty as a mountain violet, Marcy had inherited her father's deep blue eyes and dimpled smile—along with the maddening Sullivan charm.

"He . . . went away when he was eighteen," Brina explained.

Marcy blinked, her sweet mouth pursed in a frown. "You mean like Freddy Angleterre's sister went away last Christmas?"

"No, Freddy's sister went to live with Freddy's daddy in Portland. Michael went to . . . well, to a kind of prison." A juvenile camp, according to John, with tennis courts and dormitory beds instead of cells. Little more than a slap on the wrist after what he'd done.

"It's where they send gangbangers and druggies," Jay contributed with obvious relish.

Marcy's eyes grew round with a depth of horror only the innocent can manage. Overhead the rain seemed as harsh as shrapnel against the roof. "Daddy's brother was a gangbanger, like on TV?"

Brina made a mental note to monitor Marcy's TV watching more closely. "No, of course not. Your brother is just kidding." She shot Jay a look stern enough to have him slumping back against the seat again.

Firmly entrenched in what Brina had come to think of as his hulking male phase—even though he was as thin as a rail and barely topped her by an inch or so—he'd recently decided that slickers were for wimps. Framed by a mop of thick chestnut curls, his lean and angular face with its too sensitive mouth was still pale from last month's bout with the flu, giving him a fragile look that reminded her too much of her father after her brother Teddy's death. The sullen look had her stifling a sigh.

"Remember what I told you about what happened to Uncle Teddy?"

Marcy nodded. "He got killed when a truck smashed into his school bus and made it run into a ditch and got all crunched up."

"That's right. The truck that ran into the bus was Michael's." She took a breath. "He was driving too fast down Old Orchard Road and he couldn't stop when this light turned red. After they let him out of jail, he never came back to Osuma."

Marcy mulled that over before asking, "Did Daddy's brother look like him?"

"No, Michael has blond hair and gray eyes. He's taller than daddy by three or four inches and is a lot, well, broader." A natural athlete, he'd lettered in three sports and still held Osuma High School's record for most passing yards in a season, she suddenly recalled.

"Where did Daddy's brother go if he didn't come home?" Marcy looked puzzled.

"Usually he lives in Arizona, but he's going to be staying in the President's Room for the next few months. That's why I needed to tell you about him, so you'd understand if you heard someone talking about him." She took a breath, the stark image of his taut features superimposed over her troubled thoughts. "He changed his name from Michael to his middle name of Rhys. Rhys Hazard."

Marcy digested that before asking somberly, "Does that mean me and Jay are s'posed to call him Uncle Rhys?"

Brina considered. From what he'd said to John, he had no interest in renewing family ties. "I think it best you call him Mr. Hazard, both of you."

Jay shrugged. "Works for me."

"I like Uncle Rhys better," Marcy declared.

"I doubt that Mr. Hazard will be around the house much, but if you do happen to run into him, I expect both of you to be polite."

"Right, like I'm gonna go up to him and spit in his face on account of he killed my uncle," Jay muttered, his jaw tight and his lips plastered to an overbite sheathed in metal.

"Jay!" She sighed. "It's possible people will say some really ugly things about Mr. Hazard. They might even say them to you. I hope they don't, but I want you to be prepared and not take it personally."

"Why would they say bad things, Mommy?" Marcy asked, her eyes huge in her face.

"Because they're mad at him for what he did."

Marcy looked thoughtful. "When Joel Rampton hit Bobby Ruiz in the head with a rock, Mrs. Fieldstone made him say he was sorry before he could come back in the classroom. Maybe, if Mr. Hazard said he was sorry, he could be our uncle again."

Brina felt a pang of sadness. "It doesn't always work that way with grown-ups, honey."

"Do you think he's sorry, Mommy?"

Brina drew a long breath. Was he? "I don't know, Marcy."

"But if he was really, really sorry like Joel, then he could be our uncle, right?"

"If he was really, really sorry, yes, I suppose so."

"'Member when Jay broke Grandma Sullivan's pretty clock and she got all mad, even when Jay said he was sorry. And you said even if someone does something really naughty, it's not nice to stay mad at somebody after they say they're sorry and promise never to do the same bad thing again."

"Well, yes, I did say that, but—"

"So if Mr. Hazard says he's sorry, that's what's important, right? And then we can like him again."

Brina gave in with a sigh. Pinned to the mat by a five-year-old's unpolluted logic. "You're absolutely right, Marcy. That's what's important."

If only she could make herself remember that.

Chapter 7

J. T. had been born to the land, and it was to the land he always turned when he was heartsore. There was beauty there to soothe a man's deepest hurts, and strength to enable him to face one more day when all he wanted to do was lie down and die from the grieving. It was God's greatest gift to those who were wise enough to appreciate it.

Standing in front of the window at the far end of his den with his callused day laborer's hand wrapped around a glass of Irish whiskey, he trailed his weary gaze over the familiar, sharp mountain peaks.

It was a wild day, this, he decided. One minute calm with the promise of clearing, the next full of rain and bluster enough to turn the sky black, even though it wasn't yet five in the afternoon.

A man given to reflection might consider the stark contrast an omen of sorts. Good and evil, he thought whimsically before drinking in the soul-soothing view that had been the reason he'd chosen this room as his own when Marceline had gotten it into her head he needed a den like her father, the rich, sophisticated banker. As though a fancy rug and a bunch of spindly antiques that he was terrified to touch could turn a peasant Irishman into a gentleman.

Biting off a sigh, he dug callused fingertips into the back of his neck and did his best to loosen the knot that had twisted tight as soon as Lucy had called to tell him that his boy had come home. No, not a boy now, but a man of forty who'd been through the fires of hell when he'd still been as green as grass. A lad just turned eighteen thrown in with all manner of men without heart or soul or conscience.

He felt his throat tighten and his belly quake as he thought of the confining bars, cruel barbed wire and indescribable animal savagery. Such an experience could forge steel in a man or fill him with bitterness enough to shrivel his soul.

Mick had clearly made a success of his life, financially anyway, but what kind of a man had the laughing, mischievous boy with his heart on his sleeve become? It was a question that had tormented him daily since the last time he was face-to-face with his son. His fingers curled into a fist that he pounded softly on the sill. Eighteen years since Mick's release from prison, and in all that time not one word exchanged between the two of them. Lucy, damn her meddling soul, blamed him, but what choice had he had?

His chest rose and fell in a weighted sigh. *Ah, Mickey, if only you knew how it broke my heart to see them taking you away in chains, but there was nothing I could do for you, lad. It was your own actions that condemned you.*

His chest aching, he drained his glass, then turned away from the window to refill it. He had just broken the seal on a fresh bottle of Jameson's when John walked in, flushed and windblown and looking like he'd just been goosed. "Been to a funeral, have you, boyo?"

John shot him an impatient look. Never as quick as his brother's, the boy's sense of humor had developed a few more holes since his divorce. "You mean Brina didn't call you?"

J. T. shook his head. "Lucy."

"Figures." After stripping off his suit coat, John tossed it onto the back of his mother's favorite chair, then stripped off his tie and laid it carefully over the coat. "Bastard has his head up his ass if he thinks he can shove me around."

"You're not to call your brother names in this house!"

Jaw set, John took a barrel glass from the shelf and poured himself three fingers of scotch from the heavy crystal decanter. "It's the literal truth, isn't it? He was born a bastard. Adoption doesn't change that."

"It pains me to hear you say such a hateful thing."

John shrugged. "Just following Mother's example."

"Your mother was wrong to speak of it to you. We had agreed that neither of you was to know."

"You didn't say that when she was alive."

"Aye, I did, but not in your presence. What passed between your mother and me was private and will stay that way."

J. T. contemplated the whiskey in his glass and thought about the last time he and Michael had been together in this room. That excited he was, fairly bursting with the news he'd come to share. Like always, his gaze had gone to his mother first, gauging her mood. It broke his heart now, remembering how hard the boy had tried to please her when there'd been no way possible.

The lad had picked the worst possible moment to open himself up to a woman who'd stopped thinking of him as her son the moment Johnny was born. Still, she'd sworn an oath to him and to God never to let the boy know the truth. Looking back on it now, J. T. realized she'd actually enjoyed breaking her oath—and the boy's heart.

Mick had been white-faced and shaking when he'd spun around and raced for the door. Furious, J. T. had lifted the woman from her chair and shaken her so hard she'd gotten hysterical. By the time he'd calmed her down and followed Mick outside, the boy's rig was gone. The call from the sheriff's department had come thirty minutes later.

J. T.'s hand tightened around the glass as the memory of the next few hours rose to slap at him. It was bloody awful carnage he'd found at the bottom of the hill. Two boys dead and the driver dying right before his eyes.

One of the deputies at the scene knew him and pointed him toward the ambulance just pulling out. Mick was alive, the officer told him, but in a bad way.

From the skid marks he had to have been going upwards of ninety, maybe more. We won't know until the investigating team arrives. Worse, according to the deputy, it looked like Mick might have run a red light before hitting the bus.

J. T.'s knees had actually gone watery, and he'd had to lean against one of the fire trucks until he could force steel into them again. He'd prayed then, like he'd never prayed in his life. To the Blessed Mother, to the saints, to God and *His* Son. He'd begged then for the boy to live. For the others who'd been hurt. For the salvation of Mick's soul if he should die. Only later did his prayers beg the Blessed Mother to watch over the son he might never see again.

J. T. drained his glass in two swallows. He thought about a refill, then changed his mind. Whiskey dulled his mind if not the ache in his soul, and he had thinking to do tonight.

He leaned forward to take a cigar from the antique humidor bearing the crest of some hell-born English earl. Marceline thought it gave the room class. "How did Brina take to seein' Mick again?" he asked as he reached into his pocket for his lighter.

"She got emotional the way she always does." John snorted. "Can you believe it, she hadn't even recognized him when he walked in?"

J. T. puffed the cigar to life, then dropped the lighter on the blotter. "Is he changed that much, then?"

"Enough. Looks like a cowboy gimp, walks with a fancy cane."

J. T. grieved a little for the restrictions the boy had to endure. "How did he take to seeing you again?"

Something ugly flashed in John's eyes. "He acted like I was some day laborer, ordering me around."

"The man who signs the checks gets to give the orders. That's the way of the world, son."

J. T. leaned back and stretched his legs, wincing a little as his sore muscles protested. Between thoughtful puffs, he studied his son's face. The spitting image of his old man, everyone said. J. T.'s kid for sure. Except it had been Mick who had been most like him in all the ways that mattered. A mutt who fought for what he wanted instead of expecting it to be handed to him. A scrapper who'd blacked the eye of a school yard bully tormenting one of the migrant kids.

"I have half a mind to let the governor know what kind of man he's coming here to honor," John declared, eyeing the phone. "Remind him that Sullivan's contributed a bundle to his last campaign."

"Not Sullivan's," J. T. reminded him. "Me, personally."

"Same thing," John said impatiently.

J. T. contemplated the smoke curling upward from the tip of his cigar. "You ever stop to think what would happen if North Star pulls out now?"

"Yeah, my so-called brother will lose a bundle. Maybe enough to put him out of business."

"Could be, though that's doubtful." J. T. drew in a mouthful of smoke, savored the taste and the calm it brought, then tilted back his head to blow it toward the ceiling. "Without North Star, a lot of folks hereabouts will be out of work again. You included."

John flushed. "I had offers, lots of them. I just didn't want to leave the valley." His face hardened. "As for the rest of Sullivan's employees, hell, most of them are just as happy being on welfare and unemployment." John carried the decanter to the desk and sat down.

To hell with keeping a clear head, J. T. decided. He poured himself a triple and knocked back a good half before leaning back, glass in hand. It was his fault the boy was so self-involved. He should have put his foot down years ago. He should have done a lot of things years ago.

"Now, this is what a girl wants to see after a hard day, two good-looking men with their feet up."

The scent of John's intended teased J. T.'s nostrils as she entered. A tall, golden creature she was, too. Favored tight shiny workout togs, she did, designed to show off her charms. Today she wore a brassierelike thing that left her tanned midriff bare and shimmering pink shorts. Not so much as a ripple of fat marred the smooth line. A young man would need a will of steel to resist such a female when she cast her net his way. From the besotted flush on John's face as she leaned over him, J. T. doubted the boy had put up much of a fight.

"Yum, you taste like sin itself," she purred, then twittered when she caught J. T.'s eye. "I swear, J. T., this big ol' handsome son of yours has this way of making me forget my manners."

Made her forget the wife and children he'd had as well, he thought, but kept his thoughts to himself. God help him, he had enough sins on his own soul to worry about. "So will you be having a drink with us, then?" he asked politely.

"Well, maybe a small glass of wine before I hit the shower. I added a half dozen reps to my weight training regimen and I'm whipped." She flicked John a glance. "Some of that yummy Chardonnay we brought back from Vegas, please, honeybunch."

John took a quick sip–to cool himself off, J. T. figured—before setting the glass aside. "Coming right up, babe."

Sherri beamed him a smile before settling on one corner of his desk. A shameless hussy, his ma would have called her. Sweet, kindhearted Brina, with her sparkling brown eyes and honest smile, was worth a dozen Sherris with change left over.

"So what's got you two gorgeous males looking so serious?" she asked as John handed her the glass.

"The prodigal brother," John said with a sneer.

"Whose brother is that?" she asked brightly.

"Mine."

"If you don't want me to know, just say so," she chided peevishly before taking a dainty sip from one of Marceline's prized Waterford stem glasses.

John glanced his way before sighing. "I'm telling you the truth, honey. I have an adopted brother named Michael. He's three years older than me, and I haven't seen him since I was fourteen."

Sherri looked to J. T. for confirmation, and he nodded. "Michael—Mick—left town when he was eighteen and he's never been back."

"Dad's being tactful. Truth is, Mick was sent to prison for killing three people when his truck hit a school bus."

"Oh my God, that's terrible."

"Sure is," John said. "I was on that bus. Just luck I wasn't skewered, too."

"What do you mean, skewered?"

"The impact drove the steering wheel right through Mr. Gregory's chest."

"That's sick, Johnny," Sherri protested, but J. T. detected a glint of horrified fascination in her eyes. "You know how sensitive I am to gory stuff like that."

"Sorry, babe. How 'bout I take you out to dinner to make up for upsetting you?"

Her shiny lips turned down in a pout that J. T. suspected had proved to be a damn good bargaining chip when she was angling for something. "I'm not about to go to that awful Waffle Haus again," she declared. "Last time that horrible Wanda person hissed at me like I was some kind of criminal. I *know* she told that bitch waitress to spill red wine on my good silk blouse."

"I'll buy you a new one. A dozen new ones if that will make you happy."

She sipped wine, then ran her tongue over her bottom lip,

apparently thinking it over. "I'd rather have that Donna Karan evening gown I saw at Nordstrom's before we left for Vegas," she said in a coquettish purr.

"Consider it yours, sweetheart." Eyes glittering, John leaned forward to plaster his mouth to hers.

"For the love of God, John, keep it in your pants until the two of you are alone!"

The two of them drew apart like two kids caught in the glare of a cop's flashlight. Sherri giggled, then bit her lip. John rubbed a hand over his mouth. "Sorry, Dad. Guess I got carried away."

Sherri jumped up quickly and shot J. T. a flustered look. "I'll, um, just finish my wine upstairs." She gave John a quick peck on the check. "I'll be ready when you are, honeybunch," she murmured suggestively before heading for the door.

John watched her go, a hard flush rising on his cheekbones. Hooked right enough, the boy was, J. T. thought as John drained his glass. "Right behind you, babe!" John called after her as he carried his glass to the bar.

"About Michael," J. T. said, drawing his son's startled gaze. "You're not to call the governor, or anyone on his staff," he said coldly. "I won't have Mick embarrassed."

John stared at him as though he'd lost his mind. "C'mon, Pop. You know you wouldn't have sold the company if you'd known it was Mick who owned North Star."

"You're wrong, John," he said coldly and firmly. "I would have sold Sullivan's to the devil himself if it meant jobs for folks who stuck with me when times were bad." And maybe, if God and His blessed saints were with him, he'd given his son a reason to come home for good.

It was raining again, big drops that plopped on the inn's slate roof. The sound was particularly loud in the cozy room tucked under the sloping eaves where Brina was reading Marcy a bedtime story. Before Jay had decided a few years back that he was too grown-up for stories, the three of them had cuddled together. Now it was just Marcy and Mom tucked into Marcy's white-and-gold bed.

The scent of bubble bath and warm little girl teased Brina's nostrils as her plump little dumpling of a daughter snuggled closer. It was cozy here and the pillows behind her back were soft, so soft in fact she'd nearly dozed off a couple of times before the Prince swept a starry-eyed—and pathetically naive—Cinderella off into a happily-ever-after predivorce delusion of happiness.

Cindy, girl, take my advice and demand an ironclad prenup, Brina thought before giving in to a jaw-cracking yawn. In a minute she would summon the energy to uncurl her legs and dive in to the last of her long list of daily tasks.

"Time to snuggle down, sweetheart," she said as she closed the book that had been hers as a child.

"One more, Mommy, *puh-leeze,*" Marcy pleaded, looking like a scrubbed Botticelli cherub in her candy-striped jammies.

"Not tonight, sweetie. Mommy still has to make the dough for the breakfast rolls."

A frown pleated an ominous V between Marcy's brows, while her small chin jutted forward. "Why can't I sleep in Miss Merribelle's room like always?"

"Remember, we agreed you would only be sleeping in Miss Merribelle's room until the roof was patched? Now that it's fixed, Mommy needs to rent your room so you and I and Jay can go on living here."

A haggling gleam appeared in her daughter's eyes. "You could rent this room instead, 'specially if the people have a little girl."

Brina hid a smile. There was nothing she liked better than a good haggle. "Guests stay on the first and second floors. This floor's just for family. Our special nest." She smiled. "Besides, it's such a nice room. Remember how excited you were when we found the Pooh wallpaper?" For days after she'd painstakingly fitted it to the sloping walls and twin dormer alcoves, Brina had seen Pooh and Eeyore and Tigger marching through her head.

"But I like the President's Room *lots* better," Marcy protested. Brina could almost see the wheels turning behind those big blue eyes. "This dumb ol' bed's too small. I'm liable to fall out and break my arm like JoEllen when she fell off the jungle gym."

"I slept in this same bed until I was a lot older than you are now."

"Sherri said I could come and live with her and Daddy all the time when they have their own house again. She always wanted a little girl like me."

Well, she can't have you, Brina thought with a furious scowl before she caught herself. "That's because you're one extra special kid," she said as she bent to slip Tigger beneath the quilt.

"Sherri's full of shit!" Jay pronounced from the doorway.

Startled, Brina spun around to shoot her son a reproving look. Like just about everything she aimed his way these days, it seemed to bounce off without making the slightest dent. "One more statement like that, young man, and you'll spend the next month pulling KP," she promised.

"What's KP, Mommy?" Marcy demanded.

These days Jay was mostly arms and legs. Given the fact she was always having to buy him sneakers, Brina swore his feet were growing at least an inch a week. Though his shoulders showed the promise of width in a year or two, they were mostly bone now, with only a thin layer of muscle to pad the sharp angles.

"KP is an army term that means 'kitchen police,'" Brina explained. "Grandpa Eiler said he must have peeled a million potatoes before he was discharged."

Marcy looked intrigued. "Is Jay going to peel potatoes?"

"No way!" her son declared. "That's woman's work."

Brina heard the echo of his bigoted father and stifled a sigh. "It's honest work for man or woman," she corrected. "And if I say you're going to peel potatoes, John Thomas Sullivan III, you *will* peel potatoes."

Jay set his jaw. "I was just saying what's true," he declared. "Dumb old Sherri pretends she likes us, only when she thinks we can't hear, she's always whining to Dad about how much trouble we cause whenever we're around."

"You're just mad on account of she called you a wimp," Marcy chirped.

"Marcy," Brina chided. "I'm sure you must have misunderstood."

"Huh-uh. I heard her telling Daddy how she wanted to have a baby after they were married on account of Daddy should have a son named after him who wasn't such a wimp. She said it was probably all your fault, on account of you babied Jay too much. She said he was probably going to turn into a fag."

Hurt flashed in Jay's eyes before he bolted across the landing to his own room, slamming the door behind him. Brina's jaw turned to stone.

"Mommy, what's a fag?" Marcy's curious tone was unaffected by Jay's outburst. She was used to her brother's mercurial moods.

Still seething, Brina forced a smile. "It's a term very ignorant people use when they want to be particularly nasty. Sherri should have known better, and I don't ever want to hear *you* using that word again, is that clear?"

Marcy nodded, her lashes heavy. "Night, Mommy," she murmured, her voice slurred. "I love you lots."

Brina bent to kiss the soft pink cheek half buried in the pillow before snapping off the bedside lamp shaped like Pooh. "Good night, sweetheart. I love you lots more."

At the expected conclusion to the nightly ritual a sweet smile flitted over Marcy's lips.

Careful to leave the door ajar, Brina crossed the large square landing to Jay's room and knocked on the door.

"Jay, can I come in?" she called. After fortifying herself with a deep breath, she inched open the door and looked in. Jay was sprawled facedown on top of the rumpled red, white and blue quilt, his face buried in the pillow.

"Jay? Are you all right?"

His thin shoulders jerked, and he mumbled something that sounded like "Go away."

"Honey, Sherri doesn't have enough gray matter in that bleached blond head of hers to fill a teaspoon."

When Jay didn't respond, she pushed open the door and made her way through the minefield of discarded books, filthy high-top sneakers and plastic model parts. A half-built replica of a low-slung sports car Brina didn't recognize sat on an old kitchen table she'd salvaged from the inn's basement shortly after moving in. Schoolbooks were piled next to the model, unopened as usual. Jay's grades had slipped badly this year.

Frowning, she plucked a sock from the top of his desk lamp. After a testing sniff—which she immediately regretted—she tossed it toward the hamper under the large poster of the first Sting Ray, a 1963 split-window coupe like his father's.

She crossed to the bed and sat down. Though she longed to take her son's stiff body into her arms, she knew he would flinch away. Maybe it was a first step toward a necessary— and desirable—separation, and healthy for an adolescent male, but it still shredded Brina's heart every time.

"Sweetie, Marcy didn't mean to upset you. She was just re-peating something she heard."

"Whatever."

Brina clenched her jaw. Lord, how she hated that word. "You're not a wimp, Jay," she said. "You're intelligent and kindhearted and wonderfully talented. Just because your life's goal isn't to grow up to butt heads with some steroid-crazed

Neanderthal on the fifty yard line of some muddy field doesn't mean you're not manly."

"Dad's ashamed of me," he mumbled into the pillow. "He wishes I wasn't his kid."

"No, he doesn't, sweetie. Maybe he doesn't show it sometimes, but he loves you very much." As much as Johnny the Weasel could love anyone other than himself.

"Then how come he wants me to go to some kind of sports camp for retards this summer?"

Shock sifted through her, pushing away some of the weariness. "Who told you that?"

"He did, right before him and Sherri left for Vegas. Claimed it would toughen me up so I won't disgrace him when I go to high school next year."

God, what had she ever seen in that man? "This is the first I've heard of any camp, Jay. Otherwise, I promise you, I would have told Dad to forget it."

"Yeah, well, he had the brochures and everything." Jay turned his head to look at her. The wavering tracks of tears on his thin cheeks tore at her heart. Jay hated to cry. Even as a child he had preferred stony silence to tears. "He said he was going to sign me up when he got back."

"He can sign you up, but that doesn't mean you have to go."

"He'll make me, just like he made me take those stupid karate lessons. And then he'll get mad on account of I'll probably be hopeless at football too."

Brina heard the desolation beneath the sullen tone. "You weren't hopeless at karate, Jay. Just because you weren't the star pupil doesn't mean you were a failure. In fact, Mr. Wong had some very nice things to say about your tenacity."

"Tell that to Dad," Jay muttered.

She had, many times. Instead of listening, John had simply railed at her for coddling his son. *Hell, I should have known how it was going to be when you freaked out every time he so much as scraped his knee.*

But football? She shuddered inwardly. Jay barely weighed a hundred pounds. Twenty-five pounds less than her, in fact. She'd seen the boys who played these days. Glowering, monstrous hulks as big as tanks. Jay was sure to get a significant number of his parts smashed, squeezed or torn off. Not to mention the damage to his self-confidence.

Besides, John and his brother had both played football, and what had that done for them? John was an insensitive jerk, and his brother—

Don't go there, she reminded herself, biting off a sigh.

"Jay, the judge made it clear that your dad and I both have to agree on important decisions. And I give you my word, I don't intend to agree to any football camp. Not unless it's what you want."

"Yeah, right," he muttered, sitting up suddenly. Eyes narrowed, he challenged her with a look dripping accusation. "Like you cared about what I wanted when you kicked Dad out."

Expelling a long breath, Brina dug through the fog of her own exhaustion for an extra measure of patience. "I cared, Jay. I simply didn't have a choice."

"Yeah, right."

Brina reached out to touch his shoulder. "Jay, sweetheart, listen—"

In two quick, jerky movements, he rolled to his back and surged to his feet. "I gotta call Pete about something," he muttered before walking out, leaving her staring after him.

"So what do I do now?" she muttered aloud in the hope of catching the ear of a benevolent eavesdropping spirit. "Do I punish him for being rude? Do I cut him slack because he has an ignoramus for a father? Or should I just cut to the chase and lock him in his room until he's twenty-one and human again?"

When no answer rang out, she straightened her tired shoulders and stood up. Tomorrow she would ask her friend Summer Hollister, a psychologist used to handling kids, for the name of the best child psychologist within driving distance. If she had to sell a few pieces of valuable furniture to pay for it, so be it.

Her baby was in trouble, and it seemed she was the only one who cared.

After preparing dough for the breakfast rolls and cleaning up the kitchen, Brina went into her office to check her messages. There were four—three requests for reservations for the weekend of the fifteenth, which she had to refuse, and one from Henry Dunnigan. After explaining that he'd lost the paper with Hazard's cell phone number written on it, he politely requested that she ask his boss to call him at San Francisco General Hospital. Since Hazard and the others had yet to return from dinner out, she decided to slip the note under Hazard's door on her way upstairs.

After turning off the light, she crossed the foyer to the parlor. Game faces firmly in place, Ernestine and the colonel were seated at an octagonal card table in front of the large bay window overlooking the gazebo and herb garden. For the colonel, these games of Scrabble that he and Ernie played almost every night were as deadly serious as any of the battles he'd fought as an infantryman during Korea and Vietnam.

Despite her delicate features and slim body, Ernestine had proved to be a formidable opponent. Her phenomenal recall of obscure words was her secret weapon. After the first few weeks she'd suggested they "make it interesting" by playing for a penny a point. At the last reckoning, the colonel owed Ernie 6,704 dollars and some odd cents.

Both looked up as Brina entered. "Is the little angel all tucked in?" Ernie asked with a fond smile. Behind gold-rimmed glasses her pale green eyes twinkled with good humor, aided, Brina suspected, by a small libation or two, courtesy of the colonel's bottomless hip flask.

"Tucked in and already asleep, thank goodness." Stifling

another yawn, Brina crossed to the credenza between the two large double-hung windows facing Maple Street to pour herself a cup of chocolate macadamia nut coffee. After taking a thirsty sip, she wandered over to check out the board.

"'Zarf?'" Brina read aloud. "What in the world is that?"

"Exactly what I asked her, my dear," the colonel declared. "She *claims* it's some gizmo or other they use in the Middle East to hold a hot coffee cup."

"I'm not just *claiming* it, Fitz. It's a fact. And before you start again, although the word is of Arabic derivation, it *is* in the dictionary, which makes it perfectly legal."

Bowing to the inevitable, the colonel signaled his surrender by dumping his remaining tiles onto the table. "Shall I season your coffee, my dear?" he asked, reaching for his silver flask.

"Perhaps a bit," Ernie said, moving her cup and saucer closer to his side of the table. "To keep you company."

Ernie had turned forty-five last August. By her own reckoning, she was an ordinary, dull, painfully plain single woman. Not true, Brina had told her more than once. Maybe Ernestine wasn't drop-dead gorgeous, but she had a boyish figure Brina envied and a pleasant face. Even more importantly she was kind and generous and, when she was among people she trusted, wickedly funny.

Brina had never detected anything remotely romantic between her two boarders and had often wondered why they hadn't fallen in love. In her opinion, they seemed a perfect match—cultured and intelligent, with a love of books and nature and opera. Brina suspected that the colonel was still in love with his late wife, Thui.

Brina watched as the colonel tipped the flask over Ernie's cup, then glanced Brina's way. "How about you, my dear? A taste of Jack Daniel's finest this evening?"

She opened her mouth to decline as she always did, then changed her mind. "Make it a double," she added, pulling out one of the two empty chairs. Maybe the liquor would dull the pulsating stress headache she'd brought downstairs with her.

Looking first startled, then delighted, Colonel Fitz added a generous "taste" to her coffee, then did the same to his own. When the flask returned to his pocket, he lifted his cup to her, his expression both benign and intense.

"Here's to our lovely landlady, who has been working above and beyond duty for months now," he said with a fond smile. "We, who are the beneficiaries of your hard work and determination to carry on as graciously as possible, salute you, my dear." His voice thickened, and he had to clear it before adding gruffly, "Well done."

"To you, Brina," Ernie said, lifting her cup as well. Her eyes were filled with affection. "You've made a warm and loving home and filled it with kindness and generosity and laughter. I thank you from the bottom of my heart."

As the two of them drank the unexpected toast, Brina was shocked to feel tears welling in her eyes. "I . . . thank you both," she managed. "I couldn't have survived these last awful months without the two of you."

"The pleasure was ours," the colonel assured her as he re-placed his cup in the saucer. At the same time the porcelain clock on the mantel chimed the half hour. Eight thirty and all's . . . a miserable mess, Brina thought as she brought her own cup to her lip and drank deeply.

The potent bourbon burned so fiercely she instinctively sucked in air, only to break into a furious coughing fit when the last of the swallow went down her windpipe.

"Oh dear, are you all right?" Ernie cried. The colonel shot to his feet and began thumping her on the back so vigorously she nearly ended up plowing a furrow through the Scrabble tiles with her nose.

"Stop pummeling the poor girl, Fitz!" Ernie got up so quickly her chair teetered. Brina tried to nod agreement, only to find herself all but smothered by her own hair, which had escaped the scrunchy holding it atop her head. She shoved it aside and tried to catch her breath.

"I'll get some water," Ernie said before hurrying out.

An instant later, Brina heard the telltale tinkling of temple bells. Her guests were returning. *Oh no, not now!*

Still wheezing like a rusty bellows, she tried to tell the colonel she was fine, only to break into another flurry of wracking coughs.

"Is she all right?" she heard Della asking. The colonel stopped whacking Brina's back and stood frozen, his expression registering the stunned surprise Brina suspected most men experienced when catching sight of Ms. Campbell-Browne for the first time.

"I'm . . . fine," Brina managed to gasp out as tears ran down her face. Behind Della stood the no-neck chauffeur and behind him, Rhys Hazard—two large men, one as scary as a dark alley, the other annoyingly attractive despite the set of that rock-hard jaw.

"Not to worry, ma'am," the colonel jumped in, his Southern drawl suddenly far more pronounced. "Dear Brina has just had a little disagreement with Gentleman Jack Daniel himself. He can be a mite difficult for a lady to handle."

"Had a few tussles with that *man* myself when I was young and stupid." Della winced, then offered Brina an apologetic look. "Sorry, Brina, that didn't come out right."

"No . . . offense taken," she muttered between wheezing breaths. "I don't usually drink." Pressing her hand flat against her chest, she drew in a lungful of much needed air. She caught Hazard's eye and realized he looked amused. She lifted her chin and narrowed her gaze in her own version of a glare. For all the good it did, which from the appearance of the deepening laugh lines around his eyes, was pretty much zilch.

"Perhaps you should lie down, my dear," the colonel suggested, still hovering.

"You do look a little pale," Della agreed.

"Truly, I'm fine," she declared in a voice that was almost normal now. Her throat felt scalded, and her pulse was skittering all over the place. She found herself looking directly at Hazard as she added, "My *coffee* just went down the wrong way."

One side of his mouth curled up. "*Coffee* does that sometimes," he replied solemnly. His gravity annoyed her even more than open amusement, especially since she sensed he was laughing inside.

She summoned a public smile and performed polite introductions. *The Successful Innkeeper always strives to make all guests feel included in any social gathering.* Provided she wasn't choking on a double shot of the hard stuff.

During the ensuing flurry of handshakes and polite greetings, Ernie returned with the water and Brina took a long, grateful swallow while the colonel offered coffee or sherry from the cut-glass decanter.

"Sherry for me," Della said.

"Gentlemen?" the colonel inquired. "Join us?"

"I'll pass, thanks," Hazard replied before turning toward the stairs. The driver shot a quick look after his employer before shifting his gaze to the bar. "Wouldn't mind a snort of that stuff in the fancy bottle."

That *stuff* being a budget-busting Napoleon brandy, purchased especially to impress her VIP guests.

"Will we get to meet your kids tonight?" Della asked Brina as the colonel attended to the drinks.

"Unfortunately, no," she said, rising. "Marcy's in bed and Jay's pretending to do homework. I was just about to say good night and head upstairs to check on him when you came in." She swept them all with a polite smile before excusing herself.

"Good night, dear," Ernie called, her face flushed. The colonel and Della echoed her words, while the driver grunted something that sounded like "Night."

Still carrying the now empty glass, she checked to make

sure the front door was securely locked, then returned the glass to the kitchen before heading for the stairs and her last chore of a surreal day. After the activity and high good spirits in the parlor, the second floor seemed unnaturally quiet. Almost lonely.

She took a deep breath—and reminded herself of all the good things North Star was doing for her friends and neighbors, and, okay, for her and the kids, too. Then she lifted her hand and rapped sharply on the door to Number 4.

To her surprise, the door edged open a few inches as soon as she touched it. The muted glow of the circa 1920s boudoir lamp on the bedside table was the only illumination. She realized she was holding her breath and let it out slowly.

"Door's open, Del," Hazard called with that trademark impatience.

"It's Brina Sullivan, Mr. Hazard."

"Door's still open, Ms. Sullivan." Was it her imagination or was there a hint of laughter salted into that impatient drawl?

Seated on the bed, he watched her as she entered, those brutally large hands stilled in the act of unbuttoning the shirt he'd already tugged free of his jeans. She couldn't help noticing the wedge of bronzed, muscular chest so dramatically framed by the pale blue cotton. Softly curling hair glinting gold in the light covered truly awesome pectoral muscles in a very intriguing pattern. Not that she cared all that much for chest hair, she reminded herself. So it was doubly annoying when her mouth suddenly went dry.

"Uh, I'll come back when—"

"Married eleven years, two kids, you must have seen Junior without his shirt at least once," he drawled, his gaze both challenging and watchful. Unbidden, her gaze returned to that wedge of darkly tanned skin covered with silky hair. It would tickle her nose or . . . her bare breasts, she thought before pulling herself up short.

"He plucks his," she said with a frown as impatient as his.

He bunched tawny brows over a nose that was a fraction off-center. "Come again?"

An *idiot,* she decided. He thinks I'm an idiot and is even now wondering if he should ask for North Star's deposit to be returned due to innkeeper eccentricity. "His chest," she clarified with as much dignity as she could scrape together. "John plucks his chest hair."

"Yeah?" He looked as though he didn't know whether to believe her or not. He also looked reluctantly intrigued. "Why?"

"Well, he said it was because it made him too hot when he wears a vest under his suit coat, but I have a strong hunch he's ashamed because it grows so weird."

"Weird how?"

"Why ask me? You must have seen him with his shirt off, too."

"Right, like he had hair on his chest at fourteen." In a blink the hint of bemusement in his eyes vanished, and the steely hardness returned. For the tiniest of moments, however, she saw a glimpse of emotion so dark and violent it shook her.

The Successful Innkeeper is not a wimp! she made up on the spot. "I won't keep you," she said. "I just came in to give you this message from Mr. Dunnigan." At the look of alarm that crossed his face, she hastened to add, "He sounded fine, at least to me. He asked that you call him at the hospital, but I didn't sense any urgency in his voice. He left the number." She stepped forward to hand him the message slip.

"Thanks," he said, his face softening slightly. "Sorry for your trouble."

"Accommodating guests is my business, Mr. Hazard."

"Even one you hate?" he asked in a deceptively soft voice.

"Yes, even one I hate," she said just as softly before walking out.

Rhys woke up in a cold sweat, his cheeks wet from tears, his chest heaving from the effort to breathe. For a terrible few seconds he felt the walls squeezing in on him. Fighting panic, he rolled to his back and fumbled to turn on the bedside lamp. Light flooded the room, searing his gritty eyes, and yet anything was better than the smothering blackness.

He'd had the same miserable dream again. The one where he was lying shivering in the snow while blood poured from the door of the bus and voices screamed for help. He tried to get up, to help the injured, but shackles held his arms and legs immobile.

Lying back against the now sodden pillow, he stared at the ceiling, forcing himself to take slow, deep breaths until the crushing weight on his chest eased. He'd been a month into his sentence the first time he'd had the dream. It had been the first crack in the numbness that had come over him in the courtroom when the judge pronounced his sentence and he realized he was actually going to be locked up for a long time.

Prison was where they sent other people, not him, he'd kept thinking, even when the prosecutor was grilling him. He wasn't old enough to go to prison. He hadn't even finished high school or had sex for the first time or voted or gotten good and drunk. It had started to feel real when they'd put on the leg shackles. It got a whole lot more real the first time he'd been forced to submit to a strip search. He'd started to shut down then. Little by little, hour by hour he stopped feeling, stopped caring, stopped thinking about anything except getting through the next minute. Two weeks after his sentencing, they'd transported him to McNeil Island. His new home was a six-by-ten cell, shared with a taciturn ex-stockbroker doing twenty-five to life for killing his wife and her lover.

At first he'd accepted the restrictions and calculated humiliations with the dumb obedience of a trapped animal. With that first spring, when the trees he could see through the window began to leaf out, the numbness had gradually worn off. It was then, in the long, empty hours of the night with the demented sounds of other caged men echoing off the dingy cement walls, that he'd known he would never make it through four years without going crazy. Or worse, without becoming as vicious as the men around him.

All he had to do to end it was drop a few badass remarks to any one of many psychotic thugs during exercise period, then turn his back. With the guards patrolling the area, it would have to be quick, his death. A swipe of a homemade knife across his jugular, a quick thrust to the gut, he didn't much care. No one would give a damn anyway. Hell, Marceline would probably pop the cork on a bottle of that imported French champagne she liked so much and throw a good-riddance-to-bad-rubbish party. In the end it was that image that had given him the guts to stay alive. He'd refused to give her the satisfaction.

He had served every single day of his sentence. Three times he'd come up for parole. Three times he'd been refused.

When they finally had to let him out with 237 dollars he'd earned washing dishes in the prison kitchen tucked into the pocket of a cheap suit, he'd headed for the nearest McDonald's to wolf down the Big Mac and fries he'd been craving. After he'd eaten, he'd tracked down the nearest thrift store, exchanged the ill-fitting suit for jeans, a couple of T-shirts and a worn-out jacket, then caught a ride with a trucker hauling logs to California. As they'd crossed the border at Portland, he'd vowed never to return to Washington—and he hadn't. Until now.

He wiped his damp face and chest with the fancy sheet before shoving one clenched fist under the down pillow. God help him, why did it have to be *her* brother he'd killed? Why did it have to be anyone? Pressure built in his chest, the edges sharp with the guilt and remorse that never quite went away.

Of course she hated him. Why wouldn't she? He'd hated himself for years.

Chapter 8

It wasn't quite five thirty, and everyone except Rhys was still fast asleep. Outside the turret room the streetlamp still glowed an eerie blue. Once in a while a lonely bird sent out a morning greeting that wasn't returned. Even the wind that had set the leaves rattling in the predawn hours had died by the time the wispy light had turned the inky blackness to a soft charcoal gray.

According to Max, who'd checked out the first two floors with the thoroughness of a Secret Service agent preparing for a presidential visit, the kitchen was at the back of the house. The map on the back of the door designed to show the fire escapes and exits also revealed nine bedrooms on two floors, a parlor, an office, a library, a large dining room, and a utility room off the kitchen. Rhys had to assume there were more rooms on the third floor, where Brina and her kids lived. It was a lot of house for a woman alone to maintain, even with presumably half of John's assets as a cushion.

Did she have a man in her life, someone steady and reliable to pitch in when things got too much for her? he wondered. A man who didn't treat her like a child with only half a brain the way his ass of a brother had yesterday afternoon. A man who appreciated fresh flowers in his room and towels smelling of sunshine because they made him feel that he was special to her. Even though Rhys was *not* special, he reminded himself as he made his way to the kitchen.

The old-fashioned swinging door had been left open, and a hint of cinnamon tantalized his senses as he walked in. It took him a moment to find the light switch, another to check out the pretty room with its cheerful lemony walls and bright pots of herbs on the windowsill. The industrial-sized stainless-steel refrigerator was covered with crayon drawings bearing the names of both kids alongside snapshots of birthday parties and Christmas mornings.

Her coffeemaker was heavy-duty and included an espresso maker. No doubt cost her a bundle, he thought as he went about brewing a full pot, then searched the cupboards for a mug large enough to serve his craving.

He figured Brina was still asleep. Rhys was just as glad. He was a damn clam before the caffeine had worked its way to his brain, one of the reasons he always woke up alone. On the rare occasions when he accepted a lady's invitation to make love in her bed, he always left as soon as the lady's afterglow faded.

Del claimed he was afraid of intimacy, more of that femme-speak she was so fond of throwing at him. *People need to communicate, to share their feelings with one another,* she'd say, peering deep into his eyes in that unnerving way of hers. Except that while you were pouring out your guts, you were also handing the listener the perfect weapon with which to bludgeon you later on.

No, solitude suited him just fine.

Brina was never at her best in the morning. If she ran the world, civilized people would get up at noon and go to bed around four a.m. Though she'd learned how to fake cheerfulness for her guests, inside she was ready to chew nails before her second cup of coffee kicked in. Add a restless night to that equation, and this Successful Innkeeper was definitely not in a good mood.

She was halfway down the back stairs when she caught a whiff of fresh-brewed coffee. The wishful thinking of a desperate woman, she decided. A few paces from the kitchen door she realized it was real. *Bless you, whoever you are.*

Her determinedly cheerful smile died as she caught sight of Rhys Hazard leaning against the counter, a steaming mug held in one large hand. His cane was propped next to him, and she noticed he stood with most of his weight on his right leg.

Apparently fresh from the shower, he smelled of the sage and citrus soap she had custom-made for Nightingale House. His heavy eyelids suggested he'd spent a restless night.

Once again he wore cowhand Wranglers worn thin in some intriguing places and a faded work shirt stretched taut across a lean midriff. His storm-colored eyes were half-closed and sleepy. Viewed against the familiar backdrop of her kitchen, he seemed big and brawny and very, very male. All kinds of warning bells started clanging.

It was only sex. S-E-X! And therefore easily ignored.

"Morning," he said with an impersonal nod.

"Same to you," she muttered, stifling a yawn.

He set his mug on the counter, then turned to take its twin from the cupboard. "This should help," he said as he filled it, then extended it to her, handle first.

Though she usually added sugar, she was too tired to make the effort. The coffee was strong enough to snap open her synapses. A little blue sky edged into her mental gloom. Glancing up, she found him studying her through the rising steam.

"Feeling better now?" he asked.

"It's too soon to tell, but at least I have hope now."

Some of the tightness around his mouth eased. It wasn't exactly a smile, but it had potential. Not that she cared whether or not he ever smiled again, she reminded herself—and then immediately felt petty.

"Rough night?" he asked.

"Depends on your definition of rough."

He shrugged. "Bad dreams, insomnia, a mean-as-sin knot in your gut—take your pick."

"Yes."

He lifted tawny eyebrows. "Yes, what?"

"Yes, all of the above." Uncomfortable with the intimacy she felt suddenly, she carried her mug to the counter in order to add sugar from the bowl shaped like a pumpkin, stirring it in with one of the sterilized Popsicle sticks she kept in a jelly jar.

Sipping greedily, she wandered over to the kitchen sink and inspected her herb garden. Finding the lemon sage on the dry side, she took the pot from the saucer and set it in the sink, then used the sprayer to mist the leaves. After her father's death, she'd dug up the herbs from the garden her mother had planted. These few were all that remained.

After breaking off a leaf, she inhaled the pungent scent. Memories of her last years in the little house on Water Street exploded into her mind. Images of her mother's wake were hazier now, but Teddy's was still vivid. Something had died in her father when they buried Teddy. Something vital and strong, leaving him a walking, talking shell. How many nights had she labored over a special meal, only to eat it alone when her father came home too wasted to eat? How many times had she paced the floor, terrified that she would receive a call from the hospital or the morgue? Becoming orphaned had been her greatest fear.

"I know this is rough, Brina, my being here in your house," Rhys said. "If I could make this all go away, I would." The rough burr in his tone surprised her into turning. His eyes were haunted, but she didn't want to feel sorry for him.

Sorrow and an anger she welcomed suddenly brought heat to her face and passion to her voice. "What exactly would you take away, Mr. Hazard? Grief so deep it killed my father years before his time? Worry about what another media feeding frenzy could do to my children if your presence here rakes up past history? A sick feeling in my stomach when the governor calls you a hero in front of the town?"

Even as her conscience reminded her that he'd declined to attend the ceremony, his mouth flattened. "I tried to make this as painless as possible." His voice had turned cold. "It didn't work out that way, and I'm sorry about that."

She didn't want to accept his apology, damn it. She wanted him to hurt the way she'd hurt, to know what it was like to lose people she loved for no reason. "I'm sorry, too," she said stiffly. "Sorry my brother didn't get to grow up and get married and have babies."

His eyes turned hard and inscrutable. Still holding her gaze, he drained the mug in two swallows, then reached for his cane. With the quick, deft movements of a man accustomed to fending for himself, he washed and rinsed the heavy mug before upending it in the drainer and turning to her.

"I'm going to say this only once, so listen carefully." Although his voice was barely louder than a whisper, it compelled her to do as he demanded. "I've lived with the mistakes I made every damn day for the past twenty-two and a half years. What happened that afternoon was waiting for me this morning when I opened my eyes, and it'll still be with me tonight when I close them again. Most nights it's even in my dreams.

"I'm as sorry as I can be about your brother and the others. If I could die to bring them back, I would, but life doesn't always give you a second chance, no matter how hard you wish for it. If you want to hate me, that's your problem, but I'm not spending the rest of my life begging for forgiveness. Not from you or anyone else." He wrapped one big, brutal hand around the handle of his cane and walked out.

The more time Rhys spent in the office that had once belonged to J. T., the more he felt the old man's presence. He worked his way through a morning filled with one conference call after another. Della helped, consulting with him on one thing or another having to do with the hiring process, then bullied him into taking her to lunch in Wenatchee so she could check out the shopping. At the moment she was perched on the corner of Hank's desk, waiting for Rhys to conclude his conversation with Joan Majenek.

"Ms. Rodriquez phoned from the airport a few minutes ago to say that her flight was delayed," Joan said. "She hopes to still make her connection in Seattle, which will put her into Wenatchee on time."

He glanced toward the window and saw that the morning haze had all but burned off. "What about Scruggs and Franklyn?" Emory Scruggs was the new chief mechanic and Stan Franklyn was the CFO for the new division.

"They booked on a different airline, and as far as I know, they're on schedule."

"Anything else?" Rhys asked, glancing Del's way. She lifted her eyebrows hopefully. Five minutes, he mouthed.

"I have nothing else that needs your immediate attention," Joan informed him in the crisp tone he was coming to expect from her. "Mr. Grivaldo asked to speak with you for a few minutes."

"Fine, put him on."

"One moment, please."

"Make that ten minutes," he told Del.

"My stomach's gurgling," she complained.

"Forget the pitiful look, Del. I saw how many of those Dutch baby pancakes you shoveled in this morning."

Her eyes lit up. "Weren't they terrific? Brina's promised to give me the recipe."

"As if you ever cook," he said an instant before Ken Grivaldo's Kentucky twang rumbled over the line. Now in his ninth year with the company, Ken ran a department of fifty and was on the short list of employees Rhys considered too valuable to lose.

"Got a call from Paul Dominquez first thing this morning," Ken said. "He's uncomfortable about postponing the meeting we set up this week to finalize next quarter's line of credit. Seems he's taking some heat from his board about rumors floating around that the Northwest expansion is badly underfinanced." Ken paused for emphasis before adding wryly, "Rumors that we both know are well founded."

Ken had argued vigorously against buying out Sullivan's. Only after Rhys had explained his reasons had he swallowed his objections.

"Can you stall him?"

"Nope, I tried. I think he's worried he's so tied to North Star he'll go down in flames if we default."

Rhys snorted. "Man's sitting in that corner office on the executive level and driving a new Lexus every couple of years because of North Star."

"True, but to guys with calculators for hearts like Paulie, loyalty is just a word."

"Maybe." Rhys rubbed his jaw, his mind busy clicking through his options. Paul Dominquez was an executive VP of the Bank of the Desert and had handled North Star's credit for twelve years now.

Rhys knew all too well the kind of damage rumor could wreak on a customer's confidence. No conscientious contracts manager would risk valuable cargo to a carrier whose future was in doubt. Owning anything less than fifty-one percent of the stock also made him vulnerable to a hostile takeover. Paul was right, damn it. The situation was like a minefield, ready to blow at the first misstep.

"When does he want to meet?"

"Friday a.m."

Rhys leaned back and closed his eyes. Grivaldo could handle the negotiations alone, but Rhys figured he had a better shot at talking Paul out of his jitters if they were eye to eye.

"Set it up as a lunch meeting for Monday. Let Paul pick the place. Don't tell him I'll be joining you."

"Will do."

He heard the phone ring in the outer office where the switchboard was located. Del gestured that she would get it and hurried out.

"What's your projected ETA Phoenix?" Ken asked.

"Midafternoon Friday. I plan to stop off in San Francisco to check on Hank first. Joan's arranged to serve dinner before the board meeting and I'd like a meeting of the senior staff before the board meets so—" He broke off as Del came to the door, obviously intent on speaking with him. "Hang on a minute, Ken," he said before punching the hold button.

"That was Madison at the gate. He wants to know if he should pass through a visitor. J. T. Sullivan."

Rhys sucked in a harsh breath. He should have figured the old man wouldn't let things lie. Gut twisting, he punched the second blinking line. "Madison, this is Hazard."

"Yes sir." He pictured the man's spine stiffening to attention.

"Escort Sullivan to my office personally, then wait to escort him back to the gate. Be polite but don't let him make any side trips."

"Yes, sir."

The look of disapproval he saw in Della's gaze had his jaw hardening. "Rhys, I know how badly he hurt you, but he's still your father—"

"I know who he is and who he isn't." He cut her off coldly before punching line one. "Sorry, Ken, where were we?"

"Staff meeting before the board meets."

Rhys forced his mind back to business, but his gut was a mass of angry knots. "Let's keep this thing with the bank between us for now."

"No problem."

"What about the profit projections for North Star Northwest?"

"All ready for the dog and pony show Friday. I have easy-to-read graphs and some jazzy handouts to knock their collective socks off."

"Good, because Sam Phillips is primed and ready to go for my jugular." Two years ago, retired financial consultant Phillips had forced his way onto the board by snapping up North Star shares as soon as they became available. He'd been a dissenting voice ever since. So far Rhys had countered every grumble and criticism by pointing out the company's robust financial picture. Now, however, with quarterly profits flat, Phillips might be able to foment unrest among the other board members. With his energy and attention split between Phoenix and Osuma, the last thing Rhys needed was a contentious board.

"I don't think you need to worry, given how much money you've made the board members over the years," Ken assured him.

"Easy for you to say since I'm the one sitting at the head of the table." Rhys heard the sound of heavy footsteps ringing on the metal stairs leading to the executive offices and mentally steeled himself.

"Any word on Hank?" Ken asked.

"Talked to him last night. He says he's being tortured and wants me to send in Amnesty International."

Ken snorted a laugh. "Any idea how long he'll be laid up?"

"His doctor says six weeks. Hank says three. I figure the truth is somewhere in between."

"My money's on Hank. He . . . oh hell, I almost forgot. I need to run some tax figures by you. Just let me grab the folder from my files." As Ken talked, Rhys watched through half-closed lids as J. T. walked past Elena's desk with his usual confident stride. A familiar figure in a plaid shirt and twill pants held up with suspenders, he stopped short inside the door and planted his dusty work boots wide, gesturing that he would wait until Rhys was finished with his call.

Rhys' face went cold, and a muscle began twitching in his jaw. He'd still been in prison the last time he'd seen J. T. Sullivan, but he'd been looking ahead to his release in six weeks' time. He'd intended to work for J. T. in the orchard until the prison stink blew away, and then he'd planned to go to college, maybe Washington State.

J. T. had exploded those plans with a few words. *Coming back to Osuma would be a mistake right now, son. I've set up a trust fund to see you through four years of college in Oregon or maybe California, any place you choose. After that, we'll see.* The old man had still been explaining when Rhys had gotten up from the bench where they'd been sitting in the prison yard and walked inside. During the routine search that had followed he'd turned surly with the guard and ended up doing his last six weeks in the isolation unit. Ruthlessly, he scrubbed his mind free of the past and concentrated on the here and now.

"Bottom line, this just might be the worst quarter since the increase in fuel costs nine years ago." Ken's voice was carefully neutral, but the message was clear.

"Updating your résumé yet?" Rhys drawled.

"Kiss my ass, Mr. Hazard, sir."

Rhys laughed. "Point taken, Mr. Grivaldo. I'll see you sometime Friday."

"Expect me earlier than the others, so we can go over these figures one last time." Ken clicked off.

Rhys hung up, then sat back. J. T. was pushing seventy now, an old man. But once he'd been strong and vital. A big, blustery man with wild red hair and twinkling blue eyes who could work sixteen hours a day without complaint and still have enough juice left to listen to a little boy's jabbering.

"Hello, J. T.," he said when the silence grew strained. It was the first time he'd called the man something other than Daddy or Pop, and it sounded strange to his ears. "I figured you'd be by today."

The old man lifted eyebrows that had faded from bright red to silver. "Did you now? And why would that be?"

"Way I remember, news travels fast around here."

"It does at that." J. T. chuckled. "Guess you know you spooked your brother pretty good."

Rhys shrugged. "If he does the job to my standards, he'll stay. If not, 365 days from Monday, he'll be unemployed."

"That's between the two of you."

J. T. sighed before shifting his gaze to Della, who had settled into one of the two chairs on the other side of the desk. "Hello to you, lass. You certainly do brighten an old man's day."

Rhys' voice was curt. "Odella Campbell-Browne, meet John Thomas Sullivan."

Frowning slightly, Del rose to offer her hand. "Mr. Sullivan."

"I'd take it as a rare honor if you'd call me J. T., ma'am."

Her smile was polite. "In that case I'm Della."

"A lovely and lyrical name for a lovely lady, Miss Della."

"Thank you," she said before shifting her attention Rhys' way. "I'll wait for you downstairs."

"I won't be long."

Be nice, she telegraphed with a look. He ignored her. She frowned before offering J. T. a polite good-bye.

"Haven't seen the place look this good since it was just built," J. T. said over the sound of her retreating footsteps. "You've done a fine job bringing the old place back to life."

"Hank Dunnigan handled it."

J. T. jammed his hands into his pockets. "I was damn sorry to hear about his accident. Any idea when he'll be on his feet again?"

"Best guess so far, two months."

"So you'll be stayin' around these parts for a while?"

"Yeah, J. T., the mongrel bastard you disowned is back," Rhys said in a very quiet, very bitter tone.

The good humor on the Irishman's face disappeared. "Damn it, Mick—"

"My name's Rhys."

"Whatever you call yourself, you're still my son. I tried—"

"Bullshit! Your *son* is the lying SOB who crucified me while you sat there sucking up every word like it was gospel."

"What the hell did you expect me to do, jump up and call John a liar?" J. T. shouted.

"Yes, damn it!" Blood pounded in Rhys' temples.

"For God's sake, don't you think I wanted to believe you?" J. T. said after a moment of strained silence, his voice taut. "But your brother was just a kid and had no reason to lie, whereas you did."

In control again, Rhys allowed himself a cynical smile. "Funny thing was, the DA would have settled for six months' jail time and four years' probation if I would have agreed to cop a plea to a lie." His smile grew frosty. "Ironic, isn't it? John gets called a hero for lying through his teeth, and I do four years because I insisted on telling the truth."

"Mick—"

"Call me that again, and I'll have you thrown out of here." Rhys glanced toward the outer office where the security guard waited.

J. T.'s jaw hardened. "You made a mistake, son, and you had to pay the price. I hated to see you suffering so, but there was nothing I could do." He paused to take a deep breath. When he spoke again, his voice was as close to pleading as Rhys had ever heard. "About what happened with your mother—"

"Don't ever mention that witch to me again."

"It's stubborn you are, Michael Rhys." J. T. sighed. "Tell me what to do to bridge this gulf between us, and I'll do it gladly."

"Not one thing, old man, so do us both a favor and stay the hell away from me."

J. T. took a deep breath. "So be it." He turned on his heels and walked out.

Chapter 9

"Harve, if you're calling with another criticism of the seating arrangements on the platform, I swear, I will personally put you behind a potted palm." Lucy crushed a white carnation while she visualized doing the same to Mayor Harvey Kurtz's scrawny neck. Even as a teenager, Harve had been a self-important twit, but from the moment the governor had accepted the town's invitation to speak on the fifteenth, he'd become insufferable.

"This is serious, Lucille," he insisted, his voice taking on the adenoidal whine she'd begun to hear in her nightmares. "Folks in these parts have long memories. What if someone makes an ugly scene in front of the governor and his people? Or, God forbid, the media? The town could become a laughingstock, or worse."

"No one's going to make a scene, ugly or otherwise. Everyone knows how important it is to put Osuma in a positive light in front of the cameras."

"Positive light, hell. We're going all out to honor an ex-convict who made roadkill out of two kids and a father of five. Think what kind of message that would send to the tourists we're hoping to lure back. Tourists who bring their kids, Lucy. Parents have a natural aversion to mingling with a killer."

As Lucy had anticipated, word of Michael's return had spread like wildfire. The first call had come from Brina. After that, it seemed the whole town was talking of nothing else. Most of the callers had expressed shock that it was his corporation they'd been praising for three months.

Lucy's patience snapped and her voice became clipped. "Oh, for heaven's sake, Harve, have you lived in a cave for the past decade? Darn near every celebrity you can name is either an ex-convict, under indictment or covering up something lewd, illegal or addictive."

Harve snorted. "Wouldn't surprise me if J. T.'s kid wasn't setting this whole thing up to get even with folks who wanted to nail his miserable hide to his daddy's warehouse wall."

"Refresh my memory here, Harve. Exactly how much money did North Star contribute to the fund to restore the town's infrastructure?"

"Sure we got some money out of the bastard, but only after we granted North Star a forgiveness on property taxes for ten years."

Lucy gave up. The man was hopeless. "All right, Mr. Mayor, what is it you want me to do? Ask Chief Hollister and his men to frisk everyone along the parade route for rotten eggs? Call the governor and tell him to stay home because our guest of honor made a tragic mistake twenty-two years ago when he was *seventeen?* Or, here's a concept for you, Harve. Why don't we just cancel the whole thing and save us all a lot of worry?"

The strangled sound on the other end would have been far more gratifying if she didn't feel a niggling anxiety of her own.

"Don't be any more of a horse's ass than you already are, Lucille. Just be at City Hall nine o'clock sharp tomorrow morning for an emergency meeting of the town council." She winced as he slammed the receiver in her ear.

"Moron!" she grated, slamming down her own phone. She was about to step through the beaded curtain into the rear workroom when the door swept open, setting the old-fashioned shop bell jangling. She turned back expectantly, a welcoming smile on her face as a tall, powerfully built man in work jeans, seasoned leather jacket and tan Stetson entered. He used a cane and favored his left leg. She felt a funny feeling behind her sternum, followed by a wild burst of joy. "Mickey? Dear God, is it really you?"

"Hello, Lucy. The sign outside said 'Welcome,' so I took a chance."

A chance that he *might* be welcome? This from the boy who used to barge into her house without knocking, like a half-wild stallion full of energy and fire and fun, *knowing* she'd be happy to see him? *Oh Mickey, my sweet boy, what have we done to you?* she mourned silently.

"It's about time you came to see me," she said, rushing around the counter and straight into his arms. She felt him stiffen; then he was hugging her so fiercely the air whooshed from her lungs.

When he released her, she stepped back, eager to see the cocky grin that used to warm her heart. The last time she'd seen him they'd been eye to eye. Now she had to look up to meet his gaze. Unguarded now, his eyes hinted at the mischievous laughter that always seemed ready to burst out of him. An instant later, the laughter was gone. She had a hunch it never lingered long.

"You've gotten taller," she said, studying his face. "Welcome home."

"My *home* is in Phoenix."

"Ah, you're still angry because you think we let you down when you needed us most."

"Not you, Lucy. Never you."

Lucy refused to believe he was as cold and unfeeling as he seemed intent on proving. He reminded her of the gangly six-year-old who'd fallen out of her backyard maple tree and broken his collarbone, his eyes shut tight against the pain while he protested that it didn't hurt.

"Why wouldn't you let me visit you in prison?" Her voice was gentle, and she smiled to let him know she hadn't taken offense.

"I was barely hanging on, living minute to minute some days. I was afraid that seeing you would break me. I couldn't take that chance."

She was careful to hide the anguish his words aroused. "Is that why you sent my letters back unopened?"

He nodded. "I know it hurt you. I've always regretted that."

Even as a child he had tried hard never to give offense. "In that case you can make it up to me by letting me spoil you while you're here."

His mouth twitched. "Depends on what you have in mind."

"For starters, lots of home cooking. As I recall, you used to be a bottomless pit."

"I used to be a lot of things. Right now I'm filling in for a sick friend. When he's back to work, I'm outta here, and unless North Star Northwest blows up, I won't be back." It was a warning not to expect more.

"Never say never, dear." She touched his arm, and he jerked. The little boy who'd eagerly sought hugs and cuddles had become a man who mistrusted even the smallest gesture of affection. "I know you don't want to believe it, but you still have friends here. People who are very proud of what you've accomplished, who you've become."

"What I've become? How would anyone know that?"

She gave him a kindly look. *Prepare to have your world tilted just a little, darling boy,* she thought. "After you'd been in Phoenix for a year you'd saved enough to put a down payment on a wrecked, thirdhand rig. You worked at Orosco's Automotive during the day, rebuilt the truck's engine at night. Once you started getting hauling jobs, you went to night school to learn accounting so that you could do your own books. Apparently you liked learning, because class by class you eventually earned a degree in business management, although that's not something you advertise."

"Who told you that?"

"Someone who was impressed by how hard you worked." She smiled gently. Oh yes, he might be rich and powerful and bullheaded, but he still had a great deal to learn about family love. "Hauling jobs were scarce at first, but gradually, you began to put money aside toward a second rig. By your fourth year as an independent, you'd acquired a reputation for being honest, reliable and willing to take jobs other independents rejected as too dangerous. Your big break came when you got a contract to haul produce for a local growers' co-op. The ink was still wet on the signatures when you took that contract to the Bank of the Desert and applied for a loan. Two weeks later your application was approved." She grinned. "The rest, as they say, is history."

His stubborn mouth softened a little at the corners. It was only a hint of a smile, but it was a start. "Okay, I'm impressed. I'm also curious."

This time she took a chance and let her hand rest on his hard forearm. He tolerated the touch. "We'll have a long talk tonight, when you come to dinner."

Instead of the easy, even exuberant acceptance she had once received, he took time to think it through. "Guess that's an offer I'd better not refuse," he said finally.

"Six thirty. Don't be late."

"You must have missed the part about North Star drivers never being late."

She laughed. "You devil, I've missed you so much."

"Guess I missed you, too," he said gruffly.

She cleared her throat of a sudden thickness. "Have you seen your dad?"

His eyes turned hard once more. "If you mean J. T., yeah. He stopped by the office this morning."

She felt a flare of hope. "And?"

"He came; he went. End of story."

She started to reply, but at that moment the door burst open, setting the bell jangling wildly. An instant later Marcy raced in, sparkly shoelaces flapping and cheeks pink. Her eyes were bright as she called out a greeting. Brina's eyes, on the other hand, had the smudgy look that accompanied lost sleep or chronic worry.

"Hi, Miss Lucy, may I play in your potting dirt while you and Mommy visit?" Marcy asked as she skidded to a stop.

"Of course you may, puddin' pie. You know where it is."

But Marcy was staring at Rhys with wide eyes exactly like her granddaddy's. "Hi!" she said finally.

"Hi yourself," he said.

Tilting her head back a little farther for a better look at the man towering over her, she gave him a gap-toothed grin. "Are you a *real* cowboy?"

He watched her with the half-wary, half-bemused look of a man unused to children's chatter. "No, ma'am, I'm a truck driver."

Marcy giggled. "I'm not a *ma'am,* silly. I'm Marceline Anna Sullivan." She frowned impatiently. "You're s'posed to tell me your name now. It's polite."

"I beg your pardon." His eyes crinkled. "My name is Rhys. Rhys Hazard."

"I know who you are! You're Daddy's brother. Mommy said me and Jay are s'posed to call you Mr. Hazard instead of Uncle Rhys."

He glanced at Brina with cool eyes, but Lucy sensed something hot and volatile beneath the controlled exterior. "Did she?"

"Uh-huh. On account of because you don't want to be our uncle."

Lucy hid a smile. Along with his Celtic blue eyes Marcy had inherited her grandfather's bluntness.

"Marcy, that's enough," Brina said firmly, her cheeks pink. Interesting, Lucy thought, eager to see what happened next.

Marcy had also inherited J. T.'s persistence. "How come you don't want to be our uncle, Mr. Hazard?" Her pixie face was framed by soft, windblown curls.

"Marcy!" Brina repeated. Lucy saw her reluctance as she shifted her gaze to Rhys. "I'm sorry about this."

"She's honest. I respect that," he said before turning his attention to Marcy again. "Why don't you tell me what an uncle is supposed to do and then I can tell you if I know how to do that," he suggested in a tone that was serious, but not patronizing.

Marcy frowned, then looked up at her mother with beseeching eyes. The little imp, Brina thought.

"Don't look at me, kiddo," Brina told her daughter. "You're the one who started this."

Lucy chuckled. "She's got you there, puddin'."

Marcy's chin edged out as she accepted the challenge. In a reversal of roles that often had Johnny complaining bitterly, she was the firebrand while Jay was quiet and studious and inclined to withdraw instead of fight for what he wanted.

"I 'member now; last summer Beverly Freed's uncle Billy took her to this really fun fair in Ellensberg," Marcy declared. "She had cotton candy and ice cream and *two* corn dogs and rode lots and lots of rides until she threw up all over her new dress. Beverly said it was really, really yucky riding home 'cause the whole car smelled like vomit."

"I see." Rhys looked a little green. Brina bit her lip to keep from laughing. The gaze he shot her was surly, but when he directed his attention Marcy's way again, his voice was lashed with a subtle amusement. "I guess I could handle the corn dogs and the cotton candy and the rides if you promise not to throw up."

Marcy's eyes lit up. She knew a patsy when she saw one, even one as big as a lumberjack with a face hardened into bitter lines. "And Beverly's uncle reads her stories sometimes at night, too."

He considered, then nodded. "Guess that's doable." He lifted a tawny brow. He seemed to be enjoying himself, Brina realized. She wasn't sure she was pleased. "So that's it, then?" he asked when Marcy eyed him expectantly.

The master negotiator frowned, considered and then brightened. "I'm pretty sure Beverly said her uncle promised to take her and her sissy and her mommy and daddy to Disneyland for her birthday when she turned six." Her smile was angelically innocent as she moved in for the kill. "I'll be six on June fifteenth."

A trapped look came into his eyes, and this time both Lucy and Brina burst out laughing. "Don't answer that," Brina said, clamping both hands on her daughter's shoulders. "Trust me, anything you say will only get you in deeper."

His laugh lines deepened, and his mouth softened into a beguiling smile. Brina's insides were suddenly—and annoyingly—soft. "She's a definite pro, all right," he agreed. "We could use someone like her in sales." He winked at the little girl.

"Does that mean you want to be our uncle now?" she demanded, fidgeting in her mother's grasp.

"It's not that easy, honey," he said. "Your mom might not think that's a good idea."

Marcy looked puzzled before the frown lines smoothed away. "On account of you killing my other uncle, you mean?"

"Yes, on account of that."

"Are you sorry you killed my uncle Teddy?"

He didn't quite flinch, but Brina saw her daughter's innocent question hit home. "Yes, I'm sorry, sweetheart."

"Really and truly sorry?"

"Really and truly."

Marcy brightened. "Mommy said that if you were really and truly sorry, me and Jay and her would have to forgive you."

"Did she?" He glanced Brina's way, his expression unreadable.

Brina was torn. If she said no, Marcy would never understand. If she said yes, it would feel like a betrayal. Forcing a smile, she nodded. "Marcy's right. That's what I said."

"And now you wish you hadn't?"

Did she? Suddenly it was the day after the judge had pronounced sentence on her brother's killer—a shamefully light sentence, according to the front-page editorial—and her father's voice soothing her tears away was in her head again.

No, baby, Teddy wouldn't want you to hate Michael Sullivan for what he did. Way I see it, Brina Rose, if Jesus could forgive after what He suffered, we'd be pretty sorry souls not to do the same.

She hadn't understood how her father—her hero, the person she loved most in the world—could be so open-minded. At twelve she'd seen the world in stark black and white and so she'd started to rage at him, but the raw anguish in his eyes had stilled her tongue. As she lifted her gaze to Hazard's, she glimpsed a similar anguish in his. It rocked her hard.

"No, I meant what I said," she decided aloud.

His jaw clenched, and his gaze searched hers before Marcy tugged on his sleeve, drawing his attention. "See, I told you so."

He swallowed hard—twice. "Looks like you got yourself an uncle, Marceline Anna Sullivan," he said with a gentle smile that did amazing things to his face.

"Wait 'til I tell Jay!" she exclaimed before turning to race toward the back room.

"Marcy, wait!" Brina called after her. "Where are you going?"

She stopped and turned, her expression impatient. "To play in the potting dirt."

"We don't have time now, honey. I said we only had fifteen minutes before we had to pick up Jay, remember?"

"You can come back tomorrow," Lucy interjected before the gathering clouds in the little girl's eyes produced a storm. "Since I know you'll be coming, I'll have cookies."

"Peanut butter with M&M's?"

"You got it!"

"Can I, Mommy?"

"What do we say when we're asking a favor?"

"Puh-leeeeeeeze."

"Okay, but only for an hour or so. Lucy's got lots to do for parade day."

Placated, Marcy stuck her hands in her jacket pockets and ambled back.

"I almost forgot, Lucy," Brina said, conscious that Rhys was watching her with those cool, assessing eyes. Her skin felt itchy, and there was a funny humming in her head. "The reason I came by was to ask you if I could beg a ride from you to Summer's shower tomorrow night. The starter in the van is already wonky, and now the battery is pretty much on its last few volts or watts or whatever it is the stupid thing's supposed to produce."

"No problem. I'll pick you up about six forty-five."

"Let's go, Mommy," Marcy said, tugging on her hand.

"Okay." Brina gave Lucy a smile before reluctantly shifting her gaze to Rhys. The impact was immediate—a fluttering in her midsection, a tightening in her throat, an annoying tingle in her breasts. "So, uh, I guess I'll see you at home."

His mouth slanted, pushing a shallow crease into one hard cheek. "Guess you will."

"Bye, Uncle Rhys," Marcy chirped as Brina opened the door. "Don't forget about the story reading."

Brina whisked her daughter away before he could answer.

It was just past six, and her guests were having drinks in the parlor.

Two of the three North Star employees on Mr. Dunnigan's

final list had arrived around four. A man of middle years with skin the color of polished ebony, Emory Scruggs was as large as the chauffeur, but with what seemed to be a permanent twinkle in his dark brown eyes. It was as though he found life a constant source of amusement, and Brina had felt an immediate warmth for him.

Flaxen-haired, blue-eyed Stan Franklyn was in his late twenties with an aura of old money and aristocratic ancestry. Lean, athletic and very good-looking, he had perfect teeth and expensive taste in clothes. A man impressed by labels, like John, she decided after chatting with him on the way to his room. Still, she was trying hard to give him the benefit of the doubt. All but one room was full now. According to Della, the last of her guests, Elena Rodriquez, would be flying in later that evening or first thing tomorrow morning.

When Brina had taken a tray of cheese twists and crudités to the parlor earlier, Mr. Franklyn had been mixing drinks and had offered her something called a Kahlúa collins. She'd declined with thanks, pleading a tricky dinner recipe that needed constant monitoring. It was a little white lie. Chicken breasts à la Nightingale House was one of the simplest dishes in her extensive collection.

Not quite simple enough for a woman short on both time and sleep, she'd discovered while slicing her finger instead of the chicken breast she'd been deboning. The cut wasn't deep, but it was painful, which was one of the reasons she'd accepted Ernestine's offer to prepare the salad.

Now, perched on a stool at the center island, Ernie was meticulously tearing romaine into bite-sized bits to go with the radicchio, endive and pine nuts already in the large glass salad bowl. "How many RSVPs do they have so far for the governor's party?" she asked, glancing Brina's way.

"As of yesterday's mail delivery, just under three hundred." Brina took a quick sip of the white wine she'd also used for the sauce before adding, "Your basic intimate gathering, just the governor and a few of his closest friends—and campaign contributors."

"I admit I haven't been inside the new community center since it was finished, but it doesn't look big enough to handle that many people."

"I'm not sure it is—legally, anyway. Last I heard, Lucy and the fire marshal were 'negotiating.' My money's on Lucy."

Finished with the romaine, Ernestine started on the radicchio. "Dottie Krebs and I watched them raising the Maypole yesterday afternoon. I believe it's even nicer than the old one, but Dottie thinks it should have a fertility goddess at the top. To represent renewal and rebirth, of course."

"Summer did mention that Miss Dottie is going through a Native American phase at the moment." Brina grabbed a pot holder and lifted the lid on the large skillet on the front burner. After impatiently pushing back a stray tendril of damp hair that refused to stay put, she dipped a spoon into the sauce and tasted. "Needs a skosh more wine, I think," she said, reaching for the bottle.

"Beg pardon, Mrs. Sullivan?"

Startled, Brina spun around to find Max Stillwell holding the kitchen door open. Tonight he wore khaki Dockers and a blue-and-white-striped shirt under a blue windbreaker. The preppy version of a thug.

"Pull up a stool and make yourself at home," she offered, hoping she didn't sound as nervous as she felt. "Although I warn you, anyone hanging around my kitchen is expected to pitch in."

His heavy-lidded gaze lit briefly on Ernestine before jerking back to Brina. He had beautiful golden eyes. "Mr. Hazard asked me to tell you he'll be eating out again tonight."

Surely he didn't think that's what she'd meant by staying out of one another's way, she thought with an unwelcome pang of guilt. "Is he going to make that a habit, do you think?"

The burly driver looked uncomfortable. "I don't think so,

ma'am. Tonight is in the nature of an unexpected invitation from a . . . friend. I'll be leaving in a few minutes to drive him. If that messes up your plans, I can eat out."

Hazard had a dinner date already? With whom?

"Take your time, Max. We'll just wait until you're safely back." She smiled. He didn't. Instead, he dipped his head in a curt nod. Apparently he took his social cues from his employer.

She expected him to leave. When he didn't, she lifted her eyebrows. "Is there something else you need?"

"Mr. Hazard was wondering what time you lock the doors of a night."

Why didn't Mr. Hazard ask her himself? she wondered before remembering how she'd all but ordered the man to stay out of her way. "I usually lock up around eleven, unless I'm expecting a late arrival. If Mr. Hazard expects to be out later than that, I'll be glad to give him a key."

"Understood." Once again Max darted a glance in Ernestine's direction. For an instant the massive ruffian looked exactly like a bashful boy in the presence of the prettiest girl in class. When Ernie offered him a tentative smile, his battered face turned the color of rust. "Uh, I'll be back in time for dinner," he mumbled before giving Ernie a quick, shy smile. An instant later he was gone, the door swinging gently behind him.

Well now, Brina thought, exhaling slowly. *That* was very interesting indeed. "I think Mr. Stillwell has a crush on you," she told Ernestine with a smile.

Ernestine's hands stilled, and her eyes went out of focus as a becoming blush spread over her cheeks. "He is rather an imposing gentleman, isn't he?"

Imposing, maybe, but a *gentleman?* "Certainly the quintessential strong silent kind," Brina said.

"Indeed." Ernestine returned her attention to the lettuce. "You know, Brina, dear, I do believe our Mr. Stillwell is shy."

Somehow Brina managed to keep from choking on the mushroom she'd just popped into her mouth.

Lucy lived a few miles beyond the city limits in the house where she'd been born, the same house her immigrant grandfather had built with his own hands.

"Driveway's the one with the sunflower on the mailbox," Rhys told Max as their car approached. During his trial Lucy had always stopped at the mailbox to pick up her mail when they'd returned home from the courthouse. Some of that mail had been vicious—and anonymous—calling her foul names because she'd taken in "murdering scum." He suspected her business had suffered as well, although she'd shrugged off his questions as well as his apologies.

"Nice up here," Max said, slowing to make the turn. "Peaceful."

The house was set back from the road on a rise of land surrounded by towering oaks. A modified chalet made of rough-cut cedar, it sported bright yellow shutters and a glistening emerald green door. The front deck stretching along the entire front was new, as was a large prefabricated greenhouse to the right of the circular driveway. Lucy's yellow-and-green delivery van was parked in one side of the detached two-car garage, a muddy Dodge pickup in the other.

Max drew the Mercedes to a smooth stop. "You want I should come back after dinner and wait?" he asked.

"No need. I'll call when I'm ready." Rhys opened the door and got out. He reached back for the bottle of Merlot he'd picked up at the supermarket, the only place left in town that sold wine by the bottle. As a hostess gift it wasn't much, but he'd been carefully taught by his status-conscious mother never to show up for a dinner engagement empty-handed.

Lucy answered the bell before the sound faded. "Right on time," she said as she swept him into a hug, then stepped back

to usher him inside. "I made fried chicken and mashed potatoes with horseradish and sour cream, just the way you like it."

He felt a rush of good memories. "Smells great." He handed
her the wine. "The box boy at the Safeway swore this was a
good year."

Her eyes twinkled. "Which box boy was that, the one with
the nose ring or the one with the purple Mohawk?"

Rhys found himself relaxing. Maybe for tonight he could
pretend nothing had changed. "Definitely the Mohawk."

"Ah. That would be Danny Kurtz. Considering half his
genes came from his father, who is an A-number-one jackass,
it's a miracle the kid can actually tell red from white."

"Sounds like you're not real impressed with Danny's dad."

"If I had my way, Harvey Kurtz would spend the rest of his
days walking around with his fat head shoved up a certain un-
mentionable crevice." The sudden fire in her eyes had him
grinning.

"That's better," she said, touching his face. Her eyes grew
soft and shiny. Her fingers stroked his jaw. Somehow he kept
himself from jerking away. "This afternoon you looked so
closed off. So awfully stiff. I was afraid you'd forgotten how
to laugh."

He felt something tear inside. "How about we open that
wine and see if the kid guessed right?" he said, removing her
hand with his own. Her brief smile told him she wasn't giving
up.

"I'll get the glasses." Her eyes crinkled. "I think tonight
we'll use Mama's crystal goblets and make it a celebration."

The Merlot wasn't all that bad. It wasn't all that good either.
Like his memories of his childhood, Rhys thought as Lucy
leaned forward to dip a carrot stick into chunky pink stuff that
was supposed to be salmon and cucumber dip. A favorite of
the monks at a Tibetan monastery she'd visited two summers
ago, she'd informed him.

To his admittedly pedestrian palate, it tasted exactly like mashed-up SPAM. After living on the stuff for months during a bad patch, he'd sworn never to touch another bite. He managed to choke down enough to keep from offending her.

"The coroner ruled that Marceline had a massive stroke—a cerebral hemorrhage I guess is the correct term." Lucy glanced toward the grandfather clock set in its own floor-to-ceiling niche on the wall opposite the fireplace before checking her watch. "It wasn't all that surprising really, given my *high-strung* cousin had had high blood pressure for years, but you know Marceline. No matter how many times the doctor warned her she was dicing with death, she refused to take her medicine. That would be admitting that she wasn't perfect, you see."

"How long ago did she die?"

"It'll be a year next month. J. T. came home to find her on the kitchen floor."

Rhys swallowed more wine. It rocked him some to realize he actually felt sorrow over the death of a woman who'd caused him so much misery. "How did J. T. take it when she died?"

"About how you'd expect." She took a sip. "Lost so much weight his bones looked ready to poke through his skin. Dottie Hollister—well, Krebs now, since she married Dr. Gray Krebs three years ago—Dottie and I took turns inviting him to dinner, but he politely refused every single time. And then, all of sudden, when the buds broke into blossoms, it was as though he started coming alive again."

"He used to say he got his energy from the earth." Rhys smiled without humor. "And a daily slug of Irish whiskey."

"One has one's priorities," she agreed, saluting him with her glass before taking a healthy swallow. "So . . . what do you think of Nightingale House?"

"Interesting place," he admitted as he refilled her glass, then his own. "Elegant, but comfortable."

"You should have seen it when Brina bought it. Derelict, that's what it was. Mice had eaten through the electrical wires, and the plumbing was a health hazard."

My heart goes pitty-pat when I get a chance to get out my trusty plunger and go three rounds with a plugged-up john. Damn, but she'd been cute with her eyes laughing up at him. The laughter had died once she'd found out his identity. It shouldn't hurt. He didn't know why it did. "Whose idea was the divorce?"

"Brina filed—after John had humiliated her six ways to Sunday by taking up with her aerobics instructor."

He snorted. "Sounds like Junior."

Lucy stabbed a carrot stick into the dip with angry thrusts. "Selfish little pissant stiffed her on the settlement, too. Kept the Corvette and their brand new BMW, most of his stock portfolio, and the pretty yellow house Brina had fixed up so nicely. She got that old van along with half the settlement she should have gotten and a miserly child support, which is usually late. Most of her settlement went as a down payment on the inn and the rest was swallowed up by repairs."

Rhys couldn't afford to care. "Sounds to me like she needed a better lawyer."

Lucy nodded. "Even J. T. was embarrassed. He'd planned to set up a trust fund for the kids' education before the flood." She took a sip of wine. "I offered to lend her enough for her back payments, but she refused. Has her father's own pride, that girl."

"How come Mr. Eiler didn't help her out?"

"He died about four years ago. Heart failure is what Gray Krebs put on the death certificate, but that was just a courtesy to Brina and the kids. In reality Theo drank himself to death."

Was he to blame for that, too? Rhys wondered, shifting his gaze toward the view of the woods beyond the picture window. "What about his garage? Way I remember it, he did a whale of a business."

"He did indeed—until he started drinking so heavily. After he lost the contract to maintain the school buses, he was barely staying afloat. Theo's mechanic, Wayne Makepeace, did most of the work—when he wasn't half crocked, too." She sighed. "After Theo's death, Brina sold the building and the equipment to the man who'd won the bus contract. After paying her father's debts, there was only a pittance left.

"Wayne's daughter, Renee, came home for a visit and nearly had a fit." Lucy frowned. "Maybe you remember her? Won all kinds of scholarships and ended up going to Harvard Law School. She's been a superior court judge for the past three years and will probably get the nod for the state supreme court next month when Justice Greaves retires."

"Doesn't ring any bells." Rhys' mouth slanted. "Obviously we ran with different crowds."

Lucy laughed. "Anyway, where was I?"

"Daughter came home and had a fit," he prompted with a straight face.

"Oh, right. Well, Renee just waded in, got Wayne cleaned up and dried out. Eventually, he bought a little repair shop of his own."

"North Star's paying Brina Sullivan top dollar. Should help some."

"Help repay her notes at the bank, most likely." Looking disgusted, Lucy lifted her glass, only to put it down again quickly when the doorbell chimed.

"You expecting more company?" he asked when she shot to her feet.

"Yes, and I don't intend to apologize either, so save your breath," she said over her shoulder as she hurried toward the entryway.

As soon as he heard J. T.'s voice booming out a greeting, Rhys knew he'd just been sucker punched by an expert.

Chapter 10

"What part of seven o'clock sharp didn't you understand, John Thomas Sullivan?" Lucy demanded before J. T. had a chance to voice the apology he'd worked on all the way from his place.

"Ah, seven was it?" Fighting a grin, he leaned forward to plant a smacking kiss on her temper-pink cheek. "A little Highland cheer to beg your forgiveness," he coaxed, handing over the bottle of her favorite Glenfiddich.

She snatched it from his hands. "Since you finally made it, you might as well come on in and join us."

"Us?" His brows drew together. This morning's confrontation with his older son still rankled. The last thing he needed was a bloody "social" evening. "What do you mean, us?" he demanded again.

Instead of answering, she loped toward the living room with long deerstalker strides. Woman was mean as sin, he thought, following her. Always jabbing at a man about something or other.

Her living room smelled of the lilacs spilling from a crystal vase with a hint of the sage and rosemary she burned periodically to purify the air. Beyond the westward facing bank of windows, the sun shot its last rays directly in his eyes, so it took him a moment to recognize the man in a navy blazer and gray slacks seated in his favorite spot on the love seat. When he did, his breath hissed out. "What have you done, woman?"

"Stop glaring at me, both of you," she shot back, sounding anything but contrite. "It's time the two of you cleared the air."

"Bullshit." His face taut, Rhys used his cane to lever himself into a standing position. It was the first time J. T. had seen him on his feet since that last visit to prison.

"Just where do you think you're going?" Lucy demanded.

Fury flashed in Rhys' eyes, but his voice was deadly quiet. "I'm done here, Lucy. I don't like being conned, not even by you."

She stepped into his path and planted her hands on her hips. "You wanted answers; now you're going to get them."

"Don't make me go through you, Lucy."

"I paddled your bare bottom once, Michael Rhys Sullivan. Big as you are, I can still do it again if I have to."

The incredulous look Rhys shot her had J. T.'s lips quirking. "Like hell you will!"

She poked a finger into his chest, and for an instant, J. T. was so certain Rhys was about to explode he braced to come to her aid. "Didn't you ever wonder why the Gila Valley Co-op gave a struggling independent trucking company a major contract?" she demanded.

Rhys went utterly still, his eyes narrowed. "I'm listening," he conceded.

"I don't suppose you remember Chaba's youngest son, Miguelito, since he was just a kid when you left, but he happened to be at the co-op office when you showed up to talk to Jorge Mendoza about the delivery contract. Turns out he's married to one of Mendoza's daughters. Anyway, Miguelito mentioned seeing you to Chaba, who told J. T. One thing led to another, and your dad asked Mendoza for a favor, one grower to another," she said, returning her attention to Rhys. "One *father* to another."

Rhys' mouth thinned. "I know Mendoza. He's not the charitable type."

"It was mostly Chaba," J. T. amplified when Lucy looked

uncertain. "Told Mendoza he'd helped raise you. Said you'd stood up for his son more than once, and that you always shouldered your share of the work, even when no one was watching. Said if you promised to deliver on time with minimal damage to the fruit, that's exactly what you would do."

"And if I'd messed up, then what?" The question was spoken reluctantly, but at least he'd opened the door a crack.

"Mendoza would have put out the word and you would have been finished in the valley."

"J. T. would have made good the loss in full," Lucy added after shooting him a chiding look.

"Is this true?" Rhys demanded in the same lethal tone J. T. imagined had kept more than a few hard-nosed drivers in line. He met that unyielding gaze head-on with one of his own.

"It's true I helped you get that one contract. The way you handled it got you the ones that followed."

Rhys accepted that without visible emotion. "And the loan from the bank for my new rig, did you arrange that, too?"

J. T. shrugged. The kid was as smart as a whip. Let him figure that out for himself. As he'd expected, it took less than a beat.

"You guaranteed the loan." It was a statement of fact, delivered in a flat tone. His son might not carry his blood, but the boy had a full measure of Sullivan pride.

"Mendoza gave me the name of the loan officer you were dealing with. I arranged to guarantee payment if you defaulted, but only on the condition you not be informed."

"All along you knew I was behind the offer for the warehouse," Rhys said.

"I knew."

Rhys measured him steadily, giving away nothing. J. T. had a feeling he'd be a deadly poker player. "Wasn't much of a deal you cut me," Rhys said finally.

Something loosened inside J. T.'s midsection. "It was highway robbery and you know it," he said with a sardonic smile.

J. T. thought he caught a fleeting look of the boy's quick humor in the man's face. "Funny thing, I didn't see anyone else lining up to bid against me," Rhys said.

"I could have held on."

"Horse piss. The buzzards were circling."

J. T. conceded the point with a grin that felt almost normal. "They were indeed. You saved my arse, son."

Rhys shrugged. "Then we're even."

Seated at one end of Lucy's couch, J. T. stretched out his legs, letting his shoulders slump. His jaw ached from two hours of polite conversation, and his stomach was sour from all his son hadn't said.

Lucy had been stubbornly cheerful, jumping in with a leading question whenever the conversation played out. He and Rhys had talked about business and the stock market. They'd taken turns complimenting Lucy's cooking. Rhys had left shortly after dessert.

Now, curled into her favorite chair next to the fireplace, Lucy sipped espresso, her green eyes half closed. J. T.'s body stirred, remembering those clever eyes drowsy with passion after he'd plowed through her maidenhead like a bull in full rut. She'd loved him at sixteen, with all the sweetness of a first love. Obstinate woman that she was, she'd gone on loving him and believing in him, right up until the morning Marceline flashed her engagement ring in her face. He would never forget the way the love in her eyes had shattered into hurt. Eventually she'd forgiven him—and Marceline. He'd never quite forgiven himself.

"He's so controlled, so afraid to let anyone get close. It . . . hurts," Lucy said suddenly, her eyes growing dark.

J. T. dropped his gaze. "There hasn't been a day I haven't missed him—or prayed for his eternal soul."

"It was his father's belief in him he needed, not his prayers." Her voice was a whiplash, leaving its mark.

"You were there. You heard the testimony. There wasn't one scrap of evidence to prove his contention that the bus was the one to shoot the red light, not him. Only why would it? Anson Gregory had a spotless record, and according to Theo's maintenance log and Makepeace's testimony, the brakes had been replaced only the week before."

Her frown was impatient. "Bad brakes aren't the only reason the bus might not have stopped that day."

"Name one!"

"Ice on the road," she shot back.

"The trooper on scene fifteen minutes later swore it was clear."

She glared at him. "Maybe Gregory was distracted or had a heart attack."

"The coroner said not." He saw the frustration building in her and let out a low growl. "God's truth, I would have fallen to my knees and kissed the feet of anyone who could prove Mick hadn't run that red light, but the only evidence his attorney could present was the boy himself." His belly filled with acid. "We both saw the way the jury looked at him when he was on the stand. They didn't buy his story either."

"Like juries never make mistakes?" She gave an unladylike snort. "Get real, John Thomas."

He wanted to throttle the woman. "If he wasn't lying, that means Johnny was. Yet Mick's attorney couldn't shake John's story, while Mick—" He stopped and shook his head. "Judge Kaplan had the right of it, I'm sorry to say. What Mick did, trying to shift the blame onto a good man who couldn't defend himself, that was a coward's way." He gulped coffee and wished to God it was whiskey.

"That's it, then, is it? Rhys has to prove something to you that's impossible to prove before you'll forgive him, while Johnny has already proved himself to be a louse who cheated on his wife—and *lied* about it for a year."

"A sin of the flesh is . . . different."

"Oh, hell and blast, you are the most exasperating man." She sighed. "Still, you did reach out tonight, and I thank you for trying."

"As I thank you for loving the boy as you do." He took a breath. "He could have been ours, yours and mine. If I hadn't been a fool."

"But you *were* a fool, weren't you, J. T.?"

"Yes, and it's that sorry I am."

"'Too little, too late.'" Somehow he had lost himself in her shamrock eyes. She, too, seemed frozen, her gaze clinging to his. Had he really loved her? he wondered. Would they have made each other happy, two stubborn souls of independent natures that they were?

"Lucy—"

The clock struck suddenly, and she stiffened. "Drink up, J. T. It's getting late, and I have an early meeting of the parade committee tomorrow."

Reluctant to leave but knowing he should, J. T. took a final swallow of coffee, then got to his feet, doing his best to hide a wince as his sore muscles protested. "I'll help you with the washing up."

"Get in the way, you mean." She linked her arm through his and they walked together toward the entry. At the door, he turned to look at her.

"You're a good woman, Lucy Steinberg, as well as a rare lovely colleen." He felt a lump the size of County Clare lodge in his throat. "I meant what I said; it's yourself who should have been my boy's mother," he said gruffly, brushing his knuckles over her jaw.

Hurt splintered in her eyes, but her lips curved into a mocking smile. "Save your blarney for someone who needs it, Sullivan," she said with a laugh before brushing a kiss next to his ear, her usual way of sending him on his way. "Now move your bloomin' arse, boyo," she ordered, drawing back. "I'm tired."

He opened the door and stepped out onto the deck. The air was washed clean and felt surprisingly warm against his face. The scent of pine filled his nostrils as he drew in a cleansing breath. Through the haze the moon was a blurred crescent in a muted black sky. He thought about the lonely bedroom at the top of the stairs. He thought about Lucy's smile. He thought about the heaviness in his groin.

"I would stay if you were to ask," he said, staring straight ahead.

She inhaled swiftly. "Good night, J. T." The door clicked shut behind him.

After one look at Rhys' face as he settled into the passenger's seat, Max slipped Vivaldi into the CD player, then kept his mouth shut and his eyes on the road all the way back to town. Rhys was grateful for the man's tact. Before his hip had turned on him, he'd often walked off his bad moods, sometimes staying out until the early hours of the morning, tramping over the desert until his leg muscles were quivering. Now, however, he was forced to deal with his emotions in other ways. Work, mostly. Tonight, however, he had little enthusiasm for flowcharts and spreadsheets.

What he needed was a drink, a stiff one, he decided as Max pulled into the inn's small parking lot and let the engine idle. Surprised, Rhys looked over at him. "Something wrong?"

Max shook his head. In the light from the dash his ruined face seemed carved from badly weathered stone. "I was just thinkin' if you ain't gonna need me anymore tonight, I have a mind to stop for a cold one by that place across from that old mill we passed."

"Consider yourself off the clock," he said, reaching for his cane. Max would limit himself to one drink, an ironclad rule for any North Star employee who drove a company car.

"Wouldn't mind some company if you was of a mind."

Rhys was tempted, but the way his luck was running, he

was all but guaranteed to run into someone else from his past, and he'd faced his quota of demons for the day. "Another time, but thanks for the invitation."

Max waited until Rhys had gotten out and turned to shut the door, before adding, "Uh, boss, it might be a good idea to let Mrs. Sullivan know I'll be coming in late so's she won't lock me out."

"Don't worry; I'll cover for you with the warden."

Max waited to pull out until Rhys had made his way to the front steps. Hell of a strange guardian angel he had, Rhys thought, both amused and touched.

A welcome glow spilled from matching carriage lights bracketing the big front door.

The deserted entry was lit by twin lamps with stained glass shades that cast a vibrant glow on the gleaming tabletop. Music spilled from the parlor, and Rhys thought he smelled coffee. He heard the murmur of voices punctuated by Del's throaty laugh and Emory's gruff drawl.

He crossed to the arched doorway and looked in. It was a pretty room, with pale blue walls and man-sized chairs arranged in cozy groups of four or five. Twin windows covered with lacy curtains faced the street. A real lemon tree with heavily laden branches stood just to the right of the window closest to the door.

Emory, Del, and Stan had joined the white-haired, ramrod straight ex-army type and the wispy little lady with the pretty eyes at an octagonal table in front of a bay window. They were playing Scrabble, and both Emory and Stan were scowling while Del beamed at them with the Cheshire cat grin that Rhys knew all too well. Miss Whoosis looked pretty pleased with herself as well, while the colonel seemed more amused than concerned. It struck Rhys that the old gent looked exactly like a dignified, slightly potted granddad watching his grandkids squabbling.

"Who's winning?" Rhys asked when Del called out a greeting.

"Ernestine and I have effectively turned these guys into whining jelly," she replied with an airy wave.

"Jelly, hell," Stan muttered, rearranging his letters on the holder. "Rules say we have a right to protest illegal words."

"Obscure ain't illegal, rich boy," Del shot back.

"Face it, gentlemen," the colonel enunciated with the precision of a man contentedly into his cups, "we've been outthought and outfought by the ladies every game. I, for one, am willing to concede the field."

"Come join us, sugar," Della said with a grin. "We're playing a penny a point."

Rhys had had his fill of board games in prison. "Too rich for me." He glanced around. "Did Elena make it in?"

"No, she called from SeaTac to say she's due in around ten tomorrow morning."

He nodded. "Any idea where Ms. Sullivan might be?"

Della's eyebrows zoomed up. "Last time I saw her she said she had a monstrous amount of paperwork to take care of before going up to bed."

Rhys thanked her with a nod before saying good night and retracing his steps across the foyer. The office door was ajar and the light was on, but no sound came from within. He knocked, waited a beat to be polite, then pushed the door open.

Dressed in slacks and a soft yellow blouse that hugged her breasts, Brina had fallen asleep in her chair, her cheek pillowed on one arm, her face turned toward the door. Her eyes were closed, her pale lips slightly parted, her features relaxed. Light from the brass lamp shot specks of gold into her disheveled dark hair and emphasized the violet shadows under her eyes. She looked rumpled, overworked, worn out—and so lovely he felt his body stirring.

He was reluctant to wake her, but the last thing he needed

was a hysterical woman calling out the cops on his driver in the middle of the night.

Grimly he crossed to the desk and reached out to touch her shoulder. Because he wanted to stroke that hot little body until she purred, he shoved his hand into his pocket and took a stumbling step backward.

"Hmm?" Her tone was grumpy—and as provocative as the hottest moan. He made himself remember the anger in her face that morning—and all the other reasons why she was off-limits.

"Brina, wake up."

Her lashes fluttered, then slowly drifted upward. Her eyes, however, remained unfocused, giving her the drowsy, sated look of a woman who'd just been well and truly loved. A heavy pressure settled between his legs. Maybe his head knew the lady was off-limits, but his libido hadn't gotten the message.

"Rhys?" Oblivious to the torment she was causing him, she gave a few baby owl blinks, then sat up to glance around in a flurry of confusion. "What are you doing in my office?"

Suffering the fires of hell. "I came in to tell you Max will be coming home late."

"Late?" She frowned, then moistened her lips with her tongue. He realized he'd been celibate much too long if watching a woman wake up turned him on. "What time is it?"

"A few minutes before eleven."

She gave a huff of dismay, which drew his gaze to her mouth. "I was working on the program for the fifteenth and must have fallen asleep." A heavy lock of hair slipped free from the clip to puddle against her neck. Impatiently, she tugged the clip off and tossed it onto the desk. Her hair sprang free, a dark silky mass.

Fascinated, he found himself staring. Before he could stop himself, he saw himself burying his hands in all that glorious silk while he explored that tempting mouth with his lips and tongue. When he felt his heart start to slam at his ribs, he pulled back fast. Before he could make good his escape, however, she glanced up at him to ask anxiously, "I'm sorry, what did you say about Max?"

"Just that he went out for a beer and figures to be late getting back. Asked me to remind you not to lock him out."

She looked distinctly out of sorts. "I'll leave the door open this time, but as I *mentioned* to him earlier, I prefer to give a key to guests who plan to be returning later than eleven."

Though Rhys had never taken to following orders easily, he had an urge to snap to attention and salute. The more he saw of John's voluptuous ex-wife, the stronger his conviction that she and Lucy were cut from the same imperious pattern. "I'm sure it won't happen again," he said.

"It's not that I mind, you understand," she said a little too quickly. "It's just that I worry about security. After the flood, we've had some trouble with outsiders coming in to take advantage of the confusion. Several people were hurt after surprising intruders."

"I got the point the first time." He took a tighter grip on his cane and edged toward the door.

"Actually, I'm glad you came in." Her voice had cooled noticeably and the stiffness was back in her face. Even as he told himself it was better that way, disappointment crowded him hard. "I need to find out who's going to represent North Star at the festivities on the fifteenth so I can put it in the program."

He considered. "Del likes to shine," he decided aloud. "She'll be happy to meet and greet the suits."

"What's her official title?"

"Director of Human Resources, North Star Northwest."

She scribbled a note. "Full name, Odella Campbell-Browne, with a hyphen?"

"Yes, ma'am."

"Brown with an *e,* right?"

"Right."

"It's not a big production, you understand, but it would be lovely if she made a short speech."

"I'm not sure Del can do short."

"It's been my experience that exotic butterflies can do anything they like. It's the little brown moths who annoy people." She tossed the pad aside, drew a deep breath. Beneath the soft lemony blouse her nipples flirted with him. Desire slammed into him again, and he cursed silently. He was semihard already. One more of her deep breaths and he'd be in real pain.

"It's been a long day, Brina," he said a little desperately. "If you don't need anything else from me, I'll say good night."

"Actually . . . I can't believe I'm about to say this, but . . ." She hesitated, took another deep breath. "You should be the one we're honoring. You're the one who brought employment to the town. I think people need to know that."

He felt heat climb his neck. "It was a business decision. I expect to make an obscene amount of money on this expansion."

Her gaze dropped. "Ernie—Miss Winkle—thinks it's an act of contrition."

"She's wrong. I bought Sullivan and Son because the old man was too desperate to hold out for what it was worth." He leaned forward, bored in to make sure she got the message. "I stole the place, Brina. Flat out took the miserable SOB for a bundle."

"That doesn't sound like a deal J. T. would agree to, no matter what the circumstances." Her eyes were dark and troubled and held an emotion that reached deep inside a place he rarely visited. A place of half-forgotten hopes and expectations.

"Put Del's name in your program, Brina. I'm not interested in taking bows I don't deserve." Before she could respond, he got the hell out of her office.

Chapter 11

Brina stepped out of the big claw-foot tub in the family bathroom, her body still warm and soft from the jasmine-scented bubbles. Shivering a little, she reached for the towel and quickly dried herself before slipping into her nightshirt and soft terry cloth robe.

It was nearly one. The house was shrouded in a peaceful silence. Rhys' driver had returned fifteen minutes ago. Though she was exhausted, her innkeeper's soul wouldn't let her rest until she made sure he'd locked the front door.

After anchoring her steam-frizzled hair with a butterfly clip, she stepped into her tiger-striped slippers, gave the belt of her comfy robe one more tug and headed downstairs. She smiled a little as she saw that the door was securely bolted. Tomorrow she would make sure the preppy thug had his own key, she decided, turning to retrace her steps.

It was then she noticed one of her precious *Gone with the Wind* lamps had been left burning in the parlor. Frowning, she detoured to her left, only to stop short on the threshold. Her back stiffened and her chin came up.

"All your chicks are safe in the coop," Rhys said from the depths of the wing chair where he sat with his bad leg propped on the colonel's ottoman. He'd taken off the beautifully tailored blazer she'd noticed earlier and rolled up the cuffs of his pale blue oxford dress shirt. He had a balloon glass of what appeared to be brandy in his hand, the one with the ruined knuckles.

"What can I say," she admitted with a shrug. "I'm a compulsive worrier."

"Seems like worrying is the right thing to do when you have kids in the house."

"J. T. gave me a pistol as a housewarming gift when I moved in here, but I'm terrified that one of the kids will find it, so I stashed it in the top of my closet under my winter sweaters. As for the bullets . . ." She sighed. "For the life of me I can't remember where I hid them."

His laugh was rusty—and charming. "Might be a better idea to install a security system."

"I've thought about it, but I haven't had the money. Now, thanks to North Star, I might be able to swing it."

He lifted his glass and took a sip. "Years back Max worked security for a while. He'd be happy to check the doors and windows for you every night."

At the mention of his driver, her thoughts turned to Ernestine and those quick little looks her friend had sent Max Stillwell that morning at breakfast and again at dinner. She worried the inside of her cheek with her teeth for a couple of tense seconds while she debated the wisdom of confiding her concern to the man's employer.

"About Mr. Stillwell," she began, then realized there really wasn't a tactful way to ask if the man had a psychotic bent.

"What about him?" Rhys prodded.

"I'm sure he's a fine person, but . . . it's just that he's rather, um, formidable. Not that that can't be a good thing, you understand, but somehow, whenever I look at him, the words 'mass murderer' tend to pop into my head."

"Beneath that scary exterior is the heart and soul of a poet. In fact, while he was in prison, he had a few of his poems published in the local newspaper."

"He's an ex-convict, too?" The words were out before she could stop them.

He accepted them without reaction. "He did time for defending his baby sister from an abusive husband. Just so you know, Emory is also an ex-con."

Surprise jolted through her. "Anyone else?"

He hesitated. "Hank Dunnigan."

Her mouth dropped. "Why . . . I mean what did *he* do?"

"You'll have to ask *him*."

She stared at that world-worn face with the strong bones and sensitive mouth, so many emotions battering against one another. "Don't take this wrong, but does North Star go out of its way to hire ex-convicts?"

"No, but we don't turn them away the way most companies our size do either."

Even though his face was shadowed, she sensed some powerful emotion running through him. It couldn't have been easy coming back to a place where he'd been vilified. It could be arrogance, of course, but her instinct told her that it was something else entirely. Courage, for instance.

Was their being thrown together like this some kind of test? she wondered. Had she only been mouthing empty words to her five-year-old daughter this afternoon? Pretending to forgive while at the same time hanging on to her anger and resentment like a favorite shirt? Even if that was the case, did it matter to anyone but herself?

That, at least, was a question she could answer with a decent degree of certainty. Marcy, Jay—*all* children—needed to feel bedrock beneath their feet, not shifting sands. More than the expensive *things* too many parents substituted for the hard task of nurturing, children craved a sense of absolute security in a world of temptations and conflicting messages and very real danger. Her father had been *her* absolute, a man with core values that never wavered. But how could she provide that security when her own feelings were so conflicted?

One way or another she had to bring this mess to some kind of closure. She decided to start by getting to know this man who sat alone in near darkness, with only silence and his own thoughts for company.

Before she could change her mind, she walked to the sideboard and poured herself a cup of French roast from the thermos before curling up in the settee opposite his chair.

"I've always loved the feeling of this house at night when all the voices are stilled and the rooms are empty," she said, glancing around. "Sometimes when I'm here alone I get the loveliest whiff of French perfume."

"Funny, I thought it was cigar smoke."

"That, too. I have an unbreakable rule about no smoking, but every so often when I'm not around, the colonel sneaks one of those horrible stogies, then opens up all the windows and fans the smoke out with one of my pillows. It's a game we play."

"I'd give a good chunk of my stock options for one of his smokes right now."

"I thought I mentioned when you checked in that smoking is permitted on the porch. As long as you use the sand buckets and not my lawn as an ashtray."

"Actually, I quit years ago." He took another sip, then let the brandy drizzle down his throat.

"Good for you."

He shrugged, drawing her attention to those huge shoulders. "Wasn't anything even approaching good about it at the time. It was more like a choice between eating and cigarettes. It was a toss-up for a day or two, but my addiction to food won out over the nicotine craving."

She laughed softly. "I was too much of a goody-goody to ever start. I hear it helps you lose weight, so maybe I should give it a try."

A look that warmed her to the marrow lit his eyes from deep

within. "I think your weight is just fine, at least in the places that show."

Unsure how to respond, she solved the dilemma by lifting her cup and taking a tiny sip. "Why did you change your name?" she asked after a moment of silence that, this time, was surprisingly comfortable.

His mouth slanted, creasing only one cheek this time. "Is this some kind of bonding ritual we have going here, or do you quiz all your guests this way?"

"I admit to a certain curiosity about my guests, but I also respect your right not to answer."

"Most ex-cons learn to dread personal questions," he admitted. "Sooner or later your past gets between you and something important, like a job or a woman. Prison paranoia is part of the baggage you take with you when you leave, like not being able to vote in most states and always looking over your shoulder."

"I never thought about it that way."

"No reason why you should." He glanced down, then shifted his shoulders. "I changed my name because it wasn't really mine." His mouth edged up. "From the puzzled look on your face, I gather no one's told you I'm adopted."

She stared, her mind scrambling to catch up. "I had no idea. No one ever said a word."

"Guess every family has a shameful secret." He shrugged. "Way Lucy explained it to me when I was staying with her before my trial, Marceline had four or five miscarriages before she got lucky. Somewhere around the sixth month, she and J. T. took an apartment in Seattle to be near her specialist. When the baby was stillborn, she came close to a breakdown. Seems I was born the same day in the same hospital to a teenage hooker who waited too long to get an abortion. J. T. bought me to keep Marceline from cracking up. No one bothered to tell me until I made the mistake of pushing Marceline too far one too many times, and she dumped it on me in retaliation."

Brina drew a slow, careful breath. "What about John? Was he adopted, too?"

His mouth slanted. "Nope. After years of lighting candles and praying to the Holy Mother, a miracle happened and she got pregnant again. Ironically, she delivered without a problem." He lifted his glass to take a sip, then let his head fall back against the chair. "As Marceline was so eager to let me know, John was the only 'real' Sullivan son. I was unwanted garbage." He could have been discussing the weather for all the emotion he put into his voice. "I found out on the day of the accident. I never should have been behind the wheel."

His face seemed to have paled, and he looked very tired. She thought about the misery in the eyes of her friends who'd been in danger of losing everything before he'd promised them jobs. She thought about the black ink on her books because of him. A man who knew what it was to lose everything he'd ever held dear.

"Why didn't you tell all this on the stand?" she asked with a little frown between her eyebrows.

"My attorney thought it sounded too much like whining." His eyes held a look of regret so deep it brought a pressure to her chest. "He was right. My emotional state was no excuse."

"I'm not so sure about that," she said. "I'll have to give it some more thought."

Silence settled as he watched her with guarded eyes.

"Why did you pick the name Hazard?" she said a few moments later.

"I figured it didn't much matter what I called myself as long as it wasn't Sullivan. When I went to the courthouse in Phoenix to make it legal, I had to put down something. I was smoking at the time and had just lit up. I was looking at the pack, and well, you can guess the rest."

"You mean, the 'hazardous to your health' part?"

"Yeah."

It was painfully easy to imagine—a lonely young man who

felt abandoned by the only family he'd known, trying to convince himself it didn't hurt. "I've always thought that life must be so much easier for people who can look at things and see only black and white. Me, I have this tendency to see all these swirly grays. It's very annoying sometimes."

"Is that what you see now?"

She nodded. "I wonder if this is some kind of character test," she muttered. "One of those walk-the-talk opportunities that the universe takes such delight in throwing at us poor hapless humans when we least expect it."

"Which talk is that, exactly?"

"The countless talks I've had with my children about how everyone makes mistakes that hurt other people, but the important thing is to learn from those mistakes." She smiled. "The one my darling daughter mentioned to you this afternoon." She smoothed her robe over her knees, then ran her fingers over the nubby terry. This was a dream, she decided, because it was really too weird to be happening. Sitting here with a man she scarcely knew, yet had spent half her life hating, connecting on a level of intimacy she'd never once experienced with John. It was totally illogical. Since it wasn't really happening, she said honestly, "I have to admit I enjoyed watching you cut John off at the knees yesterday afternoon."

His half-closed lashes veiled the expression in his eyes as he asked, "How'd the two of you end up together?"

"He comforted me after the accident. He was sweet, and I was lonely, and then one day I realized I loved him."

"Hell of a thing, love." His mouth took on a sardonic slant. The kind she suspected his rivals had learned to dread. "J. T. claimed he was refusing to let me come home because he loved me. He didn't want me hurt, he said. Only I knew the real reason. Marceline didn't want me there, and he *loved* her more." He drained his glass, then put it on the piecrust table at his elbow.

"You sound as though you don't believe love exists."

"Everyone talks about it, so it must. Me, I'll stick with things I know something about."

"Lucy loves you."

"She loves a person who no longer exists."

Silence stretched between them, palpable with tension. The house itself had taken on a stillness so complete she could almost hear the thudding of her own heart. Beyond the thick walls, life went on. Here in this room, however, time seemed to have rolled back to the frozen moment that linked the two of them forever.

"I have to know," she pleaded, looking up at him. "*Did* you run a red light the way everyone said?"

He squeezed his eyes shut for a long moment before opening them again. "The easy answer is no. It's what I believed then; it's what I believe now." He plowed his free hand through his hair, leaving it disheveled. "I've run those few critical moments through my mind over and over, trying to see it from all angles. I swear the bus was slowing down for the red light. No, damn it, I *know* it was slowing down. In my mind I'm looking through the windshield of my rig and I see the light ahead of me clear as day. It's always green." His jaw flexed.

"Before the trial I thought maybe I'd missed some little detail, something that would prove I was right, but maybe I was just looking for an easy out so I could live with myself." He heaved a sigh weighted with more than weariness. "The truth is, I'll never really be sure, so I can't give you a reason not to hate me, though I wish to God I could. If that's where you're going with this, you'll have to get there by yourself."

She blinked. "Does it matter whether I hate you or not?"

His gaze held hers, changing slowly to something very close to a plea. "Yeah, it matters."

"Why?"

"Lots of reasons." He glanced around. "This, for instance,

the two of us ending up in the same room despite this agreement we made."

"I could make up a schedule," she joked. "Assign a time when each of us gets the living room."

His face hardened again, giving her a glimpse of the man who'd put aside the soft parts of himself in order to survive. "No thanks, Brina. I had to live that way in prison. I won't live that way ever again."

She felt her face turn hot. "The Successful Innkeeper tries at all costs not to put her foot in her mouth," she muttered with a sigh. "It's a habit I'm trying to break, without much success, obviously," she added when he frowned.

"Proves my point, though, doesn't it?" His chest rose and fell slowly. "This isn't going to work, you and me in the same house. I've got too much on my plate right now to live every day wondering if I'm going to get blindsided by another reminder, another bitter glance. A cutting remark."

His gaze found hers and held. "Some things about this mess I can't control, but this I can. I'll leave first thing tomorrow." He lowered his leg and reached for his cane. His face tightened as he got to his feet. "Good night, Brina, I wish you well," he said before limping past her.

She felt a pressure in her chest. "Wait," she cried, twisting to look at him.

He stopped and turned, his face shuttered, his shoulders braced, his expression part prideful, part defiant. It was the same look she'd seen at the trial.

"You promised Marcy . . ." She stopped, then shook her head. "No, you were honest with me; I have to be honest with you. I don't *know* if I still hate you. I know I don't *want* to, for my children's sake as well as my own. I don't think I do, but I can't promise not to . . . to have . . . flashbacks." Her lips felt stiff as she curved them into a smile. "Maybe this . . . tension between us is a variation on post-traumatic stress syndrome."

His brows drew taut. "Are you saying you want me to stay?"

Was she? "Yes, I . . . want you to stay." Because the tension was nearly unbearable, she added flippantly, "Uncles do not jump ship when the sailing gets a little rough."

His mouth curved into a crooked smile with cautious edges. "Is that right?"

"Absolutely."

He swallowed hard. "You're a hell of a woman, Brina Eiler," he said gruffly. "Don't let anyone ever tell you you're not." With that, he turned and left. To her dismay, she realized her eyes were suddenly full of tears.

Chapter 12

It was just past five. Awake since four, Rhys had read for a while, then showered and shaved before heading down to the kitchen for coffee. Now on his second cup, he sat at the center island, jotting down some ideas to discuss with Grant Goodeve when they sat down together sometime Monday.

His VP of sales was deeply involved in negotiating several important contracts, the most vital of which was MemoryData, Inc. The company was soliciting bids to haul their product to end users throughout the States and into both Canada and Mexico. Rhys was determined to have it. Determined, hell! He *had* to have it.

Although he hated putting his entire future into the hands of one man, he'd learned years ago he couldn't do it all. Goodeve had come to him from Microsoft, and what he didn't know about corporate gamesmanship didn't exist. In addition, Grant had been an all-American rugby player at Yale. No one was better at playing tough.

"Are you always up this early?"

The half-sleepy, half-grumpy voice caught him by surprise, causing the mug he'd been lifting to his lips to jerk. Coffee splashed onto the pad, turning his notes to indecipherable splotches. Before he could catch himself, he'd let out a staccato curse more appropriate to the loading dock than a woman's kitchen.

"I'll give you that one because it's partly my fault," Brina said primly as she snatched a paper towel from the roll and handed it to him. "But I would appreciate your watching your language around my children."

"Yes, ma'am." As he mopped up the spill, he tried to ignore the way her nicely rounded butt filled out an ordinary pair of jeans.

"Finished with that?" she asked when he crumpled the towel into a ball.

When he nodded, she tossed it into the trash can under the sink before pouring herself a full mug.

"About the problems with your van, would you like me to ask Max to take a look at it?" he offered.

She shot him a surprised look. "I'm not sure it would do any good. The starter's on its last legs, and I know the battery is older than Marcy."

"Marcy being what, five?"

"Yes, going on forty-five."

He smiled. "And your son—Jay, is it?"

"John Thomas III. He's twelve." As she swallowed, her face took on a soft-focus look of pure bliss.

"Are he and John close?"

"Not really. Jay's more interested in finding out how things work than athletics."

"As I recall, John wasn't all that great at either one."

"True. But to hear him talk to Jay, he was at least a super-star, if not supernatural."

Rhys snorted. "John never wanted to put in the hard work it takes to be good at anything but making excuses."

She took another greedy sip, her lashes drooping as she waited for the caffeine to kick-start her day. "Jay was extremely close to my dad," she said after a moment. "I think that's one of the reasons he's so crazy about engines and cars. Dad used to let him help with tune-ups. Even gave him a set of tools all his own. Wayne Makepeace was storing them for Jay in his shop. They were lost along with Wayne's in the flood."

Still holding her mug, she opened the pantry door and walked inside. He heard a rustling, then a sharp crack, followed by a word that was anything but muffled.

"Good thing your kids didn't hear that," he offered straight-faced when she emerged, carrying a bag of oranges and wearing a pained look.

"Successful Innkeepers sometimes resort to violence when pushed too far," she muttered as she dropped the oranges onto the center island in front of him. As she turned, he saw that the front of her peach-colored T-shirt now sported a large coffee stain over one breast.

Catching his gaze, she scowled, then swung around to jerk open a drawer and pull out a snowy chef's apron. Once safely covered, she turned around to glare at him. "Despite all evidence to the contrary, I am *not* a klutz."

Because he wanted to stay, he knew it was time to leave. "Since there's no safe answer to that, I think I'll excuse myself and get out of your way."

"Not a chance, Hazard. House rules, he who guzzles multiple pots of my special breakfast blend at dawn pays by cutting up oranges for juice." To punctuate her unexpected pronouncement, she grabbed a wicked-looking knife from a wooden holder and slapped it down next to the oranges. "Cut them in half first. The juicer is under the counter next to the fridge."

He eyed the shiny blade warily. "What the heck is a juicer?"

She shot him an incredulous look. "You've never seen a juicer?"

"I'm a truck driver, not a cook."

"So?"

He offered her a challenging look. "Tell me, Ms. Sullivan, have you ever seen a jake brake?"

"Of course, hasn't everyone?" she retorted airily before bending over to take a bowl from one of the bottom cabinets.

In his imagination he was already rubbing his palms against that world-class butt. He went rock hard. She stood too quickly and caught him gawking like a green kid.

"Well?" she demanded. "What's the problem now?"

Shifting, and damn grateful the edge of the table hid the bulge in his jeans, he cast a wary glance at the oranges. "How many do I cut up?"

A look of long suffering crossed her face. "All of them, of course."

"Sounds like a lot of work."

She lifted a dark eyebrow. "And your point is?"

He rested both forearms on the counter. "Let's talk about this, Ms. Sullivan."

"Pardon me?"

"Seems to me all that cutting *and* juicing is worth at least a week's free ride on morning coffee."

Her gaze narrowed, but not before he'd seen the eager gleam in her eyes. The lady obviously shared his love of bargaining. His heart rate quickened in anticipation.

"You're already into me for two cups," she scoffed in a traditional opening move. "More, now that I think about it. When I came down yesterday, that huge pot was nearly empty."

"Could be I only made two cups. One for me, and since I'm a real generous guy, one for the lady who supplied the beans."

Her look questioned his sanity. "In the spirit of the upcoming celebration, and because I, too, am known for my generosity, I am prepared to comp yesterday and today in exchange for one day's juicing."

He treated that with the disdain it deserved. "Seven days comp."

She nearly choked on her coffee again. "Three," she sputtered in outrage, "and that's pushing it."

Sensing victory, he decided to throw her off guard by upping the ante. It was a ploy he'd refined during the days when the only thing standing between him and an empty belly was his ability to whittle out a favorable deal. "Eight—and a generous chunk of that coffee cake you served yesterday," he proposed, leaning toward her to punch his point.

She scowled. "Five and you'll take whatever's left over."

"Done!"

She blinked, then frowned. "Wait, I . . . you *tricked* me!"

"Yeah, I did, didn't I? Must be my lucky day."

Humming along with Tony Orlando and Dawn on the golden oldies station she preferred when she was alone, Lucy was happily crafting the perfect centerpiece for Summer's baby shower that night when she was interrupted by the jingling bells announcing the arrival of a customer.

She slipped through the beads separating the front room from the back, a welcoming smile on her face. Surprised, she came face to face with J. T., who stood on the other side of the waist-high counter.

"Top o' the afternoon to you, Miss Steinberg," he said with stiff formality. "It's a rare sight you are to my tired eyes."

Suspecting a practical joke—on her, naturally—she narrowed her gaze. If she wasn't mistaken, the big fool was wearing a new blue-and-white-striped dress shirt still crisp with the manufacturer's sizing and tailored slacks with a crease sharp enough to slice bread.

The rush of desire that tumbled through her was utterly humiliating. *The man dumped you, you idiot,* she reminded herself for about the umpteenth time in recent months.

"All right, I'll bite, what's going on?"

When he continued to grin at her like a gangly boy, she leaned forward to sniff the air. The more he drank, the more shanty Irish he became. "Have you been imbibing already this morning, John Thomas?"

His grin disappeared. At the same time his brilliant blue eyes took on a defensive sheen. "There's mornin' and then there's mornin'," he hedged.

"Meaning?"

His chin edged forward. "Meaning I haven't touched a drop in the light of day," he said tightly.

"And before that?"

His grin flashed once more, a ray of sunshine in a dark sky. "Ah, Lucy love, surely you don't begrudge a man with a weeping heart the comfort of a wee dram."

Her jaw dropped, then snapped shut as hurt surged through her. What she showed him, however, was a good-natured impatience. "Given the fact that it's been almost a year since Marceline passed, it's beyond time you stopped with the Irish melodrama."

"Ah, but you wound me deeply, colleen," he protested, his craggy face crumpling into a look of deep pain. "It's your cruel rejection that's driven me to drown me sorrows in the drink."

"*My* cruel rejection?" she repeated in disbelief. "How dare you?" She sucked in a lungful of air. "You *jackass!* Coming around here all polished up and looking hangdog, playing on my sympathy."

"I—"

"Well, it's not going to work, you hear me, John Thomas Sullivan? I am not some kind of . . . of fallback lover!"

"But, Luce, I never—"

"Don't think I don't know what's going on in that arrogant male mind of yours, because I do."

The weathered lines that were gouged into his temples deepened as he stared at her warily. "You do?"

She stabbed the air with her index finger. "You think I've been carrying a torch for you all these years. Poor, pathetic Beanpole Steinberg, pining away for a man who dumped her, a homely boring old maid, drying up inside because I'm still crazy in love with another woman's husband."

By the time she ran out of words—and air—she was visibly shaking, and her chest felt like it was about to explode. Her cheeks stung with the scald of realizing she'd made a specta-

cle of herself again. Skinny lovesick Lucy, bleeding out her
emotions for him to trample over again. "Get out," she ordered, her voice vibrating with pain and anger.

"Now, Lucy love—"

"I mean it, J. T. We're finished, you and me."

"Damn your pride, woman! You're as bright as a new shamrock about most things, but when it comes to love, you're
thicker than a post."

"Who said anything about love?" she asked suspiciously.

Instead of answering, he flipped up the pass-through with one
huge hand, charging behind the counter so fast she only had time
to let out a surprised squeak before he wrapped her in those huge
work-hardened arms and crashed his mouth down on hers.

Instinctively, she slammed her palms against shoulders as
hard and unyielding as granite. At the same time pleasure
spread through her, as potent and addictive as the whiskey she
tasted on the lips now sweetly gentle and coaxing on hers.

A helpless shivering moan came from somewhere around
her toes, and her fingers crushed the fabric of his shirt in an attempt to pull him even closer. She felt his erection thrust hard
between her legs and whimpered, eager to feel him inside her
again after so many long, empty years.

An impatient growl rumbled in his throat a split second before he lifted his head, breaking the kiss. Desperate to recap-
ture the indescribable feeling she'd missed for so long, she
opened her eyes and arched upward. Instead of accepting her
invitation, however, he dropped a kiss on her nose before taking a jerky step backward. When she didn't release him, he
wrapped those big calloused hands around her wrists and
tugged them free.

"In case you haven't figured it out yet, it's courting you I am,"
he informed her with a husky note of promise in his voice.

She blinked, her heart a frantic bird fluttering in her chest
and her nerves singing a wild torch song. "You're . . . courting
me?"

"That I am."

"But . . . why now, after so many years?"

"Because being with you makes me feel alive in ways I haven't felt in too long. And because I never forgot the green-eyed colleen who made me laugh."

"But—"

"Enough talk. It's the doing you need." He ran his hands up and down her arms, then grinned. "I'll leave you now, love, but while I'm planting my trees, I'll be thinking about the next time I feel your sweet mouth under mine."

He lifted her hand to his lips and kissed it before walking out.

Rhys held his first staff meeting at two that afternoon. Max had ferried Elena from the airport to the inn, then returned after lunch to fetch her to the depot. The others had spent the morning settling in, Stan in the office next to Della's, Emory in his cubicle off the maintenance bays on the main floor. Rhys had toyed with the idea of calling Junior in for the meeting, then decided against it for a number of reasons. Mostly because he didn't want to lay eyes on the SOB again until he absolutely had to.

He'd let Del run the show, since the meeting dealt mainly with personnel. Did a good job of keeping focused and to the point, he thought with a flash of pride as she wound things up.

"You're screening data-processing and computer people, correct?" Seated at the curved end of the workstation, Della glanced at Stan, who sat next to Elena on the leather sofa facing Rhys' desk.

He nodded. Twenty-eight years old and a cum laude Cornell graduate, Franklyn was a superb CPA, but lousy with people. Though Hank still had reservations about him, Stan had had the right qualifications at the right time to become NSN's CFO.

"Most of Sullivan's office staff have already sent in applications—with the exception of Sullivan Senior's executive assistant, who moved out of state after the flood." She twinkled a smile at Elena. "Which is just as well since Elena's not about to step aside."

"Got that right," Elena replied with a chuckle. A widow with three grown children, Elena was as fiercely protective of her bachelor boss as she was efficient.

"What happening with the rigs?" Rhys asked Emory Scruggs.

"Got me a fax from Alvarez at Kenworth Sales in Seattle right before we left for the airport yesterday a.m. Says he'll supply the drivers to get the rigs here by the weekend."

"Anything else I need to deal with today?" Rhys asked, glancing at each one in turn.

"Nope," Emory declared, looking eager to get to work.

"Nothing here," Stan echoed before reaching down to snap his briefcase closed.

Della and Elena shook their heads. Della saved her work and powered down the computer.

"There's one more thing before you go." Though Rhys spoke quietly, he saw Della's head come up and smiled to himself. The woman knew him too damn well. "It's about me personally, but it affects North Star as well."

He felt a sudden twisting pain in his gut. As far as he knew, only his senior executives knew he'd done time. It was company policy that anyone who put on a North Star badge started with a clean slate. Only his head of personnel, Ben Jacobs, and Rhys himself knew which of the thousands of employees had prison records.

"You need to know I grew up in this town. It's not something I care to remember, but I can't deny it either. People here know me as J. T. Sullivan's older son, Michael. If you hear people talking about Mickey Sullivan, that's me." He caught the stunned looks and smiled slightly. "When I was just shy of eighteen, I hit a school bus in my pickup. Two kids and the driver died. I was convicted of vehicular homicide and served forty-eight months."

There was absolute silence before Emory broke it with a curse. "Must have drawn yourself a real hanging judge, seeing as how I got off with thirty months for murder two."

Rhys' stomach soured. "Let's say he and I didn't hit it off."

"And the Mrs. Sullivan who runs the inn is . . . ?" Elena asked.

"John Junior's ex-wife." Damn, he hated dredging this all up again. "It's a safe bet I'm not going to be any more popular now than I was when I left. There might be some flak, and you need to be on your guard."

Franklyn looked startled. "We're dealing with ugly words, right? Not violence?"

Emory snorted. "Maybe you ain't noticed how folks these days are blowing each other away on account of one cuttin' the other off in traffic, for crissakes. Don't take much of a stretch to see some local yahoo appointing himself avenging angel."

Suddenly Rhys needed some space around him. "If no one has anything else that needs discussing, the meeting's adjourned."

It was a few minutes after the four p.m. shift change, and Chief of Police Brody Hollister was kicked back in his chair with the phone cradled against one broad shoulder, doing more listening than talking, a habit deeply engrained in him by his lifelong struggle with stuttering.

A few minutes later, he finally hung up. Damn long-winded civil servant. "Man acted like I couldn't understand English. Made it a point to come at the same subject a half dozen different ways."

Across the desk, his second-in-command, Sergeant Slade Hingle, had the brass to grin. A bull of a man with the blue black skin of his African forebears, Hingle was Brody's go-to guy and had a nearly infallible way of reading people.

"Got to hand it to you, Chief, you were a lot more polite than I would have been." Slade paused, tucked his tongue in his cheek. "Course, that 'yes sir' you tossed in at the end there sounded a whole lot like 'fuck you' to this old country boy."

Just Hingle's luck that Office Manager Maxine Dornberger aka the Dragon Lady chose that precise moment to walk in. A large, rawboned, frizzy-haired woman of indeterminate age, she'd been ragging at Brody about something or other for the past twelve years. This month it was swearing; she'd gotten it into her head to clean up the language around headquarters.

"That will be one crisp dollar for the widows and orphans fund, Hingle," she snapped as she approached Brody's shiny new desk. Hingle tried to look chastened, but Brody caught the twinkle in the sergeant's eyes as he dug into his pocket and hauled out a crumpled single. Ignoring his piteous look, Maxie snatched it from his hand and tucked it away in the pocket of her severely tailored blue jacket.

"Don't forget you're due to collect the twins from their play date at five o'clock," she told Brody as she handed him a business card.

"Like I'd forget my girls?" he grumbled before glancing at the particulars on the card.

"'M. R. Hazard, Chairman of the Board and CEO of North Star Trucking, Inc.,'" he read aloud. "Did Mr. Hazard say what he wants?"

Maxie frowned. "He did not."

According to the background check he'd run after his wife, Summer, had filled him in on the buzz running around town, M. R. Hazard aka Michael Rhys Sullivan had an unblemished record since his release from McNeil Island at the age of twenty-two. While incarcerated, he'd gone before the parole board three times and been summarily denied every time. Each time the board's report cited both the judge's strongly worded recommendation against early release and two serious disciplinary referrals to the lockdown unit as the primary reasons for their decision. The third time he'd been eligible he'd waived his right to plead his case in person. A hard-ass with an attitude or a proud man refusing to beg? Brody figured it could swing either way. "Ask him to come in, will you, please?"

"Brace yourself," Maxine muttered before sailing out with her chin jutting.

Chuckling, Hingle climbed to his feet and stretched. "Sure would have liked to see this guy going toe-to-toe with our Maxie," he said before taking himself off, leaving the door open behind him.

As Brody rose to his feet, he wondered what kind of a man he was about to meet. One who damn well wasn't favorably inclined toward cops, he decided as Hazard came in.

As they exchanged perfunctory greetings, shook hands and sized each other up, Brody called to mind Michael Sullivan's mug shot. The eyes were the same vivid gray, but the shock and bewilderment of a scared boy were gone, replaced by a mixture of intelligence, confidence and cynicism. Despite the pronounced limp and the cane he obviously needed, there was enough muscle packed on his upper body to give the toughest badass second thoughts. Instinct told him M. R. Hazard would prove to be exactly the kind of partner a cop wanted next to him going through a door—or a formidable enemy if his inclination ran the other way.

Brody gestured politely toward the chair Hingle had just vacated. "Suppose you have a seat and tell me why you're here, Mr. Hazard."

"I've been sitting too much today, but thanks for the offer."

Brody gave him that one. Hazard obviously understood the dynamics of power, and because he did, he wasn't about to give Brody any kind of edge. Brody didn't mind playing by Hazard's rules. For now.

Deciding *he* hadn't been sitting too much, he settled into his chair again. Understanding the power of silence in an interview—or an interrogation—he leaned back, propped his feet on the bottom drawer he kept open for that purpose, folded his hand over his belt buckle and kept his mouth shut.

Hazard's gaze ceded the point to him. "How much do you know about my past history?"

"Convicted of vehicular homicide at age eighteen, served your full sentence, no arrests since."

"After I got out of the hospital and before I was released on bail I spent forty-eight hours in a cell down the hall here. Had a lot of cops wandering by to make their opinion of me known—among other things. I don't remember you being one of them."

"No reason why you would since I was working in L.A. then, but if I had been here, I wouldn't have been one of those talking trash to a scared kid. Does that satisfy your curiosity?"

"It does."

"Good. Now satisfy mine if you will. What do you want from the Osuma PD?"

"Your word that North Star personnel involved in the ceremony on the fifteenth won't be embarrassed—or worse."

A reasonable request. Impossible to grant, but not out of line and more than a little thoughtful. "You have reason to think that's a possibility?"

"There were some pretty ugly threats twenty-two years ago. Seems logical some of the people making them are still around."

"Probably, although I'm hearing that sentiment is running more toward gratitude for the jobs you're providing. Might go a long way toward keeping things mellow."

"On the other hand it might not."

"Can't argue with that." Brody debated, then dropped his feet and spun around to take a folder from the file drawer behind him. He hunted up the neatly typed list of security procedures for the weekend and handed it over. "These are the security measures we've planned. The governor's people have already added their 'suggestions.'"

"No offense, but I'd like to run this past my chief of security in Phoenix."

"No offense taken. My people think it's pretty solid, but nothing's perfect. If your man sees s-something we missed, have him give me a call."

Since Hazard struck him as a man who could hide his thoughts as easily as he could display them, he figured the skepticism surfacing in those gray eyes was deliberate. It was also subtle enough to be easily missed if a man wasn't paying attention. Brody had survived almost thirty years as a cop because he paid attention.

"Might help ease your mind to know I consider us to be on the same side in this, Mr. Hazard. You don't want anyone getting hurt and neither do I. If your man has a better way of handling things, I don't have a problem making adjustments. Hell, I've been known to take advice from my seventeen-year-old daughter when her idea was better than mine."

Hazard's slow, rueful grin took Brody by surprise. "Your daughter, does she happen to know anything about security?"

Brody laughed. "What can I say, she's a t-teenager. She knows *everything*. According to her, I'm the one who's a hopeless ignoramus." His face softened the way it always did when he thought about Kelly. "But just in case, when I go home tonight, I'll ask her. And if she comes up with something useful, I'll pass it on to your security guy. Fair enough?"

This time Hazard was the one to initiate the handshake. "Fair enough."

The butt-ugly, bunkerlike building housing Sarge's Place had taken a beating in the flood, but the concrete block construction and slab foundation had prevented it from being swept away. Never one to pay for what he could finesse, promote or steal, the owner, Gunnar "Sarge" Stenner, had mucked out the place the best he could before offering the guys of Engine Company 2 a month of free drafts if they would scour off the rest of the crud with a pressurized blast with a two-inch hose. The place still smelled like a musty root cellar, and the pressure washing had scoured off ragged patches of paint as well as dirt. Sarge hadn't bothered to repaint, but so far no one had complained.

Hunkered up to the bar with his heels hooked over the brass rail, John was killing time before driving to Wenatchee to meet Sherri at the bridal shop where they had a five thirty appointment with the frigging wedding planner. Sherri was already talking champagne fountains and white fucking doves. He didn't even want to think about how much cash he'd have to lay out before it was over.

He checked the Budweiser clock behind the bar; then figuring he had a few more minutes' reprieve, he signaled the barkeep for another draft. On the downhill side of sixty, Red Sturgess had been tending bar at Sarge's Place for as long as John could remember.

"You got the starting pitchers for the Yanks–Red Sox game on Saturday yet?" John asked as Red drew him another cold one.

"Rookie by the name of Chavez is listed for the Yanks. Has him a ninety-mile-an-hour fastball and one of them forkballs. Looked real good in spring training."

Another fucking greaser millionaire, John thought, trying to remember if he'd read anything about a new Yankee phenom. "What was his record last season?"

Sturgess set the draft on a clean napkin before whisking away the empty glass. "Nineteen wins, eleven losses."

John took a sip and considered. Red produced a rag and began wiping down the bar while keeping one eye on four bikers playing pool toward the rear. Not even the wailing country tune on the jukebox could completely drown out the exchange of crude obscenities accompanying the clicking of balls.

"How about the BoSox?" John asked. "Who they got set for Saturday?"

"Last I heard they was goin' with Martinez."

John thought about the money he'd dropped at the blackjack table in Vegas. He'd been up almost fifty grand before his luck had turned sour. By the time the house had cut off his credit, he'd lost the fifty and dropped another forty. Just about everything he'd gotten when his Dad had sold out.

His luck had been in the toilet for months, but that was about to change. He felt it.

"Get out your ledger, Red," he said with a cocky grin. "I'm feeling lucky today. Lucky enough to risk two grand on Boston."

Red shot a quick look around before leaning one meaty forearm on the bar, bringing his face closer to John's. The stench of the butts he chain-smoked oozed through his pores, and his breath stank of sour mash.

"It's like this, Mr. Sullivan. Sarge said if you was to come in while he was off to remind you that as of last night you're already on his books for more than forty Gs."

"So I had a run of bad luck." John shrugged, deliberately keeping his expression cool. "It happens. He knows I'm good for it."

Red had flat yellow eyes like a rattler's. They narrowed slightly. "Just so's you know, Sarge is not one for carrying a man beyond thirty days before expecting payment. Said to tell you by his reckoning you got until the seventeenth. Eleven more days grace at double the usual interest. After that, he's gonna collect one way or another."

John felt fear rain like ice down his spine. Somehow he managed to keep his edge as he downed the last of his beer. "You tell Sarge I don't appreciate threats," he said and slipped from the stool.

Red smiled, revealing teeth as yellow as his eyes. "Just so's you know, last man who welshed on a bet with Sarge ended up in one of them canyons up yonder with his dick in his mouth."

Chapter 13

Brina shoved the garlic bread into the upper of her twin ovens and closed the door. Tonight's dinner was lasagna and salad, with antipasto and bread. Easy, fast and fail-safe on a night when she was pushed for time.

"Petey's gonna ride with his dad in his dumb old cop car in the parade," Jay said before taking a huge bite of his cheeseburger. He and Marcy were eating in the kitchen tonight, perched on the stools at the center island.

"I'll bet he's thrilled, huh?" she said, retrieving salad from the fridge. She had forty minutes before Lucy was due to pick her up for Summer's shower.

Jay shrugged. "I guess. It's really lame, though."

Brina slanted him a curious look. "Why do you say that?"

"It's just a dumb old Taurus. Not like the 'Vette. All the guys wish they could ride with Dad and me."

"Uncle Rhys is gonna read me a story tonight," Marcy told her brother smugly. "He said."

"Big deal," Jay scoffed.

Marcy stuck out her tongue. "You're just jealous 'cause he likes me best."

"Marcy!" Brina chided. "Uncle Rhys hasn't even met Jay yet."

Marcy was undeterred. "Daddy likes me best. Grandma said."

"Grandma was wrong," Brina jumped in quickly and firmly. "Daddy likes you both exactly the same."

"Who cares what Grandma said anyway?" Jay muttered, glaring at his sister. "She's worm food."

"Mom-meee!"

"That's enough talk like that, Jay."

"I got math to do," Jay muttered, hopping down from the stool.

"Don't you want your dessert, sweetie? I got chocolate chip mint just for you."

"Ice cream makes my stupid braces hurt." He jerked open the door to the dishwasher, jabbed his plate into the nearest slot, slammed the door shut and stalked out.

As soon as Brina put dinner on the table, she rushed upstairs to change. After slipping into her slacks and best silk blouse, she grabbed the portable phone from the charger and punched out John's number.

Sherri answered, her voice cooling when she heard Brina's. While Sherri went to find John, Brina walked to the closet to pull out her only pair of Italian flats.

"Make it fast, okay, Brin," John ordered when he came on the line. "Sher and I were just heading out for dinner at the new Thai place in Wenatchee."

She forced enthusiasm into her voice. "That's perfect, actually. I was going to ask you to stop by tonight to spend some time with Jay. Since Wenatchee's on the way, you won't be inconvenienced."

"Is something wrong with the kid?"

Brina tucked the phone against her shoulder in order to button a shirt cuff. "Yes, you promised to stop by to see him yesterday and you never showed up."

"I had to run over to Seattle. We didn't get back until late. I'll explain to the kid. He'll understand."

She attacked the other cuff. "No, he won't, John. You keep

saying you'll stop by, but it's been weeks since you and Jay spent any time together."

Her ex's long-suffering sigh was heavy in her ear. "I've explained that, Brin. Once I settle into the new job, things will get back on track."

"This is a rough time for Jay," she said, trying not to bite off each word. "Now that he's hit puberty, he's feeling confused and insecure. He needs to know his dad loves him."

"Hell, Brin, he knows that."

"That's just it; he doesn't. Every time you break a date with him he thinks it's because you don't care about him. And now with this football camp nonsense, he's convinced you think he's a wimp."

"He isn't yet, but he's headed in that direction. Football camp will toughen him up."

She drew an irate breath. "Will that be before or after he gets major bones broken?"

"Oh, for crap's sake, Brin, the kid is almost thirteen. He doesn't need to be coddled like he was a baby."

"No football camp, John. That's final."

"That's bullshit, that's what it is!" John's voice exploded through the phone into her ear, making her wince. "You're trying to undermine my authority with my son to get back at me for falling in love with someone else."

"And you're ruining your son's self-esteem by making it crystal clear you won't love him unless he's pumped up on testosterone and machismo."

"Cut the psychobabble, okay? You don't know shit about how to raise a boy."

Brina took a death grip on the phone—and her temper. "Let's cut to the chase, John. I will not agree to your sending Jay to some kind of boot camp for jock Neanderthals. The court gave me the final word. If you don't like it, tough." She took great pleasure in banging down the receiver.

* * *

"More tea, Brina, dear?" Looking like a tiny hummingbird in a flowing green caftan and shimmering ruby red scarf, Dottie Hollister Krebs sat at Brina's corner of the 1930s chintz sofa, her Revere silver teapot at the ready. "It's a special blend I had made up to keep a woman's natural juices flowing."

Brina had to admit the "special blend" had a distinctly exotic aroma that evoked sensual images of lotus blossoms, ukulele music and a lover's moon rising over a sandy beach. Before Brina's increasingly rebellious imagination ran amok and added a man and woman—both gloriously naked and wildly in love—to the fantasy, she blinked it away.

"After the month I've put in, I'm not sure I have any juices left to flow, natural or otherwise," she told her beaming hostess as she held up her delicate Wedgwood cup.

"Of course you do, dear," Dottie proclaimed as she poured out with the aplomb of a highborn aristocrat. "Anyone with eyes can see that you're a passionate woman with a healthy appetite for pleasure."

Perhaps once, a long time ago. "I can't dispute the appetite part, anyway," Brina murmured, her gaze dropping to the thunder thighs presently sheathed by tailored gray slacks.

"I suspect your chakras are even more blocked than poor Lucy's," Miss Dottie asserted. "Blocked chakras cause a body's sexual energy to become dammed up."

"Ah." Feeling more like a bug impaled on a pin, Brina took several needed sips.

"That bein' the case, Miss Dottie, just how does a girl go about getting her chakras undammed?" asked Char Williams. Seated next to the guest of honor on the brightly patterned rug, Char was a transplanted Los Angeleno in her early thirties. Summer's assistant director at the Phoenix House Rehabilitation and Treatment Center and as bright as a freshly minted penny, she had a wry sense of humor, long runner's legs Brina coveted and attitude to spare.

"I have a marvelous meditation tape I'll have Gray copy for

you. After that I would strongly recommend frequent doses of prolonged and intense sexual stimulation."

"Can I have an amen to that, ladies?" Summer Hollister offered with a fond look for her husband's aunt. Dressed in a lime green tunic and slacks, she sat like a contented Buddha on a plump floor pillow amid piles of toys, little boy outfits and discarded wrapping paper. A well-respected psychotherapist specializing in adolescent drug abuse, she was everything Brina wasn't—elegant, stylish and, above all, confident. Her golden hair was sleek and glossy, her eyes sparkling green. Married three years now, she was still wildly in love with her husband, the town's top cop.

According to Dottie, big, tough, self-contained Brody Hollister had taken one look at his aunt's houseguest and fallen hard. *Crashed to earth like an old-growth redwood* had been the way Dottie had put it then.

It had been at Dottie's invitation that Dr. Laurence, as she'd been known then, had come to Osuma four years ago. When she'd begun checking out the Hollister homestead, everyone—including Brody Hollister—had thought she'd intended to establish a private practice. Everyone had been wrong. Phoenix House had gotten off to a rocky start, but now it was thriving, with a remarkable history of positive results and a long waiting list.

Although Summer's area of expertise encompassed substance abuse and rehabilitation, she'd also been darn good at counseling an emotionally battered, cheated-on wife whose self-esteem had been in the toilet. Over copious amounts of tea—and, before Summer had gotten pregnant occasional glasses of Pinot Grigio—Brina had dumped out a ton of emotional baggage on her friend's elegant shoulders. Instead of doing a heavy-handed shrink thing, Summer had prescribed shopping therapy and funny movies, lent her books on surviving divorce and infidelity and, most important of all, loved and accepted her as a sister.

Yesterday, when Brina had called her to dump the news of Michael Sullivan's sudden reappearance, Summer had been immediately—and wonderfully—supportive. *The bastard, how dare he put you through the wringer all over again!* she'd fumed. *Walking into your house like he owned it. Throwing his weight around, acting like a big shot.*

A working conscience really was a mean bitch, Brina thought sourly. Even though she'd hated admitting it, even to her best friend, Rhys Hazard hadn't done any of those things. Just the opposite, in fact.

Not that that changed the facts, she hastened to remind herself. Or the resentment that made it hard to breathe around the man.

A perfectly natural response under the circumstances, Summer had assured her when Brina had finally run out of steam. Ditto, Brina's conflicted—and contradictory—feelings toward Rhys Hazard.

The boy she'd hated no longer existed. The man he'd become—the man he'd made himself into—was a stranger. A very attractive, charismatic, sexually appealing male who'd gotten to her on a gut level. Could it be that a part of the emotional turmoil roiling her stomach was guilt? Summer had asked. Or something even more visceral—and far more unsettling.

According to Summer, physical attraction wasn't something that could be turned on—or off—at will. Like it or not, it was beyond intellectual control. On the other hand, how a person dealt with those feelings—and the needs they aroused—was something else entirely. I am woman; hear me roar, Brina thought as she lifted her teacup to her lips. She would beat back those lustful thoughts with willpower and reason.

As Summer's eyes met hers for an instant, Brina saw both sympathy and understanding reflected in the depths. However you want to deal with this publicly, I'll follow your lead, she telegraphed silently. As the chatter of the others swirled around them, Brina thanked her with a smile.

"I can see it now, the next mega-bestseller," Lucy grumbled, aiming the tines of her sterling cake fork toward Dottie, her oldest and dearest friend. *"The Wit and Wisdom of a Sixty-Four-Year-Old Sexpot.* The baby boomers are sure to lap it up."

"A sixty-*three*-year-old sexpot, Lucille," Dottie corrected with a haughty look that set the silver and tourmaline minichandeliers attached to her dainty earlobes swinging. "I'm still three months from my birthday while you, as we all know, are already *four* months past yours." She returned the pot to the matching silver tray on the country French sideboard before settling into the comfortably worn wing chair facing the sofa.

"Dot's right, Luce, you're definitely the oldest person here," said Amanda Lendel, their lifelong friend. Married for forty years to the pastor of the Osuma Community Church, Mandy had always been the most conventional and even-tempered of the four childhood buddies known as the Fearsome Foursome—and thus, by default, the designated voice of reason. Frequently she was called upon to referee when Lucy and Dottie squared off, as they'd been doing for sixty years now.

"I'm also the richest, which means I can do as I damned well please," Lucy said with a sly grin that had the fourth member of the Foursome, Florence Willis Fortier, clucking her tongue. Mrs. Fortier had been the principal of George Washington Elementary when Brina was a child. Now principal of Osuma High, the redoubtable Flossie still had the power to make her snap to attention.

"A *lady* never brags about her beaux, her beauty or her money," she lectured in her rounded schoolmistress tones.

"Or her sex life," Mandy added primly, albeit with a decidedly naughty twinkle in her eyes.

"Bah," Dottie scoffed. "At our age we have an obligation to

our younger sisters to indulge in a bit of tasteful boasting whenever possible."

Char drew up her legs and hugged her knees. "So, tell us, Brin, this Rhys Hazard who's turning this town on its collective ear, is he gorgeous as well as sinfully rich and deliciously notorious?"

"Not gorgeous, but not a troll either," she said, keeping her gaze on the contents of her teacup.

"I only remember a gangly boy with the devil's own grin and gentle eyes, but Ernestine swears he's Mr. Darcy come to life," Dottie confided.

"I do love those dark, dangerous and brooding types," Summer said.

"Actually, Rhys' hair is a sort of silver-dusted blond," Brina offered without thinking. And gloriously thick, with a natural off-center part and a hell-for-leather windblown look that just naturally made a woman long to tidy him up.

"Give us the bottom line, honey chile," Char urged. "One to ten on the sex appeal scale, where does he rate?"

"Depends on how you feel about long-legged, lean-hipped, granite-jawed cowboy/commando/loner type guys." She distracted herself with a few more swallows of tea before she remembered about the natural juices. She put the cup down so fast it rattled the saucer. At the same time she caught the surprised look that passed between Lucy and Miss Dottie.

"Don't know about the rest of you, but this committed feminist turns to quivering jelly just thinking about making it with a rough tough guy with a big gun like Dirty Harry," Char exclaimed before popping another brandied apricot into her perfectly shaped mouth.

"Speaking of big guns," Summer said, looking at Brin with sparkling eyes, "one to ten, how would *one* rate Mr. Alpha Cowboy Tough Guy on the bulge scale?"

Mandy choked on the tea she'd been about to swallow, prompting Flossie to pound her on the back until she begged for mercy. Brina realized she was enjoying herself for the first time in ages.

"You don't have to answer that, dear," Miss Dottie assured her.

"Oh, yes, you do, girl," Char said with a leering grin. "Ain't no way my natural juices can settle with that kind of question just hanging unanswered."

"'The Successful Innkeeper must be circumspect at all times,'" Brina quoted.

"Circumspect? In Nightingale House?" Dottie scoffed. "Dear heart, those rooms fairly throb with sexual energy, as I'm sure you've already discovered."

"Not really," she said. "Maybe Merribelle took it with her when she sold out and retired to Palm Springs."

"On the contrary, dear, one has only to walk into the foyer to feel it pulsing against the more sensitive areas of one's body. You've simply blocked it out. Not that it isn't perfectly understandable, of course, considering the traumatic disillusionment of recent years."

Lucy and Flossie exchanged looks before Flossie turned her principal's glare in Dottie's direction. "For heaven's sake, Dorothea, can't you see you're embarrassing the poor child?"

Brina flinched inside. She suspected she'd been called "poor child" a lot since the divorce—and not only by the Fearsome Foursome.

"I'm simply interested in finding out what kind of a man J. T.'s boy has become," Dottie countered, her surprisingly youthful face assuming an affronted look right out of a *Perils of Pauline* melodrama.

"He's clearly become successful with a capital *S*," Flossie offered without glancing up from the discarded wrapping paper she was carefully folding.

"I always knew that boy had gold in him," Dottie said. "In fact, he reminds me of Brody."

"You mean he's a stubborn mule?" Summer murmured, her smile soft.

"No, I mean he had to fight tooth and nail for even a scrap of affection from that ice maiden excuse for a mother."

"For once Dot's not exaggerating," Lucy said, her expression grim. "I remember once he talked his kindergarten teacher into helping him draw a special picture for his mother's birthday, only to find it a few days later in the wastebasket in her bedroom. Poor little guy was heartbroken. He didn't understand what he'd done wrong. J. T. told me he smoothed it over by telling Mickey the maid had thrown away his picture by mistake. But when Johnny started school, his paintings ended up in fancy frames on the piano in the living room."

"Along with about a million pictures of her 'darling boy,'" Brina added, her stomach souring at the memory of Marceline's endless supply of anecdotes.

"I still remember the look on Mick's face when he walked in and saw that big silver frame containing John's first scribbles setting there in a place of honor. He was about six then as I recall."

"Well, shee-it, I'm against hitting women, but that bitch sounds like she should have been whomped upside the head on a regular basis," Char declared. "Might have knocked some decency into her."

"Not Marceline!" Lucy and Dottie declared in unison before sharing brief smiles.

"All those weeks after the accident when Michael was in the hospital, Marceline never once went to see him," Lucy said tightly. "After that, I could never look at her again without revulsion."

Brina glanced up from the crib blanket she'd just retrieved from the floor. "Part of me thinks I have a duty to my brother to hate Rhys, but for the life of me I can't seem to manage."

"Of course you can't, dear," Dottie said, beaming at her. "Hatred isn't part of your nature."

"Like I keep telling the kids at Phoenix House, hatin' takes way too much energy," Char said, stretching out one long leg. "Loving your fellow man is just so much nicer."

Summer carefully set her empty cup on the floor next to a stuffed Pooh Bear. "It wouldn't surprise me if that rejected little boy turned into a man with serious issues concerning intimacy and trust, especially when it comes to women."

"Making him either a love-'em-then-leave-'em Don Juan, or a loner," Char said. "Either way, it makes a guy like that a real dismal romantic prospect."

"On the other hand," Summer added, "someone like that is often desperately hungry for affection. Paradoxically, their distrust won't allow them to accept what's offered."

"Sounds like a Catch-22 to me," Mandy said with a thoughtful frown.

"Sounds like an emotional battleground to me," Flossie offered.

Brina thought it sounded terribly unfair—and very sad.

Chapter 14

After locking the door to the utility room and hanging up her slicker, Brina walked into the kitchen to find Ernestine at the stove, stirring cocoa into a saucepan of milk. Looking flushed, she wore the emerald velour lounging robe Brina and the kids had given her last Christmas.

"You're home early," Ernestine said as she turned down the burner. "Did you have a nice time?"

"Interesting, but not restful. Miss Dottie sent home some of the leftover cake. It's her special coconut cream delight. Feel free to help yourself—there's plenty."

"I shouldn't," Ernie protested, even as she turned a longing gaze toward the foil-covered plate in Brina's hand. "But perhaps a modest piece."

"Don't tell anyone, but I had two—and they were anything but modest." Sighing over her pathetic lack of willpower, she placed the plate on the center island before taking a glass from the cabinet.

"Any problems on the home front?" she asked as she filled the glass from the tap. Since she couldn't afford a relief desk clerk, Ernie filled in as both clerk and baby-sitter during those rare evenings when Brina managed to get away. In return, Brina gave her a break on her monthly rent.

"No calls, and everything is in perfect order," Ernie assured her before removing two plates from the cupboard.

"None for me, thanks," Brina said, indicating the extra plate.

Ernie's pale complexion took on a pink tinge, and her lashes lowered. "I thought perhaps Mr. Stillwell would enjoy a snack," she said. "We've been playing chess in the library."

"Chess? You and . . . the . . . and Mr. Stillwell?"

"He's an excellent player. In fact, he's beaten me three games to two."

Brina's jaw dropped. "But no one beats you! Not even Jay, and he beats *everyone*."

Ernie actually giggled. "I admit I expected an easy victory—until Mr. Stillwell took my king in seven moves." She sobered, then adjusted her collar with nervous fingers. "Despite his rather rough-hewn exterior, he has a remarkably fine mind."

Brina nearly choked on the water she'd just swallowed. "He does?"

"Oh, my yes!" Behind her glasses, Ernie's eyes glowed. "He came into the library this afternoon looking for books on birds that are indigenous to this area and we had a *most* interesting talk."

"Mr. Stillwell is a bird fancier?"

The look on Ernie's face was touchingly eager. "He's thinking of joining our bird-watching group."

"I suppose that's safe enough."

"Safe?" Ernie's brow wrinkled. "I'm afraid I don't understand, dear. Bird-watching isn't the least bit dangerous, you know."

"A safe hobby for a newcomer." Brina backpedaled furiously. "Expense- and timewise, I mean. Considering Mr. Stillwell's responsibilities and . . . everything else."

Ernie looked even more confused, but was too polite to suggest that Brina was talking nonsense. "Well, yes, indeed."

Feeling like an idiot, Brina drained the glass and tucked it into the dishwasher. "Where are the kids, upstairs?"

"Yes." Ernie took a knife from the rack. "When I put Marcy to bed at eight thirty, Jay was on his computer."

"Playing games instead of doing homework, of course."

"Of course." Ernie lifted the foil, then glanced up. "Everyone else is present and accounted for, so I locked the front door and turned on the answering machine."

"Bless you!"

Ernie looked shyly pleased. "Good night, dear. Rest well."

"You, too." Brina hesitated before adding with a smile, "Say good night to Mr. Stillwell for me, too. Tell him I have a pair of binoculars he's welcome to borrow. For bird-watching."

"I'm sure he'll be grateful. We're planning to go this weekend while Mr. Hazard is in Phoenix."

"Ah." Curiouser and curiouser, Brina thought as she headed upstairs. She sent up a private prayer to the angels who looked out for gentle souls and lonely ladies.

Some kind of screeching music throbbed against the closed door of Jay's room, bringing a frown to her face. She gave some thought to pulling the plug but decided to take a quick shower first. Yawning again, she slipped the top two buttons of her best silk blouse as she crossed the landing. The door to Marcy's room was open and the light was on, so she detoured in that direction, ready to give the little stinker what for. A few feet from the door she stopped dead, startled by the sound of Marcy's wheedling plea, "*Puh-leeeeeeeze*, Uncle Rhys. Just one more."

Rhys' deep voice answered, "You sure it's not time for you to close those pretty peepers and go to sleep?"

"Nuh-uh. I *always* stay up 'til Mommy gets home."

"You do, do you?" Amusement roughed up his voice. "Even when she comes in really late?"

"Uh-huh, only Mommy never stays out late since Daddy divorced us."

"She doesn't?"

"Nuh-uh. Mostly she works so the bank won't take away our house. Here, read this one. It's my very most favoritest."

So much for being open and honest with her children about pesky financial problems, Brina thought, moving closer until she had a clear view of the room. Rhys sat a bit stiffly on the edge of the bed. He'd changed since this morning into gray sweatpants, a faded blue sweatshirt with the sleeves hacked off, and moccasin-style loafers. His hair, rumpled and thick, gleamed with gold and silver highlights in the lamplight, and his gray eyes had a lazy cast.

Looking scrubbed and adorably cuddly, Marcy snuggled against his side, her cheek pressed against one thick forearm. The lean, mean lion and the fluffy little lamb, Brina thought, bemused.

They were both looking down at the book he held. A certain tension in his face and a subtle rigidity hovering over the heavily muscled shoulders suggested a man who was clearly uncomfortable in this role of uncle, but determined to keep a promise made to an innocent little girl, no matter how casually made. Unlike his younger brother, whose promises meant less than nothing, Brina acknowledged with bittersweet emotion.

"*Goosebumps?*" he said, paging through.

"Uh-huh. Miss Winkle gave it to me for my birthday. She's a librarian, like Miss Dottie. Miss Winkle says books are our best friends."

"She's right, although I'm not real sure about this one, toots. Sounds too scary for me."

Marcy giggled. "You're too big to be scared!"

"Everyone's scared of something, darlin'."

Marcy cocked her head, and her red gold curls shimmered like spun silk in the lamplight. "What are *you* scared of Uncle Rhys?"

"Small places with no windows."

Her nose wrinkled. "Like a closet?"

"Yeah, like a closet only not as nice. I'm not real crazy about the dark either."

"Me neither. Mommy lets me keep my Snoopy light on sometimes."

He glanced at the ceramic lamp on the little yellow dresser between the dormers. "Good for Mommy."

"She says it's okay to be scared, only you shouldn't run away and hide even when you are." She frowned. "Did your mommy let you keep a light on when you got scared?"

"No." He opened the book, but Marcy was on a roll.

"Was your mommy really my grandma?"

"Guess she was, yeah." His tone was neutral, revealing nothing of his feelings.

"My grandma's in heaven. Daddy cried and cried, but Grandpa Sullivan didn't 'cause he's a man and men aren't s'posed to cry. Mommy said Grandma would have been . . . uh-oh!" Primrose blue eyes fastened on Brina's, and the earnest face broke into a sunny grin. "Hi, Mommy! Uncle Rhys is reading me a *story*."

"So I see." Before Brina could think better of it, she walked into the room. "Miss Winkle said she tucked you in at eight thirty. You should be asleep by now."

Rhys' gaze, guarded now, met Brina's for an instant before he bent his head to look Marcy in the eye. Brina gave the cagey little promoter points for bluffing, but she suspected there were few who could hold their own against those street-wise eyes for long.

"Doesn't sound like Mom knows about that staying up late stuff, toots."

Marcy's lashes fluttered down, and her stubby fingers plucked at the quilt. "You promised to read me a story, but you weren't home when Miss Winkle put me to bed, so I had to stay up 'til I heard you come home," she said in a small voice before peeking up at him through her strawberry lashes. "How come you stayed out so late?"

"I was working out at a gym in Wenatchee with Max."

"How come?"

"Exercising keeps my hip from getting stiff."

Marcy glanced at his cane. "You could do that *after* story time."

"Guess I could at that." His jaw flexed. "I'm sorry, Marcy," he said solemnly. "I didn't realize you were waiting for me." He lifted one of those large hands to gently tuck a stray lock of hair behind her ear. Brina's breath caught at the fleeting expression of tenderness on his face. "Guess we both messed up, huh?"

"Uh-huh. Only Mommy can't be mad at you 'cause you're lots bigger than she is."

His mouth took on a slow, wry slant that did annoying things to Brina's insides. "Don't count on that, toots. Mommies have ways of making even big guys shiver in their boots if they know the right things to say."

Marcy blinked in surprise before leaning forward to peek up at her again. "Don't be mad, okay, Mommy? I went downstairs and asked Uncle Rhys to read me a story, and when he asked me if I was allowed to stay up, I . . . I told a fib." Her lower lip quivered a little then, but her little shoulders pushed back bravely. Her small hand, Brina noticed, had found its way into his.

Brina felt a rush of pride. "Since you were brave enough to admit the truth, I promise not to be mad." Because she knew her daughter all too well, she added sternly, "This time. If it happens again, you're going to be in big trouble." She leveled a warning look at Uncle Rhys. "*Both* of you."

His eyes crinkled at the corners, but his expression remained serious. "Sounds like she means it to me," he told Marcy, sounding like an intimidated boy.

Marcy peeped past his formidable chest again. "Uh-oh, she's got her hands on her hips. That's a real bad sign."

"It is?"

Marcy gave her head a couple of vehement shakes. "It means she's gonna yell if you sass her back."

Rhys turned a speculative gaze toward the hand that was firmly welded to the swell of Brina's hip. Right where the two pieces of coconut cake were even now depositing yet another layer of padding, she thought with a silent groan.

He cleared his throat. "Something tells me the best tactic here is a strategic retreat."

"The quicker the better," Brina agreed, working hard at not giving in to a smile.

"Yes, ma'am." His grin came and went quickly, but not quickly enough to conceal those two creases in his hard cheeks.

Taking a breath, she deliberately focused her attention on her imp of a daughter. "Say good night, and scoot under the covers, sweetie. You have school tomorrow."

Silky brows drawn into a stubborn knot, Marcy opened her mouth to protest, but a look from Rhys had her mouth snapping shut. "Mommy's right, toots." He closed the book before placing it atop the others on the bedside table. "I have to be out of town for a few days starting tomorrow, but we'll read this as soon as I get back, okay?"

Now that she had what she wanted, Marcy was sugar and spice and dimples. "Okay."

"So . . . uh, I'd better scram so you can get your beauty rest."

"First you have to kiss me good night."

Shock flickered in his eyes. "Is this another uncle thing?" he asked in a voice that was slightly thicker than usual.

Marcy nodded smugly, and he swallowed hard before leaning down to kiss her forehead. "Good night, little darlin'. Sleep well."

"Night, Uncle Rhys," she said, throwing chubby arms around his neck for a hug. "I love you."

He froze, took a deep breath. "I, uh, love you, too," he said gruffly, drawing back. Dusky color rode high on his cheekbones.

Oblivious as always, Marcy yawned, then burrowed the back of her head into her pillow. She let her curly lashes droop. The little stinker, she looked exactly like a drowsy kitten that had just lapped up a whole bowl of cream.

Bemused, and a little shaken, Rhys caught Brina's gaze before he reached for his cane and levered himself to his feet.

Marcy's lashes fluttered open. "Uncle Rhys, make sure you come back before Wednesday, okay?"

Rhys drew his brows. "What happens Wednesday?"

"That's show-and-tell day, silly."

Clearly mystified, Rhys looked to Brina for clarification, but she shook her head. "Sweetie, what's show-and-tell have to do with Mr. . . . with Uncle Rhys needing to be back?"

"I want to show all the kids my new uncle."

Brina was pretty sure Marcy didn't understand the look of stark panic on Hazard's face, but she did. "Sweetie, show-and-tell is not for showing *people,* just *things.*"

"Who says?"

"Everyone knows that." Brina directed a pointed glance Hazard's way. "Right, Uncle Rhys?"

"Your mom's right, toots," he said a shade too quickly. "I think it's some kind of federal law."

Her lower lip edged out. "Well, I think that's really poopy," she declared.

Hazard's eyes crinkled, but he kept a straight face. "Life is like that sometimes, sweetheart," he said before leaning down to ever so gently pull the quilt to her chin. "You best close your eyes now before your mom changes her mind and busts both of us."

"Night-night," she murmured.

Hazard wished them both a good night before leaving.

Brina bent to kiss Marcy's cheek. "Mommy loves you, sweets."

"I love you, too, Mommy. Night-night."

Brina was nearly to the door when Marcy called out to her.

"Yes, sweetie?" she asked, pausing to look back.

"Now that you're not mad at Uncle Rhys anymore, does that mean he can stay here forever and ever?"

The photo of Theo Eiler stood next to those of Brina's mother and children on the bureau in her bedroom. While he'd been alive, she'd gone to him with her problems. Seated in his frayed beige recliner, he'd puffed on his pipe and let her talk until she had no words left. Occasionally he would ask a question, but mostly he just listened. By the time she'd run down, she had usually come up with the solution on her own.

"It's a mess, Daddy," she said now, her gaze resting on her father's beloved photograph. In earlier photos—those taken before her mother's yearlong battle with the breast cancer that ultimately killed her—Theo Eiler's smile had been both boyish and full of mischief. Dimmed by grief after Anna Eiler's death, his smile had disappeared almost entirely after Teddy had died. Because Brina had been taking this particular snapshot, he had tried, but the determined curve to his lips only added to the air of melancholy hanging over him.

"Marcy is such a loving child. So trusting. I'm terrified he'll hurt her, and yet I don't want to disillusion her."

Disillusionment and pain are part of the price we pay for being alive, baby girl. We fight against it, but the truth is the things that hurt us the most usually end up making us stronger—and, if we're lucky, more understanding.

But this was her *child*. What if she were irreparably harmed? "I wish I knew what you would do," she murmured, touching her father's face with her fingertip.

You're so much like your mother, Brina Rose. So determined to protect those you love. And because you're like your mother, you already know deep in your heart what's the right thing to do.

But she didn't—and there was no one to tell her.

*   *   *

Ten minutes later, Brina walked down one flight, her heart beating much too fast. Striving for calm, she took a long, deep breath, braced her shoulders, then lifted a hand and knocked on the door of the President's Room.

The door had been left ajar again. Apparently, Rhys disliked closed doors as much as he disliked small rooms. It didn't take much imagination to figure out why. Suddenly beset with second thoughts, she started to turn away. At the same time the door swung inward, startling her into a squeak of surprise. Now bare-chested and barefoot, he wore only sweatpants. In his free hand he held his sweatshirt, as though he'd started stripping before answering the knock.

Oh, dear heavens! she thought in stunned awe. Her early glimpse of his chest had been little more than a tantalizing tease. Now she saw that it was as close to perfection as her imagination could envision. His massive shoulders were equally impressive, and his arms bulged with a laborer's sinewy muscles under smooth bronze skin.

A puckered purple scar curved from his back to a spot over his left hipbone before disappearing under the low-slung drawstring waistband. The soft fleece molded more than the strong muscles of his thighs, she realized when her gaze just happened to stray a few inches lower. His sex was thick and heavy, a definite ten on the bulge scale. She went hot all over.

"If you have a minute, I'd like to speak with you." Though her insides were a mass of conflicting feelings, most embarrassingly carnal, her voice was coolly distant as befitted an innkeeper faced with a half-naked male guest.

"I have a minute, yeah," he said, stepping back. "What's on your mind?"

"It's about this uncle thing," she informed him as she edged inside. His frown gave her pause, but she plunged ahead. "I know Marcy's put you in an awkward position, and I'm sorry. From what you said to John the other day about family, it seems clear to me that playing uncle to his children is pretty much the last thing you want to do."

He tossed the shirt onto the bed before leaning on the cane. "Probably would have been if I'd taken time to think about it. By the time I remembered Marcy was John's as well as yours, that sneaky little darlin' had me down for the count."

"From the time she opened her eyes, Marcy's always had more than her share of J. T.'s Irish charm."

"And a lot of her mom's."

It took a moment for the quiet statement to sink in. When it did, she lost her train of thought. "I . . . thank you."

"You're welcome," he said gravely.

Unbidden, her gaze drifted once more to the broad expanse of bronzed male chest. He was a sculptor's dream and a woman's fantasy. The lusty part of her that only rarely struggled free was openly fascinated, and her fingers itched to explore. She quickly jerked her gaze away but not before she caught the glint of understanding in his eyes.

"It's damn inconvenient, isn't it?" he said with a rueful smile.

"Inconvenient?"

"You. Me. The last two people on the planet who should be attracted to each other."

Her heart rate quickened even more. "I didn't say that."

"You're not attracted to me?" He took an awkward step forward, bringing them close enough to touch. He smelled wonderful—clean and masculine. Deep inside her body, desire unfurled like soft, silky petals opening to the sun.

"It's just a simple chemical reaction," she asserted.

His eyes heated. "Reaction, hell. It's like a damn explosion."

Fireworks and skyrockets and a blazing heat where there'd been only dead ashes for a long time. "Call it whatever you want; it's total insanity," she insisted.

"Call me crazy, then, because I wanted you the second I saw

you at the top of those stairs. I still do." His voice was husky and deep, and her insides went mushy.

"It's very . . . flattering, but I'm not available."

He loomed over her, powerful and insistently male. With each breath, she drew in his unique scent. His skin exuded heat.

"You know how I built my business, Brina?" he asked with enough steely resolve to make it count. "By never taking no for an answer, that's how."

She reminded herself that the last man to make her go shaky and sweaty inside had ended up breaking her heart. "There's always a first time."

"Not without a whale of a fight." His gaze held hers for a long, tense moment before dropping to her mouth. He lifted a hand to brush a rebellious curl out of her eyes, reminding her of his gentleness with Marcy. And then he skimmed his hand along her throat to the curve of her neck and let it rest there while his thumb gently massaged the tight muscles. It felt so good she wanted to purr. Worse, she wanted to nuzzle that strong hand with her cheek.

"It would be a mistake," she murmured, her gaze on his mouth.

"I disagree." His voice was low and thick with need.

"I'm not in love with you. I'm not even sure I *like* you."

"You want me. That's enough."

"Not for me! I don't believe in sex without mutual respect and caring."

"I respect you and I care about you. I also want you so much I'm about to explode." He glanced down, drawing her gaze to his groin. He was visibly, hugely aroused. She couldn't quite stifle a sound of dismay. His grin was pure male cockiness. "Happens every time I think about taking you to bed."

"It's just physical," she repeated, a little desperately.

"Pleasure *is* physical."

A pink tinge spread over her cheeks, and her eyes turned

dark and vulnerable. Rhys realized she was trying hard to breathe evenly, even as that really fine chest heaved a little too hard, but it was her mouth that tipped him past reason.

"Give me a chance, honey." He lifted a hand to nudge a stray lock of wild hair away from her neck. "We'll go slow, fast, any way you want it."

"I don't *want* it, period."

"No way I can change your mind?" He rubbed his thumb over the tempting curve of her shoulder and felt her shiver. If she pulled away, he would let her go. It would kill him, but he wanted her to be as desperate for him as he was for her.

"Read my lips, Hazard. I do not want to go to bed with you."

"Not even if I laid my best kiss on you?" He lowered his head, his mouth hovering over hers until her soft lips parted. Still he waited, desire bunching like a fist in his gut.

"Not even then."

"It's been a while, though," he said before dropping a whisper-soft kiss at the corner of her mouth. "Might take me a few tries to get it right."

She froze but didn't pull away. He kissed her again, then tasted her with his tongue. She moaned, swayed, let out a sigh. "I know this is a mistake," she muttered, but her breasts were suddenly pressed against his chest and her arms were around his neck. "I want you, too."

With a silent groan, he dropped the cane, braced his weight on his good leg and concentrated on exploring the rich taste of that proud little mouth. It was so good, this feeling surging through him. Like the first wild rush of freedom after years of confinement.

"Sweet," he whispered between kisses. He buried his hands in her hair, feeling the wild curls swirling around his fingers. Her scent was fresh and invigorating, like sunshine on a meadow. He inhaled deeply, feeling pleasure swim in his head until he became disoriented, like a man who'd just had the wind knocked out of him.

Slowly, deliberately, he explored that soft, pink mouth, his tongue sliding along the sultry bottom lip he'd tasted in his dreams for two nights running. Close to the edge, he forced himself to draw back, but when she whimpered and swayed toward him again, he wanted her naked, her legs spread, her arms reaching for him. He wanted to see pleasure explode in her eyes as he took her over the edge.

Widening his stance to bring them closer, he ran his hands down her spine to the most beautiful derriere he'd ever seen, urging her upward with his palms. At the same time he plunged his tongue between her lips, seeking honey. She went wild then, rubbing her pelvis against an erection that was already painfully engorged.

He sucked in a breath, tightened his arms. "For God's sake, honey, don't move or this will be over before it starts."

She nuzzled his neck, then licked his throat. He began to tremble. "We have to move sooner or later, or what's the point?" she murmured against his skin.

He choked a laugh that turned to a groan when his body threatened to explode. "Didn't anyone ever tell you it's not a good idea to tease a man who's in serious lust?"

"Guess not." She gave a little wiggle and he trembled harder.

"Now," he demanded thickly. "I need to be inside you."

The sound of an impatient rap on the connecting door had his head snapping up and his heart thudding. "Rhys, are you decent?" Della called.

His frustrated groan came all the way from his feet.

"Oh God," Brina muttered, burying her face against his chest. With a hand that wasn't completely steady, he tucked her close.

"In a minute, Del."

"Hurry up, okay?"

"Damn, sweetheart, I'm sorry," he whispered into the wild cloud of tousled curls tickling his chin. "Next time I'll—"

"There can't be any next time," she declared, drawing back. "Thank goodness Del showed up now. We must be out of our minds!"

Her eyes were full of accusation, but her lips were beautifully plump from his kisses, and her creamy complexion was still flushed with the desire he'd aroused in her. He felt like shouting. "We're not out of our minds. It's what we both want, which makes it all the way right."

"No, it's not. It's foolish and selfish." She was still breathing hard. "I have two kids who depend on me. I can't play at being wild and crazy. I was *never* wild and crazy. It's not my nature."

"Could have fooled me," he said, his grin crooked and a little stiff.

She took a breath, then took a step back and lifted a shaky hand to brush back her hair. "Promise me you won't try to kiss me again."

"Brina—"

"Please, Rhys. If you don't give me your promise, I'll have to ask you to leave."

"Damn it—"

"Rhys, are you all right?" Del sounded worried now.

With a little cry, Brina slipped past him and out the door, letting it click shut behind her.

For the first time since he'd been fifteen, Rhys had a wet dream. He woke up gasping for air, his sheets sticky, his body drenched with sweat. Though it was obvious he'd had an orgasm, his dick was still painfully hard.

Stifling a moan, he rolled to his back. Instead of the usual postorgasm lethargy, he felt wired and frustrated. Self-gratification had never been his thing—not even in prison when the muffled moans of his fellow inmates would cover his.

Squeezing his eyes shut, he let out a long, tortured breath. His life then had been an obscenity. No matter how many showers he took after his release or how vigorously he scoured his skin, the prison stink had lingered in his lungs and clung to his skin for months. Even now sometimes in that split second between sleep and alertness, he thought he was strangling in that foul slime again. An inmate. An animal. Gutter scum, just like Marceline had claimed.

The gulf between Brina and him couldn't be plainer. He carried a permanent stain, a stigma that no amount of success or contributions to charity could erase. Brina was everything that was clean and good and sweet, a great mother, a good friend. Like a patch of sunshine in a gloomy day, she drew people to her and made them feel special.

He drew in another breath and held it until he convinced himself he could still smell her here in this room she'd given him. A light, flowery scent with licks of sunshine and spice. Class? Oh yeah. She had it all right, the real thing, the kind that had nothing to do with what she wore or drove or who she hung out with. The kind of class that came from inside. A core decency, he supposed was the best term, and a solid unwavering generosity. Whatever he called it, he'd felt her kindness and heard the compassion in her voice, qualities he'd been searching for all his life.

Problem was, he didn't belong here. He knew it; she knew it; damn near everyone in town knew it. Even if he stuck it out, tried to make peace with people who hated him, it wouldn't work. By any rational standard Brina was light years above the reach of a guy carrying his kind of baggage. But damn, he wanted to be with her so badly he ached with it.

Annoyed and still frustrated, he turned to his side and closed his eyes. He focused on his breath, the texture of the air, the rhythmic rise and fall of his chest. Gradually his breathing became quiet and deep, and his heart rate slowed. He filled his mind with images of a dense gray fog. He blocked out sound and feeling, studied the gradations of color, the currents moving along the edges, imagined the damp condensation against his skin. It was as close to blank as he could make his mind, and still he could taste her.

He ground out an obscenity that made him feel worse. He had to get out of there, clear his head. Flipping to his back again, he reached for his cell phone. Squinting in the dim light, he stabbed out Max's number.

Light filtered through the lace curtains drawn over the dormer window of Brina's bedroom, dappling the floor with silver. Curled on her side in the middle of the spool bed she'd refinished only last month, Brina rubbed her cheek against her pillow and thought about counting those fanciful splashes one by one. Since she'd already tried lulling herself to sleep by reciting tomorrow's to-do list and planning an entire week's worth of menus in her head, she was desperate enough to try anything. If she didn't get some rest soon, she'd be sleepwalking through her day.

Scowling, she turned onto her back. The slippery sheets beneath her legs had her moaning softly. Even worse was the pressure of her nightshirt against her nipples. For the first time in years she felt alive and vital, a woman who gloried in the way a man could make her feel.

Why did it have to be the absolutely wrong man who made her feel so good?

She was still asking herself that question when the sun came up.

Chapter 15

"No fog this morning. It should be a good day to fly." Della turned away from the window where she'd gone to check the weather and returned to perch on the edge of the bed.

"It's never a good day to fly," Rhys muttered as he tossed his shaving things into his duffel bag and zipped it shut. Since he was heading back to Phoenix after stopping over in San Francisco to see Hank, he was traveling light. Tanner had flown in last night, and was staying at a motel in Wenatchee where Elena had rented a room by the week for him.

"Unless all hell breaks loose, I should be back here on Tuesday, Wednesday at the latest."

"Bring me a quart of Chuey's chili, okay?"

He grinned. Both of them were hooked on the devil-hot chili made by the crusty owner of a small Mexican deli near the Tower. "If you're a good girl and keep things under control while I'm gone, I'll bring you a gallon."

"Oh, sugar, I'm good, but I ain't been a girl for the *longest* time."

He laughed. "Just make sure no one starts any brushfires while I'm gone."

"You have anyone in mind?"

"Yeah, the so-called head of sales." He turned his back, then unzipped his jeans and tucked in his shirt. "He's supposed to have a report ready for me on Monday. Make sure he leaves it

on my desk before he takes off to play with his trophy bimbo."
He zipped his fly before turning back to face her. "Max will be
available to drive you until you decide on the color you want
for your company car."

"Don't rush me, sugar. Color is vitally important to image,
you know. I'm leaning toward gold, for obvious reasons." She
tossed her head, and her enormous gold hoop earrings swayed.
"Give Hank a kiss for me, okay?"

He gave her a "not a chance in hell" look that had her
laughing, before hooking his Stetson from the bedpost. He ran
his hand through his hair, then settled the hat comfortably before reaching for his cane.

"Walk me down?" he asked as he deposited the duffel next
to his briefcase just inside the door.

"You go on. I have some calls to make before breakfast."

He nodded. "One more thing, I told Brina you'd be happy to
make nice with the governor and his cronies next Saturday.
She said something about a speech, so you might want to get
together with her and rough something out."

"Guess there's no sense pointing out I'm not exactly what
folks up here are going to be expecting?"

"None at all." He leaned down to kiss her cheek. "Take
care, you hear?"

"You, too."

He found Max in the dining room, sitting at the table sipping tea and talking in a gentle voice with the wispy librarian.
Both looked up when he entered. For the first time he noticed
the proprietary light in Max's eyes.

"Morning, Miss Winkle," he said, hoping to hell he hadn't
screwed up her name.

"And to you, Mr. Hazard." She smiled shyly, revealing twin
dimples that rocked him back a little. The first time they'd met
here in this room she'd scarcely lifted her gaze from her
breakfast plate.

"Ready to go, boss?" Max asked as he pushed back his chair.

Rhys nodded. "As soon as I let Ms. Sullivan know I'll be out of her hair for a few days." He glanced at his watch before adding, "Meet me outside in ten minutes."

"Anything you need carryed to the car?"

"My briefcase and duffel."

He turned to leave, then scowled as snatches of his childhood lessons in courtesy drifted into his mind. He'd been on his own for so long, with only his own wants and needs to consider, it took an effort to fit himself into someone else's world. One more reason why he hired men like Hank to run interference. "Uh, if you'll excuse me, ma'am?"

Startled, Miss Winkle looked at him with pretty green eyes half hidden behind gold-rimmed glasses. "Of course, Mr. Hazard. I . . . I hope you have an enjoyable trip."

Recognizing her attempt to be pleasant, he reined in his impatience and did his best to reply in kind. "I have a board meeting and three high-level staff meetings, so enjoyable it won't be, but I appreciate the thought," he said before heading on to the kitchen.

Whatever Brina was cooking for breakfast smelled terrific, and his stomach gave a protesting growl. With his schedule already getting tighter than stink on a junkyard dog, he figured to save time by grabbing something at the airport before boarding.

"Hi, Uncle Rhys!" Marcy shouted from her perch at the center island, where she was shaking cereal into a bowl. Her eyes were sparkling and bright, and she looked cuddly and warm in a fuzzy pink robe with bunny slippers on her feet.

"Hiya, toots," he said. "How's it goin' this morning?"

"Me 'n' Jay are going to see Grandda after Jay gets off school," she said before splashing milk into her bowl. "He has new kitties in the barn."

"I'll bet he'll be real happy to see you," Rhys said before shifting his gaze to the half-grown boy seated across from her.

Scarecrow gangly, he had wayward reddish brown hair, a lean, pale face spattered with freckles, and his mother's velvet brown eyes. A faded black Harley-Davidson T-shirt hung loose from shoulders that were more bone than muscle.

"You must be Jay," he said, extending his hand. "I'm Rhys."

"I figured." His nephew had a weak handshake and wary eyes.

"His real name is John Thomas Sullivan III," Marcy announced, her mouth full of cereal. "Mommy said that was too big a name for him when he was a tiny baby so that's why we call him Jay."

"He's not interested in dumb stuff like that," Jay muttered, shooting his sister a disgusted look.

"He is, too, on account of he's our uncle and uncles are s'posed to be interested in everything. Right, Uncle Rhys?"

He looked down into those trusting eyes and thought about lost chances. "Absolutely, and thank you for telling me."

"Welcome," she said demurely before shooting her brother a look. "Told you so."

Jay gave a grunt before slanting Rhys another wary look. "Rad cane. Where'd you get it?"

He'd had the cane for so many years he had to think a minute. "In a pawnshop in Amarillo on one of my first hauls to Texas."

Jay glanced down at the grapefruit he'd been eating. "Is it on account of the accident?"

"Yes, it is."

Jay frowned. "Guess people stare at you a lot, huh? 'Cause you limp real bad when you walk?"

"Some do, yeah. Since there's nothing I can do about it, I don't let it bother me."

Jay glanced up, frowned, debated before finally asking, "What if someone calls you a dumb name?"

Something Rhys didn't understand was behind the question. Just in case it was important to the kid, he gave some thought to his answer. "Time was I would have busted his jaw, or at least his nose, but that was when I was a lot younger and stupider. Now I guess I'd figure that anyone who had to build himself up by making fun of me was too pathetic to bother with."

"But what if it was, like, someone you couldn't hit? Like maybe it was a grown-up or . . . whatever?"

Definitely something going on. What now, slick? he asked himself. Since he didn't have a clue, he went with his instinct. "Guess then I'd have to find a way to outsmart that particular person."

"Like how?"

"Like laughing in his—or her—face." When the boy frowned, he plunged ahead. "See, the thing you have to keep in mind about bullies is the fact that they're really cowards at heart."

The look Jay shot him questioned his sanity. Kids, he was discovering, had a way of cutting right through a man's defenses. It scared him some. "A few years back I caught this documentary on public TV about bears. Some guy who studied grizzlies, and he said that if you're ever confronted by one of those big suckers in the woods, you should stand up straight and lift up your arms to make yourself look dangerous. Claimed that most times the bear gets scared and runs off. I figure a bully's a lot like that grizzly. If you rear up and challenge him, he'll run off."

"What if he doesn't?"

"That's when I'd bust his jaw."

Jay grinned, flashing a mouthful of braces before quickly clamping his upper lip over his teeth. Rhys sympathized. He'd spent two miserable years choking on a mouthful of wires and had hated every minute of it.

"I have a bear," Marcy said before taking a drink of milk.

"His name is Pooh, like Christopher Robin's." She wiped the milk mustache with the back of her hand. Little savage, he thought, grinning.

"Uh, is your mom around?"

"She's doing laundry. In there," she said, pointing to the door to the rear.

"Thanks."

"Welcome," she said before shoveling in more cereal.

He found Brina transferring wet towels from the washer to the dryer. His good intentions wavered some when he noticed the butt-hugging jeans and skimpy T-shirt under a man's worn-out shirt.

"Good morning," she said when she caught sight of him in the doorway. For a moment she looked flustered before hauling herself in tight. He rode out a feeling of longing.

"Morning," he said with a polite smile. "Just wanted to let you know I'll be gone for a few days."

She bent to close the dryer door, giving him another all-too-brief glimpse of her mouthwatering fanny before she straightened to press the start button. "So you told Marcy last night. I hope nothing's wrong."

"Nope, just business." He shifted, drew in the flowery scent of her glossy hair and grieved for what might have been. "I'm also out of clean clothes."

She darted a curious look at his chest. "Feel free to use my washing machine any time you like, Mr. Hazard." Her mouth twitched. "My ironing board, too, if you feel so inclined."

"You think I don't know how to do stuff like that?"

"I think I'd like to watch." She wasn't wearing any makeup he could see, which meant that her mouth was naked and pale—and so tempting his own went dry. Since he couldn't kiss her, he offered her a cocky grin instead.

"You got it, Ms. Sullivan. Prepare to be impressed."

She laughed. "Confident, are we?"

"About some things, yeah." One side of her shirt collar was

turned under, and he lifted a hand to free it. His knuckles brushed her neck, and she sucked in a breath. Her skin was as smooth as sun-warmed marble and infinitely more giving.

"Sorry," he said, drawing back. "It's a bad habit, tidying things, tucking things away. Comes from driving so many years. Anything loose in the cab has the potential to kill you if you roll."

Something came and went in her eyes before he got a read on it. Just as well, he figured. "I have an opening for a maid, in case you're interested," she said with a hint of a smile.

"I told you what interests me, Brina. You turned me down flat. Like to broke my heart, too."

Her breath seemed to come a little faster. "Seems to me you've been working hard to convince me and everyone else you don't *have* a heart."

It bothered him some that she'd seen that. It bothered him more to realize she was even more perceptive than her kids. But then, his experience with nice normal families was pretty limited. In fact, he wasn't sure he knew what normal was, given the way he was raised. One thing he knew for sure, though. Brina was as different from Marceline as wine was from vinegar. Rich, heady wine that made a man's head swim and body throb.

"Anything you want from Phoenix?" he asked when he couldn't think of anything else to say. "Del's already put in an order for some of Chuey Garcia's homemade chili."

"Is this homemade chili majorly hot?" she asked with a hopeful glint in her eyes.

"Chuey brags that his chili is as hot as the fires in the deepest depths of hell itself. First time I ate it, I sweated through my shirt. Problem was, it was the only decent shirt I owned and I was heading for a job interview at the time."

"A driving job?"

"Delivering bottled water."

After having spent two bucks for a bowl of chili, he'd been

left with forty-two cents in his pocket. Sucker that he'd been then, he'd left it for the sad-eyed waitress and walked out penniless.

"Did you get the job?" Brina asked, her head tilted up at him.

"Nope." His gaze dropped to her mouth and lingered before he remembered that was a bad idea.

"Why not?"

"Driver had to be bondable. I'm not."

"Oh, I never thought of that."

"No reason why you should."

She frowned, drawing his gaze to that soft mouth again. "Was that the only job you didn't get?"

He shook his head. "I'd been so focused on surviving prison I hadn't given much thought to life afterward. It took me a while to figure out the way things were going to be for me from then on."

There was understanding in her eyes, mixed with the wariness he figured he'd earned after the way he'd behaved last night. "Is that why you started your own business?"

"Yeah."

"Did you like driving a truck for a living?"

If anyone but she had asked that question—and no one ever had—he would have blown them off with a smart-ass comment. He respected Brina too much to give her less than the truth—as much of it as she could handle, anyway.

"I liked most of it, especially when I started picking up longer hauls. Saw a lot of the country before I quit. When I had time, I even managed some sightseeing." He smiled. "Mostly I liked the freedom to call the shots."

"Daddy always claimed that being the boss was a lot like being nibbled to death by ducks."

His laugh seemed to surprise her as much as it surprised him. It also lingered with him long after he'd gone.

*   *   *

Beyond the wall of windows, the desert sky was ablaze with the vivid colors of sunset. Far below, the city lights were winking on between the intertwining ribbons of red and white vehicle lights that marked the two freeways quartering the city. It was Saturday night, and the city was gearing up to party.

Behind his desk, where he'd been since six a.m., Rhys tucked the phone against his stiff shoulder and scrawled his name on the last letter in the folder that Joan Majenek had slipped onto his desk before leaving. In his ear the phone continued to ring. Frustrated and disappointed, he was about to hang up when he heard a click on the other end of the line.

"Ms. Campbell-Browne's phone." The voice was rushed and a little sultry—and definitely not Del's. His heart slammed his ribs.

"Brina?" he guessed.

He heard her inhale. "Hello, Rhys. Uh, Della's upstairs helping me wallpaper the family bathroom. I just came down to get us a couple of sodas when I heard her phone ringing. She yelled for me to answer it, so . . . I did." She gave a self-conscious laugh. "Obviously."

His mouth was dry, he realized. The way it had been as a gawky teenager working up the nerve to call a girl for a date. He swallowed a couple of times before drawling, "Let me get this straight. The woman I've seen reaching for a Valium if she so much as chips her nail polish is slapping up wallpaper?"

"I'll have you know we are applying an extremely complicated pattern with the skill and precision of professional wallpaperists."

" 'Wallpaperists'?"

"What would you call it, then?" Her voice seemed to fade in and out as though she were moving.

" 'Wallpaperer'?" he ventured.

"Definitely an improvement, that."

He chuckled. "How about 'wallpaper technician'?"

"That does have a certain ring, I agree, although I think I like 'wallpaper artisan' even better. What counts, however, are results, and Del and I kicked butt. Every seam is ruler straight and perfectly matched, not an easy feat, let me tell you."

"Clearly important measures of success in the wallpapering game."

Her soft gurgle of laughter made him dizzy. "Almost as important as keeping paste out of your hair. Unfortunately, we had a little problem with that, but Del assured me she intended to wash her hair anyway."

He laughed, and it felt damn good. "I'd pay major bucks to witness this project up close and personal."

"I wouldn't laugh if I were you, or you might find yourself shanghaied into helping us with Jay's room next."

Shanghaied, hell. He'd take a bath in the damn stuff if that would please her. "I take your point. No more laughing."

"A wise decision."

He closed his eyes and pictured her looking up at him with desire shimmering in her eyes the way it had an instant before he'd kissed her. Dumb mistake, slick, he decided as he went from limp to hard with the speed of light. "Tell you what, I'll call back later when you . . . when Del isn't so busy."

"No problem, I'm carrying the phone up to her as we speak." She gave a little huff of exertion, and his mind zoomed to a fantasy of those soft lips moving under his. Hard got harder.

"It's Rhys for you," he heard her say in a muffled tone.

Del's reply was unintelligible. "She'll be with you as soon as she wipes paste off her hands," Brina translated. "She mentioned that you'd stopped to see Mr. Dunnigan yesterday. How's he doing?"

He grabbed the lifeline like a drowning man. "Better. Actually growled at me a few times."

"I take it that's good?"

"Oh yeah. The time to worry is when he's being a good boy."

She laughed. "Jay's the same way."

He realized he'd run out of conversation, which, unfortunately, focused his mind directly on his rigid cock. He squeezed his eyes shut. "I, uh, saw the flowers you sent him. It meant a lot to him."

"He's a lovely man."

Lovely, hell. His brows slammed together. He didn't like the feeling curling like a poisonous snake in his gut. He thought maybe it was jealousy before rejecting that idea. "Maybe you don't know he's still carrying a torch for his wife?"

Her breath hissed in. "No, I didn't know that. Thanks for the warning." He heard the sudden chill in her voice and winced. Christ, what the hell was the matter with him? He sounded like a self-righteous ass.

"Look, that came out wrong. I—"

"Here's Del," she interrupted. Before he could smooth the waters, she was gone.

To the casual observer Enrique Colon was about as intimidating as a half-grown puppy. His soft brown eyes were full of fun, and his smile was infectious. He was also one of the toughest SOBs Rhys had ever met—in or out of prison.

He had been North Star's security chief for more than a decade. As soon as Rhys arrived at the Tower on Friday, he gave Enrique the job of vetting the security measures Brody Hollister had roughed out. Now, after four solid days of meetings, appointments and paperwork, during which he hadn't had even a few minutes to spare, he'd asked Ric to drive him to the airport late Monday afternoon so they could talk.

"It's a straightforward procedure, no holes that I could find." Ric checked traffic before accelerating into the fast lane.

"Anything you'd change?"

"Not without actually eyeballing the layout. On paper it

looks solid." He flicked Rhys a grin. "Have to admit I didn't expect that kind of savvy from a small-town department."

"The cop in charge isn't your usual small-town bubba. Earned his stripes in L.A."

"That explains it, then."

Rhys watched one of Wilshire Trucking's yellow-and-black rigs cut off a minivan full of kids and gave some thought to reporting the driver to the ICC. His deeply ingrained loathing of snitches stopped him.

"A word of caution, Rhys," Ric said as he took the airport off-ramp. "No matter how much security you put in place or how solid you make it, there's always a way to take someone out, especially if the shooter's dedicated enough or suicidal enough to die for the cause."

By the time Tanner landed at Wenatchee, Rhys was in a foul mood. A storm over the Cascades had tumbled the small jet like an agitator in a washing machine, making it impossible for him to work. Worse had been the acute case of claustrophobia brought on by the suffocating closeness of the clouds against the windows.

After an initial greeting, Max slipped Chopin into the player and kept his attention on the road. Rhys' spirits took an upward spike when he reached the depot. At least things were under control here. *His* control.

His footsteps and the tap of his cane echoed through the cavernous area as he made his way to the stairs to the loft. At the top, he stuck his head in Della's office to say hi and received an exuberant hug, which he returned with gratitude.

"Where's my chili?"

"Max took it to the inn along with my bags."

"How was the trip?"

"Bumpy."

"We missed you, especially Marcy. She was very annoyed that her uncle Rhys wouldn't be back for another whole day."

He tried to downplay the pleasure that gave him. "You explained about the problem with the plane, right?"

"I did my best, but a hydraulic system leak is a difficult concept for a five-year-old to grasp. Brina finally saved my fanny by explaining that the plane had a boo-boo and you had to have it fixed."

He laughed. "Guess that's about the size of it." He rested his aching hip on the corner of her desk and picked up a stack of résumés.

"Anything I need to know before I deal with that pile of stuff I saw weighing down my desk?"

"Nothing major. Emory expects Kenworth Seattle to deliver Friday instead of tomorrow. Man's as excited as a kid on Christmas Eve."

"I know the feeling," he admitted. He doubted he would ever forget the day he took delivery on his first brand-new rig. "Any idea what time they're coming in?"

"Sometime in the morning. Sullivan Junior's proposal is on your desk. He said to tell you he'd be in Seattle for the next two days, making sales calls."

Rhys accepted that without comment.

"Also, Stan and I need an hour of your time to discuss some amendments to the benefits package. Elena suggested three this afternoon as a possibility, since neither Stan nor I have interviews scheduled then."

"Fine. Set it up."

She made a note on her desk calendar before settling back in her chair. "How'd the board meeting go?"

"Started out okay, but by the time we'd worked through the agenda, I felt like a piece of meat thrown into a cage with a bunch of starved lions."

Her lips twitched. "Knowing you, big brother, those lions ended up more like bloody pussycats."

"I bought us some time," he admitted before pushing to his feet. He'd done the same with Paul Dominquez, but he'd had to play hardball by threatening to pull his corporate as well as his personal accounts.

"How much time are we talking about?" Del asked.

"Next board meeting is in one month. As long as North Star stock stays healthy, we can ride out the temporary drain on the cash flow for another month or so, but Northwest better start pulling in revenue, or Phillips will come at me with Uzis."

Del laughed, and he grinned. But it wasn't really much of a joke. He was juggling a lot of balls in the air. He'd done a juggling act before, but never with so much at stake.

Rhys figured he'd climbed more steps in the seven days he'd been back in Osuma than he had during the prior six months at least. Maybe more, since he generally avoided anyplace without elevators.

Problem was, Marcy had cornered him during dinner and demanded a story—after she'd made him bend down so that she could give him a kiss. Hurting by the time he made it to the third floor, he paused at the landing to let his hip rest. Marcy's room was on the left, the door closed. On the opposite side of the wide entry music pounded against another closed door. Jay's room, he figured.

He'd just returned his handkerchief to his back pocket when the second door to his right opened and Brina emerged. Her hair was loose, framing her face with silky curls, and she had on that ratty blue robe again, belted just tightly enough to emphasize those curvy hips and ripe breasts. As far as he could see, the robe was all she was wearing.

For the first time since he'd realized he would spend the rest of his life as a semicripple, he was actually thankful he couldn't walk without his cane. Otherwise, he was damn certain he'd already have her scooped up and halfway to her bedroom instead of hoping to hell his body didn't disgrace him.

It had surprised him how much he'd missed her. He'd even dreamed about her while he'd been gone. Imagined her body next to his, then woken up to find himself hugging his pillow, his cock as hard as steel. Tired as he'd been, he'd had to haul himself out of bed and into a cold shower. Now more than anything he wanted to feel those soft curves molding against him while her mouth moved under his. Not that he'd expected a hug from her, let alone another soul-shivering kiss. Still, even a bastard like him could hope.

"You do realize you can always say no when Marce asks you to read to her," she told him. "My daughter tends to be more imperious than usual after she's spent the weekend with her grandfather."

"Spoils her, does he?"

"Shamelessly." She wandered his way. The music stopped, then started again. Grimacing, she glanced toward Jay's door before letting out a sigh. "J. T. buys Marcy books and Jay CDs. I've tried to get him to do just the opposite, but you know how stubborn your dad can be."

"He's not my dad." Damn it, how many times did he have to repeat that before people started getting the point?

Her smile rebuked him so gently that he couldn't take offense. She was close enough now that he could smell the soap she'd used and another, lighter scent. Not perfume, exactly. Maybe some of that lotion women used to keep their skin soft, rubbed on while that luscious body was still dewy and pink from the shower. Picturing that in his mind had him nearly groaning aloud. Her house, her rules, he reminded himself.

"I thought about bringing the kids something from Phoenix, but I figured I'd better ask you first."

Her lips curved. She had an almost dimple at one corner of her mouth. "Something small and inexpensive would be fine. A jigsaw puzzle for Marcy, maybe a model for Jay. Just a token."

"Guess that means the Saint Bernard puppy is out."

"Don't you dare! No puppies of any kind."

He wanted to touch her. Just . . . touch her. "A kitten?"

"Alas, no. Guests can be allergic, and cats roam."

Being close to her was a mistake. Like standing too close to a stove when a man knew he'd be spending the rest of the night in the cold. "I've heard iguanas make nice pets, and they don't have dander."

"I'd rather have the Saint Bernard," she muttered.

"Done!"

She blinked, then gave an exasperated huff. "Excuse me, but we were *not* negotiating."

"Sure sounded like it to me."

"You're hearing things."

"Reneging already, are you?"

Her eyes sparked golden fire. "Of course not! I never renege."

He grinned. "Good. I'll just go tell Marcy about her new pet."

He started past her, only to have her grab his arm. Her eyes were laughing, but she'd drawn her lips into a stern line. "I'm warning you right now, Hazard, if you bring a Saint Bernard into this house, you and the dog will end up sleeping in the toolshed."

He would sleep on a bed of nails if she were with him. It was a new experience for him, this need to be close to her in more than sexual ways. "You're tough, Ms. Sullivan. Real tough."

"And you're not nearly as tough as you want everyone to think."

"The hell I'm not!"

It came again, the near savage hunger to touch her. To press a finger against the plump curve of her lower lip, to feel the satin warmth as he very, very slowly traced that crooked little smile with a fingertip. Just once couldn't hurt, he argued when the need grew unbearable.

To distract himself he let his gaze drift lower, to the sleek line of her throat, to the fragile hollow between her collarbones. Moisture was trapped there, tiny beads just begging to be lapped dry. Dumb move, slick. Real dumb.

"Rhys, is something wrong?"

It was supposed to be a laugh at his own expense. It came out as a groan. "You have no idea," he muttered.

Concern leaped into her eyes, crowding out the playful humor. "Is it your hip? Are you in pain?"

"Oh, yeah."

"Maybe you should sit down." Her hand curled around his forearm. Having *her* touch *him* was almost as good as touching her. Her clean womanly scent went straight to his head, making him a little drunk.

"I have a better idea." He slid his arm around her waist and pulled her closer until her hips were pressed against his. She gasped when she felt his erection. Though it nearly killed him, he paused to give her a chance to pull away.

"You promised not to kiss me again," she whispered, those velvet brown eyes nearly black now.

"Not a chance. I never make a promise I'm not certain I can keep."

She took a deep breath. Confusion and desire seemed at war behind her searching look. "Oh, Rhys, it would be so complicated," she said in a low, agonized voice.

"I keep remembering how you felt and tasted. Right in the middle of the board meeting I thought about how good you felt in my arms, and I got so turned on I lost my train of thought."

"You did? Really?"

"Really. It was darn embarrassing. Six guys in two-thousand-dollar suits just sat there looking at me like I'd lost my mind."

Laughter bubbled from her throat before she asked, "What did you do?"

"Well, I thought about dumping the pitcher of ice water in my lap, but I settled for adjourning for ten minutes to calm

down." He gave her a rueful smile. "As soon as they cleared
out, I hightailed it into my bathroom and took a cold shower."

"You didn't!"

"Oh, yeah, I did." He rubbed his chin against her temple.
She shivered, and he wanted to cheer. Instead, he took a
chance and lowered his mouth to hers in a kiss he tried to keep
coaxing, not threatening. She made a garbled sound deep in
her throat, then brought her hands up and clutched his shirt.
Cursing the cane now because it kept him from holding her
with both arms, he pulled her closer in an awkward one-armed
embrace.

He nibbled and then tasted. His body turned hot, and his
blood seemed to race. He kneaded her spine with his fingers,
and she rubbed against him. The music stopped suddenly. The
silence was deafening. Stiffening, she pulled away.

"See what I mean?" she said in a rush. "This thing between
us is a bomb waiting to go off, and I'm terrified my kids will
be the ones to be hurt."

"We can work it out."

"Work out what? An affair? Sex with a lonely divorcée?"

She made it sound selfish and . . . meaningless. A casual roll
in the hay. His jaw tightened. "It could never be just sex between the two of us."

Her lashes dipped. "It would be a mistake."

"Why?" No longer able to resist, he threaded his fingers
through the springy curls at her nape. He wondered how all
that dark silk would feel brushing against his chest.

"For one thing, we don't even know each other. For another,
I might live in a place that was once a bawdy house, but I'm
not part of the amenities. Finally—and most importantly—I
have two kids who've been through enough upheaval in their
lives. Having their mom romping in a guest's room is the last
thing they need."

He frowned, unsure what he was supposed to say next. Convincing a woman to sleep with him was uncharted territory for

him. He wished he'd taken more effort to figure out how to please a woman outside of bed.

He decided to take it point by point, the way he handled a contract. "First, I'll tell you anything you need to know about me in order for you to feel more comfortable. Second, this is not about guest perks, and third, I'm willing to be as discreet as you want."

"I can see why your business is so successful," she said with a smile.

"Is that a yes?"

"It's an 'I'm tempted, but I have to think about it very carefully before committing.'"

"I'll give you time, but I won't promise not to do my best to convince you."

"That's not fair."

He grinned. "Not a bit."

"Uncle Rhys, I've been waiting and *waiting* for you!" Marcy's petulant voice drew their attention before Brina could answer.

Looking sleepy and irritable, the little girl stood in the doorway of her room in striped blue-and-white pj's, a book in her hand.

"Sorry, sweetie, Uncle Rhys and I were just talking," Brina said before turning back to look up at him again. "See what I mean?" she said in a low voice.

"Uncle Rhys!"

He was beginning to understand why some of his employees with small kids often came in looking grumpy and frustrated. "Be right there, toots."

"Hurry up."

"Yes, ma'am," he called back, making her giggle. "You pick out the book and I'll be right there."

"Now *you're* spoiling her," Brina muttered.

"We'll settle this later," he said in a low voice.

"It's settled. It has to be," she said, setting her jaw. "And this time I mean it."

He glanced toward Marcy's room, saw that the doorway was empty, then dragged Brina against him again. He kissed her until his senses spun and his body was about to explode. He ended the kiss before he found out if she would grab onto him again. "Later," he said.

The phrase she muttered made him laugh. Oh yeah, this was some woman all right, he thought with a smile that came from deep inside.

One of these days you're going to turn a blind corner and there she'll be, that sweet, special lady your soul's been waiting to find. He had a feeling Del had been right—and it scared him to death.

Chapter 16

It was a perfect day for a parade, clear and bright. Rhys had hoped for a downpour that would keep anyone with any sense indoors. While the coffee brewed, he leaned his butt against the counter, crossed his arms and sulked.

"Mommy always lets me have Lucky Charms while the coffee's cooking."

Startled by Marcy's sleepy voice, Rhys spun around to see her padding toward him in her bunny slippers. Her eyes still a little glazed and her baby soft hair sticking up in wisps, she was bundled in her fuzzy robe with striped pj's peeping out from the hem. It shook him to discover how much he'd missed her.

"You're up early," he said as he took the pot from the burner to fill his mug.

"Uh-huh, on account of me 'n Kelly Hollister are going to the parade."

"Kelly's your best bud?"

She giggled. "No, silly, she's my baby-sitter."

After pouring his coffee and taking a sip, he stared glumly at the sunshine flooding the tile floor, his mood as black as pitch. As a boy he'd spent a lot of sunny Saturday afternoons during festival weekends hanging out with his buddies. Ogling chicks, acting like hot stuff. He'd known who he was then and what was expected of him as J. T. Sullivan's older son. His life had made sense. It had been comfortable. Hell, it had been a great life.

In contrast, Rhys Hazard had no past, no roots, no family besides the one he'd cobbled together from outcasts like himself. Until he'd come back to Osuma, he would have sworn on a stack of Bibles that he didn't miss the life he'd led here. That he wasn't lonely. That he didn't wish that he could make things right so he could stay.

"Uncle Rhys, you forgot the Lucky Charms!" Marcy exclaimed as she climbed onto a stool. She pointed to the pantry door, princess to devoted subject. "Mommy keeps 'em way up on the top shelf 'cause I ate a whole box once and then threw up in the parlor right before Grandmother came to visit, and she stepped in it with her new shoes. She made the awfullest face, and Mommy laughed, only she really tried not to."

It was a hell of a visual, he thought, and let it replay a couple of times while he found the cereal, then a bowl and a spoon. Chattering a mile a minute, Marcy filled the bowl almost to the top, then glanced up expectantly. "*You* have to pour in the milk. It's a *rule,* on account of it's too heavy for me."

He found the gallon jug. "How come Mommy's not watching the parade with you?" he asked, pouring.

"She's baby-sitting, too, only with grown-ups it's called being a hostess." Marcy pushed back the floppy sleeve of her robe before picking up her spoon. "You can have some, too, if you want," she said, pushing the box toward his side of the island. "Only promise you won't take it all, okay?"

"I promise, and thank you for sharing," he said, hoping he didn't sound patronizing. This uncle thing made him edgy as hell. That bull in the china shop had it easy compared to a bachelor whose only contact with kids came at the company Christmas party. Even then, there'd always been a mom or dad around as backup in case he said or did something dumb.

"People are s'posed to share," she said with her mouth full. "Mommy said."

He wondered what kind of advice John passed on to his kids. Nothing nearly as kindhearted or admirable, he suspected. He'd been taught that coveting his brother's wife was a mortal sin, but what about the wife his brother had thrown away?

"What are those colored things?" he asked as he filled another bowl for himself.

"Marshmallows. They're the bestest part. Mostly I save them 'til last, like dessert."

He settled himself on the stool and reached for the milk.

"You're s'posed to put your napkin on your lap, 'cause we're polite at our house," Marcy informed him.

It took effort, but he kept his expression suitably chastened. "I beg your pardon, Ms. Sullivan," he replied gravely, plucking a napkin from the holder in the middle of the butcher-block top.

She giggled. "You're funny, Uncle Rhys. Like Grandda, sometimes."

The smile that had started to bloom faded. Why the hell was everyone always comparing him to his . . . to J. T.? he thought irritably.

"Is Jay doing parade stuff, too?" he asked.

"Huh-uh. He's riding up front with Daddy in the Corvette. He's real excited 'cause Amy Fieldstone is gonna be watching and he promised to wave to her."

"Is Amy a babe, then?"

"Huh-uh, Amy's his *girlfriend,* only he doesn't want anyone to know so don't tell him I said so, okay?"

"Cross my heart," he said before digging in. The little stars and moons were already bleeding colors into the milk, turning it a sickly gray. The whole mess looked anything but appetizing, but he'd eaten worse. Besides, he didn't want to offend the little darlin' watching him with bright expectation. "Hey, this stuff is really good," he said when he'd swallowed.

"Course it is, silly," she said with another giggle that reached right down inside and wrapped another Marcy ribbon around his heart. It was going to hurt like hell when he left this place.

Hurrying down the back stairs a few minutes later, Brina inhaled the lovely aroma of strong coffee. Though she hated to admit it, she'd missed sharing her first cup in the morning with Rhys.

In even the short time she'd shared her house—and her kitchen—with him, she'd been impressed by his willingness to pitch in. Came from living alone for more than half his life, she suspected. He'd even made up his own bed when Cindy had had cramps and had to go home early.

As usual, he was perched on a stool, his boot heels hooked in the rungs, his broad back to the stairs. He'd gotten a haircut while he'd been gone, she realized. Though she missed the shaggy ends, she had to admit the shorter style fit the image of a high-stakes power player. On the other hand, the plaid Western shirt and cowhand Wranglers were far more consistent with the truck driver he'd been.

At the moment, however, he was playing straight man to Marcy, who appeared to be delighted to have this big tough male firmly under her pudgy thumb.

"Hi, Mommy," she piped up with a grin. "I'm *sharing* my Lucky Charms with Uncle Rhys."

"That's my good girl, sweetie," she mumbled, following her nose to the coffeemaker. The "Innkeepers Do It with Reservations" cup she preferred was already waiting on the counter, along with the sugar bowl and a spoon. While Rhys had been gone, Marcy had asked Brina at least a dozen times how many more days till he returned. Marcy had asked that same question about her father during the months after the divorce, but recently she rarely mentioned Johnny.

Still, John would always be her father, and to someone like Brina who had adored her own father, the relationship between father and daughter was immeasurably precious. John's preference for his little girl had always been evident, but beyond exerting his bragging rights, he'd shown very little interest in getting to *know* her. Probably because that would have taken time away from more important things—like racking up gambling losses.

"Decided to sleep in, did you?" Rhys asked, glancing up at the clock. So did she, only to discover she was a good half hour behind schedule.

Fighting off panic, she spooned in sugar, then attacked the cobwebs with a couple of sips of coffee before answering, "My clock radio must have crashed and burned during the night."

"Best thing is one of those old-fashioned alarm clocks you have to wind up every night," he said. "The one I have is loud enough to empty cemeteries in a fifty-mile radius."

"May I be 'scused, Mommy?"

"You may indeed, sweetie."

"Can I watch cartoons in Miss Winkle's room?" Marcy asked, slipping down from the stool before reaching up for her bowl and spoon.

"It's awfully early for Miss Winkle, sweetie. Best watch upstairs."

"Miss Winkle's already gone to work," Marcy said as she opened the dishwasher door and stowed the bowl and spoon.

"What do you mean, gone to work?" Brina asked.

The dishwasher door closed with a thud. "I peeked in to say hello and her bed was already made."

As part of the rental agreement she and Ernestine had worked out, Ernie made her own bed, did her own laundry and cleaned her room herself. "But she's going to the parade with—" Brina stopped short when suspicion dawned. She shot Rhys a look. "You don't think that she . . . that they . . . you know?"

His face was solemn, but she detected a glimmer of amusement in his eyes. "You mean the librarian and the chauffeur?" One corner of his mouth hitched up. "Sounds kinky to me."

"There are little pitchers here, remember?"

"Little . . . oh right. Sorry." In unison they looked at Marcy, who looked back impatiently.

"So can I, Mommy?" she demanded, shuffling from one foot to the other.

"Can you what, sweetie?"

"Can I watch cartoons in Miss Winkle's room?"

Oh right, cartoons! "I think it's best you watch upstairs this morning."

"Our TV's too tiny," Marcy protested. "You can't see people's faces like you can with Miss Winkle's."

"Then sit closer," Brina suggested.

"Nuh-uh. Sherri says I'll end up cross-eyed if I sit too close and then I'll be ugly and then nobody will marry me."

From the corner of her eye Brina saw Rhys' head come up and his nostrils flare. Like a papa wolf defending a cub, she realized with a start. "You could never be ugly, toots," he declared. "Anyone who says so is full of . . . beans."

Brina wanted to hug him.

"That's what Jay says, only he says Sherri's full of shit," Marcy said.

"That, too," he agreed with a perfectly straight face before flicking Brina a look. "Bright kid, your son."

"Uh-oh, I gotta go poop," Marcy announced before taking off running toward the back stairs.

Brina shot the ceiling an exasperated look before venting her frustration with a sigh. "No doubt about it, I expect to be totally gray by the age of forty."

"Gray, green or bald, you'd still be a knockout," he said,

skimming his gaze to the hair piled atop her head in a hasty attempt at casual chic. "Although I have to admit I liked burying my face in those crazy curls of yours the other night."

She'd almost forgotten what it felt like to want a man's hands on her body, almost as much as she wanted to get her hands on his. Her fingers itched to experience the various textures, to explore the massive shoulders, that broad, furry chest, and—

"Fair warning, Brina, stop staring at my crotch, or you're going to find yourself spread-eagled right here on this counter in two seconds flat."

Acutely embarrassed, she jerked her gaze to his face, only to feel a scalding blush from her hairline to her toes. "Shhh, someone might hear you," she ordered, looking around quickly.

His eyes held hers, dark and turbulent—and frustrated. "I meant what I said, Brina," he warned with a gritty impatience that had her sucking in a harsh breath. "Every time I think about the way you felt in my arms, I get hard and stay hard. It's damn uncomfortable, and I'm not in the mood to play some adolescent 'Will she—won't she?' game with you."

Adolescent? *Adolescent?* After she'd bent over backward to give him that . . . that second chance he seemed to want so badly? She slammed down her mug, sloshing coffee over the counter.

"Allow me to reassure you, Mr. Hazard. She most definitely *won't!*" She took a hurried breath, her chest heaving like a bellows. "As for your precious . . . crotch, if you don't want anyone looking, stop wearing those tight jeans!"

That's telling the insensitive jerk, she congratulated herself as she stalked to the cupboard where she kept her waffle iron. She indulged herself by rattling pans before setting the iron on the counter. Damn him, damn him, *damn* him!

He caught her just as she turned toward the pantry. Before she could gasp, he pulled her against his chest with a one-armed wrestling hold, ducked his head and covered her mouth with his.

Liquid fire shot through her, leaving a trail of sizzling sparks. This . . . possession was nothing like the coaxing kisses he'd given her last night. *This* was the kiss of a man who'd reached the end of his patience, the kiss of a man used to getting what he wanted. In this case, he definitely seemed to want *her,* she realized with wonder.

Desire slammed into her the likes of which she'd never experienced with John. Heat seared the inside of her skin and skittered along her nerve endings. She clutched his shirt, twisting the cotton. She couldn't breathe. There was nothing civilized about the desire clawing at her, nothing remotely gentle.

His erection pressed between her legs, and she gasped into his mouth. Large? Oh yes, *yes!* And as hard as iron. Despite the layers of clothing between them, she felt his heat and she was suddenly desperate to feel him inside her. She made a sound in her throat, a guttural plea that had him lifting his head to stare at her. His mouth was vulnerable, his eyes glazed with a hunger that matched her own.

"Not here," he ground out in a thick voice before kissing her hard and long again. "Tell me where," he ordered when the kiss ended.

Not her room. Or his. The den? "The laundry room," she managed to get out between harsh breaths. "Hurry, Rhys. Hurry—"

But it was too late, she realized as a sudden flurry of morning greetings drifted toward them from the direction of the dining room. The household was up and expecting breakfast.

"Damn it to hell!" he exclaimed in a hoarse tone that had her choking out a laugh.

"This is not funny," he warned, but the straining muscles in the arm holding her relaxed. He dropped his forehead to the crown of her head and pulled her closer. "We'll finish this tonight, after you get back from the governor's shindig."

She wanted to protest, but she couldn't. She wanted him too much. "Tonight," she said, and ached when he stepped back and let her go.

"How much longer 'til Kelly comes, Mommy?" Like a little dervish in pink tights and a pink-and-purple Barney sweatshirt, Marcy whirled away from the window and ran to jump on the bed.

Brina tucked a pair of socks into the *Pocahontas* backpack on the bed before checking her watch. "Twenty minutes."

Picking up the clipboard from the bed, she checked socks off the list. Ta-da! She was ahead of schedule! *The Successful Innkeeper is always prepared for unexpected glitches.* Like forgetting to pack Marcy's toothbrush the last time she slept over at the Hollisters'. Now, however, she had The Clipboard on which she put The List.

"Mommy, you forgot to pack Pooh!" Marcy exclaimed.

"Well, he-eck," she muttered.

"Nice recovery, Mom."

She nearly dislocated her neck turning her head toward the door. Rhys stood just beyond the threshold, watching her with a definite glint in his eyes. Her heart did a Snoopy dance, leaving her a little breathless. "I've had lots of practice," she said ruefully, dropping the clipboard next to the pink-and-purple backpack. Sexual desire had a beat of its own, she realized— hot, insistent pulses rippling along her nerve endings and squeezing her chest.

"Guess what, Uncle Rhys? I'm sleeping over at Kelly's house!" Too antsy to sit still, Marcy bounced up and down on the bed as she talked. "They have a new baby horsy."

His face softened and his eyes turned silver with tenderness. "Boy or girl horsy?"

"A girl. Kelly gets to name her 'cause her horse is the mommy, only she hasn't decided yet."

While Marcy chattered away, Brina tucked Pooh into the

backpack and zipped it closed. "You're good to go, sweetie," she said when Marcy finally exhausted the subject of the baby horse.

"Can I wait downstairs on the porch with Jay?"

"Yes, but if Kelly shows up early, don't leave without saying good-bye. And remind Jay, too, if your dad happens to arrive while I'm up here."

"Okay." Marcy picked up the backpack and headed for the door. Rhys stepped into the room to let her pass.

"No running in the house," Brina called after her, but Marcy had already disappeared. Rhys shifted his gaze from the landing to her. She felt the impact of those enigmatic eyes in every part of her tired body.

"Hectic morning?"

There was nothing in his voice to remind her of the sizzling kiss they'd shared less than six hours earlier, but suddenly her face began to tingle. It took all of her willpower to keep from running her tongue over her lips, where the taste of him lingered.

"Days around here are always hectic. It's the downside of running a business from your home."

"You have dark circles under your eyes." He lifted a hand to adjust her collar, then surprised her by rubbing his thumb over her cheekbone. "You're spreading yourself too thin. You need more help around this place."

Though his clipped tone had her wanting to bristle, she saw the genuine concern buried in those sometimes steely, sometimes icy eyes. This was the man both Della and Marcy had recognized behind the tough, hard-bitten exterior. Wasn't that one of her recently avowed criteria for allowing herself to care for a man again? Enough inner strength and self-assurance to allow himself to show tenderness?

Right now, however, she needed the strength more than the gentleness. It would be so easy to wrap her arms around that lean waist, lay her cheek against that bulwark chest and draw in some of his steel.

Though no one in the inn "family" had been thoughtless enough to say anything to her face, she suspected they knew all too well how much she hated the idea of going unescorted to the governor's gala, especially since John would be there with Sherri all but surgically attached to his hip. She could already feel the looks of pity following her everywhere she went.

"Actually, a permanent part-time assistant just happens to be in the top five on my wish list," she said, pulling back just enough for him to get the hint and drop his hand. "The very next item after I take delivery of that shiny new Suburban with my name on it."

He looked surprised. "You bought a new Suburban?"

She laughed. "I wish. But the tape on visualization my friend Summer gave me says you're supposed to picture exactly what you want as though it were already yours, and I have a great imagination." She let out a lustful sigh. "My Suburban is frosted silver with a maroon interior, although sometimes I picture the interior in navy instead. I haven't quite settled exactly which is right yet."

His sigh was long-suffering. "This is a woman thing, right? Like rolling your eyes when a man even dares to offer a helpful suggestion?"

"I personally would never do that," she declared, striving to look dignified. "I can't speak for my fellow sisters, however."

"Yeah, well, one of those fellow sisters, named Odella Campbell-Browne, is about to drive me crazy changing her mind about the color of her company vehicle a dozen times a day."

The frustration in his voice had her lips wanting to curve. It was so cute, the big rough-edged self-made tycoon buffaloed by a dainty female a good foot shorter and definitely half his weight. Her father had been like that with her mother. Her heart tumbled.

"Personally, I think she should choose the burgundy Outback with the tan interior," she declared, "but as of yesterday she was leaning toward the bronze with the burgundy interior."

"You're a day behind. Today's color is pewter over black."

"Oh no, pewter is much too drab! That's not Del at all."

"It's not?"

"No way! She would absolutely loathe it before the new-car smell wore off. I'd better make a note to talk to her before she makes a terrible mistake."

Looking mystified, he eyed her warily. "Why is it a man can walk into a showroom, check out what's available and make a decision on the spot while a woman acts like the fate of the world depends on choosing the right color?"

She tossed him a pitying look. "I would think a man who owns about a million trucks—plus a muscle Mercedes—would understand the dynamics of vehicle bonding."

He gave her one of those infuriating "just like a girl" looks Jay had recently perfected. "Sounds to me like something out of that New Age babble Del's been spouting lately."

Now, *that* was an insult to a sister she couldn't allow to go unchallenged. "Okay, answer me this, big guy. How come every mode of transportation you own is the same color of blue?"

His expression turned cagey. "Who says they are?"

She ticked down the fingers. "Your rigs, your Mercedes and . . ." She pursed her lips, considered and then nodded her head. "And your company plane."

"You've never seen our plane."

"Am I wrong?"

His gaze narrowed, and she was pretty sure she saw a muscle tighten in his jaw. She was going to enjoy watching him try to wiggle out of the blind canyon she'd just led him into so brilliantly.

"What can I say. I like blue." The "aw shucks, I'm just a guy" shrug was a nice touch—she had to give him that—but after eleven years of living with a compulsive gambler, she could spot a bluff at a hundred paces in a snowstorm.

Careful not to overplay her own hand, she contrived to look more curious than triumphant. "So when you went truck shopping the first time, you're telling me you walked in, saw the blue truck and bought it?"

He shook his head. "My first rig was mostly rust colored, but best I could make out, the original color was brown. When I finally had it painted, the guy who did it had some paint left over from another job and he cut me a deal. Turned out to be garbage truck gray."

She wondered if he knew how impressive that was, going from a rust bucket rig and a cut-rate paint job to owning his own award-winning high-rise. About a hundred questions popped into her mind. Just in time she recognized the diversionary tactic of a pro. Reluctantly, she accorded him a point in his favor.

"Okay, when you bought your first *new* rig, did you choose the color or take what was available?"

"Guess I chose it." It was very subtle, just a slight flicker of his lashes. Sensing victory, she bored in.

"Did you choose it from stock colors?"

"No, I special-ordered." He hesitated, then added, "Kenworth calls it midnight blue."

"Aha. So you didn't just walk in and point?"

"No." His eyes turned dark, his jaw hard. Like a door slamming, he closed up. It stunned her, how fast he could withdraw. Looking up at him, at the tension turning his jaw hard, at the lines at the corners of his eyes and the deeper ones bracketing his mouth, she saw suffering. He kept it fiercely hidden, she realized, and he would just as fiercely deny its existence if challenged.

Her father had looked very much like that when he'd spoken of Teddy. Near the end of his life, when he'd been drinking too much, he'd spent hours poring over family albums, tears streaming down his ravaged face. Lucy said he was reliving the past because the present had become too painful. Brina suspected it was just the opposite with Rhys. The past was too painful, so he shut out anything that made him remember.

"I'm sorry, Rhys," she told him. "I didn't mean to poke into places where I wasn't invited."

He grew very still. His gaze was fixed on the window, where the ruffled gingham curtains fluttered slightly. His jaw flexed, then relaxed. "The room in the prison hospital where they took me to recuperate after a couple of mainland surgeries on my hip had a window," he said in a voice ironed flat of all emotion. "They weren't much for pain relief inside, especially at night when they were short staffed. I spent a lot of time staring out that window."

"You could see the North Star," she guessed.

He looked a little surprised at that—and not altogether pleased, she realized. "Yeah, right after midnight. I got so I waited for it because that meant Mrs. Wilcox would be coming on duty."

"Mrs. Wilcox was . . . ?"

"One of the civilian nurses." His lips curved briefly. "Looked like an aging flower child. Used to talk about inmate rights and cruel and unusual punishment, like there really were such things." He drew a breath. "Guess she meant well. Volunteers from the outside usually did. Me, all I cared about was the dope she passed out. Regular as clockwork, one hour after she showed up, I was swallowing two of the sweetest pills ever turned out by the pharmaceutical industry."

Suddenly, he flashed her a mocking grin. It warned her that Rhys Hazard was one tough dude, too hard to be broken and dangerous to cross. She almost believed it—until she saw the sadness lurking deep in his eyes. Anyone vulnerable enough to feel sorrow could be broken.

The boy in that bed, that was the Michael Sullivan her father saw and wanted her to forgive. Deeply shaken, she managed to keep her expression light. "Well, there you go, you've just proven my point perfectly," she declared with a grin of her own.

The hidden sorrow vanished in the face of sheer befuddlement. "I can't wait to hear the rationale behind that."

"Color is vital in choosing one's vehicle because it's symbolic. I picked silver because it symbolizes independence, a shiny new life after divorce." She offered him a level look softened by a mischievous grin. "Ironic, isn't it? You picked midnight blue for exactly the same reason—freedom from pain."

He stared at her in blank silence before scowling at her. "No wonder you and Del hit it off. Psychobabble junkies, both of you."

She did her best to look like an empowered female. "If that's supposed to sting, Hazard, you're wasting your time. I'm raising a son, remember? I know that it's genetically impossible for a male of any age to admit when he's wrong."

He contrived to look offended but there was a hint of mischievous laughter in his eyes. It took years from his face and did disturbing things to her libido. "Not impossible, honey," he said in a husky, suggestive tone. "It just depends on what's in it for him."

Though he hadn't moved, he was crowding her again. She thought about the resilience of smooth bronzed skin over hard muscle, the hair-rough texture of his chest, the coaxing pressure of his mouth on hers. She slid her gaze toward the bed, only to blush furiously.

He hooked his free arm around her waist, pulled her close and rested his chin on her topknot. "What . . . what time is this dog and pony show this afternoon scheduled to start?" he demanded.

A little thrill ran through her. "The official ceremony starts at one o'clock. The parade is supposed to follow at three but like Lucy says, that all depends on how long-winded the speakers are. Everyone but the governor is supposed to hold their remarks to five minutes, but with the exception of Del, we're dealing with politicians, so who knows when the parade will actually get under way."

Since she had nothing better to do with her hands, she wound them around his neck, pushed to her tiptoes and kissed his mouth until she ran out of air. His chest rose and fell in harsh breaths, and color flooded his cheekbones. His eyes were a little glazed as he studied her face. With a heavy sigh, he pulled her against him, but instead of kissing her, he tucked her under his chin again.

"Honey, your sense of timing is so bad it's not even on the scale," he muttered into her hair.

"Feels pretty good to me," she murmured. For good measure she wiggled a little.

"Behave yourself, woman. I want you too badly to settle for a quickie, and we don't have time for anything else."

"But we do! Kelly and John are both due any minute to pick up the kids. Everyone else but you is going to the ceremony. Del's representing North Star and I'm just holding down a chair as acting president of the chamber of commerce, so no one will care if I'm late." She had a thought and grinned. "Since Lucy has the programs, my job's officially done, so I don't really have to show up at all."

Unable to help herself, she circled her abdomen against his erection. A tremor shook him, and he let out a strangled groan before pulling away. "But I do," he muttered, his voice lashed with black humor.

She blinked. "Come again?"

His jaw flexed. "Del isn't representing North Star this afternoon. I am."

Chapter 17

Three blocks of Alpine, from Main to Third, had been closed to traffic and now teemed with families in a party mood. The pocket park where the band shell stood occupied the north side of the middle block, and Osuma's trademark Maypole with its crown of flowers and greenery stood in its own specially constructed island at the intersection of Alpine and Main. The streamers were still wound around the pole's length, ready to be unfurled during the dance on Sunday at noon and again at three. At the pole's top, multicolored ribbons fluttered in the breeze.

Passing it on her way to the band shell, Brina felt a sentimental tug. Like her mother when she'd been sixteen, Brina had danced around that pole herself in her sixteenth year. Before she knew it, Marcy would do the same.

"Yo, Brin, is this a great party or what?" Wanda's husband Jackson yelled when she waved at him on her way past the Waffle Haus. Sensing a windfall in the making, Wanda had set up a stand in front of the restaurant to sell blackberry blintzes and the deep-fried sinfully rich, diet-busting waffles dusted with powdered sugar that Brina loved. After eyeing the line, which was a good twenty eager souls long, she made a mental note to stop back later.

"Just like the good old days," she called back.

After sidestepping a young couple doing a mean salsa to the

steamy beat throbbing from a boom box atop a large cooler—and narrowly averting a collision with a couple of roughhousing boys—she quickened her step. Seconds later, she heard someone behind her call her name. Reluctantly, she stopped one more time and turned to see Wayne Makepeace weaving an unsteady path toward her.

Her heart contracted at the changes she saw in the man who'd been her father's best friend and an honorary uncle to her when she was growing up. Wayne had always been thin, but now he seemed little more than skin stretched over bone. His normally ruddy complexion had taken on a pasty look, and his puppy dog brown eyes were rimmed in red.

Sparse black stubble covered his jaw, and his thinning hair stood up in gray clumps. He wore a stained khaki work shirt with WAYNE'S AUTO REPAIR stitched over one pocket, and his baggy brown pants had a rip over one knee. In his hand he carried a bottle in a wrinkled paper bag.

It had been three months since she'd seen him, she realized now. He'd stopped by the inn one afternoon to tell her he'd taken a job at a Chevy dealership in Wenatchee. He'd been sober at the time. She felt both frustration and sorrow at seeing him this way.

"Just seen that boy of yourn with his daddy and that blond chippy over by Klein's beer garden," he said when he reached her side. "Growin' like a weed, ain't he?"

"I'm convinced he's going to be even taller than both of his grandfathers."

"Has Theo's donkey's ears, too," he went on, oblivious to her discomfort. "Course they ain't as large as his grandpop's, but they stick out the same."

"I know, but don't tell him that, okay? He's already self-conscious about them."

"I remember you being the same way about your hair when you was his age. Bought every kind of straightening stuff there was, as I recollect. Your daddy and me were afraid you'd end up bald." His smile was filled with an affection that had her own smile wobbling.

"Look, I have to do this ceremony thing right now, but maybe we could meet for something to eat later?" she suggested, thinking he could use a good meal.

His gaze skittered away again, darting here and there before coming back to her. "I'd like that, sure enough, but I need to get myself back to Sarge's in a few minutes. Got me a job there doing odd jobs 'til I find something else."

"Have you applied at North Star?"

He shook his head. "Ain't qualified to work on them big diesels."

"How hard can it be?" she asked before digging into her bag for her wallet.

"Now you just put that away, missy," he ordered in a gruff tone. "I don't need no handout from Theo's girl or anyone else."

"It's a loan. Heaven knows you were there for Daddy when he was in such bad shape and—"

"Anything I did for Theo and you, you paid me back in full when you gave me the money to start my own place. I wouldn't feel right taking more."

Aware that time was getting short, she opted to postpone her arguments for later. Somehow she would find a way to help him. Perhaps a call to his daughter . . .

"Testing . . . one . . . two . . . three." The voice boomed over the area, followed by an earsplitting feedback squeal. She shot a quick look in the direction of the park. The new bandstand was a third larger than the one washed away in the flood and had a reinforced foundation that the other had lacked. Constructed of local cedar, it had been left unpainted, and the rusty color was still unchanged by the elements.

The stage was already crowded. In addition to the governor and Fat Harve, she recognized Amelia Richwine, a former schoolteacher and now county coordinator for the Democratic

Party. Several locals were there as well, including all three members of the city council and Phil Potter of the *Osuma Recorder.* Sawhorse barricades ringed the entire structure. Brina counted four state troopers and two Osuma police officers standing guard around the perimeter.

"You better get on, now," Wayne said quietly, sounding far less inebriated than she had first thought.

"Look, why don't you come for dinner sometime next week? The kids would be thrilled to see you."

Shame flickered across his sad brown eyes. "I'd rather wait until I get on my feet, but I thank you for the offer."

Mindful of his pride, which had always been considerable, she didn't press. "I hope you know we consider you family, Wayne. Anything you need, you only have to call."

"You've got your father's heart, sure enough." He dropped his gaze to the pavement beneath his worn work boots. "What you done, being so decent to Michael Sullivan after what happened to Teddy . . . your daddy would be real proud." When he looked at her again, she nearly gasped aloud at the stark pain in his eyes. "That's what I come to say," he added before she could comfort him. "Now I've said it, I'll be on my way."

"Thank you for that. It means a lot."

He nodded once before turning abruptly and walking away, his gait unsteady now. Oh yes, she would definitely phone his daughter in Seattle on Monday, she decided as she hurried toward the park.

Rhys had made some dumb-ass decisions in his life. Deciding to participate in this circus sideshow today had to be one of the dumbest, but he hadn't been able to get the words of North Star's security chief out of his mind. Perhaps the risk to Del was minimal, but it was still a risk, one he didn't dare take.

By one o'clock when Lucy stepped to the podium to address the sea of faces staring up at them, sweat had already pooled in the hollow of his spine. Not since those first days at McNeil had he felt so powerless to control his fate.

At least Lucy kept things moving. After starting things off with some pithy words of welcome, she introduced her friend Mandy's husband, who gave the invocation. Then came the guy Lucy called Fat Harve, who reminded Rhys of a toad crammed into a blue suit. According to the program, His Honor was supposed to introduce Governor Luan.

Between the concrete crowd control barriers and the stage, representatives of the media crouched with their cameras and minicams ready. A lightning storm of strobes and clicking shutters greeted each speaker in turn.

Del was still handling the PR stuff. Shortly after they'd arrived, the woman dealing with the media had taken her off to be interviewed by local TV. It went without saying that she wouldn't discuss North Star's CEO and his personal connection to the town. That kind of personal publicity was the last thing the company needed.

He wished Brina were sitting next to him instead of Luan, but Lucy had put her four chairs to his right, at the end of the front row. When he'd left the inn, she'd been in the shower. A few minutes ago, when he'd seen her walking toward him in a power suit the color of ripe peaches, he'd been struck dumb by the transformation. From adorable, harried innkeeper to sophisticated, stunningly beautiful career woman. He'd wanted her with a ferocity that rocked him hard. He'd managed to turn down the heat to a degree that wouldn't embarrass either of them, but the flame was still there.

If he eased forward an inch or two and slanted his gaze right, he could see those world-class legs she'd kept hidden until now. As a distraction they were first rate—as long as he didn't let himself think about skimming his palm over those silky calves and higher. With a silent groan, he shifted his attention to the sea of faces below the platform.

He saw Del and Emory in the front row, along with Lucy's

best friend, Miss Dottie Hollister, and a man he took to be her new husband, the doctor. There were other faces, too, people he thought he recognized, although names eluded him.

After the governor finished came the key ceremony. Only instead of giving him the key to the city, which would have been laughable, he was to receive a symbolic key to the warehouse—from J. T. himself.

He'd damn near walked off the platform when he'd seen that in the program. Only his reluctance to embarrass Lucy had kept his ass in the chair. He'd steeled himself to get through the next hour by icing down his thoughts to the basics. Now he reminded himself again that it was his company these people were honoring, and he would represent his company with as much dignity as the bastards allowed him.

"And now it is my very great honor to introduce the governor of the great state of Washington, Jonathan P. Luan!"

Applause erupted from the crowd as the governor rose to shake the mayor's hand. After the ritual slap on the back, Luan stood before the podium, one of the chosen receiving obeisance from lesser mortals.

"Thank you for that warm welcome! I can't tell you what a pleasure it is for me to be here today, joining with you in celebrating the rebirth of your wonderful community. As I look around this afternoon, I am reminded of that horrible day last September nineteenth when so many lives were irreparably changed. When the waters receded, I grieved with you for all that had been lost . . ."

As the governor continued, J. T. surreptitiously checked his watch. Fifteen, maybe twenty minutes and he could loosen his collar and dump the tie. Next to him Lucy kept sending him anxious looks, the same anxious looks she shot in Mick's direction. *His name is Rhys now,* he heard Lucy chiding him. For damned sure *Rhys* was enjoying this about as little as he was. A man could chip flint on that hard jaw of his.

Easing back, J. T. slipped his hand into his jacket pocket to touch the key that had been on his ring for nearly thirty-five years. Rhys had been at his side when he'd unlocked the warehouse door the first time. His son had been that excited, taller than most even at the age of five—and so proud to be a Sullivan it brought an ache to his father's heart.

Tell me again how when I'm big enough I can be your best helper, Daddy. Sullivan and Sons. It was to be his memorial and his legacy. Now it belonged to that wide-eyed little boy who'd rejected everything and anything that made him a Sullivan.

J. T.'s stomach spilled acid. Ah, but it had been that humiliating that day he'd gone to welcome his son home, only to be stopped at the gate like an intruder, having to beg for permission to set foot on land that had been his for longer than Rhys had been alive.

Narrowing his gaze against the sunlight, he looked to the mountains. There was majesty in the soaring peaks and permanence in the granite slopes. Men had died on those slopes when their courage and strength failed. Others had been brutally tested, only to emerge stronger in both body and spirit.

Much as it grieved him to admit it, the boy he'd loved was lost to him forever. He'd turned to stone inside. There was no give to his pride, no warmth behind those cold gray eyes, only a sharp and lethal bitterness.

J. T.'s chest rose and fell in a heavy sigh that pained him. Rhys Hazard had made it plain how little he cared about the man who'd raised him. So be it, then, he thought. When he handed over the key this day, that would end it between them.

"You're next," Lucy whispered in Rhys' ear, jerking his mind back to the next few minutes. Then suddenly, the governor was finished, and Lucy was getting to her feet.

After shaking Luan's hand, she waited until the governor was seated again before stepping to the microphone to introduce J. T. Looking like a man taking that last long walk to the execution chamber, J. T. rose and stepped to the podium. The crowd roared when he leaned down to kiss Lucy full on the mouth.

Cheeks stained the color of a bad sunburn, she shot him a murderous glare before returning to her chair.

"Do *not* say a word!" she muttered to Rhys.

"No ma'am."

Brina caught his gaze and grinned. He did his best to grin back, but his facial muscles had suddenly seized up. As J. T. reminisced about the people who had worked for Sullivan's over the years, his brogue boomed out over the crowd, more pronounced than usual, a sign, Lucy had told Rhys once, that the big Irishman was wrestling with emotions he didn't want to reveal.

This had to be hell on the old man, he thought with reluctant sympathy. He told himself J. T. still had his orchards. He told himself it wasn't his fault J. T. had been forced to sell out. He told himself he'd paid the SOB a damned good price. He told himself he no longer loved the old man.

"So all in all it's been a grand and glorious thirty-five years, and I thank all the good people who helped make it so. I will always treasure your loyalty and hard work more than I can say. And now—"

The applause that erupted seemed to take J. T. by surprise. Even as he gestured for quiet, he had to swallow several times before he could speak. "And now, like all good things, Sullivan and Son has come to an end. A new opportunity has presented itself for all of you. An excellent one, by all accounts. I've been told many of you have already hired on, with more hires to come."

This time he seemed to expect the applause and waited it out with a poise that rivaled Luan's. "There's a lot more I could say, but Lucy made me promise to keep it short." He turned to look at her, the devil's own grin creasing his weathered cheeks. He winked before turning front again. A smattering of applause rose, causing Lucy to clamp her jaw tight.

"In truth, what she said was 'None of your Irish blarney,

John Thomas Sullivan, or I'll be booting you in your blooming arse.' So, in the interest of protecting my posterior—"

Laughter rose in a wave. J. T. paused to let it swell. Lucy stared straight ahead.

"As I was saying," J. T. continued when the laughter died down, "I'll keep it short." He paused to clear his throat. "Before I received a call from a representative of North Star Trucking, I'd already turned down several offers to buy us out. Not because the offers weren't good from a financial standpoint, but because I suspected the outfits offering them weren't up to Osuma's high standards."

Cheers erupted again. Rhys took a deep breath. God, where was the old man going with this?

"You have my word on this, North Star is an outstanding company, with an excellent reputation in the transportation industry, and just because the man who built it is my son doesn't mean I didn't check it out."

The buzz that arose had Rhys gritting his teeth. Damn, why did the man have to throw his past in their faces? "An article on employee-friendly corporations in *Fortune* a few years back rated North Star in the top five," J. T. went on as though oblivious to the rising noise level. "So it's with great satisfaction that I turn over the key to what was once Sullivan and Son to the man responsible for putting so many of my friends back to work, Rhys Hazard."

Rhys took a deep breath and got to his feet. Face impassive, he limped to the podium. J. T. took the key from his pocket and held it up, prompting a wild melee of flashing strobes and frenzied shutter clicks.

J. T.'s grin was filled with charm, but when he turned that grin Rhys' way, the sorrow in those bright blue eyes whipped Rhys right back to the day J. T. had come to see him in the hospital. He realized he was trembling inside and tightened his abdominal muscles until it stopped. Only then did he take the key J. T. held out.

"Guess you've already changed the locks, but maybe you can hang this on the wall," the Irishman joked.

Conscious that the two of them were being observed by half the valley's residents, most of whom had to be aware of their past history, he managed a smile. "In a place of honor," he said, winning him a flurry of cheers and applause. J. T. didn't offer his hand before he returned to his seat.

Alone at the podium, Rhys slipped the key into his jacket pocket. "I appreciate the warm welcome you've given North Star today and during the two weeks since the transition team relocated from Phoenix. As many of you know, the man who is the guiding force behind this new depot, Henry Dunnigan, was on his way here when he was seriously injured in a car accident in San Francisco. I spoke with him right before coming here today, and he asked me to tell all of you how much he's looking forward to becoming a part of the community." He smiled briefly. "He's doing fine, by the way."

While he waited out the cheers, he found himself glancing Brina's way. Funny how something as simple as a woman's smile settled a man, he thought as he braved the front again. "I have been told that in some cultures when someone gives you a gift, it's only good manners to give one in return. So on behalf of Hank Dunnigan and everyone at NSN, I would like to present J. T. Sullivan with his own NSN badge, which will allow him to check up on us any time he gets the notion. Maybe his name isn't on the building anymore, but because he built it solid and strong, it survived. And because it survived, North Star is able to provide the jobs he talked about. So in a very real sense he is the reason we are here today to celebrate a new start."

He fished the badge from his jacket pocket and let it dangle from the chain so that everyone could see it before he turned toward J. T. It was as close to an apology as years of resentment and bitterness would allow.

The old man looked stunned for a moment before he got to

his feet. Rhys felt a sudden tightness in his throat. Old tapes, he told himself as J. T. took the badge and slipped it over his neck while the crowd cheered and whistled. J. T. hesitated, then held out his hand. Rhys steeled himself and accepted the handshake—and the gratitude shimmering in his father's eyes.

The photographers jostled one another, trying to get the front-page shot. The bright light from a minicam hit him. As he withdrew his hand, he heard his name and J. T.'s being called over and over. Just what he needed, another fifteen minutes in the spotlight's glare, he thought grimly, turning to invite the governor to join them. Luan offered his hand, and they shook before Luan pulled Lucy forward to stand with them.

With The Man center stage, Rhys felt safe stepping back. He started to sit down again, only to realize that everyone else on the stage was now standing, applauding right along with the crowd. His gaze sought Brina's. Turned out she was looking at him, her eyes suspiciously shiny. Had he done that? he wondered with dark dread.

A hole opened in his gut. Before he could stop himself, he gave his head a little jerk, and she walked toward him. "Are you okay?" he asked when she reached his side.

Nodding, she sniffed like a little girl. "Are you?"

"Since no one's thrown any tomatoes yet, I guess I am." He shifted his weight to his good leg and did his best not to flinch. A look of alarm crossed her face.

"Don't say it," he warned.

"Stubborn," she muttered, narrowing her eyes at him.

"Anyone ever tell you how cute you are when you're steamed?"

Her face turned pink. A feeling of tenderness ran through him, surprising him. With the exception of his feelings for Del, he'd thought that emotion was beyond him. Before he could give that more thought, the governor claimed his attention, and Brina slipped away.

Chapter 18

It was a little past two thirty when Max dropped Rhys off at Nightingale House. The inn's front door was locked, so he used the key Brina had given him. He was closing the door behind him when he heard a strangled cry from the direction of the parlor. Heart pounding, he went to investigate.

Jay stood in front of the bar with his back to the door, with smashed lamps and overturned end tables scattered all over the fancy Oriental rug.

"Jesus, Jay, what the hell's going on here?" he demanded.

The boy spun around, his face contorted and white. Tears glistened on his cheeks and dripped from his chin, but it was the raw agony in the kid's brown eyes that had Rhys hissing out a curse.

"Leave me alone!" the boy shouted before bolting for the door.

Rhys dropped his cane, braced his weight on his good leg and lunged. The kid was as slippery as an eel, but Rhys' size made up for his lack of agility. Still, he took a vicious hit in the gut—an elbow, he thought as the air whooshed out—before he managed to contain the kid in a bear hug. "Talk to me, Jay," he ordered when Jay stopped struggling. "What's going on?"

Jay muttered something against his chest before straining to get free. "If I let you go, will you promise not to take off?" Rhys asked, trying to keep his voice nonthreatening.

Jay hesitated, and then he nodded. Rhys released his hold but stayed ready to grab the kid. Jay stepped back, his arms wrapping around his skinny chest and his head hanging.

"Jay, I'd like to help you if I can, but I need to know what's got you all riled up."

"Nothin'," he mumbled in a low tone. The scuffed toe of one sneaker worked at rubbing a hole in the Persian carpet.

"Wrong answer, son. I don't know you all that well, but I have a hunch you wouldn't destroy your mom's treasures on account of nothing."

A mottled red flush spread across his pale cheeks. "It's all her fault!" he cried out, jerking up his head. His eyes blazed with anger and betrayal. "She said Dad *wanted* me to ride with him in the 'Vette, only she lied! He wants Sherri!"

"What makes you think that?" Rhys had to work to iron the anger from his voice.

"I heard them arguing, only they didn't see me 'cause I was behind a float. Sherri was all bummed 'cause she wanted to ride with Dad and he was telling her how he really wanted her, too, but how Mom made him take me and he had to say okay or Mom would take him to court for more money. And he got this look like he was smelling something dead and called me a . . . miserable little m-mama's boy." Jay's chest heaved, and he lifted a hand to dash away another rush of tears. "He . . . he hates me because I'm not good at football and stuff like that."

Rhys felt his stomach knot. His brother was a self-centered prick who deserved to be stripped naked and put on display in the town square as a pitiful example of a husband and father. "Hell, son, your dad hates me, too, because I'm illegitimate. I figure that's his problem, not mine."

Jay's head shot up and he stared, his eyes widening. "How can you be illegitimate if you're his brother?"

"*Adopted* brother," he corrected. "Your granddad bought me right out of the hospital."

Jay blinked. "Bought you how?"

"Paid money to the woman who'd given birth to me." His
grin felt almost natural. "Ten grand, according to your granddad. He never said if it was worth it. Probably not."

"Bummer," Jay muttered.

Rhys laughed. "Yeah." He rubbed a hand over his sore
belly, scrambling to take advantage of the wedge he'd managed to shove between the kid and the raw edges of the hurt.
"So, about this parade, was it riding with your dad that was
important or would it embarrass you to ride with me?"

"With . . . you? You mean in the Mercedes?"

Rhys started to nod before another thought occurred to him.
"Nah, that's too tame. What I'd really like to do is take out one
of the new rigs, see what it can do." He grinned. "What do you
say, son? Want to kick a little parade butt with your uncle
Rhys?"

It was almost three. After calling Max and asking him to return to the inn, Rhys shed his jacket and tie and made sure his
class two license was still in his wallet.

Five minutes later Max pulled up with Ernestine in the passenger's seat, looking flushed and young in a frilly gold blouse
and long flowered skirt. She took one look at Jay's face and
sent Rhys a stricken look. *Later,* he mouthed over the boy's
head and she nodded.

The staging area for the parade participants was in the parking lot behind the City Hall. He spotted the governor and his
entourage near an antique fire engine. Del was there, too—surrounded by men as usual.

The Osuma High band in their blue-and-white uniforms
milled around behind the fire truck, tuning up and clowning
around. Lucy, clipboard in hand, was busy shepherding a half
dozen giggling cheerleaders into position in front of the flag
bearers. Nearby a dozen or so brightly colored floats stood in a
ragged line.

Several still and TV photographers were shooting pictures

of the scene. A skinny woman in a red suit carrying a microphone crossed between two floats and bore down on the governor, her photographer and his lackey trailing after her like eager puppies.

The North Star rigs were lined up at the end of the parade, just as Lucy had ordered. The chrome of the upright exhaust pipes was as shiny as polished mirrors, and as far as Rhys could see, there wasn't so much as a fingerprint on the gleaming paint jobs. Emory and his people had done North Star proud. Rhys shifted his gaze toward the sparkling windshield. It had been nearly six years since he'd been in the cab of one of North Star's Kenworths, longer since he'd inhaled the new-truck smell he loved. It had been too wearing on his soul, sitting behind the wheel and not being able to take her out.

Fighting a rush of conflicting emotions, Rhys glanced past Max's shoulder toward the crowds lining both sides of the street. Kids licked dripping ice cream cones, and dads pushed strollers. Teenage boys in baggy clothes and caps worn backward swaggered past a gaggle of girls as bright as spring flowers, who giggled and called out flirtatious comments. Older folks gossiped and smiled, enjoying the show. It was the kind of day—the kind of *memory*—that had tormented Rhys for years after he'd left this place.

"Might as well bring up the rear," he said, beckoning to the rig's driver, who was having a last smoke with some of the others. As the man approached, Rhys realized he looked vaguely familiar.

"Name's Walt Harrison, Mr. Hazard," he said when he reached Rhys' side. "You likely don't remember me, but I started driving for your daddy the same summer you started working in the warehouse."

Rhys sifted through memories that he'd pushed away so many times they were frayed and blurred. Gradually a younger version of the seamed face clicked into place. The hair that was now gray and thinning had once been black and bushy. "I remember you very well, Mr. Harrison," Rhys said, his chest tight. "You had twin daughters, right? Two little redheads? Used to come down with their mama to welcome you home from a haul?"

The older man broke into a grin. "Sandra and Sharon. Had them a double wedding a couple of years back. Both their husbands worked for Sullivan's. Now they're gonna be working for you, same as me." His grin faded, and he shifted, looking down for a moment before clearing his throat and lifting his head again. "I just want to thank you for keeping my family together, Mr. Hazard." He stuck out his hand.

Rhys managed a smile as he took it. "Call me Rhys, okay?"

Harrison seemed surprised. "Be glad to, only it might take me a while to forget it used to be Mick."

"Yeah, I know the feeling," he said as the handshake ended.

"Can I get in now, Uncle Rhys?" Jay called, already stretching a hand toward the handle.

"Yeah, just watch your step," he said before turning to Harrison again. "I'll take her, Walt, thanks."

"Sure thing, Mi—Rhys. It'll be real nice to enjoy the show from the sidelines." Harrison dug into his pocket for the key and handed it over. "Careful with her," he said with a grin. "She's a honey."

"I promise to bring her back without a scratch," he said before circling around to the other side. He only hoped to hell he could get himself and his gimpy leg into the cab without making a jackass of himself.

Two and a half hours later, Brina stood with one hand pressed to her suddenly churning stomach, staring in disbelief at the parlor she'd labored over for weeks in an attempt to make it a perfect gem. Now it brought back memories of the flood's destruction.

She took a jerky step forward, then jolted back to her senses. Whoever had done this might still be in the house! Her heart in her throat, she spun around and rushed across the foyer to her office, her heels clattering loudly. The door was closed. A piece of notepaper imprinted with the North Star masthead and the name M. R. Hazard had been taped at eye level on her office door.

Brina: Don't panic and don't call the cops. Will explain when Jay and I return.

It was signed with a bold *R*.

Jay and Rhys? Responsible for this? She spun around to stare at what appeared to be some kind of frenzied destruction. Rhys had been talking with the governor when she'd headed toward the chamber of commerce float. On her way to the staging area she'd run into Jay walking with a girl in a floppy denim hat and cutoff overalls over a skimpy T-shirt.

Jay had turned bright red when he'd spotted his mother, mumbling an introduction to Amy Someone-or-other, who gave her a shyly dimpled grin. Before Brina had excused her-self to find her assigned float, she'd reminded Jay that his fa-ther was to bring him back to the inn in time for Kelly Hollister to pick him up on her way home.

Maybe John would know what was going on, she decided, opening her office door. After checking her messages and find-ing nothing about Jay, she hit the speed-dial button for John's pager number. It took three attempts before he finally called her back. The impatience in his voice set her teeth on edge. She'd no sooner explained her reason for calling than he turned on her.

"How the fuck should I know where they are? The kid didn't show when he was supposed to, and Sherri took his place in the 'Vette."

"What do you mean, he didn't show? He's been looking for-ward to riding with you since you decided to drive in the pa-rade."

"Yeah, right. That's why he was a no-show." He took an im-patient breath. "Look, Brin, the kid's been acting weird ever since we split. Sher thinks he's trying to make me feel guilty and so do I."

"He's not acting weird; he's grieving! He misses his father."

John's sigh was long-suffering. "Once this new job settles into a routine, I'll have more time to be with the kids. Until then, you'll just have to handle it." He severed the connection before she could say another word.

After dropping the phone into the cradle, Brina sat frozen, trying to decide what to do next, when she heard the front doorbells jangling. "Mom, where are you?"

She spun around and scrambled to her feet, banging her knee and tearing her panty hose in her haste. "Coming," she called, hurrying into the foyer.

Jay still wore his sloppy cargo pants, but he now also wore what appeared to be a brand-new midnight blue T-shirt with the North Star logo silk-screened across the front. His face was flushed, his eyes dancing. For once he'd forgotten to keep his upper lip over the braces he hated. "It was *awesome,* Mom. You should have been there."

"I *was* there, sweetie—right up front on the chamber of commerce float," she reminded him as she caught sight of Rhys closing the door, a wary look on his face.

"Not the parade, except that was gnarly, too. But after the parade, Uncle Rhys drove out to the old road by the quarry." His grin flashed. "Man, oh *man,* that big old Kenworth really hauled ass!"

Her mouth went dry. "How much . . . ass did you haul, exactly?"

Before Jay could answer, Rhys came forward to place a warning hand on her son's bony shoulder. "Uh, Jay, might be your mom's not all that interested in the boring details."

"Oh yeah, right." He shot Rhys one of those "us against them" looks. "I'm real sorry about the mess and all, Mom," he said in a subdued tone. "Uncle Rhys is gonna give me a part-time job in his office weekends so I can make enough money to pay for the stuff I broke."

"I see. You'll also clean up this mess—right after you get your stuff ready so Kelly won't have to wait when she comes to pick you up."

Jay liked Kelly a lot, and he liked being around Brody, especially when Brody let Jay help him tinker with his monster Harley-Davidson. In recent months, however, Jay had started complaining that he didn't need a sitter. Brina marshaled her reserves to deflect an argument, or at least some heavy grumbling. What she got was another metallic grin before he took off.

She compressed her lips and blew air into her cheeks before turning again to confront the man at her side. "*Someone* has some explaining to do," she enunciated slowly and carefully. "I pick *you*."

Looking like a man who wanted to be someplace else, he leaned more heavily on his cane. "I got it in pieces, but best I can make out, Jay overheard John and his girlfriend talking. Seems she was put out because she thought she should ride with him instead of Jay. John blamed you, something along the lines that you'd threatened to take him to court for more child support if he didn't let Jay ride in the 'Vette. Jay bought it all and ran." His gaze narrowed slightly. "Him riding with John, you set it up, didn't you?"

She nodded. "But I didn't threaten to take John back to court." She frowned. "Well, I did, but not because of this. That was John taking the easy way out."

"Jay made a mistake and he needs to take some serious heat as a consequence. But he's also pretty mixed up right now. Might be a good idea to get him some professional help."

"I intend to, but so far I haven't found the right therapist." *Meaning one she could afford,* she added silently before asking, "He believed John, didn't he? That I blackmailed him?"

"Probably."

"And this acting-out behavior?" She gestured toward the parlor. "Was this to punish me?"

He chewed the inside of his cheek, a habit he had when he was thinking things through. Finally he nodded. "I'm no shrink, but I'd say that's a pretty good guess, yeah."

She realized she'd been harboring a faint hope that Rhys would somehow absolve her of the guilt burning in her chest. "Jay blames me for the divorce," she admitted with a sigh. "Knowing my weasel ex, I imagine Jay's had some help reaching that conclusion."

"Yeah, well, John always was good at laying off blame."

"Is that what he did with you?"

"Oh yeah." His mouth curled at one corner. "Started before he was old enough to go to school. It took me a while to figure it out. Not that it did much good. Marceline wouldn't hear anything bad about her perfect son." His voice was entirely flat, without a hint of emotion. His eyes, too, were carefully shielded.

"I must have read ten books about children and divorce, maybe more," she admitted. "Every single one talked about how important it is not to put the kids in the middle. Don't let them hear you saying nasty things about your ex. Don't use them as weapons. Don't tear down the other parent in their hearing." Getting agitated all over again, she shot him an exasperated look. "Not one of them said anything about what you're supposed to do when that *other parent* isn't following the same rules!"

He didn't smile, but she could tell he wanted to. "From what I've seen, you're doing okay."

Despite the gruff praise, he was beginning to get that trapped-in-the-headlights look she'd seen on Brody's face a time or two when discussions with Summer got a little too heavy. Men! she thought with a private huff of female disdain.

"I'm sorry for dumping this on you, Rhys." She was careful to keep her shoulders from slumping, and her chin high. "If you hadn't been here, I hate to think what else he might have done. He might he have hurt himself or . . . worse." The sudden tightness in her throat squeezed off further speech.

"Today was just a Band-Aid, Brina. He's still plenty raw." His jaw turned hard. "Don't take this wrong, but he's feeling like he's just so much unwanted garbage in the Sullivan family."

A chill ran down her spine. He'd used similar words when describing his own childhood. "Marcy's always been John's favorite, probably because she looks so much like him," she admitted with heavy reluctance. "J. T. tries, but he's been busy." She realized she was making excuses and sighed. "Oh Rhys, what would you do if he was your son?"

"Thank God every night in my prayers," he said a little gruffly.

"You would, wouldn't you?" she said softly.

His eyes were suddenly dark with feeling. "Yeah. He's a great kid."

An odd sensation ran through her. Like the sweet bubble of emotion she'd felt an instant before she'd held each of her babies for the first time. Seconds later she'd started falling in love. It shook her to realize she had that same feeling now. Her heart stuttered, and her chest hurt. Breathing took more effort than it should, and her gaze slid away.

"I have a feeling he's going to be spending more time pestering your mechanics about horsepower and pistons and all those other mysterious engine type doohickeys than working off his debt."

Rhys shifted his weight, something he did often, as though standing was difficult. "Look, Brina, I know you're probably steamed because I didn't get your permission to take Jay with me, but I didn't have a lot of time and—"

"No."

The furrows deepened. "No, what?" he asked cautiously.

"No, I'm not steamed."

He didn't look convinced. "I swear it was safe, Brina. No one rides in a North Star rig without being belted in."

"Definitely a good rule to have." He really had beautiful eyes, she thought. Deep-set, and the color of Mexican topaz, with thick golden lashes that would have looked almost feminine on another man. On those rare occasions when he allowed himself to relax his guard, they crinkled with irresistible humor. At other times, when he thought himself unobserved, they seemed full of bleak shadows. Now they watched her warily.

"I wasn't anywhere close to topping out the speed," he said a little stiffly. Apparently he wasn't used to explaining himself.

"Of course you weren't. You wouldn't do that."

His face tightened. "I did once, and three innocent people paid. What makes you think I won't again?"

"For that very reason—you don't want anyone to get hurt again."

His mouth turned vulnerable, but only for a moment. "Jay's trying to find a way through some pretty rocky ground right now, but there's nothing mean or vicious about him." His face tightened. "I figure that's because of his mom's influence."

"Thank you, but my father gets a lot of the credit," she said with a self-conscious smile. "He was the kindest person I've ever known."

"I remember."

She'd never seduced a man. She wasn't sure she knew how. Probably just make a joke of herself. A plump, inexperienced pigeon lusting after a lean and dangerous hawk. Laughable, really. Completely absurd. Infuriatingly tempting.

Her breathing changed again. "So, uh, just how fast does one of the huge trucks go, anyway?"

Looking as though he expected a trap, he cleared his throat. "One thirty, one thirty-five. But I kept it under a hundred." His mouth flattened. "Mostly," he added in a stiff tone, as though forcing himself to own up to the whole truth.

"Aha, the 'hauled ass' part."

A boyish look of cocky pride crossed his face. "Your son can be very single-minded." His eyes crinkled again, and her insides melted. "A lot like his mom."

Not always. "Well, anyway, thank you for being there for him." Before she lost her nerve, she went up on her tiptoes, braced one hand on his rock-hard shoulder and kissed his cheek. "Like Della says, you have a pure heart and a gentle soul."

His eyes turned stormy. "Don't count on it," he grated an instant before he hooked one burly arm around her waist, trapping her.

His thighs were hard against hers, and his belt buckle was gouging her stomach. His arm was steel against the hollow of her back. None of that seemed to matter at this particular moment. Not when his beautiful mouth was so very close to hers, and his eyes were hungry and hot.

"I've been thinking about this since I saw you on that damned stage this afternoon." His mouth came down on hers. She felt a jolt, and then a wave crashed. It was wild excitement and the sweetest sigh. His mouth was demanding and hungry. However, it was a savage need she tasted beneath the passion. A desperate aching need. With a strangled moan, she plastered herself against him, her arms twining around that strong neck. She wanted heat and power and raw passion, the kind that ignited skyrockets and made her want to scream. She wanted to soar, but just as she felt a welling of urgent fluttering inside, he drew back. His eyes were glittering, the planes of his face taut.

"God almighty, you're something. Just when I think I have you figured, you do something to knock me flat."

"I know the feeling," she said, her voice unsteady.

His hand splayed against her spine, his fingers massaging muscles that felt about as powerful as melting wax. He dipped his head and kissed her again, a long, sweet, cherishing kiss that made her head swim. Her fingers ruffled through his hair, feeling the silky thickness. He shivered, and then drew back, but his arm was still warm around her waist. "This bash the governor's putting on tonight—you're going, right?"

She was careful to move only her head when she nodded. "It's not really my thing, but Lucy bullied me into it."

"Is there anyone I have to fight?"

Mystified, she gave him an inquiring look. "Fight?"

"Before I can ask you to be my date?"

She blinked, her thoughts tumbling like glass in a kaleidoscope. It must have been the fumes from the spilled alcohol clouding her thinking. "I thought you weren't planning to attend."

"That was before I saw your legs. I figure if you looked that great in a suit, you'd have to be a knockout in a party dress."

Her stomach bottomed out. "The last time I wore a dress John claimed I looked like a sausage tied in the middle."

Sudden anger slashed his sharply defined features. "On the evolutionary scale, I figure John is a couple levels below pond scum."

She sputtered a delighted laugh. She was beginning to love that half-shy, half-amused smile of his.

"Who am I to argue with such a perceptive observation?" she said.

"So it's settled, right? You and me tonight?" The smile disappeared as he added in a voice suddenly devoid of all emotion, "Unless you'd rather not be seen with me. It could get messy. Probably will, in fact."

She shot him her best "watch it, buster" look. "Do you *really* think I'm that hypocritical?"

"A man like me learns to expect the worst. That way I'm always prepared—and rarely surprised."

In light of his past experiences that made perfect sense. It also made her hurt for him. "That's the difference between us,

I suppose. I keep expecting the best. I admit to being disappointed sometimes, but I'm willing to take that risk."

His jaw flexed. "I'm a long way from the best, Brina, but I'd rather go back to prison for the rest of my life than do anything to hurt you or your kids."

"I know that," she said in a low, shaky voice. When he didn't look convinced, she added more forcefully, "'The Successful Innkeeper must become a shrewd judge of character.'"

"What's with these pithy quotes you're always tossing out?"

"Words of wisdom from Montgomery Meegs, my mentor in this hotel game. They're from his book *The Successful Innkeeper's Guide to Gracious Hospitality* that Ernestine found for me on some dusty shelf in the library's storage room shortly after I bought this place. Bless her heart, that sucker's saved me from disaster so many times I've lost count." She sighed, her gaze fixed on the comma-shaped scar on his chin. "Unfortunately, some of his advice is a bit dated." Despite the herd of butterflies beating their wings against the inside of her chest, she lifted her chin and tossed him a teasing grin. "Like the one about Successful Innkeepers making sure the guests' horses are treated as well as the guests."

The twinkle in his eyes all but melted her backbone. "Something tells me this guy isn't working on a sequel."

"Alas, you're right. I suspect he's up there whipping St. Peter into shape as we speak." She took a breath, then took a risk and straightened his collar. "This thing tonight is black-tie, although I don't imagine anyone would care what you wear."

"Is that a yes on this date thing?"

"It's a yes."

His brow cleared. "Just don't expect party manners, okay? I'm damn rusty."

She drew a shaky breath, one hand going to her wildly tumbling stomach. "As long as you don't expect Brittany Spears."

This time his grin was blazing white with definite licks of

boyish mischief and big-boy sex appeal. "Trust me, honey, Brittany Spears could strip naked and beg, and I'd still want you about a thousand times more."

Her insides turned deliciously soft. "Are you always so irresistible to the women you ask out?" she murmured self-consciously.

"Nope. This is all new territory." He hiked up one of those sun-kissed brows. "How'm I doing?"

"So far so good." She drew air into her oxygen-starved lungs. "I'll meet you in the parlor at six thirty."

He dropped a kiss on the tip of her nose before letting her go. She waited until he disappeared up the stairs before she exhaled. As she raced up the back stairs to the family quarters, she wondered if it was too late to lose twenty pounds.

Chapter 19

Despite his good mood, by the time Rhys made it to the top of the stairs, the muscles of his hip and thigh, traumatized by driving the rig, were already tightening. Unless he did something immediately, those same muscles would twist into spastic knots.

He filled the old-fashioned footed bathtub with hot water and the Epsom salts he bought by the case, then stripped down and climbed in. Thirty minutes later the water had gone tepid and some of the tightness had eased.

Nevertheless, climbing out of the tub was a slow, clumsy process. Even leaning heavily on his cane, it took him several more painful minutes to get from the bathroom to the bed. It cost him, but he managed to pull back the covers before easing his sore, naked body onto the big mattress. As much as it infuriated him, he would have to break his date with Brina.

Hating the disability he'd fought for more than half his life now, he pulled up the sheet, then called Del's name. After giving her a couple of seconds to answer, he was about to reach for the cell phone on the night table when the door opened a crack. "Did you call me, Rhys?" she asked through the opening.

"Yeah, come in a minute, please—if you're decent."

"Sugar, I'm always decent," she declared as she opened the door wider.

His breath hissed in when he caught sight of the scrap of shiny green material with no back and not enough front to matter that she called a dress. "Jesus, Del, if that's decent, I'd hate to see what you call *indecent.*"

"I'll have you know this is a Donatella Versace original straight from Milano and—" She stopped in midsentence, her grin giving way to a look of alarm. "Oh shit, I was afraid of this when Max said you'd driven one of the rigs in the parade."

"Don't fuss," he ordered, doing his best to scowl as she hurried around the foot of the bed.

"I'm calling Max," she declared firmly. "You need to see a doctor."

"What I *need* is for you to let Brina know I can't take her to this thing tonight." He thought it through before adding tersely, "Don't make it into a big deal, but make sure she understands I expect a rain check."

Ten minutes later, Del joined the others in the parlor.

"What time does the boss want to leave?" Max asked as she accepted a glass of champagne from Colonel FitzHugh.

"Actually, he won't be able to go after all," she said before turning to Brina to add, "He asked me to make his apologies for him. His bad leg is acting up on him again, and he's gone to bed."

Disappointment and anxiety replaced the anticipation in Brina's dark eyes. "Is there anything I can do? A heating pad, maybe?"

"His doctor has prescribed medication, which he hates but which I finally bullied him into taking. He should be fine in the morning."

"Oh dear, it doesn't seem right to go off to a party and leave him all alone," Ernestine murmured, glancing in Max's direction.

"Be worse if we don't," Max said, patting the small hand that had sought his. "Boss hates anyone making a fuss over him. Makes him real testy. Even threw this old-fashioned alarm clock at my head once when I suggested maybe he should cut down from working sixteen hours a day to fourteen so's he wouldn't hurt all the time."

"Oh dear," Ernestine murmured.

Della patted the sweet lady's shoulder. "Not to worry, Ernie, Max is real good at ducking." She grinned. "We all are."

Brina offered her a thoughtful look that made Del very uneasy. "Do you think he'd mind if I peeked in on him before we left? If he's sleeping, I won't disturb him."

Del started to discourage her, then thought better of it. "Max is right, he can get pretty grumpy, even, um, explosive at times." She grinned. "But if anyone can handle him, you can."

The grandfather clock had just chimed six as Lucy stood in front of the mirror affixed to the entryway umbrella stand, fastening her mother's amethyst teardrop to her earlobe. The doorbell rang. She took a moment to calm her racing heart. A thousand doubts suddenly assailed her. Was she wearing too much eye makeup? Did the rinse she'd let her stylist put on her hair make her look like an old lady trying to be young? Had she dabbed on too much perfume?

She shot a panicked look at the floor-length skirt. The Empire waist actually made her small breasts look voluptuous for once in her life. When she walked, the soft organza skirt seemed to float around her ankles.

The bell rang again, and the ball of nerves in her chest expanded until she felt as though each breath was a major struggle. The last time she'd put her heart on the line, the big, insensitive ox on the other side of the door had trampled it flat.

She could still back out. It wasn't too late.

A hard fist hit the door, thudding with such force the windows rattled. *Oh, for heaven's sake!* Temper surging, she jerked open the door so fast, she nearly took a punch in the face before the man pulled back that enormous fist.

"Jay-sus, Lucy, what the hell do you think you're doing, surprisin' a man like that," J. T. exclaimed.

"Me?" she shot back. "You're the one trying to batter down my door, you . . . you ill-mannered dolt."

His crooked grin rattled her all the way to the utterly impractical silver high-heeled sandals Dottie had bullied her into buying. She'd be lucky if she survived the evening without a sprained ankle.

"Ah colleen, you do have a way of bruisin' a man's ego. A less besotted man would have taken himself off to lick his wounds long before now."

"Horny is more like it."

His eyes took on a rueful gleam that had her nerve endings tingling. "Ah, there is that as well," he said, pulling a florist's box from behind his back. "For you, me beauty."

Bemused, she recognized the name on the box. Seattle's finest and most expensive by far. "You bought me flowers from a competitor?" she demanded, both outraged and deeply touched.

"A necessity. For the surprise, you see."

Though her mouth wanted to curve into a giddy smile, she feigned an irritable frown as she opened the box with hands that weren't quite steady. Inside, nestled on a bed of golden tissue paper, was the most beautiful orchid she'd ever seen. It was a delicate peach color with a ruby center, and the frilly petals seemed to pulse with passion. "My first orchid," she whispered in awe.

His weathered face took on the look of a bashful boy. "For my first love," he replied, his voice suddenly thick.

"Oh, J. T.," she murmured, her gaze clinging helplessly to his. "This isn't fair."

"Ah, but you have to admit it's exciting, colleen," he said, framing her face with his big hands. Her lashes drifted down an instant before his mouth whispered a tender kiss over her lips. "You'll be the prettiest girl at the ball, my love," he said. "And I'll be the luckiest man."

"You're full of blarney and you know it," she said, her voice shaky. Suddenly she was very glad she'd let Dottie bully her into buying the impossible dress. Maybe the magic would all disappear into a puff of smoke at midnight, the way her dreams had evaporated forty-five years ago. For now, however, she intended to pretend she really was Cinderella in her frightfully expensive designer original, with her very own Prince Charming offering his arm.

It was just after eleven when Brina rapped gently on the door to Rhys' room, which was ajar as usual. "Rhys, it's Brina," she called softly. "Can I come in?"

When he didn't answer, she felt her stomach clench. He'd been sleeping when she'd looked in on him before leaving for the party. Even though both Max and Della had assured her that sleep was the best thing for him, she'd spent the last four hours seesawing between guilt and worry.

"Rhys?" she called more loudly.

After deciding her need to make sure he was all right overrode her respect for a guest's privacy, she eased the door open wide enough to stick her head inside. Fortunately, the drapes on every window had been pulled back, allowing the glow from the security lamps to spill into the room, providing more than enough light to see by.

Rhys was lying on his back with his face turned toward her, one arm flung wide, his big hand curled into a loose fist, the other tucked under the pillow. His eyes were closed, his facial muscles taut. The sheet was bunched just below his navel. She hesitated, unsure how he would feel if he woke up to find her creeping into his room. She'd just decided to leave when he opened his eyes and looked directly at her.

"Brina?" His sleepy voice had a seductive quality that shivered all the way through her.

She drifted toward him, a vision in a dress the color of a vanilla milk shake. Made of some soft material that shimmered in the dim light, it had a plunging neckline in the shape of a V that showed a stunning amount of cleavage, long fitted sleeves and a swirly, just-above-the-knee skirt that moved when she moved. One side of the cock-teasing creation wrapped over the other, hugging her ripe breasts snugly before tying at her curvy waist in a floppy bow. One little tug, he figured, would free that mouthwatering body from the pretty gift wrapping. When blood rushed to his loins, he realized the pain in his hip had eased back to a dull ache.

How long had it been since he'd had a woman? Six months, seven? Probably longer. How long had it been since he'd wanted a woman with this kind of shuddering ferocity? He rubbed his cheek against the pillow and tried not to groan. He could smell her, that special mix of cinnamon and soap and living, breathing woman.

"Rhys?"

His heart rate went from normal to redline in two seconds flat. "Brina?" he demanded, struggling to clear his mind.

"I'm sorry; I didn't mean to wake you," she said in a low tone. "I just needed to make sure you were okay before I turned in."

Real. She was definitely real. God help him. "What time is it?"

"Just past eleven," she said as she walked forward on those tall streetwalker heels that did great things for her ankles, her hips swaying just enough to have his breath jamming in his throat. Oh yeah, she had great legs, all right, as well as the sweetest ass he'd ever seen.

"Is the party over already?"

"Heavens, no. In fact, when I left, Del and Emory were entertaining everyone with their Fred and Ginger imitation."

It took a moment for her words to build into a mental image of Del and the ex-gangbanger *dancing*. The picture refused to stick. "Del and . . . Scruggs? You're joking?"

"Not at all. For such a huge man, Emory is wonderfully

light on his feet. And Della had every man in the room breathing hard—including the governor."

That he could believe. "Did Max bring you home?"

"No, he offered, but a friend and her husband were leaving then and I caught a ride with them." She glanced at the vial of painkillers on the night table. "I heard Max telling Ernestine that you shouldn't have driven the rig today. He said that's why you have a full-time driver, because driving hurts you too much."

"Max is a fussy old woman."

"He's right, isn't he?"

"I knew I might have a few twinges, yeah." He frowned. "Don't look at me like that, Brina. I'm no hero, just a guy who's been where Jay is more than once. Lucy and J. T. tried to be there for me, so I tried to be there for Jay, that's all."

"Oh, Rhys," she said with a melting look that went a long way toward soothing more aches than the one in his hip. "You really are a love."

He felt something tear inside, releasing feelings he hadn't thought he would ever have again. Feelings that aroused a longing in him so powerful he had trouble breathing. "So, have I squeezed enough sympathy from that soft heart of yours to deserve a kiss?"

"Only one," she murmured before leaning forward to brush her lips over his. His body responded instantly, and he wrapped his arms around her to keep her from escaping. Her body was soft and pliant, and she tasted like wine and chocolate. He was suddenly starving.

"More," he growled an instant before capturing her mouth again. He kissed her until his lungs burned, forcing him to come up for air. His hand shook as he freed her hair from some kind of shiny clip. It sprang free to ripple over his chest.

"I love your hair, honey. It's beautiful and wild, like the passionate woman who lives inside you."

She made a helpless, yearning sound before drawing back.

Her eyes were glazed, her lips parted. He wanted to rush right past foreplay to the part where she took him inside and rode him hard, but despite the urgent little moans, something told him she needed more petting before she would allow herself to shatter for him.

Pulling back, he found the bow at her waist and tugged. "Damn, if I didn't score the prettiest girl at the party." One end of the bow pulled free. His mouth went dry. "I wish I could have danced with you."

Brina's pulse skittered. At the same time he turned slightly so that his erection prodded her thigh. "You're impossible," she protested as she reveled in the feel of the rigid hardness she'd aroused in this self-contained, powerfully confident man.

"But lovable, right?" He smiled to show her he was teasing.

"Infinitely lovable." She inched forward until her mouth hovered over his. Very gently she touched her lips to his mouth.

"More," he murmured while at the same time slipping one hand behind her head, trapping her. "Give me more."

She wanted to do just that, she realized as she leaned into the next kiss, just enough to feel his mouth give under hers. Just enough to send a jolt of heat sizzling through her. Then, because it felt so good, she parted her lips and ran her tongue carefully over the delicious curve of his lower lip, the one that was slightly fuller and definitely sexy.

He went still, and then he groaned, a low, helpless sound that came from deep inside. Simultaneously, his hand cupped her breast. This time she was the one groaning as his thumb worked her nipple back and forth until it was hard and throbbing.

She felt a slow drizzling feeling begin inside her and pressed against the hand doing such wonderful things. Just when she knew she couldn't take any more, he slid his hand inside her dress. She uttered a startled yelp as his fingertips eased beneath the wispy, low-cut bra.

"God, you feel good," he murmured, his voice thick. "I want to see you."

Like a dash of cold water, all the derogatory things John had said about her body came flooding back. She drew back, only to have Rhys frown up at her.

"What?" he asked. "Did I hurt you? I know I'm out of practice, but—"

"You didn't hurt me," she blurted out. "I . . . it's just that I'm out of practice, too." As well as being way, way out of her depth.

He kneaded her thigh, his gaze soft on hers. "So we'll practice together, sweetheart. That's what people do when it's their first time, isn't it?"

She swallowed. The pressure of his hand and the erotic sensations he was arousing in her made it difficult to concentrate. "I don't know. I've only had one first time."

Something changed in his eyes. "My first time was in a brothel in Mexicali when I was twenty-three. The girl who serviced me did just that, serviced me." His brief laugh was tinged with self-mockery. "It wasn't exactly the experience I thought it would be." A significant chunk of his personal view of the world was encapsulated in that terse statement, she guessed.

"What did you expect?" she asked softly.

"I'm not real sure. Maybe to feel something besides disappointment." He lowered his gaze to the hand curled around her thigh. "If you were into fantasy, we could always pretend it was the first time for both of us."

"We could?"

He nodded. "There's something else you need to know." He lifted his hand from her thigh, only to slip it beneath her skirt. Only a sheer layer of nylon came between them.

"What's that?" she asked, intensely aware of the weight of his big hand pressing her flesh.

"This thing with my hip. Mostly I can compensate, but in bed, I'm pretty much stuck with being on the bottom." Though he flavored his words with a laconic humor, she heard the embarrassment under the light touch. "Some ladies find that too much work."

Some ladies were crazy, too. "In other words, forget the *Kama Sutra*?" she said with a teasing smile.

His eyes crinkled. "That's about the size of it, yeah."

"Uh, I suppose we should talk about safe sex."

"I believe in it, if that's what you mean."

"Me, too." She drew a shaky breath. "I should probably tell you I had myself tested after I found out that John had been cheating on me. I'm . . . um, well, safe."

"Me, too," he said, sliding his hand up her thigh. She gasped when his fingertips brushed the delta between her thighs. "Feel good?" he asked, watching her eyes to see what pleasured her best.

"Wonderful," she murmured in a dreamy voice.

"Think it might feel even better without the panty hose?"

She took a breath and nodded. "Does this mean I have to strip in front of you?"

That odd look appeared in his eyes again. "Oh, honey, that would make this old boy purely ecstatic, but seeing that it's your first time and you might be shy, there's a robe in the bathroom yonder if you want to use it."

It seemed downright silly for a woman who'd been married eleven years and borne two children to feel awkward in the bedroom, but silly or not, that's exactly how she felt. "If you wouldn't mind."

"Honey, I don't care what you do as long as you do it quick." For emphasis, he rubbed his erection against her, only to let out a shuddering groan. "That just might have been a mistake," he said, his eyes glittering.

She laughed as she got off the bed. "I'll hurry," she promised, matching her actions to her words.

"Brina?"

She stopped and turned. "Change your mind already?"

"God, no! I just wanted to tell you that you'll find a package of condoms in the black leather kit on the shelf."

After she disappeared into the bathroom and closed the door, Rhys slipped one hand under the pillow. He figured it wouldn't last, this miracle. Nothing he cared about ever did. The secret was not letting himself feel too deeply or want more than he could produce on his own. As long as this thing between the two of them was grounded in sex, he could handle the fallout okay when it ended.

The door creaked open, and she walked out, bundled from neck to toe in the navy blue robe Del had given him last Christmas. The hem trailed on the floor, and she'd rolled back the sleeves.

"Honey, maybe you'd better put the Do Not Disturb sign on that connecting door yonder and lock it, too, just in case Del decides to check on me before she goes to bed."

"Oh Lord, I never thought of that," she muttered as she hurried across the room.

When she returned to the bed, she took the foil packet from the robe pocket, then looked at him shyly. "Do I give this to you now or what?"

"Put it on the table." He smiled. "John never used rubbers before you were married?"

"I made him wait until we were married. By that time I was on the pill."

Fighting a deep envy for a jerk who didn't come close to deserving such a gift from this very special woman, he reached up to tug on the robe's sash. "I really need to see you," he said, watching her eyes for a sign of reluctance—or, God forbid, fear.

The vulnerable look that crossed her face broke his heart. "Don't expect too much, okay?" she said.

"Would it help if I told you I think you are the most beautiful woman I've ever wanted to take to bed?" he asked, letting her hear the need in his voice. He opened the robe a few inches, watching her reaction. When she didn't protest, he opened it far enough to glimpse her breasts. Desire shot through him like a high-voltage jolt, and his breath hissed in. Her breasts were lush and full, tipped with dusky nipples just begging to be sucked.

"Take off the robe, Brina," he ordered, struggling to keep his voice steady. "Please."

She frowned slightly, then stood up and removed the heavy robe, letting it fall to the floor at her feet. In the subtle glow of reflected light her skin had a porcelain perfection he longed to touch. In contrast to her full breasts, her waist seemed tiny before flaring into hips so curvy his mouth watered. Her legs were a work of art, sleek and sexy, with perfect curves and slender ankles. "God help me," he murmured, skimming his gaze over the luscious shape.

His hand actually trembled as he lifted the sheet to let her scoot in next to him. Her hair brushed his jaw and he drew in her scent. "How about another kiss to get us in the mood?" he prompted, playing with a lock of dark, silky hair.

"Are you always this bossy?" she asked as she snuggled closer.

"Yep. It's in the CEO manual." He kissed her then, taking the initiative away from her. He was too close to exploding to wait much longer. But first, he wanted to see her shatter for him.

"You taste sweet," he murmured against her mouth as she relaxed against him. The soft pressure of those glorious breasts against his chest felt about as good as anything could, he thought as he threaded his hands into her hair and angled her head to give him better access.

Her mouth was soft and eager and hot, moving under his. Her hands found his shoulders, her fingers opening and closing against his skin like a kitten kneading a rug. The pleasure-pain sensation aroused by her blunt nails raking his flesh was as erotic as anything he'd ever had done to him before.

Gently, reverently, he ran his hand down her spine, enthralled with the ripe female shape that seemed made just for him. Her skin was warm and satin smooth. She shivered when he ran his finger over the cleft separating her rounded buttocks.

He drew back, needing to see her face. Her eyes were pleasure glazed, her lips full and slightly parted. There was a sexy little frown between her brows, and a frantic pulse fluttered in her throat.

"You feel so good," he managed to get out through a throat constricted by feelings almost too powerful to accept. "I wanted this the moment I saw you."

"Me, too." He heard the truth in her voice and was lost.

With a harsh groan, he took her mouth again, kissing her until her lips were as swollen as his. At the same time he reached between them to stroke her belly, moving lower and lower with each stroke, his fingertips ruffling the soft hair between her thighs. Her breathing became labored as she rubbed herself against his hand.

He thrust a finger into her, and she gasped, drawing her mouth from his in order to bury her face against his shoulder. Calling on every ounce of control he possessed, he managed to block out the demands of his own body as he stroked her into readiness. Her fingers clutched at his hair, tugging and kneading in a private frenzy she couldn't seem to control. When she was wet and panting, he inserted a second finger and stroked faster.

She cried out incoherently, close, so close. He strained against a violent need to seek the release his body demanded as he stroked deeper. He felt the tiny tremors shivering against his fingers an instant before she shattered, her mouth pressing against his shoulder to muffle her scream.

He winced, his control stretched whisper thin. Her legs trembled, and he kneaded the soft mound at the apex of her thighs, bringing her to climax quickly this time. She shuddered, then went limp, her mouth open against his shoulder. He felt her moist breath as she murmured his name.

He wanted to hold her, to savor the feeling of her warm, sweet body covering him like a blanket, but his engorged penis felt as though it would burst if he didn't bury himself deep inside her now.

Awkwardly, he reached out a hand and fumbled for the foil packet. Using his teeth, he ripped it open, then managed to work it over his penis with one hand. When he was ready, he used both hands to raise her hips. As she murmured something indistinct, he cursed his lack of mobility before saying thickly, "Lift up a little, honey."

She went to her knees, then slowly moved down his body, her breasts pulling the hairs on his chest. Her thigh slid fluidly over his, brushing his penis as she straddled him. He shuddered, then arched his head back, fighting to hang on long enough to feel himself sliding into her.

"Help me, sweetheart."

"How?"

"Guide me in."

He felt her hand curling around him while at the same time she adjusted her hips and spread her legs wider. He clutched the mattress and arched his back against the desperate need to thrust into her. Soft pubic hair whispered against the tip of his penis as she settled over him, taking him inside little by little until he was nearly crazed with the need to move.

"Sweetheart, I . . . can't . . . wait . . . much . . . longer," he managed to push out through a tight jaw.

When she was fully seated, she leaned forward, sliding her thighs against his. Her hands clutched the pillow as she began to move. He fought to hold off his climax until she reached hers, but his mind was fogging. Just when he knew he would fail her, her breath came out in a long, incoherent rush and he felt the internal spasms telling him she'd reached a climax again. His own came in an explosion of pleasure so great he couldn't seem to stop shuddering. Only then did she collapse against him, her skin wet from exertion and her hair plastered to her head.

His hand trembled as he smoothed the damp silk away from her face. He felt emotion well up inside him, along with words he'd never said to any woman. He bit them back, knowing that to actually say them would be a mistake. In his mind, though, they shimmered just beyond his reach, like the elusive miracle of home and family that would never be his.

Brina was still sleeping when Rhys made the trip back to bed after disposing of the condom. Her hair was spread out on the pillow with the fussy lace that had made him feel like a sissy whenever he'd felt it brush his face in the night. Tonight, however, it seemed appropriate, somehow—a bed fit for a lady. *His* lady, at least for the time he was allowed to be in her life.

Emotion bunched in his chest once more, so strong it was a physical ache. Setting his jaw, he lowered himself carefully to the mattress. He sat unmoving, wondering if he should wake her. Since her kids weren't home, he gave in to the need to feel her next to him for a little longer and slipped in next to her. He longed to stroke her awake and make love to her again, but anything more strenuous than breathing was beyond him. Tomorrow, he promised himself as he curled himself around her and closed his eyes.

Brina woke to find the room still bathed in moonglow, her body drenched in heat and sweat. Rhys' sweat as well as his body heat, she realized as she lifted her head and looked at the man sprawled next to her. He was on his back, the covers bunched below his navel again, one hand buried under the pillow. The other clutched the sheet between them as though it were a lifeline.

In the silvery light she could see drops of sweat glistening on his chest and pearling on his forehead. His chest rose and fell in a jerky, fast rhythm, and a low, guttural sound came from his throat, as though he were struggling against some unseen enemy. He was clearly suffering, but was the pain physical or emotional?

She gnawed her lip, unsure how to help him. Finally, she reached out a hand to touch his shoulder. "Rhys, wake up," she whispered in the same nonthreatening voice that soothed her children from their occasional bad dreams.

At the sound of her voice he jerked violently, his eyes snapping open. His entire body tensed as one hand came up to grab her wrist. Pain shot up her arm from the viselike grip of his strong fingers, and she cried out. The unfocused look in his eyes disappeared instantly, replaced by a confused concern.

"Brina?" His voice was rusty. "What's wrong?"

"It looked like you were having a nightmare."

"Sorry," he said, easing his grip. "Happens sometimes." He drew her hand to his mouth and kissed the place on the inside of her wrist that still tingled from the pressure of his hand.

"Would it help to talk about it?"

"Nope. I'd rather kiss you good night again." He rolled to his side and found her mouth.

Chapter 20

At six fifteen the next morning Rhys had just taken the first sip of his second cup of coffee when he heard her footsteps on the back stairs. It was downright pathetic, the way his heart took off racing and his body quickened at the thought of holding her again. Which was exactly what he intended to do as soon as possible.

"Good morning," she murmured, her still drowsy gaze searching his face before skittering toward the mug he'd laid out for her.

"How are you feeling?" she asked as she filled the mug, then stirred in sugar.

He studied the soft contours of the throat he'd explored with his mouth. "Guess that depends on you."

That brought her gaze back to his. "On me? Why?"

He could smell her, roses and warm, sleepy woman. "Because I've spent the last two hours wondering if you were having second thoughts about sleeping with me."

"Only constantly," she blurted out.

A grim disappointment was a hard-knuckled fist grinding against his sternum. He covered it by taking a slow sip of coffee. "Is that why you were gone when I woke up?" he asked when he had himself in hand again.

She gave a little laugh. "No, that was strictly an act of mercy."

He frowned. "You want to explain that?"

"Oh my, you really do have a way of turning dangerous from one instant to the next. It's rather . . . amazing actually." She took a sip, watching him with eyes that were no longer drowsy. "It's the eyes, mostly, and the way your mouth gets stern. If I didn't know what a pussycat you are under all that prowling intensity, I'd be hightailing it for cover right about now."

"The term 'pussycat' refers to a female feline," he said stiffly, only to have those brown eyes sparkle even more brightly.

"You idiot, can't you tell when someone is teasing you?"

He felt some of the frustration ease off. "Evidently not," he said carefully.

She sighed. "I went back to my own bed because I very much wanted to make love again, and I knew you needed time to heal." She smiled. "*That* was the aforementioned act of mercy. Which I am now in the process of regretting."

He hid his relief behind a grin. "Someone told me once that regret is a useless waste of energy unless it's accompanied by an act of contrition." He reached out to tug on a stray curl caressing her jawline, deliberately allowing his fingers to brush her throat. Her breath caught, sending his hopes soaring.

"I've always hated to waste anything, especially energy," she said in a breathy voice.

"In that case . . ." He set his mug on the counter, plucked hers from her hand and put it next to his before pulling her into his arms. "Good morning, sweetheart," he murmured before bending his head. "I've missed you." Her lashes fluttered down, and at the same time she made a soft, yearning sound that wound around his heart.

Her mouth was soft and eager, sending a jolt of pure elation running through him. To his surprise, the joy was more consuming than the heat gathering in his groin. Her small, capable hands skimmed up his arms to his neck, and she pressed closer, crushing those gloriously full breasts against his chest. Another soft, helpless moan escaped her lips as she rubbed her pelvis against his erection.

The kiss turned wild, a frantic mating of lips and tongues that had his lungs starved for air and his skin turning hot. Barely hanging on to his control, he pushed backward until she was jammed against the counter. Bracing on his good leg, he tugged her T-shirt free of her jeans, and cupped his palm over her breast. Her skin was hot silk under the lace of her bra, her nipple hardened by a response as involuntary as the bulge straining his fly.

He'd only intended to kiss her, he reminded himself as he slid his hand down her smooth, warm midriff to her waistband. *It's foolish to do more than kiss her,* he told himself as he slipped the button free. *In the kitchen.* He slid down the zipper. *Where anyone could surprise us.* His hand splayed over her belly even as he struggled to pull back. "Brina, we need to stop."

Brina heard the strangled note of desperation in his voice and knew what it was like to be female in the most primitive sense. His hand trembled where it was spread wide against her navel, his palm warming her skin. She felt the heat of him pouring through his shirt and saw the hot licks of hunger in those flint gray eyes.

"Jay and Marcy are still asleep, and anyway, not even a ghost can get down those back stairs without being heard."

"Sweetheart—" She smothered the protest she sensed was coming by opening her mouth over his. He made a dark sound deep in his throat and then his free hand gripped the back of her head, holding her still as he plunged his tongue deep into her mouth.

Her hand fumbled with his belt buckle, then his zipper. When his jeans fell open, exposing his dark blue boxer shorts, she reached through the opening to free his thick, engorged erection. He was hot and hard and when she squeezed him gently, he jerked; then with an inarticulate cry he stilled her hand with his own.

"You sure you want to do this now?" he demanded, his face taut.

"Very sure," she managed, reaching for him again. "In fact, I . . . insist."

He choked a laugh as he deflected her hand with his. "Patience, sweetheart. First I need to get you as ready as I am." He kissed her hard, then tugged first her jeans, then her panties over her hips. She felt the cold wood against her buttocks as he slipped his hand between her legs, spreading her thighs far enough to allow his fingers to stroke her.

She gasped at the sheer sweetness of the sensation surging through her, and her head fell back. Deep inside, some secret, fragile part of her that had lain dormant even during her marriage burst free, allowing indescribably wonderful ripples and surges to flow through her.

"That's it, love, let it go," he ordered, his voice low and urgent. "Let me see what you feel." He inserted one finger, then two, working them in and out in a smooth, slow rhythm that seemed to spiral around and through her. At the same time his thumb rubbed her engorged clitoris, and she felt a restless urgency building inside, forcing her to move against his hand.

She clutched his neck, her body trembling. "My knees are jelly," she whispered shakily, then whimpered when he withdrew his hand.

"Easy, love." She felt his hands on her waist and then she was suddenly sitting on the counter. He pushed her jeans lower, splayed her legs wider. Embarrassed, she tried to close her legs, only to have him slide his hands over her inner thighs. Her protest was swallowed by his mouth as he kissed her long and hard and deep.

At the same time he explored her with his fingers, rubbing the sensitive bud slowly at first and then, when she moaned, faster and faster until she felt herself squirming.

He stopped then, replacing his fingers with the velvet tip of his penis. She gasped as he pushed a few inches into her. He trembled, then moaned as he withdrew.

"No, don't go," she protested, clutching his shoulders to pull him closer.

"I can't protect you," he said, his voice thick. "I had no idea—"

She groaned, only to gasp as he suddenly pushed her onto her back. The counter was cold against her back, and her head banged into the flour canister. At the same time she felt his mouth on her, sucking and kissing her, his tongue thrusting into her. She felt the climax coming, and pushed her fist against her mouth to keep from crying out. His hands held her hips as he thrust deeper, driving her over the edge.

She gasped, then gasped again as another, stronger climax shook her. Tiny ripples surged through her as she threaded her fingers through his thick hair. She whimpered with pleasure as he kissed her thigh.

He straightened then and gazed down at her. "You look just like the picture over the fireplace in the room where I sleep," he said with a crooked grin, his eyes dark with tenderness. "My beautiful, sexy, mysterious lady."

"I feel beautiful," she whispered, reaching for his hand. "And deliciously naughty." She kissed his palm and smelled herself on his fingers. It was amazingly erotic. Almost as erotic as the sight of his still engorged body thrusting through the opening in his shorts. "Let me return the favor," she said, sitting up.

Rhys felt his body react, even as he caught her hand before she could touch him. "Tonight, after everyone's asleep," he said, his voice thick. He heard the thud of sneakers on the top stairs a split second before she stiffened. His mind yowled in protest as they drew apart like guilty teenagers impaled by a cop's flashlight.

"Damn," he muttered, pushing his privates into his shorts and zipping his jeans, buckling his belt.

Her face was flushed and her eyes were still cloudy with passion as she leaped down and pulled up her panties and jeans.

"Go away with me this weekend, any place you say."

"I can't," she said, fumbling to tuck in her shirt. "Cindy has tonsillitis, and I don't have anyone to substitute for me."

"Put the colonel in charge."

"Colonel Fitz? Running the inn?"

"Why not? He's spent half his life giving orders. Give him forty-eight hours, and he'll have this motley crew spit polishing shoes and bouncing quarters off beds."

She shot him a startled look, then broke out laughing. "It would almost be worth risking my reputation as an innkeeper to see that."

"Say yes, sweetheart," he urged as sneakers pounded down the next set of stairs.

"I want to say yes, with my entire heart and soul and still quivering body, but I just can't. But I love you dearly for offering."

When Jay burst into the room a few seconds later, she was in the pantry, humming to herself as she banged pots around. Rhys hadn't moved. He was still trying to deal with that damn word. Love.

J. T. figured it was the smell of frying bacon that had drawn him out of the best sleep he'd had in years. With his Lucy love curled up next to him, sated and warm from his loving, it hadn't mattered a fig that the bed was too small for the likes of his hulking great body. Life could be sweet, he thought, turning onto his back. Sunlight warmed his face, drawing his gaze to the window. She'd opened the drapes, he noticed, affording him a perfect view of the mountains.

He yawned, then stretched before throwing off the covers.

Saints be praised, he'd been as randy as a boy last night, and randy he was again this morning. Twice he'd loved her last night, and twice she'd shuddered and shrieked as passion had ripped through her. Wild she'd been and wild she'd made him. Sixty-nine he was now, yet she'd made him feel spring green and joyful.

Padding naked into the bathroom, he vowed to bed her often from now on, but not as his mistress. No, he wouldn't shame her that way, he decided as he turned on the shower and stepped under the spray. This very morning he would ask her to be his wife.

Lucy had just set a steaming frittata on the table when J. T. walked into her white-and-yellow kitchen. To his immense surprise—and delight—she wore only a thin red robe splashed with bright orange and pink roses. Every time she moved, the material seemed to shimmer like a sunset over water.

"It's about time you stirred yourself into action," she grumbled, but her eyes held a sated smile that warmed his soul.

"Top o' the morning to you, me beauty," he replied, and hooked his arm around her waist. She let out a startled squeak an instant before he covered her mouth with his.

She resisted for only a moment before returning his kiss with a satisfying fervor. By the time he ran out of air and was forced to draw back, she'd wound herself around him like a bright ribbon, and his cock was standing at eager attention.

"Come back to bed with me, darlin'," he urged while framing her face with hands he feared were too rough for her still flawless skin.

She shook her head. "It's tempting, I admit, but I have to open the shop in a little more than an hour."

"So you'll be a little late. It's your shop."

"It's been my shop for the past forty years. Starting it, making a success of it, helped me regain my self-esteem. Just because we've had one night of sex doesn't mean I'm going to change my entire life."

"But that's exactly what I woke up intending to ask you to do." He was suddenly beset with an attack of nerves. "Marry me, darlin'," he blurted out before courage deserted him. "Lie with me every night and wake with me every morning. Let me show my love in all the ways a husband can and should."

Her jaw dropped, and her eyes went blank for the span of a breath before she regained her composure. "It's sweet of you to ask, and I'm perfectly willing to sleep with you as often as we can arrange it." Before he could gather his wits, she had broken free of his grasp to fetch the coffeepot. "We'd better eat before this gets cold," she said as she poured. "Oh, the juice. It's in the fridge."

"Hang the juice, woman, it's a wedding I'm wanting!" he roared in rising frustration.

"Stop glaring at me and pour the juice." After returning the coffeepot to the warmer, she pulled out a chair and sat down.

He stalked to the table and loomed over her. "You, a respectable woman all your life, you're telling me you'd rather live in sin than marry me?"

"Sin has nothing to do with consensual sex, John Thomas!" Her jaw set and her chin edged out. Her green eyes warned him not to push her.

"It's in love with you, I am, Lucille Steinberg, and I refuse to dishonor you by sleeping with you again without benefit of clergy."

"I didn't see any priest in my bedroom last night blessing the marriage bed," she declared. "And you certainly weren't reciting any vows when you were pounding me into the mattress at three this morning."

"Blast it, woman, didn't you hear me? I love you!"

"Bah! You're just horny."

"That I am. And I'll stay that way until it's my ring on your finger and the priest has given us God's blessing."

"Never!"

In the back of his head he heard the clamoring of generations of Sullivan men, urging him to throw her over his shoulder and carry her off to the nearest justice of the peace. Because he knew she would never forgive him if he did that, he turned on his heel and stalked out of her kitchen.

"Don't you dare walk out on me again, John Thomas Sullivan," she shouted as he jerked open the front door.

Grinning, he took great delight in rattling the very shingles on the house as he slammed the door behind him.

Sherri had already left for her morning workout when John stumbled into the bathroom to take a shower. She still hadn't returned by the time he went downstairs in search of strong coffee and an even stronger Bloody Mary. He went to the kitchen first, only to find it empty and the coffeemaker untouched, a sure sign his old man hadn't come home last night.

It was disgusting as hell, thinking about his dad screwing that dried-up old prune he'd taken to the governor's party. Still, if Lucy did manage to snare the old man, she sure as shit wouldn't move into a home with another woman's stamp on it, which would leave this place for Sherri and him. Like Mother always said, Lucy had the taste of a peasant, which meant she probably wouldn't want the furniture either. Wouldn't take much to convince J. T. to leave it here.

Heading for the den to fix the Bloody Mary, John ran his fingers over his mother's prized rosewood table next to the front door. According to the insurance appraisal he'd "just happened to see" on her desk a few years back, it was worth a cool six grand. He figured it would bring in a lot more at auction now. Selling it, as well as some of the other antiques on the list, would help, although he doubted he could raise the entire nut he owed Sarge. Maybe if he showed the bastard the appraisal and promised to sign over the 'Vette once the loan was repaid, Sarge would be willing to wait for his money. It might not be the best angle to work, but it was the only one he'd come up with so far.

Giving thought to how to nudge his old man into making an honest woman out of judgmental old Lucy, John poured vodka into a water glass, added a splash of Bloody Mary mix and stirred it in with his finger before taking a fast drink.

The sharp crack of the kitchen door slamming had him letting out a groan. "Rise and shine, honeybunch," Sherri called up the stairs. "You promised to take me to brunch at that new place in Cashmere, remember?"

"I'm in here, babe," he called, only to wince as pain crashed through his head.

She was smiling when she entered, a towel looped around her neck, her fantastic body encased in hot pink spandex shorts and a matching sports bra.

"Mmm, yummy, a Bloody Mary! Fix me one, too, will you, lover?" she said before kissing him full on the mouth.

Gallantly he extended his glass. "Here, take this one, babe. I'll make myself another one."

He watched as she swallowed, then licked the residue from her lips. "Guess what, honeybunch?"

Her expression reminded him of a little girl bursting with a secret she couldn't wait to tell. "What, baby doll?"

She set her glass on the bar in order to put her arms around his waist. "Well, see, I just *happened* to stop by the Lexus dealership a couple of weeks ago, to check the new models, you know? There was this totally gorgeous silver LS 430, and this really sweet guy Dick said his manager was in a dealing mood so why not take advantage of it. I think he thought he could talk me into going out with him if he did right by me." Her eyes took on a lustful glow that had icy fingers clawing John's gut.

"Jesus Christ, Sherri, tell me you didn't sign anything!"

"Now don't you go getting all stern with your Sherri Bear, love," she protested, eyes full of promise as she rotated her pelvis against his groin. "Hmm, you feel good, lover. And you do owe me a fuck from last night."

He broke out in a cold sweat. The heat in his loins made it hard to concentrate. "Just how good a deal did this guy make you?"

She bubbled over with pride. "With all the extras I wanted, the list price was just under sixty. The manager—Jim—knocked off almost fifteen for the Beamer, which was way above blue book and—"

"You traded my BMW?" he exclaimed hoarsely.

"You said it was mine, remember? You even signed it over to me."

To keep the debt collectors from repoing it, you stupid—he pulled himself up short. Sherri had no idea how precarious things were right now.

"Did I do wrong, Johnny?" The mouth that could suck him dry in minutes turned down in a little-girl pout. "Do you want me to go back to that nice Dick guy and see if I can cancel the deal?"

He could just hear the talk now. *John Sullivan's fiancée had to cancel the deal on a new Lexus because John's ass is deep in debt and sinking fast.* Never mind that it was true. If word got out, his credit would dry up faster than an old lady's twat, and then there'd be no way in hell he'd ever get well.

"Hey, I was only joshing with you, babe. I'm as proud as I can be at the way you fast-talked such a sweet deal out of that guy."

She gave a delighted squeal and fastened her mouth to his. Whatever he'd intended to say went right out of his mind. He took her right there on the floor, with his mother in a portrait looking down at them.

By midnight John still hadn't come up with a way to raise the money he needed. Deciding to sleep on it, he downed the last of his drink and got to his feet. The fact that he staggered over that simple act took time to register on his scotch-fogged brain.

The cell phone he'd left on the bar earlier rang just as he reached for the light switch. "Has to be a wrong number," he muttered and considered ignoring it before deciding he would enjoy ripping the hide off the asshole on the other end.

He changed his mind when the caller identified himself.

"Hello, Sarge," he said coolly, despite the fear wedged like a lump of greasy meat in his throat. "What can I do for you?"

"Now you asking that question, that surprises me some. Yes sir, it surely does, considering our agreement."

"What agreement is that?" he bluffed.

Sarge's voice took on an ugly edge. "Don't try to jack me around, Johnny boy. According to my book, what you dropped yesterday brings you up to fifty-two large owing. I've given you more wiggle room than most, but your time has about run out."

John swallowed the sudden surge of panic. "I've told Red and now I'm telling you, I'm no welsher."

"Red thinks you are. Me, I'd be willing to accept your word, but Red's the nervous type. Might be a good idea to come by tomorrow early to reassure him. Otherwise, he just might have to come looking for you."

Chapter 21

Sarge's Place opened at six a.m. Most mornings when Red Sturgess unlocked the door, the hard-core regulars were already waiting. This Monday in May was no exception.

An early riser since his boot camp days, Sarge Stenner had been in his cramped office at the rear of the bar since daybreak, toting up the wins and losses on the action he'd taken over the weekend. By his rough count the house was ahead by some twenty grand. Fifty percent of that was his, while Red got forty. The remaining ten percent would go into the contingency fund.

It was the same arrangement him and Red had had since meeting up in the late seventies in Mexico City, where they'd both been assigned to the security detail at the American embassy. Smuggling had been their game then, usually duty-free cigarettes stolen a few cartons at a time from embassy supplies. In those days they'd used courier planes shuttling daily from Mexico to Washington, D.C., to move the merchandise.

Once Sarge had retired after his twenty years in the service, he'd come back to Osuma and bought a run-down café across from the old Hollister sawmill and turned it into a bar. Red joined him three years later after his own retirement. Times had been great those first few years. The two of them had their own version of a cartel right here in the valley. Instead of coke, they'd dealt mainly in blue-collar dope like hash, pot and crystal meth. Payments from the contingency fund to the then chief of police had made them bulletproof.

Then, twelve effing years ago, the ungrateful cop bastard had choked to death on a chicken bone at a Kiwanis dinner, and his replacement, a former Osuma High School classmate of Sarge's by the name of Brody Hollister, had brought down the hammer on drug trafficking in his jurisdiction. Since then, the stuttering ape had conducted a systematic campaign of harassment that Sarge managed to laugh off. Privately, though, he'd given serious thought to taking the man out. Only the fact that Hollister laid off on busting him for his bookmaking as well as the back room poker game was keeping the man alive.

Feeling pleased with his morning's work, Sarge locked his tally book in the bottom drawer of his desk along with the cash he'd taken in payoffs yesterday. The contingency fund had been seriously depleted over the past weeks, having paid for false IDs and passports for him and Red as well as two first-class one-way tickets from Pangborn to Suva on the island of Fiji. The dates on the tickets had been left open, but if everything shook out the way he'd planned it, him and Red would be on a plane by this time next month, a cool two million plus tucked away in their accounts in Lucerne.

After taking a cigar from the wooden box on the desk and lighting up, he punched out a number in Vancouver, B.C. Pacific Rim Trading Post, Ltd., had been in business for nearly sixty years, importing cheap novelties and gifts from China and Taiwan for resale to markets in both Canada and the Western U.S. Both warehouse and offices were housed in a turn-of-the-century brick structure located near the Port of Vancouver where the goods were off-loaded.

Three months ago Pacific Rim had been bought out by Cascade Imports of Oakland, California. The buyer's name was William G. Jones—aka Gunnar "Sarge" Stenner. It was a name he'd used before for his various schemes. Although the company was little more than a paper shell, it had the one thing Sarge needed to make this deal work—a dilapidated warehouse in an industrial section of Oakland.

"Pacific Rim Trading." The voice on the other end was young and female.

"Get me Chang, will ya, dollface?"

"Hang on, okay?"

He had to hand it to that sneaky slit-eyed SOB; the man figured all the angles. *I hire only the young and stupid, my friend. They soon tire of working and quit. I then hire another. No one is around long enough to remember faces or names.*

"Chang here."

"Po, it's Sarge Stenner. How's it going?"

"Very well, my friend. The ship arrived as scheduled on Saturday. The merchandise was transferred to our warehouse without—how did you put it?—without a hitch."

"Very good." Good? It was fucking *great!* His highest payoff yet.

"And of course you checked the quality?"

"Of course. It was as promised, the highest grade available." Chang paused, then asked, "May I inquire how arrangements are proceeding at your end?"

"Slick as snot." Still smiling, Sarge swiveled his chair toward the window. "My guy in California is eager to take delivery, and I'm working on transportation. I know it's a pisser having to wait for a few more weeks, but like I said, it's a damn sight smarter to wait for the perfect setup instead of taking a chance on second-best."

"We Chinese invented patience, my friend." Chang chuckled. "I shall await your call, shall I?"

Yes, you fucking well shall. "Sounds good, buddy. As soon as things are nailed down, I'll give you the heads up."

After hanging up, Sarge flexed his tight shoulders and felt some of the tension ease off. Like he'd told Sturgess when they started tossing around the idea of this gig, *No guts, no big payoff.*

The endgame starts now, he thought, taking a cigar from the box on his desk. After biting off the tip, he lit up, then drew in a mouthful of smoke. As he savored the taste, he watched Sullivan's Corvette pull into the lot.

Rolling the cigar between his pursed lips, he watched that arrogant A-hole lock the driver's door. Like he'd told Red, he'd worked Sullivan real careful-like, counting on the man's arrogance and compulsion to play long odds to lead him deeper and deeper into debt.

A grimace tightened his facial muscles as he recalled yesterday's Giants-Cubs game. Red had handed him a ration of shit for taking Sullivan's bet, but Sarge had had confidence in Sullivan's ability to pick losers. Still, he'd been sweating bullets before Sosa had nailed a hanging curve, sending it over the center field fence to win the game for the Cubs. Even Red had let out a yell.

Face relaxing into a grin, he drew the pigsticker from its hand-tooled sheath and placed it on the desk blotter so that it would be the first thing Sullivan saw when he walked in. Then, anticipation building, he picked up the phone and dialed the number that rang behind the bar.

Red answered on the first ring. "Sarge's Place."

"Our pigeon's just arrived, right on time. Appreciate it if you'd send him on back for his plucking."

Red chuckled. "Got to hand it to you, partner. You called it right."

Oh yeah, Sullivan thought he could outsmart God, and maybe he could. What he couldn't do was outsmart a marine. Semper fucking fi!

Instead of parking in his usual spot in the northwest corner of the lot, John pulled around back where the easily recognizable Corvette would be hidden from view—at least from passersby. The last thing he needed was a reputation as a morning boozer.

A couple of late-model 4WD pickups sat near the rear exit, along with an overflowing Dumpster and a pile of empty booze cartons. After turning off the ignition he sat behind the wheel for a couple of seconds while his stomach settled itself. The two fingers of scotch he'd downed before leaving the house had taken the edge off his raw fear, but they had played hell with his empty stomach.

After mulling over possible options, he'd come to realize that running was the worst thing he could do. A man starting a new job didn't disappear for no reason. If he cut loose, his dad would be sure to suspect foul play and file a missing person's report. He didn't know how such things worked, but it was a good bet the cops would want to dig into his past history looking for clues—including his financial records. What if it all came out then? The gambling losses, eight years of taking kickbacks from Crank Brothers Fruit Brokers for throwing them sweetheart deals? The thought of his dad finding out that his partner—his son—had been systematically cheating him for almost as long as he'd worked for Sullivan's made him shudder inside.

After locking and carefully covering the Corvette against the dust, he pocketed his keys and headed around to the front door, his stride confident, his head high. Anyone watching from the bar's dirty windows would see a man clearly in charge of his own destiny—and *not,* like that bastard Sarge thought, a loser with his balls in a vise.

Inside the barroom, the air was already dense with smoke. Behind the bar, Red Sturgess flicked a quick glance at him. The look in those slanted yellow eyes didn't change, but John was immediately reminded of a rattler hiding in the weeds, coiled and ready to strike.

Poker face in place, John scanned the faces of the hard-core boozers gathered at one end of the bar, drinking their breakfast. Relieved to find none of them looked familiar, he headed for his favorite spot near the TV.

Sturgess ambled over, eyes glittering malice beneath the pronounced brow ridges. "Come in for an eye-opener, did you, Mr. Sullivan?"

John bit back the foul insult that came to mind. "Has Sarge come in yet?"

Red leaned closer, his lips taking on a mocking twist. "In his office. Said if you had the guts to show up, you was to go on back."

Without bothering to respond, John walked toward the rear where twin pool tables stood side by side, the balls racked and ready. Beyond the tables was the entrance to the hallway separating the barroom proper from three medium-sized rooms and a unisex bathroom. The hallway itself was a dark, narrow tunnel leading to an emergency exit, presently blocked by cases of beer stacked shoulder-high.

The bathroom door, the only one visible from the barroom, had been propped open, presumably to allow the fumes of strong disinfectant to escape. Inside the dingy cubicle, Wayne "Spider" Makepeace was cleaning the urinal. His clothes were dirty, and like always, he stank of sweat and stale booze. Christ, didn't the man have any pride? John thought as Makepeace glanced up.

"Well, if it ain't the Golden Boy hisself." Makepeace had a cracker accent that never failed to grate on John's nerves.

During his marriage, whenever Brina had had her father and his chief mechanic to dinner, John had made a point to be someplace else. After dropping the grungy toilet brush in a dented bucket of dirty water, the skinny old sot pulled a pint bottle from the back pocket of his filthy work trousers and twisted off the top. "A bit early for poker, ain't it, Johnny?" he taunted before tipping the bottle to his lips for a long swallow.

"Finally found yourself a job suited to your talents, did you, Spider?" John tossed off as he strode past.

"Leastways I never sponged off my old man like you done all your life!"

The taunt caught up with John as he passed the door labeled STORAGE. Furious, he was sorely tempted to shove that dirty brush up the old man's ass, but he couldn't afford the distraction. Prioritization was one of the three major keys to his success—along with focus on the job at hand, and the guts to take calculated risks.

The door marked OFFICE was closed. Aware that Makepeace was watching, he rapped impatiently.

"Come," Sarge called from within.

Nearly identical in size to the room next door, the office appeared to do double duty as a storage space. A large built-in cupboard covered most of the east wall, while cases of cheap Washington State wine stacked three high lined the west. Several broken chairs had been piled in one corner.

The son of a logger, Sarge Stenner was a massively muscled man with a brutally short buzz cut the color of dirty grease, thin bloodless lips and a meat hook nose. His huge arms sported tattoos, some patriotic, some obscene. Dressed in a tight black T-shirt and black jeans, he sat behind a gunmetal gray desk, a half-smoked cigar burning in an ashtray fashioned from the brass casing of an artillery shell.

Dead center on the worn blotter where John couldn't miss it lay a Bowie knife. The obvious attempt at intimidation was more amusing than effective.

"Now, ain't this a nice surprise," the ex-marine drawled in a tobacco-ruined baritone.

Deciding his only hope lay in seizing the initiative, John pulled up one of the wooden straight-backed chairs and settled into it. "Tell you what, Sarge, seeing as how we've been doing business for a long time, I'll cut you for what I owe. Double or nothing."

Sarge took another drag before butting the smoke in the tray. "You got *cajones* the size of baseballs—I'll give you that." He leaned back, his eyes hard on John's face. "Come to settle your account?"

"I'm selling the 'Vette this afternoon," he lied. "I'll have the money for you by eight tonight."

Sarge snorted. "I'm not that gullible, asshole. By eight tonight you could be in Rio."

"By eight tonight a lot of things could have happened."

"True." Sarge took a cigarette from the pack in his breast pocket and lit it with an old-fashioned nickel-plated lighter. Exhaling, he tossed the lighter to the blotter and leaned back. He took several more drags, a thoughtful look on his battered features while the air grew thick with smoke. "Might be you have a point, about us doing business for a while now. Might even go so far as to say you've been one of my most faithful customers, and like the saying goes, us marines set great store in being faithful."

He took a quick drag before flicking a glance toward a large framed photograph hanging on the wall to the left of the grimy window. "See them guys in that there picture? They're what you call four-oh gyrenes. Real loyal, every last one of 'em. The corporal on the end, the one holding the M16, he was one hell of a good guy. Always trying to work a deal to make life sweeter for himself and his buddies, if you know what I mean."

John played along. "Hey, I'm in sales. Working deals is what I do best."

Sarge laughed. "Yeah, I figured that already. Which is why I'm willing to let you work off what you owe—and, while you're at it, make yourself richer than you ever imagined."

Five minutes after Sullivan left, Sarge returned his blade to its sheath and left his office, locking the door the way he always did, even when he was only a few steps away.

As he withdrew the key, he heard a faint sound and sensed a presence. Whirling, he found himself eyeball to eyeball with Makepeace. Furious at being caught flat-footed by an old drunk, he grabbed a fistful of the man's shirt and jerked him to his toes. "Damn it, asshole, next time you sneak up on me, I'm gonna tie your scrawny neck in a knot!"

To Sarge's surprise, the man didn't cower, or even flinch. In fact, he actually dared to shrug one bony shoulder. "Sorry, I thought you seen me coming. I come to ask if you want me to clean your office before I put the stuff away." His downward glance indicated the bucket of cleaning supplies.

Sarge's anger drained away. The man was a lousy janitor, but he didn't cost much neither—a C-note a week plus free booze and a cot in the corner of the storeroom next door. Besides, Makepeace had served his country just like him—in the U.S. Army instead of a real man's outfit, but still he'd been in combat in 'Nam, even had the scars to prove it. By his way of thinking, that put Makepeace a notch above Sullivan. "Next time sing out or rattle the damn bucket," Sarge ordered before releasing his hold.

"Roger that, Sarge," the old man said with a pathetic excuse for a salute.

Sarge started down the hall, then stopped and looked back. Makepeace was reaching down for his bucket of cleaning supplies. "I'll let you know when I want my office cleaned," he said before heading for the barroom.

Nothing he liked better than paying customers, Sarge thought as he made his way through the maze of tables and chairs. This morning most of the stools were occupied and even a few of the tables. Someone had plugged the jukebox, might even have been Red who got antsy when things were too quiet.

He would treat himself to a cup of Red's strong java before heading to Wenatchee for a meeting with a real estate broker, a fellow marine who owed him a favor. If things went like he expected, he wanted to unload the bar as fast as he could. Shouldn't be much of a problem, though. Since the flood, business had picked up, most likely on account of more working stiffs being out of work.

"Did he go for it?" Red asked as Sarge slipped onto a stool at the far end of the bar where the two could talk without being overheard.

Sarge allowed himself a satisfied grin. "Does a starving dog beg for a handout?"

To celebrate opening day Del had arranged for a continental breakfast to be served in the lunchroom, which she'd decorated with blue and silver streamers and balloons. True to form, she had poked and prodded Rhys until he'd agreed to give an informal welcoming speech, which was received with enthusiastic cheers and whistles, probably because he kept it short.

By seven thirty he was back in his office, going over the day's scheduled appointments with Elena Rodriquez. "At four, Del is meeting with the man Emory wants to name day shift foreman. She would like your opinion," Elena said, her gaze on the neatly typed list in front of her. "Sometime before that, Stan would like an hour. You have time at two—unless you have a problem with that." Her tone told him he damn well better not.

"No, ma'am, no problem."

She amended his schedule before getting to her feet. At the same time, her phone rang. She hurried to answer, pausing at the door to ask, "Open or closed?"

"Closed, please," he said. As soon as he was alone, he pulled out his notebook and looked up the inn's number. He was reaching for his phone when the intercom buzzed.

"Yeah, Elena?"

"Mr. Goodeve's on your private line."

His VP of sales was deeply involved in negotiating several important contracts, the most vital of which was still Memory-Data. The contract wasn't due to be awarded until the end of the month, but it was Grant's belief that it was the unwatched pot that boiled over.

"Thanks." After punching the blinking button, Rhys eased back against the chair back. "How's it going, Grant?"

"On balance, good. On the downside, we might have a problem with MemoryData."

Turning cold, Rhys turned to stare out at the storm gathering over the Cascades. "Problem how?"

Grant cleared his throat. "As you know, Jimmy Wu in their contracts department is actively lobbying Ito to swing the contract our way. While I was in Houston, he gave me a call. Seems some jackass has been spreading it around the Silicon Valley that you're dangerously leveraged because of this expansion and might even be facing bankruptcy."

Rhys felt tension bunch between his shoulder blades. A lucky guess or a leak from someone at the bank? "Do you have a name on this SOB?" he demanded, capping his pen.

"Robert Cresswell. According to Jimmy he's a senior broker with a small local firm. Rumor has it he's tight with Mark Digeneris."

Rhys let out a vicious curse.

Wilshire Trucking was his only serious competition, and although Wu shared his contempt for Digeneris' way of doing business, MemoryData's CEO, Don Ericson, had refused to rule Wilshire out. "What do you know about this Cresswell?" Rhys asked.

"Nothing more than I've just told you, but I've already asked Lou Kerrey to check him out."

"When's Kerrey supposed to report back?"

"No later than Monday."

"You've been keeping in touch with Ericson as well as Wu, right?"

"As luck would have it I found out Ericson's kid is crazy for baseball, so I commandeered the company skybox for Thursday night and pulled a few strings so the boy can sit on the bench during the game. Sometime during the game—after Ericson's had a few drinks—I figure to set up a meeting at the

Tower. A high-end show-and-tell to counteract rumors of our imminent demise, maybe Friday afternoon. While he's there I'd like to offer him a one-year-only discount of two percent off our initial bid."

Rhys ran some rough figures in his head. "That doesn't leave much room for profit, Grant."

"True, and I could give you a whole bunch of clichés that apply. Bottom line, though, it shuts Digeneris out."

Rhys closed his eyes and rubbed at the scar on his chin. He preferred a low profile for a lot of reasons, mostly because he didn't have the patience to play corporate games, while Grant was a master. In this case, however, he needed every penny of the profit built into the current bid.

"Set up the meeting and offer Ericson and his family the use of our suite at the Ritz Carlton, but hold off on changing our bid for now."

Rhys braced for the argument he expected Grant to mount. Instead his VP sighed. "I figure you know best so I'll just say 'yes sir' and suck it up."

"Appreciate it." He paused, thought. Frowned. "Would it help if I took that meeting with you?"

The line fell silent once more while Grant considered. "It would, yes, but it has to look like you're in town as a matter of routine so he doesn't smell panic."

"In other words, Tanner had better be fueling the plane as we speak."

Grant chuckled. "Exactly!"

"Expect me sometime Wednesday afternoon."

"The guy pacing the corridor outside your office will be me."

Rhys made a note to have Elena contact both Tanner and Joan Majenek to set up his travel plans.

"How's Hank doing?" Grant asked just as Rhys was about to end the conversation. "Still giving the medical types fits?"

"Same fits, different medical types. Moved him to the rehab

unit, casts, back brace and all. The doctor still says six more weeks. Hank says three."

"What's shaking up there? Got any contracts locked in yet?"

"Not yet, but things are shaping up well enough for you to put out the word we're ready to haul freight."

"Be happy to, but it might be a good idea for your marketing guy . . ." Grant broke off suddenly to ask, "Sullivan, right?"

"Right."

"Like I said, it might be a good idea for him to fax me a list of the contacts he's already made as well as the calls he plans to make, so we're not plowing the same ground. Last thing we need right now is a perception that we're desperate to hustle up new contracts."

Rhys glanced at the folder containing Junior's proposal. The arrogant SOB hadn't been in his office when Rhys arrived. "Expect a list before close of business today."

"Good deal. I don't have to tell you that a positive cash flow would go a long way toward easing Ericson's reservations."

After hanging up, Rhys punched John's extension. It rang several times before switching to his assistant's extension. "This is Hazard," he said when she answered. "Get me Sullivan, please."

"S-sorry, Mr. Hazard. Mr. Sullivan hasn't checked in yet."

Rhys made an effort to keep the frustration out of his voice. "Do you have a cell phone number for him?"

"No, sir."

Rhys told her to switch Junior to him if he phoned in, and then because it wasn't her fault she worked for a jerk, he made it a point to put extra warmth in his voice as he thanked her.

After disconnecting, he flipped through his Rolodex for the number of the inn.

Brina answered on the third ring. The lilt in her voice warmed him all the way through. "It's Rhys, sweetheart. How's it going?"

"Actually, I'm changing your bed as we speak. It looks as though you were wrestling alligators most of the night."

The memory of his restless night brought a frown to his face. The familiar nightmare had been particularly vivid. "Kept dreaming you were pestering me for sex. Guess I must have been fighting for my life."

Her strangled gasp of outrage had him grinning. "I seem to recall a mutual pestering."

"Hold that thought," he said. "In the meantime, can you give me Junior's cell phone number?"

Twenty minutes later, Rhys had just finished filling Hank in on his conversation with Goodeve when John walked in and sat down.

"When do you expect the first trucks to roll?" Hank asked in his ear.

"Why don't I let your marketing director field that one? Hang on, let me put you on speaker." After switching over, he hung up the receiver. "Can you hear me okay?" he asked, easing back.

"Clear as crystal," Hank replied.

"Hey, Hank, buddy, how's it going?" If Junior felt any guilt for rolling in halfway into the morning, it wasn't reflected in his cocksure tone.

"All things considered, pretty good, but not as good as I'd be if we had a half dozen hauling contracts in the works."

"Not to worry, I'm on it."

"I haven't seen your marketing proposal yet, but Rhys tells me it's a good one."

Rhys caught the flare of surprise in his brother's eyes. "That's very gratifying to hear. I started on it as soon as I accepted North Star's offer, and I've spent a lot of time since then fine-tuning it."

Rhys had to admit John had all the moves of a bright, hard-

charging go-getter down pat. Looked the part, too, in a gray
suit, pale blue shirt and yellow tie.

"What companies have you set up appointments with so
far?" Hank asked.

John's cocky edge slipped a little. "Nothing's been firmed
up yet. I'm waiting for several people to get back to me."

"Which is the most promising?"

"Case Automotive Supply. So far their major markets are in
the Northwest and northern California, but they're hoping to
open up southern California. I met their CEO, George Case,
Saturday night at the governor's bash. Seems he contributed
big bucks to Luan's reelection campaign. Soon as I found out
who he was, I made a point to do some networking. I'm meeting with Georgie boy at his flagship store on Wednesday
morning."

"Sounds like a good start. Guess I don't need to tell you
how much is riding on you, especially during these next cru-
cial ninety days."

Rhys caught the edge of weariness in Hank's voice. "You
got what you need, *compadre*?" he asked Hank.

"For now. Tell Del I had one of the nurses buy me a new
PowerBook so she can e-mail the daily reports directly."

"Right." Rhys made a note. "Now get back to work, so you
can get your ass in this chair and I can get back to Phoenix
where I belong."

"Three weeks, take it to the bank."

"I'd rather hang on here an extra week or two if that means
I'll get you back a hundred percent."

"Three weeks, tops," Hank promised before disconnecting.

Rhys did the same. The resultant silence was as thick as the
morning ground fog. Fully aware of the impact of his icy stare,
Rhys kept his chilly gaze on Junior's face and let the silence
stretch out.

Dropping his gaze, John shifted in his chair, then caught
himself. "Nice guy, Dunnigan. Comes from the closest thing

California has to aristocracy, I'm told. It shows, too. Like I told Dad the first time Dunnigan approached us about a sale, the man is a class act."

"I'm sure Hank will be glad to hear you approve of him, but if you think you can work him the way you worked J. T., forget it. Under all that class you and your mother set so much store by, Dunnigan has the instincts of a street brawler and a way of sniffing out stink that's uncanny."

"Point taken." Glancing down, John flicked a piece of lint from his trousers before settling back. "Change of subject. I stopped by the inn one morning last week, but Brin was at a meeting of the parade committee. I wanted to see how things were going between you two."

Rhys ignored the unspoken question. "You stop by often, do you?"

"As often as I can, yeah. She's a terrific mom, but a lousy businessperson. As much as she'll let me, I've been giving her pointers. We might be divorced, but I still care about her, you know?"

"Funny, last time I saw you two together I got the impression you could barely stand her."

John gave a good imitation of a man doing his best under trying circumstances beyond his making. "To tell you the truth, she's been hassling me a lot lately, and I guess I flashed a little temper her way." For an instant he looked exactly like the petulant brat who thought the world revolved around him.

"How come she's hassling you?"

"What else? Money. She's always wanting more for that monstrosity of a house she's so crazy about preserving. Then she's claimed the kids at school were teasing Jay about his overbite. I told her I couldn't afford to spend money on orthodontist bills right now, but she went ahead and had the kid fitted for braces. Naturally, she expects me to pay."

"Sounds reasonable to me."

"Bullshit. Another coupla months wouldn't have made

much difference. Hell, I got teased, too, before I got braces and so did you. We both survived."

"I remember you pulling such a fit your mother threatened to take the orthodontist to court if he took off my braces before you were done," he said with deceptive mildness.

John chuckled. "I admit it. I was a jerk."

"I'd use a different word."

"Yeah, well . . ." He rubbed his hands together, looked at the floor, sighed. The humble act was new. Rhys wasn't buying, but it was an interesting show. "Thing is, Rhys, I was hoping to get an advance on my salary so Brina will back off long enough to give me some breathing room."

For his own amusement Rhys played along. "How much of an advance?"

"Five large should do it."

"Seems like a lot."

"I agree, but . . ." John sighed. "You've seen Jay, right? Much as I hate to admit it, he'll look a whole lot better when his teeth are straight."

Considering, Rhys sat back, let the silence play out long enough for an uneasy look to tighten John's pretty boy features.

"I've seen Sullivan's books. I know how much was left from the buyout after settling with your creditors. Or didn't J. T. share the profit with you?"

"I had expenses. Back child support for one, and Sherri had to put her mom in a nursing home."

"Sherri being your mistress, right?"

"Fiancée. Obviously, Brina has whined to you the way she's whined to everyone else."

You pathetic excuse for a man, Rhys thought, all but choking on the disgust he felt. "Actually, Lucy was the one who told me you'd been screwing your wife's aerobics instructor for what, a year before Brina found out?"

"I admit I'm not proud of that. Truth is, though, Brina and I had been having trouble for a long time. She's not exactly frigid, but real close, you know?"

Rhys controlled a flare of anger. "So it was her fault you cheated."

"I swear to God, Mi—Rhys, I fought it for a long time. So did Sherri. She's a real moral person, you know? It tore her up, thinking how hurt Brin would be."

"Big of her."

John frowned. "I know it sounds bad. Hell, Pop chewed my ass bloody when he found out, but he ended up loving Sher as much as I do." His expression turned smug. "Wait until you meet her. Then you'll understand what a prize she is."

"Because she's such a moral person?"

John laughed. "Just between you and me, bro, the woman has the greatest ass I've ever seen, and you wouldn't believe her tits. I'd almost forgotten what it was like to fuck a woman who actually turns me on." He offered Rhys a man-to-man look. "Told her I wouldn't marry her unless she agreed not to have kids. No way do I want that body ruined by those ugly stretch marks." He grimaced. "Believe me, I learned my lesson with Brina."

"Seems to me a man should be grateful a woman wants to have his babies, not disgusted when they leave a few marks on her."

"Hell, you sound just like the old man."

"Well, shit. If that's all, I have people waiting for a conference call."

John sighed. "Twenty-two years is a long time to hold a grudge. I was hoping we could clear the air, maybe become friends."

Rhys kept his expression impassive. "Admit you lied to the cops and the jury, and I'll think about it."

"I wish to God I could." John drew in a breath, then let it out slowly. "You weren't in any shape to remember what happened, so I understand how you might think I had some kind of Cain and Abel thing going. But I swear on Mother's soul, I simply told it the way I saw it."

Without seeming to, Rhys studied the face that blended J. T.'s bold features with Marceline's arrogance, but try as he might, he couldn't detect even the faintest hint of deception. The possibility that his memories of that day had been skewed by the shock and pain of his injury had tortured him on and off for years. If John hadn't lied, that meant *he* had. Not deliberately, because he'd told his story exactly as he'd seen it, but still, it was possible that he'd put his hand on the Holy Bible and sworn to a falsehood.

Rhys fisted his hand on his thigh. It was his left, the one he'd smashed into the wall in isolation. Suddenly he felt a little sick.

Conscious that John was watching him, he forced himself to retrieve the marketing plan from the briefcase next to his chair With a flip of his wrist, he tossed it onto the desk. "I made several changes and a couple of suggestions, but overall it's solid." It cost him to say even that much.

After eyeing him warily for a beat or two, John picked up the folder and glanced inside. "Does that mean I get a gold star?"

"It means you get to keep your job one more day."

John grinned, rose, smoothed his tie. "You can dump a badass attitude on me all you want, big brother. You might look tough, but you can't hold a grudge worth a damn."

"Don't count on it."

Grin widening, John headed for the door. Rhys waited until he had his hand on the knob before calling his name. John turned.

"About the advance on your salary, for Jay's braces? Tell Stan to make out that five-thousand-dollar check to Brina, since it's for her anyway."

It was there in Junior's eyes finally—hatred. Gone almost as quickly as it came. "Sure, right. No problem."

When he was gone, Rhys settled back and waited for the satisfaction to settle in. Instead, he found himself feeling emptier than ever. Revenge, it seemed, wasn't always sweet.

Chapter 22

After leaving two messages, Brina finally connected with Wayne's daughter just before eleven. Although they rarely saw each other now, Renee's voice was warm with pleasure when Brina reached her in her chambers. It cooled several degrees after Renee learned the reason for the call. "I'm sorry, Brina, Dad's used up all the compassion I had for him."

"I understand how you feel, Renee, really I do. But if you could just talk to him—"

"I *have* talked and pleaded and threatened. After he lost his job at the Chevy dealership in Wenatchee, I set up an appointment for him at a rehab clinic near our place in Bellevue so that I could offer personal support. He promised to sign himself in the next day. Instead he disappeared for three weeks. I was nearly out of my mind by the time he surfaced again." She sighed. "Brina, believe me, I *hate* feeling this way. Before that . . . that damn bus accident changed him, he was the best dad a girl could ever have. Afterward . . ." She let her voice trail off. Brina understood all the things she wasn't able to say.

"A lot of lives changed because of that accident, probably more than we know." Brina shifted her gaze toward the array of family photos on her office shelves. The four Eilers, then three, and finally just Brina and her dad. Two survivors clinging together. At least they'd had each other.

Rhys had had no one.

Sympathy ran through her for that lost boy. "Daddy always told me that if you want something bad enough, you'll do the work to make it happen," she said. She thought about the strength in Rhys' face and the steely look that sometimes came into his eyes. Her father and Renee's had bent under the load they'd been given to bear, but Rhys had squared those huge shoulders and fought back.

"Are you saying Dad's motivated to change now?" Renee's tone was skeptical, but Brina thought she detected faint hope as well.

"I have absolutely no proof to offer, Renee, and maybe it's just wishful thinking, but yes, I think he's—well, hit bottom, I guess you'd call it. Maybe going back to work would restore his pride in his abilities—and himself."

Renee snorted. "Who's going to hire a practicing drunk?"

"North Star might." Brina turned her chair so that she could see her rose garden. "I'd have to get him cleaned up and he'll probably need some new clothes." She grimaced. "Would you be willing to front the money to make him presentable for an interview?"

There was a pause before Renee sighed. "It's probably an exercise in futility, but all right, send me the bills."

"This permit is valid for today only, Ms. Sullivan." Unsmiling but polite, the uniformed guard handed her a yellow placard and waited until Brina had placed it on the dash before adding, "The visitors lot is to the left of the main building. Park in any of the spaces marked with yellow lines, then proceed to the main entrance next to the first set of large double doors. Offices are on the second level. Follow the yellow stripe on the floor to the stairs."

Driving slowly, Brina had just spied the sign for the visitors section when a familiar black Corvette shot out from behind a full-size extended-cab pickup, stopping directly in front of her to allow John to shift gears.

With a cry of alarm she jammed on the brakes so hard her thighs strained against the tight lap belt. The van shuddered to a stop scant inches from the 'Vette's fiberglass body.

Behind the wheel, John glared at her. Swallowing an absurd urge to laugh, she unclenched her fingers from the steering wheel to give him a jaunty wave.

In return he mouthed the despised *c* word before jamming the 'Vette into first and peeling out, narrowly missing the rear of a shiny new Explorer.

"Next time I won't stop, you miserable *moron!*" she yelled after him. Still seething, she debated for no more than a millisecond before zipping into the space he'd just vacated. It wasn't until she'd removed the keys that she remembered the guard's instructions to park in the yellow spaces.

"So let them tow it away," she muttered as she hopped out.

"Darn, I thought you had him that time, sweetheart." Rhys' voice came from her right. He stood in front of the building. The benevolent rays of early spring sunlight brought out the warmth in his deeply bronzed skin and burnished his rebellious blond hair.

He wasn't touching her. He hadn't even violated her personal space, and yet she felt as though those great-looking hands were stroking her breasts and her belly and her thighs.

Tightening her grip on her purse, she abandoned the sex-crazed meanderings and smiled. "I, uh, hope you don't mind my dropping by without an invitation."

"Nope." His eyes warmed as he lifted a hand to carefully tuck a strand of hair behind her ear. As tender gestures went, it was . . . endearing. Darn the luck, she'd always been a sucker for endearing.

"I . . . there was a reason . . . ," she began, only to find her mind going blank. "Rhys, please stop looking at me like that."

"Like what?"

He was crowding her again. "Like you want to throw me down right here on the asphalt and have your way with me."

"Right goal, wrong place." His grin never failed to catch her off guard, maybe because it was so rare. "How about I show you the sleeping compartment in one of the rigs?"

"That's an offer I really wish I didn't have to refuse, but I came to ask you a favor and I'm on a tight schedule."

"Got time for coffee? Del ordered donuts."

"I shouldn't, but . . ." If she sat down, so would he. "One cup," she decided. "And only one, repeat, *one* donut." She sighed.

"It's a deal."

Rhys watched Brina licking donut glaze from her fingertips. Her eyes were half closed, her lips parted, and her expression was blissful. He couldn't remember when he'd been so turned on. Hell, just watching Brina *breathe* turned him on. But he knew that this frenzied need for each other would eventually fade. Nothing lasted forever. Not even great sex.

"So, what was this favor you wanted to ask me?"

"Do you remember Wayne Makepeace? He used to work for Daddy?"

He felt an upsurge of violent emotions—anger, betrayal, hurt. He didn't care to sort them all out. "Yeah, I remember him. Testified for the prosecution at my trial. Surprised the heck out of me when he showed up at my first parole hearing to tell the board what a great human being I was. Not that it made any difference. That particular deck was about as stacked as it could get."

Her gaze flickered, but held on his. It was Brina's way, he'd discovered. When life threw hardballs, she might flinch, but she didn't duck. "I don't know what to say to that."

"Not much you can say. Life sometimes kicks you in the nuts." He took a sip of the lousy coffee. "Your choice whether to lie there and wait to die or get up and fight back."

"Not everyone has your strength, Rhys. Wayne, for example. Since the flood wiped out his garage business, he's been depressed and drinking too much. Even his only daughter has become so disgusted she's written him off as a lost cause. But . . . well, I was thinking that if he had a job he loved, it might give him a reason to feel good about himself again."

"This is important to you?" he asked when she began gnawing at her lower lip.

"Very. Wayne was . . . *is* like an uncle to me."

"I'll set up an interview with Del, but he'll have to get the job on his own. Be sure you let him know we have zero tolerance for substance abuse, which includes alcohol. Before he's put on the payroll, he has to pass a tox screening. If he shows up dirty, he won't be hired."

She dropped her gaze. "I don't think he'll pass. I know he was drinking on Saturday."

Rhys had put those rules in place himself, along with an ironclad requirement that all requests for exceptions were to come directly to him. Over the years he'd received several dozen requests. He'd turned them all down.

"Do *you* believe he's willing to get sober and stay that way?"

She took time to consider, then nodded. "I do, yes. I sensed something in him Saturday, a kind of, well, emptiness, as though he were being eaten away inside."

It was a feeling Rhys knew all too well. "If Del thinks he's a strong possibility in all other regards, and if he agrees to get treatment for the drinking, we'll make an exception—but just this one time. Company policy, a person who hires on starts fresh. Anyone who wastes that second chance doesn't get a third. Make sure Makepeace understands that, Brina. First time he comes up dirty, he's gone."

Although it was midafternoon, the parking lot surrounding Sarge's Place was nearly full. Just her luck, an audience, Brina thought, as she walked into a wall of noise and cigarette smoke so thick it stung her eyes and scoured the inside of her nose.

Doing her best to ignore the curious stares, she made her way to the bar. "Buy you a drink, dolly?" someone called out of the haze, causing her to flinch.

"If you're looking for a good time, honey, I'm your man," another drawled. Heart slamming, she kept her gaze fixed straight ahead. Most of the stools were occupied. She hesitated, then made her way to an empty place at one end of the bar.

The red-haired ogre in the guise of a bartender who materialized in front of her eyed her with open suspicion. "Something I can do for you, ma'am?" Despite the pretense of courtesy, his raspy voice was as unfriendly as the look in his eyes.

Painfully aware that the men on the nearby stools were hanging on every word, she lowered her voice to a near whisper. "A friend of mine works here, and I was hoping to talk with him for a few minutes."

"Which friend would that be?"

"Wayne Makepeace."

"Well, don't that beat all," one of the spectators exclaimed. "Old Spider's got himself a gal friend. A real looker, too."

Brina shot him a fulminating look that had him grinning like a particularly repulsive hyena. "Wayne worked for my father," she said stiffly. "He's also a family friend."

"Your daddy wouldn't be Theo Eiler, would he?"

She nodded. "Wayne helped raise me."

The spectator's disgusting grin disappeared, replaced by a look of respect. "Beg pardon, ma'am. If I'd a knowed you was Theo's girl I never woulda said nothing."

After accepting his apology with a gracious nod, she turned her attention to the bartender once more. "Is he here?"

He jerked a huge thumb toward the rear. "Has him a bunk in the storage room. Down the hall, second door on the right."

"Might be a good idea if you wait outside while I go and fetch him to you," the man who'd apologized to her suggested almost too quickly. "It bein' so loud in here and all."

Brina cast a wary look toward the shadowed hallway. After discovering that her feminist leanings didn't extend that far, she nodded gratefully.

"I'll wait by my van," she said as he slipped from the stool.

Five minutes later, Wayne appeared, eyes nearly closed against the glare. He looked tired, but he didn't seem drunk. "You shouldn't have come here, Brina," he said. "It's not fitting."

She made her expression stern. "You have an interview at North Star this coming Thursday at three. I've gone way out on a real skinny limb for you, Wayne Makepeace, and I'm not taking no for answer, so you might as well save your energy and pack your things. I'll give you ten minutes, and then I'm coming in to do it for you."

Because Wayne smelled more than a little ripe, Brina took him back to the inn, hustling him up to the family quarters by the back stairs. After bullying him into taking a shower and washing his hair, she threw his filthy clothes into the washing machine. Now, an hour later while they tumbled dry, he sat at the kitchen island wrapped in a blanket, sipping hot chicken soup as she mixed the batter for a cherry Bundt cake.

"I won't even get through the interview," he said. "I can't hold a pen to fill out the application." To prove his point, he held out his hand, which trembled visibly.

"Can you hold a wrench?"

"Course I can!" His shoulder twitched. "Hands don't shake then. Don't know why exactly."

"Well, there you go. Obviously you were born to fix things."

"Things with cylinders and pistons and valves, maybe. Don't seem to be much good with anything else." He wrapped both hands around the large mug and brought the soup to his mouth for several slurping sips. "Ain't got me no references. A company like North Star's bound to want references."

"I'm your reference. I've already told Ms. Campbell-Browne how talented you are. She's eager to meet you." Brina poured the batter into the pan and shoved it into the oven before setting the timer to start baking. She would drive Wayne to a bare-bones motel in Wenatchee where she'd already made a reservation. On the way they would stop at Penney's to pick up clothes suitable for an interview.

"It's not like I don't appreciate all you're doing, missy," he mumbled, sounding even more miserable than he looked. "But I hate for you to be going to so much trouble for nothing."

Brina turned to wave the wooden spoon she was washing at him. "None of that, Wayne. Merribelle and I only allow positive thoughts under our roof."

"Ain't enough positive thoughts in the world to change the past, missy. You ought to know that as well as me."

"No, but you can put it behind you and concentrate on making the present better."

"I got to think you musta forgot about how I testified against that boy in court. Ain't no way he's gonna give me a job."

"You're wrong, Wayne. Rhys arranged the interview himself." The message from Del setting the time for the initial interview had been on her machine by the time she'd arrived home.

Wayne swallowed hard. "That fella, O'Brien—the prosecutor, I guess you'd call him—he insisted. Wanted me to back up what your daddy said about the brakes being changed just the week before." He kept his head down and his gaze on his empty mug. "I didn't want to, on account of how Mick Sullivan was always real polite to me when I worked for J. T. Not like that spoiled brother of hisn." His shoulders hunched even more. "Beg pardon, Brina."

"I agree. John was spoiled rotten." Needing to think, she took her time washing up. "I can't believe Rhys would penalize you for telling the truth," she said finally.

"I just don't want you to be disappointed if it don't work out."

"It'll work out," she assured him before hanging the towel on the rack. "Next to Daddy, you're the best mechanic in the whole valley. They'd be nuts not to snap you up."

To her dismay the words she'd meant to buck him up seemed to depress him more. Before she could explore further, the dryer dinged, causing him to flinch. "I never wanted to hurt no one, and that's the God's truth."

She acknowledged that with a smile. "Rhys did make one condition, Wayne. You have to get sober and stay sober. North Star has a zero tolerance rule for substance abuse."

He let out a ragged sigh. "I ain't making any promises, but I'll do my best."

Joan Majenek's end-of-the-day list of calls Rhys needed to return and other matters requiring his attention was masterfully concise. But even as the soft strains of Mozart's Wind Serenade in E-flat flowed from the sedan's four superb speakers, he found his mind wandering. Instead of making productive use of the thirty-five minutes it took to travel from the depot to the gym in Wenatchee where he and Max worked out daily, he was thinking about Brina.

Yesterday, when she'd shown up at the depot he'd been damn near giddy with pleasure at seeing her. Like a kid with a crush, he'd wanted to show off for her. It was pathetic. Worse, it was dangerous to give her or anyone that much power. Eventually, it would twist back on him, and unless he was very careful, he could end up bloody.

"What the hell is *that?*" Max muttered, slowing to a crawl.

Rhys glanced up. A reluctant laugh escaped his lips. "Looks like a billboard to me."

"Don't look like no billboard I've ever seen," Max grumbled.

"Maybe it'll look better up close," Rhys suggested before ordering Max to pull over and stop.

Made of a plywood sheet painted gleaming white, the signboard had been attached to four-by-four posts sunk into the one corner of the newly planted field where it was easily spotted from the road. While two of J. T.'s planting crew slapped preservative on the posts, J. T. stood atop a makeshift scaffolding, paintbrush in hand. Spelled out in red block letters a couple of feet high were the words *I love you, my darlin' Lucy. Please marry me.*

"Hope Ernie don't—*doesn't*—set eyes on that thing," Max muttered. "Might set her thinking into the wrong grooves."

As Max was speaking, one of the men drew J. T.'s attention to the Mercedes. A grin split his face as he handed over the brush he'd been using to fill in the center of a lopsided red heart before climbing down the ladder propped against one end of the scaffolding.

"Shut her off for a minute," Rhys said before getting out to meet the man halfway. Wind ruffled his hair, bringing with it the mingled scents of paint and freshly turned earth. He felt a sharp pang of nostalgia. Ruthlessly, he shoved it aside.

"That's one way of getting a lady's attention," he said as J. T. approached.

"It's an act of sheer desperation you're witnessing." J. T. tugged off his cap and wiped his damp forehead with his sleeve. "Woman's got herself barricaded behind a damn wall of pride, and nothin' I've done or said so far has made a dent. I figured maybe if I put my own pride on the line it would convince her I'm serious."

"Or daft."

J. T. grinned. "Ah, but it's psychology I'm using, don't you see? Even the most sophisticated woman finds it impossible to resist a man who's so crazy in love he does daft things to win her."

Rhys shifted his attention to the sign. The letters were crooked, and the paint had run in several spots. Still, he supposed it got the point across better than a coupla dozen roses. "I'm no expert on psychology or women, but I'll give you the crazy part."

J. T. plowed a big hand through his thick hair, and then settled his hat with the brim low over the bridge of his nose. Rhys had seen him go through the same unconscious ritual countless times in the past. Seeing it again after so many years made him edgy. The past was dead, and he had no interest in unearthing memories he'd worked hard to bury.

He turned to leave just as a rabbit darted from beneath a pile of uprooted trees and debris ready to be burned. A split second later a black-and-white dog jumped to his feet and gave chase, barking furiously.

One of the men shouted encouragement. The other exchanged amused looks with J. T. *"¿Es un perro absurdo, verdad?"*

J. T. laughed. *"Si, claro,* Juanito. Foolish Dog is just living up to her name."

Obviously enjoying the challenge, the rabbit doubled back, cottontail flashing white against the bare earth. The dog followed, streaking past in a blur of white and black, her tail waving like a black plume tipped in white. Her muzzle was white, Rhys saw now, and dotted with black. Although he knew it couldn't possibly be his old dog, Freckles, his chest muscles tightened until it hurt to breathe.

Bored with watching the dog, J. T.'s men wandered over to admire the Mercedes while Max glowered like a protective father warning off unworthy suitors.

"Freckles was her great-grandma," J. T. explained when Rhys' gaze swung his way again. "Her ma died shortly after weaning the litter. This wee one was the runt and so far has lived up to the name given to her by Lupe's grandson, Pepe. She's a holy terror, that one, but I'm partial to her because she looks like her grandmother."

Freckles had been a holy terror, too, wearing herself out during the day, and sleeping like the dead at night. Contemptuous of mixed-breed dogs, Marceline had decreed that Freckles had to sleep in the utility room or on a pallet outside Rhys' door. Not on his bed. So Rhys made sure that his bed was exactly where the dog spent most of the night, setting his alarm to make sure she was back on her pallet before daylight.

"How . . . long did she live?" Rhys asked, his fingers clenched tight around the handle of his cane, gaze fixed on the black dot far in the distance.

"She was near fifteen when Doc Lucas had to put her down." J. T.'s voice turned gruff. "Had a bad heart, she did, and it pained her to draw breath."

Rhys shifted his gaze toward the west. He'd been a tow-headed boy of seven the summer Freckles had come into his life, a fat wiggly ball of fluff and spirit with a floppy yellow bow tied around her neck. Although Rhys had begged and begged for a dog, Marceline refused to have a filthy beast in the house. However, Freckles was a birthday present from Rhys Dubois and therefore safe from Marceline's wrath.

Or so Rhys had thought, until the day he'd come home from school and found Freckles gone. Lupe must have left the door open, Marceline had said with a disinterested shrug when he'd confronted her. Frantic and terrified, Rhys had run to J. T. for help. The trees were in first bud, and J. T. had his crew out from early to late, spraying the vulnerable blossoms against the many diseases that could destroy an entire crop.

J. T. hadn't even hesitated. For two critical days the equipment sat idle while twenty men searched for one small, scared mixed-breed mutt. It was J. T. himself who found Freckles stuck in a cast-off irrigation pipe. According to the vet who saved her, in another hour or two they would have been too late.

"At the end, did she suffer?" Rhys couldn't keep from asking.

"She went peacefully. Doc made sure of that."

It helped, knowing that. Believing that. "Did you bury her on the property?"

"I did. Near the rosebush she'd tried for years to kill by burying her bones among the roots." J. T. adjusted his cap again and cleared his throat. "Right to the end she insisted on sleeping outside your room. I'm thinking she never got over missing you."

If Rhys allowed it to matter, the pain would be unbearable. "I'm surprised Marceline didn't make you get rid of her."

"Oh, she tried, right enough. Swore she would take Johnny and leave me if I insisted on keeping the pup under her roof." J. T.'s voice was as cold as Rhys had ever heard it. "It was that calm I was, when I wished her the joy of her new life. She would need to get a job as soon as possible, of course, since no Sullivan male from Adam to this day ever paid out hard-won coin to support a wife who refused to live under his roof." A twinkle started deep in those familiar blue eyes. "It was right about then she experienced a sudden change of heart about the matter."

Rhys felt a reluctant smile tug at his lips, only to have it die half formed when a blur of black and white caught the corner of his eye. Racing past him, the pup nearly missed his cane by inches. After circling the two of them, barking full out, she ran to J. T., her hindquarter wagging along with her tail as she accepted the praise she so clearly believed she'd earned.

"Saved us all from another bloodthirsty beastie, didn't you, girl?" His eyes soft, J. T. bent to rub the sweet spot behind her ears. Freckles had one there, too, Rhys remembered.

When J. T. straightened, the pup came over to sniff Rhys' boots. She was broad in the hindquarters like Freckles, with the same soft wavy pelt and liquid brown eyes. Knowing he shouldn't, he held out his free hand palm down for her to sniff. No pushover, she took her time making up her mind.

The sudden swipe of her tongue across his knuckles startled him into a grin. "Behave yourself, Foolish Dog," he ordered sternly. After offering a soft "woof" in response she gifted him with another sloppy kiss. "I'll bet Marcy's crazy about you, isn't she?"

"Jay, too," J. T. said. "First time I saw the two of them playing down by that rock retaining wall you helped me build one summer, the boy looked so much like you I damn near broke down."

Rhys' head jerked up. His heart pounded. "He's not like me. I'm the—"

"Enough!" J. T. bellowed, his cheeks reddening rapidly and his eyes fiery with anger. "I'll not be responsible for my actions if you throw that blathering nonsense about you not being my son at my head one time more."

"It's not nonsense, damn it!"

"Ballocks!" Chin down, brows drawn, J. T. covered the ten feet or so between them in three furious strides. "For nigh onto two weeks now, you've been throwing your Irish temper at me every chance you get. And don't tell me you're not Irish or that you don't have a temper for that matter, because you'd be wrong."

Rhys clamped his jaw tight and let the look in his eyes speak for him. J. T. glared back, his eyes giving off blue sparks beneath thick rust-colored brows drawn into a murderous scowl.

"You've been mine since the wee nurse put you into my arms for the first time. It was sleepin' peacefully you were, but when I said your name, the same name as my father and his father before him, you opened your eyes and looked right into mine. 'Twas then I felt my heart burst open and spill out love for you. It's the same feeling I've had for the last forty years."

Heat rose to scald Rhys' cheeks. "Oh yeah, you loved me all right," he shot back, his quiet voice under rigid control. "Loved me so much you let that woman treat me like dirt, and then when I was scared and hurting, you turned your back on me."

Impatience crossed J. T.'s face. "What else could I have done, son? Ordered John to lie under oath? Taken my fists to one of the finest men I've ever known because as God is my witness, that would have been the only way I could have stopped Theo Eiler from doing what was right." Hands clenched at his sides, he took a swift breath. "I'm asking you again, Michael Rhys Sullivan, what should I have done?"

"You should have believed in me!"

"God help me I tried, but the evidence—"

"What about all those years when I busted my butt to make you proud of me? All those miserable times when I let that witch slice into me without fighting back because I knew it would upset you? Or the times I cleaned up Johnny's messes and took the heat for him because that's what you did for your brother and I wanted to be just like you?" He ran out of air and stopped to take a breath. The sudden flare of rage had burned itself out, leaving him feeling hollow inside. "I won't deny I messed up when I was a kid, maybe more than most, but I never lied to you. Not ever."

J. T. dropped his gaze, but not before Rhys saw the naked truth in those blue eyes. "You still think I'm lying about the bus driver running the red light, don't you?" Rhys said.

Shoulders stiffening, J. T. let his silence answer for him. The pup who'd settled at Rhys' feet got up suddenly and went to stand next to J. T. "Looks like Foolish Dog agrees with you, too, old man. But what else is new, right?"

Without waiting for an answer, Rhys covered the uneven ground to the Mercedes. Face poker tight, Max stood stiffly by the open passenger door, staring straight ahead. The two guys on J. T.'s crew stood nearby, pretending they hadn't heard every word.

"Rhys?"

Biting off a sigh, he turned around and waited, one hand braced on the heavy door for balance.

"Foolish Dog was always intended for you." The big man's smile was weary. "You see, I always hoped you would come back someday."

"Dogs need love just like people do. I'm fresh out." Appreciating the irony, he shifted his gaze to the sign that had set all this in motion. There was that damn word again. *Love.* What a crock.

"Good luck with the lady," he said curtly before climbing into the seat. He kept his shoulders back and his gaze straight ahead as Max shut the door and hurried around to the driver's side.

"You okay?" Max asked a few minutes later.

"No, but I will be." Just as soon as he could put this place behind him. For good, this time.

"A sign, he actually put up a *sign?*" Lucy shouted into the phone at the exact same moment that the shop door flew open.

"Lucy, where are you?" Dottie shouted as she charged inside, her gauzy mauve-and-turquoise skirt swirling around her favorite pair of sequined sneakers. The silver and turquoise bangles stretching from wrist to elbow clanged almost as loudly as the bells. "Bloody hell, you already know," she muttered when she caught sight of Lucy's frozen features.

"I'll kill him, I swear I will."

"Grab your purse and let's get a move on."

"Don't be ridiculous, Dot. I refuse to participate in this farce."

"Oh, for heaven's sake, Luce, don't be a butthead. You've been desperately in love with that man for forty years."

"Everyone's entitled to her opinion, even you."

Dottie's eyes flashed. "Now you listen to me, Lucille Steinberg. The universe has given you one of the greatest gifts anyone can receive, a second chance for happiness. Don't let stiff-necked pride keep you from grabbing on with both hands, because I promise, if you do, you'll go to your grave regretting it."

"Oh my, it's even more wonderful than I imagined," Dottie said as she stared with ridiculously starry eyes at the worst piece of manipulative garbage Lucy had ever witnessed.

"He doesn't mean it," Lucy declared. "It's . . . I know he doesn't mean it. *Everyone* knows he doesn't mean it."

"Of course he means it, Luce. The man is smitten. Anyone with eyes can see how it's written all over him when he looks at you."

"She's right, Lucy love."

Lucy whirled around, her heart slamming against her chest. Surprise at seeing J. T. warred with a feeling of betrayal that was beyond measuring. "How did . . . ?" She broke off when the truth dawned. Heat rushed her face as she turned accusing eyes on her so-called best friend. "You rat fink traitor, you *called* him, didn't you?"

"Oh, for heaven's sake, Lucy, stop glaring at me," Dot exclaimed. "At our age we don't have so many years left that we can afford to waste even a minute." Dottie tossed her head, sending her gypsy hoops swinging, but her eyes were soft with affection as she gave Lucy a hug.

"All this excitement has gotten me so worked up I think I'll stop by the hospital and seduce Gray right there on his office sofa. I might not even give him time to lock the door before I jump his gorgeous bones." She beamed encouragement in J. T.'s direction and received a silent thank you in return. "Living on the edge is so good for the complexion, you know," she tossed off before slipping behind the wheel.

"Dottie Krebs, don't you dare leave me here with this madman," Lucy cried, her Birkenstocks slipping in the loose dirt as she bolted toward the Olds.

With a bull-like roar that rattled her eardrums, J. T. caught her midstride and swung her into his arms as though she were as dainty as Dottie. "It was that patient I intended to be, you vixen, but I'm through waitin'."

"Let me go, you big idiot," she shouted, slamming a palm against his granite shoulder.

"Not this time, love," he said before crashing his mouth down on hers.

Chapter 23

It was raining on Wedneday afternoon when the Gulfstream landed in Scottsdale, where North Star rented a hangar. The warm spring shower had cleansed the air and raised winter sour spirits. Beyond the metropolitan sprawl, wildflowers had exploded overnight to form a sea of brilliant multihued blossoms amid the sand, sage and saguaro of the Southwestern desert.

The view from the top floors of the North Star Tower was superb in every season, but in the two days since his return, Rhys had found little time to enjoy it. Mostly his time had been taken up meeting with his department heads. This morning first thing he and Goodeve had spent two hours hammering out the points they needed to make when they met with Don Ericson at noon on Saturday.

Now, at a few minutes past noon, another shower had just rolled in from the south, drenching the city and limiting visibility. Alone in his office, Rhys signed the last letter in the folder Joan had put on his desk before leaving for lunch. Feeling virtuous, he removed his glasses and tossed them on the desk before flexing his tired shoulders. Nothing wore him out faster than a marathon session of paperwork.

After pouring himself another cup of coffee from the pot on the credenza behind his desk, he hit Del's private number on speed dial. "How's it going?" he asked when she answered.

"Which do you want first, sugar, the good news the even better news or the really and truly great news?"

"Start with the good and work your way up."

"Well, first, I hired an assistant who starts Monday. She's just out of business school and eager. I'm planning to mold her the way you molded me."

He said something rude, earning him a smart-ass comment in return. "Moving along—and ignoring that really uncalled-for remark—I finally settled on metallic gold over burgundy for my company vehicle. I'm taking delivery this afternoon, and I can hardly wait."

"Thank God that's settled!"

She laughed. "Brina was right about the pewter over black. The vibrations were all wrong for me."

"So far the good and better than good are marginal. I hate to think what you consider really and truly great."

"Okay, Mr. Hotshot, how about this for great? We have our first hauling contract. The first truck is set to roll on Tuesday."

"Who's on the other end of this deal?"

"Case Automotive Supply out of Tacoma." Del's tone was crisper now, no doubt in response to his lack of enthusiasm.

"Hauling what to where?"

"I don't know, Rhys. Sullivan just dropped the news on us this morning. Stan has the signed contract on his desk now. Want me to transfer you?"

Rhys glanced at his watch. "No time now. Ask him to call me tomorrow morning, please."

"Any particular time?"

He'd spoiled her surprise and he regretted that, but until he knew more about Case Automotive, he couldn't work up much pleasure. "Anytime before eleven. After that I'm due at a meeting."

A dawn-chilled drizzle beat against the window of Sarge's office as John placed the bound contracts on the desk. Pacific

Rim was about to become North Star Northwest's second customer. "You'll need to sign all four copies," John said.

"Make sure you spell your name right," Red Sturgess joked as Sarge picked up his pen.

The surgical gloves Sarge slipped on made signing awkward, but he figured that was good. If the deal was blown, the feds would play hell connecting him to W. G. Jones. Once he'd finished, he shoved the contracts toward John.

"Your turn, partner."

"Don't mind if I do, partner." Grinning, John bent to place his signature below Sarge's illegible scrawl. If, by some remote chance, the DEA caught on, he would plead ignorance. As far as he knew, the man who'd met with him "in a motel restaurant in Wenatchee" had been on the level.

"Chang will want to know when to have the goods ready for transfer," Sarge reminded him.

John nodded before tucking his pen into the inner pocket of his Armani suit coat. "I'll claim the client is in a hurry, that I had to promise delivery within a week's time to close the deal." He paused to mentally trace the Osuma to Vancouver to Oakland route in his head. "Today's Friday the twenty-first. Say it takes today and tomorrow to walk this through channels. The rig heads to Canada sometime Sunday. The way you described the size and weight of the cartons, it shouldn't take more than a couple of hours to load them. Factoring in extra time to allow for delays at the border, the rig should arrive Oakland sometime Wednesday." He considered the mind-set of the two men watching him and gave himself wiggle room. "Give or take a day either side."

"Sooner is better than later," Red declared with a scowl. "Longer the goods sit in the warehouse, the more chance shit can happen."

"Red's right. Until the merchandise is delivered to the consortium's buyer in Oakland, our asses are on the line. After

Rostov hands over the cash, whatever happens next is on him and the rest of them Russian goons."

Looking relaxed, Sarge propped his filthy sneakers on the desktop and stacked his hands behind his head. "Be sure you give me heads up in plenty of time so's I can be in Vancouver to supervise the loading. Chang seems like an upstanding guy, but he's not above holding out a few kilos to peddle on his own if he thinks he can get away with it."

Aware that his partners were watching him closely, John put on a confident face. "I won't know for sure until it hits the dispatcher's desk and he puts the pickup and delivery dates on the schedule. At Sullivan's that took a good day, but Dad didn't believe in computers, so everything was done manually. North Star's state-of-the art, computerwise." Adrenaline running hot in his veins, John slipped the contract into his briefcase and snapped it shut.

"How 'bout you pour us all a drink, Red?" Sarge suggested, indicating with a glance the bottle of Chivas Regal and three glasses set on a tray on one corner of his desk.

"Sure thing, boss." While Red poured, John set the case on the floor next to his chair. These men and their "associates" were playing for high stakes, and now he was in the game. The numbers Sarge had tossed around so casually when he'd proposed this partnership had staggered him, although he hadn't let on.

"Three fingers of Chivas, just the way you like it," Red said, handing him the barrel glass. "Me, I'm partial to rye myself, but then, I ain't got your class neither."

"Red's right, Johnny," Sarge said as Red poured out twice more. "Nobody sniffing around would connect the likes of you with the likes of us."

A red flag popped up at the back of John's mind. He hadn't allowed himself to think about the consequences if he should get caught, but suddenly he saw himself in handcuffs and shackles on his way to prison while Mick and Dad watched.

His gut twisted with both fear and hatred. "That's not likely, though, right? Someone getting suspicious?"

"In this burg?" Red scoffed as he handed Sarge a glass. "Not a chance."

"How about you doing the honors, Johnny?" Sarge suggested, holding up his glass.

As Sarge's cold eyes met his, John felt an adrenaline rush like none he'd ever experienced before. His fears drained away. Pitting his intelligence and skill against the odds was what he lived for. "Here's to success," he said, saluting them with his glass before throwing the smooth scotch down his throat. The others did the same.

John glanced at the Rolex knockoff that had replaced the one he'd hocked to raise his last Vegas stake. "Mind if I have another?" John asked Sarge, tapping his glass against the bottle.

"Be my guest."

John sipped this time, savoring the spreading glow. "I've been wondering why this has to be a one-shot deal," he said, relishing the smoky taste. "Given the way you've gone to so much trouble to set it up, buying up Pacific Rim and setting up a dummy parent company, I mean."

"Risk of getting caught gets greater the longer you're in operation. I'd rather be semirich and a free man than a multimillionaire rotting behind bars."

"That being the case, would you have any objection to me taking over your setup with Cascade after you're gone?"

An alligator's smile had more warmth than the one Sarge sent his way. "Won't be no operation left. Once the goods have been delivered and payment received, the warehouse in B.C. will burn to the ground. Same goes for the storage space in Oakland."

The look in Sarge's eyes warned him not to argue. John hid his disappointment behind a shrug. "Man's got to do what a man's got to do."

Sarge lit a cigarette and blew out smoke. "Maybe you ain't got the point yet, Johnny boy, but I'm really doing you a favor here. Amateurs like you almost always slip up sooner or later."

"You're probably right," he said after draining his glass. "Got to get a move on. Don't want to get my ass fired before this all goes down."

Red suddenly went on alert, like a hound sniffing the air. "Not much chance of that, right? Given the man in command is your close kin."

John felt fear clutching at his throat, but his game face held. "Don't worry; I know how to work him. I've done it all my life." He caught the look flashing between the two men. The fear deepened. He was a dead man if he was wrong, it said.

Red made a show of checking his watch. "If'n you boys don't need me no more, it's time I got my ass behind the bar."

"Go ahead. I'll finish up loose ends with Sullivan, " Sarge replied.

Red turned his attention John's way. He was smiling, but his eyes were as cold as a tomb. "Pleasure doing business with you, Mr. Sullivan."

"You, too."

John kept his gaze on the other man's back as he lumbered out and closed the door behind him.

Only then did he turn to Sarge. "Sometimes I get the feeling Sturgess doesn't like me," he joked.

"Don't worry about it. Red's been mad at the world a long time," Sarge returned before jerking his chin toward the bottle. "Another drink before you take those contracts to your office?"

Taking the hint, John shook his head. "No, thanks. Like you said, I need to get these babies into the right hands." He rose to his feet.

"Just so I'm clear on the drill," John said, "once the goods are authenticated, Rostov hands over the money to one of Chang's people in Oakland, who carries it across the border to

Chang himself, who takes his cut. The rest we split three ways."

Sarge nodded. "After I take my sixty large outta your share."

John smiled briefly. "So best-case scenario, by this time next week we're richer by close to a million dollars each."

"That's the way I see it playing out."

John picked up his briefcase and smoothed his tie. "If it's all the same to you, I'd like to take some of my share in merchandise."

Sarge's gaze sharpened. "*Some* being how much, exactly?"

"I don't know kilos. Say enough to fill my briefcase."

"Any particular reason?"

"This is just between us, right?"

"If that's the way you want it."

Despite the concession, John pretended reluctance. "This isn't easy to admit, you know? But, well, like you said, we're partners so you have a right to know." He let out a pained sigh and hoped it wasn't overkill. "It's for some friends of mine."

Sarge sat watching him for so long that sweat began beading in the hollow of John's spine.

"You'll have your kilos." Sarge dropped his feet and sat up. "One more thing you ought to know before you haul ass out of here. The last man who figured he could scam me took twelve hours to die. I made sure he was conscious the entire time."

Rhys lay with his spine pressed against a padded weight bench in the private workout room behind his office. The muscles of his arms and shoulders fought against gravity and searing fatigue to lift the weighted bar over his head.

Positioned at the head of the bench, his big hands poised to catch the bar if Rhys faltered, Max was both spotter and royal pain in the butt. "Put your back into it, man," he snarled while fifties rock music pumped from the sound system. "Way you're huffing and puffing you'd think I woulda put an extra twenty on each end instead of a piddling ten."

Making a piddling twenty added to the two sixty that was his personal best. The veins on his biceps were threatening to burst. The daily regimen of exercises and weight training the physiotherapist had laid down for him was designed to slow the gradual decline in mobility common in his kind of infirmity. He hated working out, but he hated the idea of ending his days in a wheelchair more.

"C'mon, man, just get it done. I ain't had my dinner and my belly's rumbling something fierce."

"Screw . . . you," Rhys muttered through a clenched jaw. His lungs burned and salty sweat stung his eyes. Suddenly furious at the limitations and frustrations and humiliations that were an everyday part of his life, he squeezed his eyes shut and little by little straightened his arms until with the last ounce of his strength, he tipped the bar over into the holders.

"Took you long enough," Max grumbled, handing Rhys a dry towel.

"Like . . . hell," Rhys rasped out between laboring breaths.

"Since you don't look like you're goin' to be moving any time soon, you mind if I hit the shower first?"

Rhys merely grunted. Although he'd tried to keep to his schedule, he'd missed more than a few workouts, and he was paying for it now. When he returned to Osuma next week, he would make sure he remedied that, he vowed, mopping the sweat from his face.

He'd just maneuvered himself into a sitting position when the cell phone he'd left on the floor next to his cane rang.

"Hazard," he grated.

"Surprise!" It was Marcy. Instantly, his mood took a one-eighty shift.

"It sure is, and a mighty nice one, too," he said with a smile. "Just what this beat-up old uncle needed."

Marcy giggled. "Grandda's old," she protested. "You're just half old."

"Thank you, sweetheart, that makes your *half-old* uncle feel a lot better."

"You're welcome," she said in the grave little voice she used when she was lecturing him.

"So, uh, how's everything going at Nightingale House?"

"Della's got a new car and she took me 'n Jay 'n Mommy for ice cream so she could break it in and Jay said she has rad music." She sneezed suddenly, and he smiled. "When are you coming home, Uncle Rhys?"

Rhys wiped his face with the towel looped around his neck. "I'm not sure, sweetheart. Another week or so, maybe longer. I've got a whole bunch of meetings scheduled."

"You have to be here to see me graduate from kinnygarden on account of I get to wear a cap with a tassel and Mommy's planning a party and everything."

"When is this momentous event happening?"

"On June the twelfth."

A little more than two weeks. "I'll do my best, but I can't promise."

"But . . . uh-oh, Mommy's got her hands on her hips again."

He mentally pictured that and hungered to touch her again. "Can I speak with her, please?"

"Okay," Marcy said a little sullenly before adding in a brighter tone, "I love you."

Because he still wasn't used to hearing the words, let alone saying them, he had trouble getting them out. "I, uh, love you, too, sweetheart."

He heard muffled voices before Brina came on the line. "I hope we didn't interrupt anything important?" she asked.

"Not a thing. How's it going?"

"Good, actually. Summer has offered to include Jay in one of the therapy groups at Phoenix House for a nominal cost, and I've lost five pounds."

Her voice reminded him of sunshine and champagne bubbles. "These five pounds, they didn't come off of any of the prime parts, I hope."

"Depends on your definition of prime."

"Everything from the top of those wild curls to the place where your feet hit the floor."

She choked out a laugh, and he felt a little giddy. He'd been seventeen and innocent the last time he'd bantered with a woman on the phone. "You might not carry J. T.'s genes, but you've definitely inherited his gift for blarney."

He waited for the customary bitterness to darken his thoughts. Instead, he found himself grinning. There were worse things to inherit, by association if not blood. "No blarney, fact. I'm crazy about every inch of your body, and if I were there now, I'd feel compelled to conduct a very thorough inspection of those prime parts."

"We'll discuss that when you get home."

Home. First Marcy had said it, now Brina. Before the idea could take hold, he changed the subject. "So, this thing with Lucy and J. T., did the sign work?"

He pictured her smiling before he heard the smile in her voice. "She hasn't said yes, but her 'absolutely not' is now a 'maybe.'"

"Got to hand it to the old man, he's persistent."

"And imaginative. The entire town's talking about his sign. When I drove Petey home yesterday, I was fifteen minutes late because of all the folks driving past for a look-see."

"Man claims he's in love. Maybe he is." Rhys did his best to hide the cynicism in his tone.

"Lucy certainly is, even if she won't admit it." Brina laughed, then asked him to hold on a minute. "I've just been informed that it's time for me to read your niece her bedtime story," she said when she came on the line again. "Even though I can't seem to do the voices nearly as well as Uncle Rhys."

A feeling of longing came over him. He would be there soon.

"Give Marce a kiss for me, and Jay, too, if he'll let you."

"I'll sneak up on him," she promised.

"Take one for yourself, too. Anyplace where you need it most, although my preference would be just above that cute little birthmark on the inside of your left thigh. I like the way you shiver when I put my tongue there."

Her breath hissed in. "I want you to know you have just ruined any chance I might have had for a good night's sleep."

"Try a cold shower," he suggested, his voice strained.

She sighed. "Just remember one thing, Hazard. The Successful Innkeeper develops devious methods to deal with stubbornly exasperating guests."

"One question, do any of these devious methods involve bare skin and a licking tongue?"

"That's for me to know and you to find out."

"God, I hope so," he said with real feeling.

She was laughing when she hung up. He held the phone to his ear for a moment longer before reluctantly letting her go.

Chapter 24

Saturday was another perfect day in the desert Southwest. Above the Tower's gleaming silver spire the sky was a deep cerulean blue. While tourists and locals prepared to enjoy a day off, North Star ran a full shift. Unlike most, freight hauling was a 24-7 business. Everyone who hired on to North Star understood that days off were on a staggered schedule and some weekend work would be required.

Although Rhys had arrived at his office a little past six o'clock, he had scarcely made a dent in his IN box by the time Stan Franklyn called at seven to give him chapter and verse on the Case contract. It wasn't the worst deal he'd ever okayed, but it was close. Still, it was a wedge into the Northwest market.

"I don't suppose Sullivan is working today?" he asked when Stan finished.

"Actually, he is. Want me to switch you over?"

"Please." Through the open door to his office Rhys saw that Joan had arrived fifteen minutes early as usual.

"Break out the champagne, big brother!" John gloated when he came on the line. "I just landed customer number two. An import-export company called Pacific Rim Trading out of Vancouver, B.C."

Rhys jotted down the name. "What kind of cargo?"

"Novelties from Taiwan and Hong Kong mostly. Sold to gift

shops in tourist locales. The parent company is out of Oakland, California. We'll be delivering the goods to their warehouse. First shipment is scheduled for this coming Wednesday."

To Rhys' surprise, his stomach knotted the way it always did when something didn't pass the smell test. "Why so soon?"

"Luck, really. Freight line they'd used for years out of Vancouver went under during this last fuel hike. Left 'em high and dry. I heard about it from an old customer of Sullivan's."

"Have you checked with Scruggs to make sure we're covered on all the customs and international shipping permits?"

"C'mon, Rhys, I've been handling deals like this for Dad for the last ten years. I know the drill as well as you do, and yeah, I checked with Scruggs."

"Are you saying Scruggs has already signed off on this deal?"

"Hell yes, he signed off," John shot back, his tone belligerent. "Ask him yourself if you don't believe me."

"I intend to. In the meantime, fax me copies of the contracts."

"Done." There was a pause before John asked buoyantly, "Hey, aren't you going to congratulate me, big brother?"

"Not until I see the numbers."

"Numbers aren't great for the first year, but like you said at last week's staff meeting, idle rigs are costing money, not earning it."

Rhys' jaw clenched, but he couldn't fault the man's memory—or his logic.

"Point taken." Rhys' hesitated before adding, "Congratulations."

"Tastes like shit, doesn't it, that big fat crow you've got wedged in your mouth." Rhys could almost see John's mouth curling into a "gotcha" smirk, just like old times.

"You've gotten your attaboy, John. Take my advice and don't push it."

Hank had been unavailable when Rhys called him a few minutes before noon on Monday. When his executive VP finally got back to him ninety minutes later, Rhys was reading his E-mail, monitoring the stock ticker running along the bottom of his computer screen, and eating his lunch, a double pastrami on rye.

"I haven't had time to go over the fine print, but it can't be any worse than the sweetheart deal Junior handed Case Automotive," he concluded after filling Hank in on Junior's latest.

"I admit I had hoped our inaugural run would have been more high-end," Hank offered with his customary temperance. "On the other hand, given we'd factored in the possibility of a negative cash flow the first six months into the start-up costs, we're slightly ahead of the game."

"Yeah, there is that." Rhys tipped back his can of Mountain Dew and took several fast swallows. "To tell you the truth, I'm not as concerned about Case as I am about this Canadian deal."

"Concerned how?"

"Wish I knew. It's just a feeling I have. Maybe I'll have a better idea what's got me spooked after I go over the contracts point by point." He took another quick bite and chewed. "Or maybe I'm nitpicking because Junior's the one who made the deal."

"Could be I was wrong about Sullivan's being a lightweight," Hank mused. "From zero to two contracts in less than two weeks is a more than decent percentage, especially for a marketing director who's new to the industry if not the job."

Rhys found himself irritated to find that Hank's thoughts ran along the same vein as his own. Still, fair was fair. "Maybe he has more of J. T. in him than I thought."

"Is that a compliment or an insult?"

It annoyed the hell out of him, the way Dunnigan had of asking the questions that made him dig deep for the answer. "A compliment," he admitted. "I might resent the hell out of the man, but he grew ten acres of pear trees into a hell of a good business."

"Maybe we should put him on as a consultant."

Scowling at the phone console, Rhys crumpled up the sandwich wrapping and tossed it into the trash. "Stick a sock in it, Dunnigan. One painful concession per day is my limit."

Hank laughed. "Wish I could be there when the first truck pulls out."

"If I know Del—and I do—she'll have it on video."

When Rhys was in Phoenix, he started his day with a pot of coffee and a stack of papers from all across the country left outside his door by the FedEx driver. By the time the pot was empty, he invariably had a list of leads for Goodeve to check out, ideas he'd gotten from reading the business sections.

Since returning to Phoenix, however, he rarely made it through the *Arizona Register* before he found himself thinking about his private time with Brina every morning and how cute she looked when she stumbled into the kitchen, her eyes only half focused, and her mouth pulled into a surly pout. Instead of checking the closing price of his own stock and that of his competitors, he was picturing that mouthwatering fanny as she bent to pull out her pots and pans. He liked her best in jeans, the tighter the better. His own personal favorite, hands down, was the paint-spattered pair she'd been wearing when she'd checked him in.

Since he'd been away from her, he missed the sex, but he missed the other things more, like the way she made him laugh, and the feeling of contentment it gave him to hold her in his arms while she slept. Although he wasn't ready to push for more than they had now, he suspected he might be edging that way.

After checking the time, he refilled his mug and reached for his phone. Brina answered on the third ring. The lilt in her voice warmed him all the way through. "It's Rhys, sweetheart. According to the Weather Channel it's pouring down rain where you are while here in Phoenix it's seventy-two degrees and sunny."

"You are a very cruel man, Rhys Hazard."

"A guy I know has a vacation place in the foothills. Not fancy, but private. Has its own pool and a skylight over the bed."

"I'm not listening."

"I'll do the cooking—and the cleaning up after."

"You never said you could cook." Her aggrieved tone had him grinning.

"You never asked."

"Not that it matters, because it's impossible."

"How long has it been since you've spent a weekend doing exactly what you want? With no phone calls to answer or meals to prepare or meetings to attend?" He leaned back and closed his eyes. "You won't even have to make the bed, since I doubt we'll be spending much time out of it."

"Now, that's low, Hazard. Totally unworthy of a man in your position."

"You know what they say, sweetheart, all's fair . . ."

In the sudden silence, the rest of the quotation hung in the air, unspoken. He'd never promised a woman love; he never would.

"I'll think about it," she conceded finally. "And now I'm going to hang up, because I'm already behind schedule and a Successful Innkeeper is always efficient."

"A Successful Innkeeper would be even more efficient after a weekend of uninhibited sex. Hazard's Rule Number One." Figuring to quit while he was ahead, he hung up while she was still laughing.

"Did you get the tape I overnighted?" Del demanded on the following Monday during their daily seven a.m. conversation. "Wasn't it fantastic?"

"Yes, if you say so," Rhys answered.

"Scoff all you want, but not five minutes ago Elena came in to tell me she's taken four calls already this morning from prospective customers who heard about us through the TV publicity. She routed the calls to John Sullivan, but I think she wanted you to know as well."

"Smart woman." Rhys made a note on his calendar to suggest to Hank that he give the woman a raise.

"What about the customers we already have? How did the actual runs go?" Rhys asked.

"Case Automotive went like clockwork. All deliveries were made early or on time."

"And Pacific Rim?"

"Not as good, unfortunately. Harrison had some trouble at the border."

"What kind of trouble?"

"Seems Canadian Customs picked Wednesday morning to conduct random searches, so Walt was late getting to the shipper's warehouse. He lost almost half a day and couldn't make it up on the turnaround trip. Sullivan wanted to fire Harrison for being late with the delivery, but as Harrison was only following company rules, I explained—with admirable restraint, if I do say so myself—that firing our senior driver without cause would bring on a lawsuit. Furthermore, I explained that you would no doubt be *extremely annoyed* if such were to happen and did he really want the shit to hit his personal fan?"

"Classy, Del, real classy."

"You bet, sugar."

The ancient GMC pickup reeked of baby puke and refried beans. The rig belonged to Paco Fuentes, a new hire up from the San Joaquin Valley. John had paid him ten bucks for a couple hours' rent and ten more for his silence.

It had been Sarge's idea to use nondescript wheels for the meeting tonight at his place, and John had to admit it made sense. The Corvette was too easily identified. As an extra precaution, John had stolen a straw hat out of one of the greaser's rigs a few days back, hiding it under a blanket in the 'Vette's trunk until tonight. One size too small, the hat dug into his forehead where he'd pulled it low over his eyes. He felt like a character in a cheesy movie. A character who was about to become very rich.

A smile creased his cheeks as he pulled into the lot and parked next to Sturgess' candy-apple red Dodge Ram 4WD. Sarge's silver Dakota was parked on the other side of the rear door, screening from view anyone who entered or exited.

Barely able to contain his excitement, John killed the ignition and lights, grabbed his briefcase and slipped from the rig. After taking a quick look around, he walked to the door and knocked, just the way Sarge had ordered. Even before he lowered his hand, the door opened only wide enough to allow the barrel of a sawed-off .12 gauge to poke through.

He took a quick step backward. "It's John Sullivan," he said, his heart thundering. The barrel was withdrawn and the door swung wide.

"Sarge is in the office," Red grated, stepping back into the dimly lit hallway like an eel oozing back into the rocks. As soon as John passed through, the barkeep locked the door behind him.

The office door stood open. Seated behind the desk, Sarge glanced up as he entered, but John scarcely noticed. Eyes locked on the three neat stacks of wrapped C-notes on the desk, he moved forward. One stack was noticeably smaller than the other two, but it was still more cash than John had ever seen in one place—and it was all his.

"Ain't nothin' prettier than fresh-minted greenbacks," Red said from behind him.

"Imagine you can guess which stack is yours," Sarge drawled.

John nodded. "Are you sure it's not counterfeit?" he blurted out before thinking.

"Hell, no, it's not counterfeit," Red declared. "What do you take us for, greenhorns?"

"No, I'm the greenhorn," John said, forcing a humble note into his voice. "A greenhorn who's about to piss his pants at the sight of so much lovely money."

Red stepped past him to place the shotgun on the desk before leaning down to pick up a small cardboard carton imprinted with the name Pacific Rim Trading Post. "Sarge had Chang wrap up the dope on account of most customs agents are too lazy to do anything extra, like slitting a strip of tape."

Faster than John could blink, Sarge pulled a wicked-looking skinning knife from a sheath strapped to his ankle, flipped it handle to blade, and held it out toward John.

Even as John's hand closed over the surprisingly warm black rubber handle, his blood ran cold. It would be easy for them to kill him and take his share. Aware of the mercilessly cold eyes watching his every move, he drew the box closer and slipped the blade point under a side flap. Honed to a razor-edge, the blade slipped easily through the banded tape.

After returning the knife to Sarge, handle foremost, John lifted the stiff flaps. Inside, he discovered twelve tightly packed four-by-four-inch Baggies, three layers deep. The black tar heroin inside each Baggie reminded him of coarse brown sand.

"Street value's anywhere from 500,000 dollars to 2 mil, depending on how you—or your friends—cut it," Red said.

"Feel free to count your share of the money," Sarge said. "After deducting what you owe and the value of the goods, it came out to 515,000 dollars."

John's breath hissed in, and when he snapped open his briefcase, his hand shook.

"Not too shabby for a coupla hours' work," Red offered as Sarge thumbed the old Zippo into flame and touched it to the tip of his cigarette.

John grinned as he began transferring the cash. "Easiest half mil I ever made."

Brina powered down her bookkeeping program, shut off the computer and reached for her emergency bag of Hershey's Kisses. The windfall from North Star that had seemed so enormous when she'd signed the contract had been eaten away by expenses like increased insurance premiums and the past-due payment to the orthodontist. At least she was still in the black, if only by a few hundred dollars, she consoled herself as she tugged on the paper tab to open another Kiss.

The front door opened with a jangling of temple bells a split second before Marcy's exuberant shout exploded into the afternoon quiet. "Mommy, Mommy, look what Daddy got me!"

"I'm in here, sweetie. In my office." A quick glance at the clock had her heart sinking. John had promised to take the kids to the auto show as a special treat for Jay. Brina hadn't expected them back until seven at the earliest. Since it was only a few minutes before five, the odds were pretty good Johnny had broken his promise to his son once again.

"Mommy, look!" Marcy demanded as the door slammed back against the office wall. Rain glistened on her slicker as she bustled inside, an unfamiliar cat carrier clutched in front of her.

"It's a baby bunny. I'm gonna call him Mopsy, like in the story in my book. Because of his ears and all. See, Mommy, see?"

It was a rabbit, all right. Mostly gray, with darker patches splattered like paint on the silky fur, the poor little creature was huddled into the corner, one long ear standing straight up like a semaphore flag, the other hanging limp. Hard little pellets littered the newspaper lining, rolling from side to side like marbles as Marcy manhandled the carrier onto the desktop.

John appeared in the doorway, looking impatient and handsome. "Not to worry, babe," he said as he perched on a corner of her desk. "Marcy girl's promised to take care of Mopsy all by herself. Haven't you, princess?" His face softened as he reached down to ease the hood back.

"Yes, Daddy." Marcy turned her face up to receive her father's smile.

Brina turned the front of the carrier to the side, but the smell remained. "Marce, why don't you take Mopsy up to your room while Daddy and I have a talk?"

"Might be better to take him to the utility room until you change the paper," John said. Brina was surprised by his thoughtfulness.

"Okay." Marcy grabbed the handle with chubby fingers and bumped the carrier off the desk. "C'mon, Mopsy. Let's go outside and play."

When she was gone, Brina leaned back and regarded her ex-husband with cold eyes. "What happened to the auto show?"

"Sherri's in bed with a migraine, so we didn't go."

"You couldn't take the kids alone?"

"Of course, I couldn't. Jay understood."

That was exactly the trouble. Jay understood all too well that his father could barely stand him. "Where is he now?"

"I dropped him off at Eric's place."

At least he'd be sure of a warm welcome in his friend's large family. "What kind of a pet did you get *him?*"

John frowned. "What the hell does that mean?"

She reined in her impatience. It was a familiar ploy, turning on her when she challenged him. "We had an agreement, John. No favoritism between the children, which means equal attention, equal presents."

"For crissakes, Brin, Jay's almost thirteen. He doesn't need a present every time he comes over to the house."

"Neither does Marcy."

His mouth slanted, and his eyes turned smug. "You wouldn't happen to be jealous of your own daughter, would you, babe?"

Brina glanced down at the chunk of old brick she used as a paperweight. "John, you are the father of my children, and since I would do just about anything to spare them pain, I am working very hard to keep from bashing your head in."

"Very funny, Brin," he said, but he slipped off the corner of her desk and took a step backward. "You'd do well not to piss me off, lady, because I can still petition for full custody."

Brina felt the blood drain from her face. That had always been her secret fear, one she suspected John knew all too well. "You'd never win," she declared with false bravado.

The cocky smile she'd once swooned over now seemed sickeningly smug. "Don't be so sure. Especially if the court finds out you have a convicted felon living in the same house with my children."

"You bastard!"

"No, that's my so-called brother, the one who smashed in Teddy's chest. Remember that day, Brin? Remember how Teddy's blood turned your pink parka red?"

Brina picked up the brick and drew back her arm. "Get out of my house, you miserable hypocrite. Now!"

He turned tail and ran. Slowly she lowered her arm, her heart thudding and her stomach roiling. The burst of temper was already fading, and in its place was a growing uneasiness. John wanted full custody the way she wanted a chronic yeast infection. Still, he was fully capable of doing exactly as he'd just threatened. It all depended on what he hoped to gain. Last time they went to court, he wanted to rid himself of an unwanted wife so he could diddle his trophy bimbo openly.

This time, though . . .

The pressure in her chest decided her. Leaning forward, she flipped through her Rolodex for the number of her bargain-basement attorney, Jonah Maccafee. It wouldn't hurt to find out what he thought about John's threat. No matter what John said, he wasn't going to take her children away from her.

Chapter 25

By Wednesday Rhys had tied up enough loose ends to feel comfortable about returning to Osuma. It was midafternoon when they landed. Rhys had a taxi take him to the depot while another ferried Max to the inn in order to pick up the Mercedes.

Since the day shift ended at three thirty, and they had yet to inaugurate a swing shift, the parking lot was all but empty when he arrived. SUVs still bearing temporary plates were parked in both Del's slot and Emory's.

The lights were on inside the building, and the walls gleamed white in the glare. The smell of fresh paint was overlaid by a familiar mix of oil and grease and stale coffee. In the maintenance area adjacent to the huge doors, all but one of the service bays were empty. Rhys stopped short when he recognized Brina's van. The hood was up, and a skeletally thin man in worn, grease-stained coveralls was working on the engine.

"Bad starter?" Rhys asked after going closer for a look-see.

The man's head came up fast. Twenty years ago Theo Eiler's chief mechanic had been a nice looking man, with a ready smile and a fondness for corny jokes. The years had taken their toll, Rhys saw now, gouging lines in the man's thin cheeks and rounding his shoulders. After a stunned moment of mutual recognition, Rhys tamped down his bitterness and offered his hand.

"Nice to see you again, Wayne."

Exhibiting all the signs of a man who wanted to be anywhere but where he was, Wayne swiped his hand over his thigh, before taking Rhys' hand. "Uh, you, too, Michael, uh, I mean Mr. Hazard."

"Call me Rhys."

"Yes, sir."

It seemed important that he meet Rhys' eyes squarely. Rhys saw a mirror image of his own nightmare in those faded brown eyes—and something more, something he had seen in the eyes of every lifer he had encountered during his four years inside. It was an odd blank quality, part acceptance, part despair and, in Wayne's case, part embarrassment.

"I'm real sorry about what happened. Theo, too. It pained him for the rest of his life. I know he wished he hadn't had to say them things to the jury."

Now Rhys wanted to be someplace else, too. "I buried that a long time ago."

Wayne gave a nervous look around. "You done good, that's for sure. I reckon your daddy is real proud."

Rhys bit back bitter words and shrugged instead.

"Uh, in case you was wondering, Mr. Scruggs said it would be okay, me working on Brina's van on my own time."

"Can it be fixed?"

"It can, yes, but it'll cost dear, even with me not charging any for labor."

"How dear?"

"Upwards of four, five hundred to get her running good. Brakes are about shot, too, and the tranny don't sound right neither."

Rhys studied the ugly green junker for a long moment. "When did you promise to have it back to her?"

"Not until Friday sometime. On account of the age of this baby, I had to order the starter special from a place down in L.A."

"What's she doing for wheels in the meantime?"

"Borrowed Miz Steinberg's rig." The hollow echo of heavy footsteps approaching from the right drew Wayne's startled gaze.

"Thought I heard voices," Emory Scruggs said as he approached. "Welcome back, boss. We missed you."

"According to what Del's been telling me, you've been doing great without me."

"Been lucky, that's all. Got another run due for Case Automotive on Friday. That's the rig yonder. Had her checked out this morning and figured to keep her inside in case one of them clouds that kept going by overhead decides to unload between now and the time she's due to pull out."

Rhys nodded. "In case you haven't figured it out, Wayne, Emory's as fussy as an old maid about those rigs."

"Nothing wrong with that by my way of thinking. I used to feel the same way about them school buses." He stopped abruptly, his facial muscles freezing. "No offense," he muttered, dropping his gaze.

"None taken," Rhys said before turning Emory's way. "See if you can find Walt Harrison and ask him to stop by my office."

Scruggs' expression turned wary. "Rhys, if it's about him being late with that delivery, I know John Sullivan's making noises about firing him, but it ain't right."

"Don't worry, Emory. I'm not going to fire him. I'm going to give him a raise."

It was just past ten o'clock. For the past hour Rhys and Jay had been working on the model of a freight depot Jay was making for his science project. Marcy was asleep, and Jay had promised to wind it up in five minutes.

After returning from a particularly fractious PTA meeting, Brina had made espresso for her guests. She carried two cups upstairs to the third-floor family room.

Settling into the lumpy sofa bed that had been the first item of furniture she and John had bought, she propped her feet on the old trunk she used as a coffee table and leaned back. She was drifting in a dreamy haze when she heard Jay's door open and close.

Rhys wore those really sexy sweatpants that had her all but hyperventilating and a faded North Star sweatshirt with the neck ribbing ripped away. He had gone to the gym after leaving the depot for a massage to loosen the knotted muscles of his hip and thigh.

"How's the model progressing?" she asked as he used the arm of the sofa to steady himself so that he could ease onto the lumpy sofa's cushion.

"Like most construction projects, it's looking to come in late and over budget." His face tightened as he bent into a sitting position. "In this case the architect is saddled with an inexperienced crew of one, who happens to be all thumbs."

She waited until he put aside his cane before handing him the espresso. "For the crew."

His smile was slow but potent. "This is nice, thanks."

He leaned back before taking a sip. It hadn't taken her long to realize he preferred silence to meaningless chitchat. When he had free time, he usually chose to sit down with a book. His tastes were wide-ranging and he retained an amazing amount of what he read.

"I miss the good old days when Jay loved to snuggle up next to me and beg for one more story the way Marcy does now," she admitted. "Now I'm lucky if I get a good night kiss."

"Won't be long before he'll be snuggling up to some sweet little honey, begging for more than a story." He set his mug on the end table before slipping his arm around her shoulders. "Lord, but you smell good," he said, nuzzling her neck. Delicious shivers ran through her, and she suddenly knew what compelled a cat to purr.

"I'll give you three hours to stop that," she threatened while her eyes drifted closed.

"What if I don't?" His breath was warm against her throat and she arched.back her head to give him better access.

"Then I'll give you three hours more."

His laughter came easier now, and more often. "You drive a hard bargain, honey. I'll have to think about that some. In the meantime . . ."

He kissed her until she felt as though all the air had been sucked out of the room. When he finally drew back, her head spun.

"Remember the wallpapering Del and I did?" she asked after she had managed to draw in enough breath to allow speech. "I think it's time I showed it to you."

His knuckles brushed her neck as he played with a disobedient tendril of hair. The indulgent smile in his eyes warmed her all the way to her toes. "You want to show me your bathroom now?" he drawled with bemused disbelief.

She smiled with just enough wicked cheekiness to whet his interest. "Actually, I want to show you my bath*tub*. With both of us naked and deliciously slippery."

His eyes kindled with a hunger that thrilled her to the core. "For someone who keeps telling me she's not wild and crazy, you sure do have a thing about stripping a man out of his jeans every chance you get."

She let her feelings shine through her eyes as she ran her fingers over his thigh to his fly. "My friend Dottie Krebs swears it's the leftover sexual energy in the house that's affecting me." She rubbed the hard ridge behind his zipper, and he sucked in a harsh breath before capturing her hand with his.

"Whatever it is," he said, "I'm damned grateful."

They got each other naked in record time. He grumbled when she dumped in gardenia bath beads, claiming they made him sneeze; then he proceeded to lick her nipples into hot, swollen nubbins while the water churned the beads into soft, fragrant suds. When the tub was full, he slipped in first, his erection moving through the suds like the fin of a shark. He scowled at her when she giggled, then got even by pulling her down on top of him.

It was the first time she had ever made love and laughed at the same time. She climaxed three times, the last time taking him with her. Now, with a delicious afterglow still shimmering through her, she lay nestled in his arms.

He lay with his back against the slippery white porcelain, his skin damp and glistening. Tiny drops of water clung to the golden chest hair surrounding the flat brown nipples. Water lapped gently against her bottom as she snuggled against him, too content to move.

"I've never made love in a bathtub before," she murmured. "It could get to be a habit."

His smile was indulgent and tinged with a lovely masculine arrogance. "I'm willing whenever you are." His sexy male dimples deepened. "Only next time, you think we could do without the sissy bath stuff?"

"Oh no, the sense of smell is the strongest aphrodisiac there is, and gardenia is a very provocative scent. That's why tropical islands are so romantic."

"Romantic, hell. If I was to walk through the maintenance shop smelling like this, my guys would never let me hear the end of it."

"Then what do you suggest we use instead, motor oil?"

"You said you wanted slippery, didn't you?"

"Not that slippery," she murmured before kissing his jaw. "How about we compromise on Jell-O. Lemon is a very macho scent."

He turned his head to kiss her nose. "So is transmission fluid," he said, drawing up one leg. She felt him flinch and frowned.

"Is your hip hurting?"

He hesitated, then said evenly and without inflection, "I'm used to it."

"Can't they do something? Replace it with plastic or whatever?"

"Tried a hip replacement once about ten years back. The anesthetic put me in cardiac arrest, so they scrubbed the procedure. I'm not real eager to try that again."

She gave a little shudder. Instantly, his arms tightened. The solid muscles cushioning her tensed, then relaxed. "I missed you, wildcat," he murmured in her ear.

"I missed you, too. I—" She was interrupted by a loud thump coming from the direction of the landing outside, followed by rapid footsteps and an urgent whisper as Marcy called her bunny's name.

Brina turned her face into Rhys' throat to muffle her heartfelt groan. "I swear, if that rabbit gets out one more time, she's going to end up fricasseed."

She felt his chest shaking as he laughed softly. "Wouldn't it be easier if you just had someone build you a bunny run?"

Grinning, she pulled out of his arms before turning carefully to look up at him. "Why, bless my soul, Mr. Hazard, sir. What a *brilliant* idea!"

A look of pure panic glinted in his eyes. "Oh no you don't, wildcat. I'm a truck driver, not a carpenter."

"I have confidence in you." She trailed her nail along the narrow line of golden hair arrowing down from his midchest to his navel. He sucked in a breath, and she went lower. "I'll trade you one of those chocolate walnut cheesecakes you liked so much."

"I can't be . . . bought." His body jerked when her hand closed around his penis. For good measure she gave a little tug that had his body swelling and his breath rushing from his chest.

"Think of that poor little bunny locked up in that tiny cage. Surely you can empathize."

"Dirty pool, sweetheart," he muttered, glaring.

"No, this is dirty pool, big guy." Smiling serenely, she bent her head and licked the hot tip of his penis like a particularly tasty ice cream cone.

Swallowing his groan, he bucked like a stallion, and his hand clamped down around a thick hank of her hair. "Honey, do that again, and I'll give you anything you want."

All I'll ever want is for you to let yourself love me, she longed to say. Instead, she bent her head and did it again. And then again.

Figuring he deserved some downtime, Rhys took Thursday afternoon off. After working out, he and Max went shopping for building materials, which took longer than he'd anticipated, so it was going on three o'clock before he actually began construction.

Fortunately, it was a sunny day and he could work outside. Brina had left earlier in a taxi to pick up Marcy, who was off somewhere on something called a play date, and Max had taken the Mercedes in for an oil change. Rhys and Mopsy had the backyard to themselves.

The plywood, two-by-fours and chicken wire he and Max had picked up at the lumberyard were stacked to one side of the brick patio, along with a quart of pale blue paint, the closest to the color of the inn's siding he could find. After checking Brina's pathetically meager selection of tools, he had also bought a power saw, a battery-powered drill and a good hammer, along with nails, screws and hinges.

A methodical man by necessity if not inclination, he figured a detailed plan would save on both time and aggravation. Using the redwood picnic table as a drafting table, he drew his own version of a blueprint, while nearby, the rabbit hopped back and forth in its tiny prison.

"What do you think of a peaked roof, Mopsy?" he wondered aloud. "Maybe with a little porch in the front, too?"

In answer the bunny hopped to the rear of the carrier, and then back again to give him a pleading look. "Yeah, I know, baby, it's hell to be in a cage, but the thing is, I have a strong feeling the minute I let you out, you'll hightail it for the hills and no way can I catch you." He stuck a finger through the grill to rub between the baby's long ears. "Much as I hate to keep any living thing penned up, it would flat-out break my heart to disappoint that little darlin' who loves you so much."

Mopsy lifted her head to lick his finger with a tiny pink tongue, and he grinned. "What say I give you a skylight so you won't feel so shut in?" He and the rabbit exchanged a moment of perfect accord before she sat on her fat bottom and began diligently grooming one floppy ear.

Twenty minutes later he had the design for the rabbit house roughed out and was sawing the last of the pine two-by-fours to length when Jay wandered outside, his hair standing up in odd clumps. He ambled across the patio, munching on a granola bar.

"What's up?" Rhys asked as the saw whined to a stop.

The boy shrugged both shoulders. "Nothing much."

"How was school?"

"Bogus like always." He kicked the stack of boards with the toe of his Air Jordans. "Some of the guys went downtown to practice skateboarding behind the library or hang out at the Dairy Queen, but me, the only place I'm allowed to go is home or to a friend's house."

Rhys strapped on the tool belt he'd bought along with the other materials, then filled the pouch with nails. "You like skateboarding, do you?"

"I tried it a few times, but I crashed into the back of a moving van and split my skull open. Mom gave my skateboard to the Salvation Army. The guys still rag me about it sometimes."

Rhys fitted a board, then hammered it in place. "Might be she's not real sure she's doing the right things by her kids, so she goes a little overboard with the hovering thing, just in case." He shifted his gaze to Jay's face. "Seems kinda nice to me, having someone care enough to worry about you."

"I guess she's mostly okay." Jay handed him another two-by-four. "She's a lot happier now that my dad's not telling her what she's doing wrong all the time like he used to."

Rhys consulted his blueprint before fitting the board into place. "How about you, are you happier, too?"

"I guess. Only sometimes there's stuff a guy can't talk about with his mom, you know?"

Rhys kept his gaze on his work, but he had a sinking feeling in his gut. A dad he wasn't. Didn't even pretend to be. Still, the kid seemed to need a friend. That he could probably handle okay—as long as they didn't get into real heavy shit.

"What kind of stuff is that?" he asked as he took another nail from the belt.

Jay shoved his hands into his pockets and dropped his gaze. "I don't know, just stuff."

Rhys hammered the nail home. "Jay, we haven't been around each other long enough for you to have figured out whether you can trust me or not, so I'll let it drop. Just so you know, though, I'm on your side. Anything you tell me stays with me."

"I trust you, " Jay mumbled in a nearly inaudible tone.

Rhys cleared his throat. The lump was still there. "That means a lot to me, Jay. There was a time when I was afraid no one would ever trust me again."

Jay lifted troubled eyes to his for a moment before glancing down again. "It's like I might not be . . . normal, you know?"

Rhys flicked him a glance and saw that the boy's face had turned so pale his freckles looked like drops of blood. Damn, now what? "Normal how?"

"I don't know, maybe like sex stuff, you know?"

Christ, you had to ask, didn't you, slick? Taking his time, Rhys put down the hammer and reached for the icy cold can of

Mountain Dew he considered his own special reward for the hours of hard labor he'd put in.

"What kind of sex stuff?" he asked before taking a long, thirsty sip.

The boy drew a ragged breath. "It's like Petey and some of the other guys have these dreams."

Rhys nearly choked. Lord save him, this was way beyond anything he had ever dealt with before. "Are we talking about wet dreams?"

Jay bobbed his head, his gaze still fixed on the ground. "If a guy never has one, does that mean he's . . . like a . . . a faggot?"

Hell, what's going on here? Rhys wondered, fighting panic. "Are you saying you think you might be gay?"

"I don't know. Sherri said I am." A look of misery settled over him as he worried a rough edge on one of the patio bricks with the toe of his sneaker. "Maybe she's right on account of I'm pathetic at sports and . . . fighting and dumb stuff like that."

Rhys set the soda can on the table, then lowered himself to the bench so that he and Jay were eye to eye. "Jay, being gay or straight has nothing to do with how good you are at sports."

"How do you know?"

"Well, for one thing, one of my drivers in Phoenix used to be in a committed relationship with a defensive lineman who plays for the Oakland Raiders. They broke up because the guy was cheating on him with a wide receiver from the Chargers."

Jay stared. "No shit?"

"No shit." Rhys picked up his Dew and rolled the can between his hands, buying a little time. Finally, he made himself ask, "Marcy says there's a girl you like. Amy, is it?"

Jay nodded, then blushed so violently the tips of his ears turned red. "Only she's like really, really popular. Mostly she sits with guys on the soccer team at lunch, but sometimes she, like, talks to me before geometry class and she's real sweet and all."

Rhys remembered those shy days. "So when you look at her, how do you feel?"

Jay shrugged one shoulder. "I don't know. Mostly good, I guess, only sometimes I feel really scared that I'll say something dumb and she'll hate me."

Rhys took a few more sips before asking, "Do you ever think about how it would feel to kiss her?"

Guilt flashed in the boy's eyes before he glanced down. "Sometimes, yeah," he mumbled.

"Think you'd like it if you did?"

Jay nodded, but he was clearly in puberty hell. Rhys managed not to sigh. "In that case, sounds to me like you don't need to worry about being gay."

Jay glanced at him through his lashes, a look of desperate hope on his face. "Really?"

"Really." Rhys hesitated, trying to remember what his dad had told him. The words were lost to him now, but the feeling of relief and comfort he'd felt then came rushing back. "About those wet dreams, don't be in such a hurry to go down that road."

"Why not?"

"Well, for one thing, it's a damn hassle trying to sneak the sheets to the washing machine without anyone knowing."

Jay's face went blank for a beat or two before he ducked his head and grinned. "Mom would find out sure enough."

"Probably would, but from what I've seen, she'd be cool about it."

"Yeah, I guess," Jay acknowledged, though he didn't sound convinced. "Was Grandmother cool?"

"No, she went ballistic. Called me worse names than 'faggot.'" Rhys finished off the soda before putting the empty aside. Overhead a big old crow scolded a squirrel, and the squirrel returned the favor. Late afternoon sunshine slanted through the leaf canopy to dapple the newly mowed grass, and the air smelled like flowers. He realized he didn't want to leave this place. Ever. His mouth went dry before he pushed the thought aside.

"Dad said he was fifteen when he had sex the first time." Jay picked up a scrap of two-by-four and picked at a loose sliver. "He said the girl was in college already, only she still had a crush on him."

"Did he?"

"Uh-huh." Jay tossed the wood onto the discard pile under the picnic table, startling the crow into another scold. Squinting against the sun, Jay watched the irate bird for a moment before shifting his gaze back to Rhys. "How old were you the first time?"

"Twenty-three." Hoping the kid didn't ask for a play-by-play account of his first fumbling encounter, Rhys levered himself to his feet and picked up his hammer. He was in uncharted territory here and hoped to hell he didn't blow it. "Hand me that one-by-four there . . . no, the short one."

Jay handed it over, and Rhys thanked him. "How come you were so old?" Jay persisted.

He should have figured the boy would have his mother's curiosity. "Just happened that way, I guess."

"Mom says if guys want girls to be virgins when they get married, then guys should be, too."

Brina had told Rhys she'd been a virgin when she married John, but until now he hadn't allowed himself to think of her in bed with his asshole brother. He wasn't real eager to think about it now. "Your mom has a point," he hedged. "Especially now, when sex with the wrong person can end up killing you."

Jay frowned. "Do you think guys should be virgins?"

"I'm sure there are guys who think like your mom, and some who don't." Damn few, he suspected. In fact, he didn't personally know a single one, but hey, he was no expert when it came to stuff like that. On the other hand he remembered all too well those scary days when his body was changing and he was stumbling his way toward manhood. Truth to tell, he felt flattered the kid would trust him enough to ask. "I also think there are girls—women—who want a guy to have experience. Makes 'em feel more secure, I guess. Me, I think a man has to figure out what's right for him."

Furrowing his brow, Jay mulled that over. Rhys hoped to hell he'd said the right thing. At any rate, he'd told the truth as he saw it. He'd learned a long time ago that honesty usually saved him a lot of grief.

"Dad says chicks like guys who have big peckers."

Rhys nearly groaned. The boy was relentless. "I'm not sure you should use that term around your mom."

Jay shot a quick look around before risking a grin. "Yeah, she'd bust a gut, all right. Mom's kinda funny about a lot of things. Dad says she's a prude."

He would, the scumbag. "Tell you the truth, Jay, I think it's kinda nice having to watch my language. Makes things more civilized, somehow. Then again, I'm no expert on women. Del says I'm a typical *guy*." He rubbed his thumb over the scar on his chin. "Way she says it, I figure women rate a *guy* maybe one notch above pond scum."

"Yeah? Why's that?"

He slammed a nail home, then set down the hammer and flexed his hand. "Well, best I can make out, a *guy* is dense as a post when it comes to women." He leaned against the table and rested his hip. "Del says he listens but he only hears what he wants to—whatever the hell that means."

"Maybe it's like when Mom says I act like I'm deaf when she's telling me to do something and I don't want to."

"I think you might be on to something there, son. I'm not real good at taking orders."

"Me neither. Mom says I'll probably end up running my own company like Grandda so I can *give* the orders." He slanted Rhys a look. "Like you did, right?"

"Right."

Looking a little cocky now, Jay picked up a board and rubbed his finger over a knot in the pine. "You probably don't need any help with this thing?"

"You offering?"

"Nah, I'd probably just mess up."

"Way I see it, you couldn't mess it up any worse than me." He picked up the hammer, flipped it and extended it handle first toward the kid. "Besides, this way we can blame each other if it turns out lousy."

"Okay, but you have to explain to Mom why I haven't finished my homework."

"I'll handle it."

"You like her, don't you?"

"Yeah, I like her."

"She likes you, too. I can tell. I used to hear her crying sometimes at night even before the divorce. She doesn't do that anymore."

"I'm glad."

"Yeah, me, too. I think it's 'cause you make her happy." Before he ducked his head there was a look in his eyes that made Rhys hold his breath. Love, he thought, stunned. The kid loved him.

Chapter 26

Fog was still thick on the ground as John drove down Old Orchard Road early the next morning. Beyond the chain-link fence the depot was a blur of white in the hazy dawn light as he turned onto the short access road. Although it was past daybreak, state-of-the-art security lights still blazed atop the guard shack and around the perimeter of the twenty-acre lot.

After halting at the gate, he shifted to neutral and let the engine idle as the guard emerged from the hut. Unlike the G.I. Joe who worked days, the night man was more laid-back, an ex-cop of no more than average height with a stocky build just going to fat. After a perfunctory look at the parking sticker affixed to the Sting Ray's bumper, he strode with clipboard in hand to the driver's side.

Smile at the ready, John rolled down the window. "Morning, officer," he said, handing over his ID.

"Morning, sir."

"Anyone beat me in yet, someone who might have put on the coffee?"

"No, sir. Expect Mr. Hazard right soon, though. Heard he got back Wednesday sometime."

John had heard the same thing, which was why he was here now. "Guess it doesn't hurt to impress the boss now and then," John tossed off as he shifted into first.

"No, sir, that's a fact right enough." The guard hung the

clipboard on a hook by the door before walking to the gate and swinging it open.

"Have a good day," he said as John drove past.

Good? Hell, he intended to have a fucking *great* day, John told himself, gunning the 'Vette across the row of neatly out-lined spaces to his spot.

He got out quickly, frowning as the damp air hit his face. After retrieving his briefcase from the trunk, he slammed it shut and headed for the entrance. With the security moved to the perimeter, the doors were no longer kept locked. Minimal lights illuminated the depot's cavernous interior, casting the corners into shadows. As he strode purposefully toward the rig still parked in the far bay, John couldn't help grinning. Very soon NSN would be a distant memory and its asshole owner would be back in a jail cell where he belonged.

The rig rolled out at seven o'clock, exactly on time. Stand-ing at the window in his office, his hands jammed in the pock-ets of his tailored trousers, John watched the long length of tractor and trailer traveling along Old Orchard Road until both were swallowed by the fog. In his mind's eye he traced the eighteen-wheeler's route along Highway 2 to U.S. 97 and Blewett Pass to Interstate 90.

According to the timetable in the dispatcher's log, the rig was due to arrive at Case Automotive in Tacoma no later than 1:00 P.M. Plenty of time, John reminded himself as he pulled his hands free and returned to his desk. At 7:20 he opened the bottom drawer, pulled out the cheap cell phone he'd bought in Wenatchee last week under an assumed name, and called the Osuma Police Department.

Using a thick greaser accent, he told the woman who an-swered that he had important information to share, but only if he could speak to *el comandante* himself.

"Hollister, here. Understand you wanted to talk to me?"

*   *   *

"The letter of intent Ericson signed has to be ratified by his board before the contract can be officially awarded," Rhys said into the phone as he scrawled his name on the last letter in the folder.

"Guess that means you'll wait to do your celebrating until the signed contract hits your desk," Hank said.

"That's about the size of it, yeah." He heard the sound of Max's heavy tread on the flooring outside an instant before his driver appeared in the doorway.

"Ready to roll when you are, boss," he said before he realized Rhys was on the phone.

"Is that Max's voice I hear or is your stomach growling extra loud?" Hank asked.

"Say hello to Hank, Max," Rhys said as he locked the workstation desk.

Scowling, Max tossed a disgusted look at the space-age speaker on the desk next to the phone console. Max didn't trust anything invented after he'd reached puberty.

"Hello, Hank," Max muttered.

Hank returned the greeting before drawling, "Am I hearing things, or did you just tell our mutual employer that you were ready to roll when he was? Surely the man isn't actually leaving his desk in the middle of the day?"

"Couldn't hardly believe it myself," Max said.

"Cut it out, you clowns," Rhys grumbled.

Max ignored him. There was nothing his driver liked better than a chance to rag the boss. "Man even had me on the phone all morning, talking to car dealers," he said, speaking louder than necessary.

"Planning to trade the 600 already?"

Max snorted. "Not hardly. The boss is fixin' to buy Ms. Sullivan a Suburban."

*　　　*　　　*

Rhys waited until the Mercedes had purred past the guard and headed south before fixing Max with an icy stare. Although Max kept his attention on the road, the tip of the one cauliflower ear Rhys could see turned red. "Don't say it, boss. I know I screwed up," he mumbled, scarcely moving his lips.

"Worse than big-time. Thanks to you, I'll never hear the end of this from Dunnigan." He was already bracing himself in anticipation of the next time he and his VP spoke.

"Guess I wasn't thinking real clear. Won't happen again."

Squinting against the glare of midday sun bouncing off the Mercedes' gleaming hood, Rhys opened the glove compartment and retrieved the sunglasses Max kept for him because he could never remember them on his own.

"You haven't been *'thinking clear'* since you started playing musical beds with Miss Winkle." As he slipped on the glasses, Rhys took perverse satisfaction in watching that hard slab of knuckle-busting granite shaped like a jaw turn red. "Why don't you just buy her a ring and make it official?"

Max flicked him a look full of misery before jerking his gaze back to the road. "Already got a ring while we was— were—back in Phoenix. From that diamond broker Del sets such store by, you know? Nothing fancy, but all the way quality. Only . . ." His voice trailed off.

"Only what?"

Max's hands tightened around the wheel. "The time or two we done circled around the idea of maybe getting married, she . . . she made it real clear she wanted to adopt some kids— and she doesn't want to wait long before getting them."

"Yes, so?"

"C'mon, boss. Can you see a palooka with my mug with kids? Probably give 'em serious nightmares."

Rhys heard something in his driver's voice that dammed the smart-ass remark in his throat. "Marcy doesn't seem bothered by your mug."

"Marcy's special, you know? On account of she's got such an exceptional mom."

One thing Rhys knew how to do was seize an opportunity and turn it to his advantage. "Guess Ernestine would be a pretty sorry mom at that."

Max's head whipped his way. Raw fury glinted in eyes the color of fire. "Anyone else said that, I'd stop this car right now and take him apart."

"Could be I was wrong about that," Rhys said, his tone deliberately mild.

"Damn straight," Max declared before fixing his attention on the road again. "Ernie can't see it clear enough, the kind of hell it would be for a kid growing up with an ex-con for a dad, but I can. Might not be bad when he or she was little, but soon as the kid started school, the ugly words would start." His throat worked. "It would kill me, knowing my kid was being beat down on account of me."

The Mercedes swayed imperceptibly as Max negotiated the turn onto Highway 2. From the corner of his eye Rhys caught sight of the memorial stone and tightened his stomach muscles. No matter how many times he passed this spot, guilt slammed like a hard, fast fist dead center in his gut.

"I'm right, ain't I, Rhys? About saying no to adopting kids?" Max's gaze swung Rhys' way again. Before he could answer, a siren shrilled behind them. Max jerked his gaze to the mirror.

"Shit, where'd he come from?"

Rhys glanced at the speedometer before casting a quick look over his shoulder. He had never known a cop to go lights and siren for a mere traffic stop. "Probably on his way someplace else."

Max slowed to let the Bronco pass. Instead, it stuck to his tail like a leech. "It's me he wants," Max grated a moment later.

"Better pull over then."

"Tags have another six months before they expire," Max muttered. "Damn sure wasn't speeding neither." He braked to a stop on the graveled berm.

Rhys took the folder containing the registration and proof of insurance from the glove box and passed it to Max, who had already taken his wallet from his back pocket.

"Hell, it's the head guy. Hollister," Max said, his gaze glued to the side mirror.

What had been a simple annoyance now sharpened into a real concern. Hollister hadn't struck Rhys as a power-drunk yahoo who got his jollies harassing unsuspecting motorists. Max slid down the window, his expression grim.

Rhys knew better than to release his seat belt. He knew ex-cons who had ended up spending a night in jail—or worse—because a cop with a burr up his ass had wanted an excuse to vent some frustration on ex-offender scum. Max had learned the same lesson.

"Sorry about the lights and siren, gentlemen," Hollister said with an *aw shucks* grin that Rhys suspected hid an impressive will. "Just can't resist sometimes."

Max offered him the folder, which he refused. The cop was so tall he had to bend awkwardly to speak to them directly. "Truth is, Mr. Hazard, I showed up at your place looking to have a talk with you, and the guard said you'd just left."

"Talk about what, Chief?"

"I understand you sent out one of your rigs this morning headed for a pickup in Tacoma?"

"That's right. Something wrong? Did the driver have an accident?"

Hollister used one finger to push up the brim of his Stetson. "Now, that's an interesting question. Same one I came out this way to ask you, as a matter of fact."

Rhys frowned. "Do you always take the long way around a subject, Hollister, or is this something you worked up just for me?"

"Point taken. Thought you'd like to know your rig is on its
way to DEA impound in Wenatchee and your driver is on his
way to the county jail. Charge is felony possession of an illegal substance and suspicion of possession to sell."

Rhys went cold. "What kind of illegal substance?"

"Black tar heroin. Eleven kilos, to be precise, tucked real
neat under the mattress in the sleeping compartment."

Rhys was on the phone with his corporate attorney, Pearl
Silverman, when Elena stuck her head in. "The guard at the
gate says there's a news crew from a Seattle station asking to
talk to you about Mr. Harrison's arrest. He wants to know if he
should pass them through."

He swore silently. "Tell him it'll cost him his job if one of
those bloodsuckers sets a foot on North Star property. Also tell
him to pass it on to his relief when he leaves."

The reporters hung around until late afternoon when a sudden squall sent them on their way. J. T. called him a few minutes before five to tell him they had shown up at his place,
demanding an interview. He had scared them off.

"Someone will talk with them, Rhys," J. T. said with audible concern. "It's just a matter of time before they rake up all
the old garbage and throw it at you. I think you'd better be
prepared."

The gaze meeting his through the wire mesh separating
Rhys from the prisoner was desperate. "It was a setup,
Mickey, I swear it was. I never even seen heroin before!" In
his agitation Walt Harrison had forgotten that Michael Sullivan no longer existed.

"I believe you, Walt. The company will pay for your attorney and your bail once the judge sets it at the arraignment tomorrow. Our attorney in Phoenix, Ms. Silverman, is already
making calls on your behalf."

"For what it's worth, I was never one of them saying bad things about you during that sorry mess all those years ago."

Rhys stiffened. "Anything else I can do for you before I go?"

Harrison ran a sun-weathered hand through his thinning hair. "My wife, she had rheumatic fever as a child, and having the twins took a lot out of her. She's been sick on and off since then. Doc Krebs has done a good job of keeping her alive, but he's warned her about too much stress."

"Has someone contacted her?"

He nodded. "I always call her from the road at least twice a day. If I hadn't called, she would have started worrying, only I don't know which is worse, you know?"

"Have you seen her yet?"

"No, she's on her way here. I told her not to come, but she made my daughter Sharon drive her over. I'm afraid, if she sees me in this place, it'll kill her." He cast a quick look around the dingy visitors room before dropping his bleak gaze to the orange jumpsuit. "God Almighty, this is a nightmare. I'm not much of a churchgoing man, but I keep the Commandments and I've never hurt anyone."

"I believe you, Walt," Rhys said. The mesh that separated them didn't look anything like cell bars, but he was beginning to feel the first fingers of panic clawing at him. "Don't take this wrong, but if there's anything you can tell the DEA agents that you haven't already told them, even something you consider trivial, it might help."

Harrison shook his head. "Ain't anything to tell, I swear. I showed up like always, punched in, and then me and Mr. Scruggs went over the rig one more time before I fired her up and went out to hook up to the trailer." He took in air, let it shudder out. "Them DEA boys kept asking me why I never checked under the mattress." His gaze narrowed. "I heard you used to drive long-haul. Did you ever think to check under the mattress in your sleeper?"

"Yeah, but only because that's where I kept my spare jeans and my petty cash—when I had some."

The guard left his post near the door and walked over to stand behind Walt, a silent warning that the visit was nearly over. Rhys hated giving away even that much control, but he didn't want Walt to take the heat, so he pushed himself to his feet.

"Try to stay frosty, Walt. You'll have an attorney by morning, maybe sooner. In the meantime, I'll do what I can to make things easier on your wife and daughters."

Walt compressed his mouth to keep his lips from trembling. When he had himself under control again, he, too, rose. "One more thing, Mick. Uh, beg pardon, Rhys. It means the world and all to me, just knowing you believe in me, you know?"

Rhys nodded. Oh yeah, he knew exactly how much it meant.

The story was on the ten o'clock news. While watching TV in her room Ernestine and Max saw the tease at the beginning of the newscast and roused Rhys and Della. Brina was in the kitchen making up her grocery list and heard the commotion. By the time she followed the noise to Ernie's room, everyone but the colonel was crowded around the TV set. As soon as Della noticed her in the doorway, she filled her in.

Brina glanced Rhys' way, but he'd effectively created a no-man's-land around himself that not even Della had dared cross. As the commercial ended, Brina returned her attention to the set.

It was the third feature. The reporter was Marina Danvers. Part Diane Sawyer wanna-be, part Barbie Does the News, she related the details of the arrest, which had been precipitated by an anonymous tip phoned in to Osuma's chief of police. The caller was reported to have been a male Hispanic who hadn't stayed on the line long enough for a trace.

A candid photo of Walt Harrison flashed on the screen as

Danvers related the particulars of his life, none of which suggested anything but a hardworking husband and father. The motive, according to the DEA agent handling the arrest, was the mortgage company's threatened foreclosure of his home after his months of unemployment.

"This is not the first time a North Star driver has been arrested on suspicion of smuggling drugs. The first arrest occurred in 1991 and involved a driver who had used a false identity during the hiring process to hide a previous arrest. He was subsequently convicted on drug charges and served ten years. No one else at the company was ever charged."

The screen changed again to a one-shot of Danvers. "Although North Star's chairman of the board and CEO, M. Rhys Hazard, was not implicated in that incident, he does have a prior conviction on three counts of vehicular homicide."

Brina felt the air change. No one but she looked Rhys' way. His face had gone hard, but he kept his gaze on the screen. He flinched when a full-color photo of the mangled bus came on the screen. His lashes flickered, but he didn't look away.

In a few short minutes, using old stills of the accident and archival footage of the funerals and Rhys' trial, Danvers effectively painted a picture of a modern tragedy. An image of the memorial appeared, the names standing out in stark relief. The shot dissolved to a two-shot of Danvers and a stocky, ruddy-faced man with thinning blond hair identified as Eugene Gregory, "the youngest son of bus driver Anson Gregory who was killed instantly in the collision."

Carefully phrasing her questions as those of a sympathetic listener, Ms. Danvers elicited a poignant story of a sad little boy growing up without a father.

"I'm not a vengeful man, but it don't seem right, glorifying a killer just because he passed out a few jobs." His face crumpled, and for an instant he looked young and vulnerable. "My son will never know his grandfather because a spoiled rich kid shot a red light and crushed the life out of a man who spent his whole life taking care of children."

The picture dissolved into a stand-up shot of Danvers in front of the North Star gate. "Our request for an interview with Mr. Hazard was summarily refused."

Danvers' face assumed a martyred expression before the camera panned to the guard shack, where the guard Brina had met stood with his arms folded over his massive chest. Behind him storm clouds obscured the view of the mountains, giving the entire scene a foreboding aura. "This is Marina Danvers reporting from the Osuma Valley." The screen went black as Ernestine cut the power on the remote. No one spoke.

His face impassive, Rhys turned and left the room. Della started after him. "Let me," Brina said, her heart in her eyes. Della hesitated before nodding. Brina caught up with him at the foot of the stairs, only to realize that Max was just a step behind her.

"Do you need me, boss?" he asked.

Rhys nodded, his gaze skimming past Brina as though she didn't exist. "Five minutes."

Max nodded before heading back the way he'd come.

"Where are you going?" Brina asked, alarmed.

"Out," he said in a clipped voice as he ascended the stairs.

"But—"

"Let it be, Brina," he said, his features taut. When he reached his room, he paused. The look in his eyes was both bleak and dangerous. "Don't make me shut the door in your face," he warned.

"Okay, I'll wait for you to come back."

"The hell you will," he said. "I'm not in the mood to argue."

"Fine. I'd rather make love anyway."

He stared at her, his gaze hard. "I don't want that."

Every self-protective cell in her body screamed for her to turn around and walk away, but her instinct told her that for all his air of strength and self-containment, Rhys desperately needed the intimacy and caring of another human soul tonight.

"You were there for my son when he needed you. Please let me be here for you."

"I'm not in the mood to be gentle, Brina. You could get bruised."

"I'm willing to risk it if you are."

The room was bathed in the soft glow of the light she'd left burning in the bathroom, and the house was wrapped in a peaceful silence. Outside a night bird cooed to its mate, who answered with a seductive warble.

Brina lay in the circle of Rhys' arms, her cheek pressed to his chest, where his heart beat in the slow, even rhythm of sleep. Despite his warning, he had made love to her with a slow, thorough tenderness that had left her limp and damp and utterly satisfied. But even gripped in the throes of an explosive climax, his body buried deeply inside of hers, he'd remained emotionally separate, a man who gave her his naked body but not the most private part of himself.

She fought the ache of sadness that had settled over her as she'd watched him surrender to exhaustion, his arms still holding her close. Even in sleep, his features had a taut, controlled look that made her hurt deep inside.

A better man than he knows, Della had said, and she'd been right.

Sometimes when he looked at her, she could swear she saw love deep in those wary gray eyes. Of course, when she'd been six and anxiously peeking out her window on Christmas Eve, she'd been absolutely convinced she'd seen Santa Claus and his sleigh taking flight from the neighbor's roof.

A part of her still believed in Santa and good fairies and angels who watched over children, lovesick women and one lonely, stiff-necked Prince Charming who needed love most of all.

She rubbed her cheek against the soft chest hair before lifting her head to see the red numerals of the clock. It was nearly two a.m. Soon she would have to return to the family quarters and her own bed.

"Don't go," he muttered, his arms tightening. "Not yet."

"All right," she murmured, resting her head against him again. His heartbeat had speeded, and his skin had grown hotter.

"I don't want any of this mess to bleed over onto you or your kids," he said, his voice rusty.

"I know you don't." She ran her fingers through the soft curly hair surrounding his flat nipple.

"There's a strong possibility this will get worse. Either someone planted that heroin to cause trouble for the company, or someone saw a quick way to get rich. Either way, I have to figure that someone works for me. Because of my record, the media is bound to do a real smear job. If I'm not living in your house, they might leave you alone." She heard a stark flatness to his tone, as though he expected her to leap at the chance to be rid of him. She wanted to assure him that she never wanted him to be anywhere else, but she suspected he wasn't ready to believe her. Then again, why should he?

"Are you saying you want to leave?" she asked.

"No, but I think things would be easier for everyone here if I went back to Phoenix."

"Well, I don't. It would look like you were running away, and that would only give the media jackals more to feed on. Besides, you have responsibilities here, and I don't intend to let you slide out of them."

"What responsibilities?"

She recognized that unemotional, indifferent tone as a shield to keep himself safe from something or someone he thought might hurt him. "For one, you promised to help Jay with his science project. For another, Marcy graduates in five days and she would be devastated if you weren't there to see her wearing her cap and gown."

He was silent for a moment, and then she heard him swallow hard. "If I'm with you, people are bound to think we're connected, you and me and the kids. Are you sure you want to risk that?"

She thought about John's threat to sue for custody. It was her greatest fear. On the other hand she wasn't about to let someone as morally deficient as John "the Weasel" Sullivan bully her into abandoning a friend in need. "If you're asking me if I'd be ashamed to be seen with you, the answer is an emphatic no." Beneath her ear his heart rate speeded. "When I was talking to Wayne's daughter, she told me she didn't believe her father had it in him to turn his life around. That in her experience as first a prosecutor and then a judge, she'd heard a lot of promises to that effect, but in the end only a very few highly motivated and enormously strong-willed individuals were able to succeed. You're one of those special people." She lifted her head and looked directly into his eyes. "I can't think of anyone I'd rather be connected with more than you."

He stared at her through the soft gray haze created by the outside lights. "This is new territory for me, Brina. I've never wanted anything more than a casual relationship based on convenient—and safe—sex."

"I . . . see."

"No, you don't. I want to be more than a paying guest in your inn." The gruff note in his voice had her heart slamming. "I want the right to sleep with you openly, without sneaking around. And I want to be there for your children."

"You do?"

"When school's out, maybe you and the kids could come down to Phoenix and stay for a while. The desert is different, but it has its own kind of beauty."

She closed her eyes on a fervent wish. "We'd like that," she said. "Provided you promise I won't come face to face with a rattlesnake. I really don't think I could handle that."

"Don't worry. I'll protect you."

She let him see in her eyes and on her face the trust she had in him. "I know you will. It's what you do best, protect the people you care about. That's one of the reasons why I love you so very dearly."

His face stilled, and his gaze bored into hers. Longing shimmered for a moment in the dark pupils before he shuttered it away. "Brina, I know this is where I'm supposed to say I love you, too." His brows drew together and he gave every indication of a man suffering from a deep pain. "Believe me, I want to, but I don't think I'm capable of the kind of love you deserve." He drew a breath that wasn't quite steady. "I know I care about you more than I've ever cared about any woman, but maybe that's not enough."

Tenderness ran through her. "It's enough," she whispered, sliding up his body until she could touch her mouth to his.

His body shuddered against hers, and his arms tightened as he deepened the kiss.

The sun was reaching for the horizon before she finally returned to her room.

Chapter 27

Saturday was customarily the busiest day for an innkeeper. Guests who'd arrived Friday night often liked to sleep in, while guests checking in on Saturday often liked to get an early start. Either way, Brina's housekeeping schedule ended up scrambled.

The reverse was true with the North Star group. Elena had flown home yesterday to spend the weekend with her family. Stan was spending the weekend in Seattle, and Emory had gone out running a few minutes before Brina had headed upstairs. Colonel Fitz had a seven a.m. tee time at the Wenatchee Country Club, Jay had spent the night with Petey, Max and Rhys were at the gym in Wenatchee, and Della was house-hunting with a broker friend of Lucy's. Only Brina, Marcy and Ernestine remained at home.

Normally, Cindy cleaned the upper floor while Brina did the lower, but Cindy had menstrual cramps again. Before Brina had gotten a good start, the dishwasher drain had gotten plugged, and by the time she'd found the reason—a cherry pit from the breakfast compote stuck in the drain valve—she was already running behind.

After reassembling the drain unit, she tossed her one-size-fits-all, super-duper wrench into her toolbox and got to her feet. Hoping to hear the latest on the investigation, she switched on the small TV tucked into a corner of the counter and flipped to the local cable news station.

During the commercial she nuked the mug of coffee that had grown cold while she'd played Ms. Fix-it. When it was ready, she carried it to the island, where a covered basket of banana-nut muffins left over from breakfast sent out a siren song.

In contrast to Marina Danvers' in-your-face intensity, the weekend anchor delivered the news with an objective calm Brina found refreshing. The North Star story was the lead, featuring a statement by Walt Harrison's attorney.

The story ended with an interview with a grim-faced DEA agent named Rooney tossing out the customary, "pursuing all leads," etc. By the time the screen switched to a commercial, Brina had wolfed down two muffins and most of her coffee.

She had just tucked the mug into the dishwasher's top tray when she heard Marcy's frantic cry. She took off running. Ernie stuck her head out of her room as Brina ran past.

"What's wrong?" she called after Brina.

"Don't know yet," Brina tossed over her shoulder.

"I'll get dressed just in case."

Marcy met her on the stairs halfway to the second story. "It's Mopsy," Marcy wailed, one small hand tugging on Brina's to hurry her along. "She got lost again and I found her in Uncle Rhys' room eating brown sugar from this bag under the big cupboard. I tried to stop her, only then she started to shake all over and her eyes got funny."

Brown sugar? A terrible suspicion exploded in Brina's chest an instant before she and Marcy burst into the room. The bunny was on her back in front of the armoire, her legs extended, her body jerking in what appeared to be a seizure. A Ziploc bag lay near her, but it was the pale brown powder that covered the floor and the bunny's fur that had Brina's heart trying to tear through her rib cage.

"*Do* something, Mommy!" Marcy begged, jerking on her hand.

Brina realized she'd frozen in place and made herself move

forward. There were no phones in the room and no sight of Rhys' cell phone. "Marce, run downstairs to Miss Winkle's room and ask her to call Dr. Ambrose's office. The number's in the book under Osuma Veterinary Clinic. Can you remember that?"

"Call Dr. Ambrose in the phone book." Marcy took a few steps before turning back. "Mopsy's not going to die like Grandpa Eiler and Grandmother Sullivan, is she?"

"I don't know, sweetie, but I do know we need the vet, so hurry, okay?"

Without another word, Marcy raced out.

Rhys had just put one foot on the stairs when Marcy came barreling down, her hair flying and her eyes wild. He caught her an instant before she would have slammed into him.

"Whoa, toots, not so fast, okay?"

"It's Mopsy, Uncle Rhys," she got out between heaving breaths. "She's real sick 'n I have to tell Miss Winkle to call the vet!"

Rhys shot a look upstairs. "Where's Mopsy now?"

"In your room. Mommy's with her." The terror in her eyes tore at him.

"Go," he said, giving her a gentle shove. "I'll see if I can help Mommy."

Gritting his teeth, he grabbed the railing and all but manhandled himself up the steps faster than he'd thought possible.

He heard Brina's crooning voice before he saw her crouched over the inert rabbit she'd wrapped in a towel. "Jesus, what—"

He stopped dead, taking in the woman now cradling the swaddled rabbit to her chest, the shredded plastic Baggie, what had to be heroin spilled on the rug. His gaze jerked to Brina's face. To the soft brown eyes that slid from his—and the suspicion he saw there.

"You think I put that shit there, don't you?" He rubbed

every hint of emotion from his voice, but the hurt was already ripping through him. "The same shit I slipped into the sleeper before Harrison took it out?"

Her gaze snapped back to his. "No! Of course not." Unlike his brother she couldn't lie worth a damn. Every nuance of thought was visible on her face and in her voice.

Already bleeding inside, he pulled his cell phone from his back pocket and tossed it to her. He had broken Hazard's number one rule. *Never let yourself care about something so badly you end up bleeding to death if it goes away.* He had a strong hunch he was about to pay a heavy price for breaking that rule.

"Call Hollister, Ms. Innkeeper," he said coolly. "I'll wait for him downstairs."

"You have the right to remain silent. . . ."

Rhys shut out the words and instead concentrated on his breathing. If he could control the flow of air, he could keep the panic at bay.

"Do you understand these rights as I've recounted them to you?" Brody Hollister's expressionless voice forced his attention.

"Yes."

Two detectives, male and female, were upstairs processing the crime scene. Not that there was much to process. He doubted there would be fingerprints on the clear plastic bag, and sure as shit there weren't any on the rabbit. Besides, Mopsy was already on her way to the vet, riding in a taxi with Ernestine and Marcy serving as paramedics.

Before she'd left, Ernestine had called Max, who had been on his way to the Chevy dealership in Wenatchee to finalize the deal for the Suburban. He'd arrived only moments later, his face a study in barely suppressed fury.

"Ain't no *way* the boss was involved in this!" he'd declared in a furious growl while going toe-to-toe and chin-to-chin with Hollister, who, for his part, showed remarkable restraint.

"Stand up, please, Mr. Hazard."

Rhys had to hand it to Hollister. Nothing of his personal feelings or beliefs bled through the professional mask. Despite the occasional stammers that seemed to take him unawares, the chief possessed a deep-seated confidence Rhys envied.

Layering his fear with ice—and hoping to God it was thick enough—Rhys reached for his cane and got to his feet. At a nod from the chief, the big African-American sergeant, Slade Hingle, stepped forward, handcuffs dangling from one hand. Rhys' breathing turned ragged. Now it starts, he thought, his worst fears playing out in real time. His heart felt like it would burst at any moment, and a thin layer of sweat had formed on his skin. Somehow he kept his terror locked inside.

"You use those cuffs, I can't use my cane," he told the sergeant coldly.

"What he ain't saying right out is he can't walk without the cane." Max spoke up from his place just beyond the parlor door. "Ain't right, treating him like a criminal when it's as plain as day he's bein' framed."

Ignoring Max's outburst, Hollister regarded Rhys through narrowed eyes. Though he wore the same khaki uniform shirt as Hingle, his long legs were sheathed in range-tough Wranglers. Instead of a cap he favored a Stetson. Clearly not a by-the-book type of lawman. Could be good, could be bad. Rhys figured he didn't have long to see which way Hollister leaned. "Is it true you can't walk without the cane?"

"Last time I tried, I couldn't, but that was a few years ago. Maybe it's different now." He knew it wasn't, but he'd be damned if he would beg. He'd crawl to their frigging cop car first.

"I think we can bend procedure just this once, Slade."

"Yes, sir."

"Time to go, Mr. Hazard," Hollister said.

Rhys nodded. He would walk out of Brina's house with his head high and his back straight.

"Who did it, boss? Who set you up?" Max's brutalized features twisted into a mask of helpless frustration.

"Your guess is as good as mine." At least one person on the benighted planet was willing to stand up and be counted on his side, and Rhys found himself grateful.

"Call Pearl Silverman," he told Max as he walked out of the parlor flanked by the two large, unsmiling cops. "Tell her to call Melvin Bailey and see if he'll take me on as a client in addition to Walt Harrison." Bailey had gotten the driver out on bail. Rhys prayed he could do the same for him.

Max nodded. "Consider it done."

"Don't let Del get crazy over this," he added in a low tone.

"I'll keep things cool. "

When they reached the foyer, Brina stepped into his path, forcing him to stop. Her face was pale and drawn; her eyes were shadowed. She looked ill.

Stupid ass that he was, his first instinct was to take her in his arms and comfort *her*. He couldn't think of the lack of faith she'd shown him—or his own idiocy in letting down his guard. It would break him if he did.

"Brody, can I talk with Rhys for a few minutes, please?" Brina asked.

Hollister turned his way. "Okay with you?"

Rhys shrugged. "Why not. I'm in no hurry to be locked up again."

"Five minutes, no more." At a sign from Hollister, the sergeant stepped back a couple of paces, giving them a modicum of privacy, while Brody wandered over to the foyer table, where he selected one of the brochures in the rack and paged through it. Max glared at Brina for a long moment before propping a massive shoulder against the doorjamb and fixing his gaze on the floor.

Now that she was face-to-face with Rhys, Brina's throat was so tight she could scarcely breathe. Rhys had become a different person, an aloof stranger whose very coldness was more frightening than the hottest fury. Somehow she had to break through that icy shell and make him understand.

"Rhys, I had to call Brody, but that doesn't mean I don't believe in you because I do, with all my heart."

"Sure you do, honey. That's why you looked at me like something you needed to scrape off the bottom of your shoe."

"I can't help what you thought you saw. I know what I feel, what I believe." When he would have turned away, Brina grabbed his arm, her fingers digging in. "Someone else put that heroin in your room. I don't know who or why, but it wasn't you."

Rhys wanted to believe her, but he'd learned the hard way never to take anything on faith. Actions were what counted. Last night she'd said she loved him, and he'd come very close to believing her. "If you really mean that, prove it."

She blinked. "How?"

"Last night you said you didn't care if this mess bled all over you. Okay, fine. Marry me. Stand with me against the crap that's bound to be thrown my way again."

He meant it, Brina thought with both shock and wonder. *Yes, oh yes!* The words were there, clamoring to escape, but the thought of the emotional damage an impulsive decision like that could wreak on her kids held her back. "Rhys, please understand, if it were just me, I'd agree in a heartbeat, but I have Marcy and Jay to think about. I can't make a decision like that on the spur of the moment."

Something intense and frightening flared deep in his eyes before that awful chill set in again. "Wrong, you just did." The icy anger in his voice was as stinging as a whiplash across naked flesh.

"I didn't! I need time to think it through."

His mouth took on a bitter twist. "Fine, you do that."

"Rhys, don't be so stubborn—"

Before she could finish, the door flew open, setting the temple bells flying from the hook to land with a cacophonous clatter on the floor. Both Hollister and his sergeant were already moving into a defensive crouch when J. T. barreled into the foyer, breathing audibly. His eyes blazed blue fire, and his blunt features were touched by a wild Celtic fury.

"What the hell is this nonsense about you arresting my boy here?" he roared, his militant gaze pinning Hollister like a blade.

The chief took his time meeting J. T.'s gaze. He was fully as burly as J. T. and, from the sudden hard edge to his jaw, just as tough. But when he spoke, his voice was as calm as a mountain morning. "Do us all a favor and bring it down a few degrees, J. T. I'm just doing my job."

"Hauling a man off to jail for something he hasn't done is a damn poor way of doing it!"

Hollister regarded him without visible emotion. "How do you know that when you don't know what he's being charged with?"

"The hell I don't know! Brina called and told me what happened. And I'm here to tell you right here and now, there isn't a chance in hell he's guilty."

Instead of taking Rhys to a cell, Slade Hingle led him to an interrogation room not much larger than a cell. As soon as he saw it had no windows, he knew he was in trouble. If they closed the door . . .

"Something wrong?" Hingle asked when Rhys stopped dead a few steps past the threshold.

"Give me a minute," he managed to get out through a throat that had all but shut tight.

The sergeant's gaze narrowed. "Your leg bothering you?"

"Something like . . . that." His skin turned clammy, and his stomach churned. Next would come the icy jaws of a vise, squeezing his chest until his lungs were incapable of drawing in air.

"You suffer from claustrophobia, don't you?" It was Hollister's voice.

Rhys jerked his head in the affirmative. His breathing was faster now. Soon he would be gasping, unable to control the harsh sounds.

"My office isn't much bigger, but it didn't seem to bother you."

"It has . . . windows."

Hollister muttered a rank obscenity under his breath. "We'll talk there, then."

Brody caught the curious looks sent their way as he stepped aside to let Hazard precede him into his office. Turning his back to the bullpen, he gestured Hingle to his side.

"Tell reception no press statements, no comment if anyone calls," he told his second-in-command. "Last thing we need is a media circus."

Hingle frowned. "Soon as we book him, it'll go on the log. Maybe Phil Potter over to the *Recorder* ain't the fastest bloodhound in the pack, but sooner or later he catches the scent."

"Put out the word. I want a lid on this."

"What about that DEA Rambo? Way I read him, he's fixing to hype this into a promotion."

"Not on my watch." Brody stopped to think it through. "We'll keep this local jurisdiction as long as we can, give Mel Bailey time to maneuver."

Hingle's astute gaze sharpened. "You sound like you think Hazard's innocent."

Brody resisted the urge to glance at the man in his office. "Way it looks, this whole thing is shaking out like a bumbling crook movie. Whatever Hazard is or isn't, he's not stupid."

"Does seem like the perp was almost begging to be caught, don't it?"

"Or set it up so Hazard would take a fall."

"Might be Hazard's smart enough to figure we'd end up thinking along those lines and set it up to look like a frame."

"Let's just play it loose and see how it turns out."

Hingle cast a quick look into the cubicle. "You want me to handle the interrogation or the paperwork?"

Ordinarily, his second-in-command wouldn't have asked. Brody's closest friend on the job, Hingle knew that interrogation was dead last on Brody's list of favorite things to do. Controlling his stuttering took a great deal of energy and concentration. One lapse and he could suddenly find himself doing a great imitation of Porky Pig. After a half dozen humiliating failures, during which prisoners had laughed in his face, he almost always let others ask the questions.

"Get started on the paperwork," he told Hingle now. "I'll talk to Hazard."

Hingle hid his surprise. "Yes, sir."

After Hingle departed, Brody waited a beat or two to let Hazard catch his breath before he himself entered the office. Not surprisingly, Hazard had seated himself in the chair with the best view of the door and the bullpen where the plainclothes personnel had their desks. The eyes meeting his head-on were the color of storm clouds.

Brody recognized the look of defiant pride. "Coffee's not fresh, but it's strong," he told Hazard as he crossed to the coffeemaker on the credenza behind his desk. "I'm guessin' a man who's spent half his life on the road takes his coffee black," he said, handing the spare mug to Hazard.

"You guessed right," Hazard acknowledged before taking a sip. "Right about it being stale, too. Not that I'm complaining."

Brody settled behind his desk and propped his feet on the corner he kept clear for just that purpose. After crossing one ankle over the other, he leaned back, rested his mug on his belt buckle and regarded the prisoner dispassionately.

Hazard regarded him the same way. Brody suspected the

man could be both ruthless and tenacious if pressed. On the other hand, so could he. "We can do this a coupla ways, Mr. Hazard. I could follow accepted procedure, ask a bunch of questions designed to trick you into incriminating yourself." He paused to take a couple of much needed sips. "Or you could save us both some time and aggravation and explain why a kilo of heroin was found in your room." He offered Hazard a slight smile. "Since you're the guest, you get to choose."

Hazard's mouth curled, but his eyes were chilled steel. "I gave you my statement at the inn."

"You never saw the smack before and you have no idea how it got there. Is that a fair summary?"

"Fair—and true."

"Not much there to work with."

"Not my problem, Chief."

"Would it help loosen you up some if I told you I'm inclined to think Stillwell's right about you being set up?"

"Number one, you haven't actually said that, and two, there's a Constitutional amendment granting the right against self-incrimination."

"Man who has nothing to hide doesn't usually incriminate himself just by answering a few questions."

"Bullshit. Last time I answered a few questions, I ended up doing hard time."

"Is it cops in general you don't trust or just m-m-me?"

"Cops in general. I'm reserving my opinion on you."

Spying Hingle approaching, Brody sat up.

"Beg pardon, Chief. Mr. Bailey has arrived." Hingle's gaze flickered toward Hazard. "Claims he's representing Mr. Hazard. He's insisting on seeing his client ASAP."

Brody glanced at Hazard. "I can let him use this office, but once he leaves, Sergeant Hingle will have to put you in a cell."

"I understand."

Brody shifted his attention to Hingle. "Give me five minutes, Slade, then escort the counselor here to my office."

Hazard waited until Hingle left before saying, "Most cops in your position would have already called a press conference to announce my arrest."

"Can't argue with that. Four years ago I'd probably be doing just that, only I'd have Hingle doing the announcing." His mouth took on a self-mocking slant. "I'm not much for public speaking. There's another reason I'm inclined to believe you, Mr. Hazard. I'd bet my pension against a vintage Harley that a man as smart as you could come up with a dozen places in one of those eighteen-wheelers to stash contraband where it would be damn near impossible to find. No reason to stash it under a mattress where even a rookie customs agent could fish it out blindfolded." Brody finished his coffee before getting to his feet. "I'd win that bet, wouldn't I?"

"You would."

The fact that Hazard hadn't hesitated was in his favor. Brody felt some of the tension leave the spot between his shoulder blades. "I'll help you all I can, Mr. Hazard, but if it turns out my instincts were all wet about you and you're guilty, I'll bust my ass to make sure you never draw a free breath again."

Brody used Maxie's office to call Brina.

She answered on the first ring, making him wonder if she'd been waiting by the phone. "Brina, it's Brody. I—"

"How's Rhys?" she exploded without letting him finish. "I called earlier to find out if he was there, but no one would answer my questions and that . . . *person* who answered the phone wouldn't put me through to you."

"That *person* was only following my orders. And, yes, he's here."

"Can I talk to him?"

"Maybe later. Right now, I need to ask you some questions, okay?"

"What kind of questions?"

"Questions that might help Mr. Hazard out of this mess."

"In that case, what do you want to know?"

Brody plucked a pen from the Mariners cup on the desk and flipped to a clean page in his notebook. "Who has access to the guest rooms besides you and the other guests?"

"Cindy Tsung, who works part-time, and my kids, although I'm trying to teach them the concept of privacy. No one else."

"Spell Tsung, please."

Brina complied, adding, "Her folks live on Water Street. Father's name is Ling."

Brody noted both on the pad. "Anyone besides the guests have keys to the front door? Someone who could come in when you're not there, for example?"

"No, no one." She took a quick breath. "I'm very careful about making sure the key is returned when a guest checks out."

"A guest could easily make a copy, couldn't he? Or she?"

"Yes, but not in Osuma. One of the books I read on security measures for inns who don't want to convert to programmable key cards suggested having distinctive keys made that would alert a locksmith or, uh, key-making place. Mine are oversized and brass with the inn's name and telephone number etched into the, uh, fat part. Since only Brevard's Hardware and Jack's Locks and Keys make keys around here, I made it a point to tell them not to duplicate any of those keys."

Brody made a note. "Any strangers around lately? Maybe someone asking to use the phone?"

"No one." There was a brief silence. "Lucy stopped by last Saturday to bring my order of fresh flowers, and Summer dropped off one of Marcy's socks that had gotten mixed in with the twins'. Oh, and John picked up the kids last Sunday

morning and brought Marcy home late Sunday afternoon—
with the rabbit. We had some heated words and he left."

"Any way he could have gone upstairs during either of
those visits?"

"No. The kids and I were waiting for him on the porch in
the morning, and in the afternoon I heard the bell over the
door ringing when he left."

An old trick, Brody knew, but he'd said enough for now.

"Brody, surely you don't think John planted that filth?"

"Just covering all the bases, Brina." He tossed down his pen
and leaned back. Maxie's chair was too small. "Why do you
ask? Do you think John might have planted it?"

"John's a weasel, but he's not a *criminal.*"

"Do you think Hazard put the stuff there himself?"

"No, I don't. Not in a million years!" Her distress was
clearly audible, and he found himself sympathizing. "Brody,
what's going to happen to Rhys now?"

"That's up to the DA. Best guess, he'll have a bail hearing
on Monday followed by an arraignment to show cause why he
should be bound over for trial."

Her sigh tore at him. "Tell Rhys . . ." She broke off abruptly.
In the sudden silence the phone line seemed to pulsate with
anguish. Twenty-five years a cop and he still wasn't able to
shield himself from the pain of the innocent. "Tell him I believe in him."

John had the house to himself. J. T. was hanging out with
his skinny mistress, and Sherri was shopping. He sat behind J.
T.'s desk, sipping the drink he'd fixed while Brina was calling
Jay to the phone. Now and then he glanced at the TV his
mother had ordered placed in a cupboard because it spoiled
the look of the den. He'd tuned it to the Wenatchee station and
muted the sound.

The early news had just ended. To his acute disappointment,
there had been no further mention of North Star or the investi-

gation into the drug smuggling. That was when he'd picked up the phone and called the inn.

He wasn't stupid enough to ask right out if Brina had found the kilo of heroin he'd planted, but as soon as Jay came on the line, the kid told him about Mick's arrest. The little twerp sounded close to tears. John had to work to hide his jubilation.

"I'm sure it'll all work out," John said after Jay had finished rattling on. He'd gotten the information he'd been after and was ready to hang up when the kid asked him if he was planning to attend his middle school graduation on June fourteenth. "Yeah, sure. Tell your mother to call my assistant at work so she can put it on my calendar," he said before hanging up.

Hot damn, he'd pulled it off! he thought, before giving in to the urge to laugh. The bastard was in deep shit. It was time to send him down for the third time.

Grinning, he leaned forward and pulled his wallet from his back pocket. From an inside pocket, he took out the card Marina Danvers had given him when she'd covered the dog and pony show Mick's mulatto bitch sister had put on last week when the first rig had rolled. The sexy reporter with the silicone tits had written her cell phone number on the back—and let it be known she'd welcome a call anytime.

"This is your lucky day, babe," he said with a grin as he took the cell phone from his briefcase and flipped it open. His heart raced, and his mouth went dry with anticipation. When she answered, he slipped once more into the persona of a Mexican laborer and started to talk. Even before he finished, she was all but hyperventilating with excitement.

After hanging up, John freshened his drink before settling into his mother's favorite chair. As she smiled down at him from the painting with that special glow in her eyes, he lifted the glass in reverent salute. "It won't be long now, Mother, and the mongrel will be back in a cage where he belongs."

*   *   *

Seated in one of two mismatched chairs at the table in his motel room, Wayne Makepeace forked another bite of chicken and pea pods into his mouth and washed it down with his last bottle of soda. It was the third night in a row he'd eaten take-out from the Chinese restaurant down the street. The food was lousy and gave him heartburn besides, but it was plentiful and, even more important, cheap.

His rent was paid for another week, thanks to Renee, who had been cool but encouraging. After he'd gotten the job, she'd paid for a thirdhand Toyota truck so that he could get back and forth to work. After he'd filled the baby pickup with gasoline, the pay he'd collected from Sarge was nearly gone. The little he had left had to last until Friday when he collected his first check from NSN. Recalling the conversation he'd had with Mick Sullivan on Wednesday brought a grim smile to his lips.

"Have to remember he calls hisself Hazard now," he muttered aloud before taking another bite. Wasn't much left of the boy he'd known in the man—not that he'd been able to pick up on during their five-minute conversation, anyway. Mickey had been a sweet boy with puppy dog eyes and a grin that made you want to grin back no matter how foul the day had been. Rhys Hazard weren't no puppy to be kicked around now, not unless you wanted to lose your leg.

Guilt as sharp as a skinning blade sliced through his belly. It weren't right, the way the town worked up a hate against that boy. A flash of blue in the periphery of his vision drew his attention to the ancient TV set he kept on for company but seldom watched. He froze, his gaze fixed on the clip of a North Star tractor-trailer driving through the gate at the depot. After hastily putting down his fork, he grabbed the remote and turned up the volume.

". . . and a spokesman for the Osuma Police Department has just confirmed that M. Rhys Hazard, North Star Trucking's founder and CEO, was taken into custody earlier today by

Chief of Police Brody Hollister himself after a kilo of heroin was discovered in his room at Nightingale House in Osuma, where he and several other North Star employees are currently residing." The picture changed to a shot of a pretty lady reporter standing in front of Osuma's City Hall.

"According to a reliable source inside the Osuma PD, the heroin discovered under an armoire in Hazard's room is identical to that found in the sleeping compartment of one of the company's trucks early yesterday morning. According to that same source a decision has yet to be made if Hazard will be charged with smuggling as well as possession. A bail hearing is scheduled for Monday morning in Superior Court."

As the picture dissolved into a commercial, Wayne got up from the table, walked back to the scarred desk and picked up a pen and paper. It took only a few minutes to write an anonymous letter addressed to Brody Hollister of the Osuma Police Department.

Chapter 28

Because Rhys couldn't pace, he counted—the holes in each square of ceiling tile, the diamonds forming the grid over the long narrow window, the bars keeping him caged. He had started on the beats of his own heart when a skinny, red-haired officer with a face full of freckles appeared to tell him he had visitors. "Mr. Bailey and a lady lawyer name of Silverman. You want I should send 'em in?"

"Please."

Both carried briefcases. Bailey's was clearly hand-sewn and expensive. Silverman's had come from L.L. Bean. With her five-foot-nothing figure, twinkling brown eyes and benign smile, Pearl Silverman, Esq. seemed about as dangerous as a dumpling. Until you looked past the twinkle in her eyes to the ruthless take-no-prisoners determination.

A Martin Sheen look-alike, Mel Bailey had shrewd blue eyes, the polished air of an Ivy League professor, and a love of the limelight. According to Pearl, his ego was nearly as inflated as his fee, both of which were more than justified by his recent streak of twenty acquittals in a row. Rhys only hoped he wasn't going to be the one to spoil the counselor's winning record.

Keys rattling, the cop unlocked the cell and stepped back. "Chief says I have to keep the cells in sight when the prisoner has visitors."

"Of course you do, Officer Keegan," Pearl told him kindly, grandma to grandson. "I'm sure the chief also would want you to remain out of earshot, since eavesdropping on an attorney-client conversation would be a violation of Mr. Hazard's rights."

"Uh, yes, ma'am. I'll just get me a soda from the machine yonder. Give a holler when you're finished."

Pearl placed her briefcase on the shelf and zipped it open. Instead of a legal pad, she withdrew a plastic container and a spoon. "Chicken soup from my grandmother Shoenvik's recipe."

Rhys was both touched and annoyed. "Leave it. I'll eat it later."

"You'll eat it now. You can listen at the same time."

He had to admit the soup smelled wonderful. After twenty-four hours of rebelling against the mere thought of food, his stomach suddenly gave out a distinct rumble. "When can I get out of here?" Rhys demanded as he picked up the spoon.

Bailey clicked open his briefcase. "Your bail hearing's set for nine o'clock tomorrow morning. I figure you'll be on the street by nine thirty."

Walking into the courtroom at 8:50 on Monday morning while bracketed by unsmiling marshals in crisp khaki uniforms was rougher than Rhys had expected. Although he tried to empty his mind, memories came at him like bullets.

He wasn't sure it was the same courtroom, although it had the same high ceiling and paneled walls. The suffocating smell of dust, old wax and overheated bodies was as painfully familiar as the sudden silence that came over the large chamber when he entered. A silence that was broken a heartbeat later as conversation swelled even louder.

"This is where you sit," one of the marshals said before a sudden look of recollection crossed his face. "Forgot you've been here before, so I guess you already know that." His expression said he expected a reaction, even relished the idea of getting a rise out of a man wearing a two-thousand-dollar Savile Row suit and a custom-tailored shirt. What he got was an icy stare that wiped the eager anticipation from his face in less time than it took to blink.

Rhys' attorneys stood to shake his hand. "We drew Judge Kaplan," Pearl said quickly and urgently. "We'll fight, but you need to be prepared for the worst."

Rhys' gut twisted. Twenty-two years ago, Hiram Kaplan had seemed as old as God when he'd thundered self-righteous vitriol at Mick Sullivan from the bench. Now Rhys realized he'd probably been no more than thirty-five.

"Worst being what?" he demanded.

"Hard to say," Bailey hedged.

Rhys was about to blast him when Pearl touched his arm. The bailiff had just entered through the door leading to the judge's chambers behind the bench, a sign that court was about to begin. Rhys hadn't eaten much of anything since downing Pearl's chicken soup. Now, as his stomach tightened, he was grateful for his lousy appetite.

The buzz behind him seemed to fade as the bailiff watched the clock. At the stroke of nine, he stepped forward. "All rise . . ."

By nine thirty it was over. By ten thirty Brina was back at the inn. J. T. and Lucy had insisted on accompanying her. To her surprise, Della was there as well. After leaving the courthouse, her other guests had taken themselves off to parts unknown.

Despite the early hour, J. T. had poured a "wee dram" for all of them from Brina's liquor cabinet in the parlor. "We have to do something," Brina raged as she paced back and forth across the brightly patterned rug. "How do you get a judge impeached, anyway?"

"With a great deal of difficulty, I'm afraid, dear," Lucy said from her perch on the arm of the chair where J. T. sat bolt up-right, his face fixed in grim lines. Since leaving the courthouse he had removed his navy blazer and necktie and unbuttoned his collar. His rusty hair was wildly disheveled from the nervous action of his big hands.

"As soon as the judge took his seat and I saw that death's-head mask that passes for a face, I knew we were in trouble," Brina declared. "I admit there was some rationale, although slight, for denying Rhys bail, but Kaplan set out to deliberately humiliate him. If I could have gotten to the man at that moment, I would have used that stupid gavel he kept banging on his head."

"I hear that!" Della spoke up, dark eyes flashing. "Talk about a hanging judge! Forget due process and trial by jury. What I saw today was a perfect example of guilty until proven innocent."

"Rhys hates small spaces," Brina said. "He even leaves the door to his room ajar."

"At least Brody managed to persuade the DA to allow him to remain in the Osuma lockup instead of county jail," Lucy put in.

Della leaned forward to set her empty glass on the table in front of her. "Pearl Silverman intends to file a writ or brief or whatever to make sure Kaplan doesn't preside over the arraignment—or the trial, if God forbid, it goes that far."

"The self-important bastard ought to be hung up by his . . . judicial robes!" J. T.'s impassioned outburst expressed the feelings of the three others in the room as well.

Brina stopped at the window and stared out, her eyes still filled with images of the man she loved. "It was so patently unfair, referring to Rhys as a flight risk simply because he owns an airplane. Even Mr. Bailey's offer to have him surrender his passport didn't sway Kaplan."

"Not only unfair, but pejorative," Lucy added. "He had to

have known how his remarks would be perceived by any potential jurors."

"Not a doubt in my mind," Della said.

"The man has a black heart for certain," J. T. muttered. "Calling a man who's done nothing but good in the last eighteen years a menace to society."

The phone rang again in Brina's office across the foyer. Automatically, she listened to the machine pick up.

"Ms. Sullivan, this is Marina Danvers again. I would really appreciate a few moments of your time in order to get your reaction to the decision by Judge Kaplan not to grant bail this morning. In case you've misplaced my number, it's 566 . . . ."

"Bloody reporters ought to be lined up and shot like the vermin they are," J. T. muttered.

"Or . . . used for our own purposes the way the politicians do," Brina cried, whirling around as a sudden idea possessed her. "Maybe we can't get Rhys out on bail, but we can counteract the negative publicity by . . . by telling all the good things he's done, like buying out J. T. to give people jobs."

Della's face lit up. "And starting Second Chance!" Met with blank faces, she laughed self-consciously. "That's a foundation Rhys set up years ago to help ex-offenders get a new start. Not only do the counselors set up interviews, but there are also classes in interviewing techniques and anger control, things like that. Four years ago it added a literacy program to help ex-felons learn to read and write. Rhys pays for a full third of the operating cost, anonymously, and only a handful of people know he's the one who started it and handpicked a board to run it."

"So that's why North Star hires so many ex-cons," Brina thought aloud. "Wayne Makepeace isn't an ex-con, but Rhys did give him a second chance—and probably saved his life." Excitement rolled through her. "His daughter is a judge in Seattle. Maybe she can help."

"Rhys hates drawing attention to himself and the donations

he makes almost as much as he hates small places," Della warned them before narrowing her attention to Brina alone. "He'll hate it if you put him in the spotlight."

"He's already in the spotlight, Della—and for all the wrong reasons," Brina countered.

"Brina's right," Lucy declared. "The media hyenas smell blood. By the time they're finished feeding, Rhys will be little more than a bloody carcass." She hesitated for several beats before turning to look in J. T.'s direction. "Rhys has already gone through hell once and survived, although only God knows how—or at what cost to his soul."

J. T.'s face tightened. Brina realized she was holding her breath and let it out slowly. "Rhys is just beginning to trust again," she found herself saying aloud. "He needs to know you believe in him, J. T. Maybe more than any of us in this room can even imagine." *Please, don't let him down again,* she added silently.

The big Irishman's eyes filled with tears. "Thickheaded I might be, but I'm not so dense I can't recognize a second chance when the good Lord sees fit to send it my way." He and Lucy exchanged a long, healing look before J. T. shifted his attention Brina's way. "Well, lass, now that we're all with you on this, what's your plan?"

Brina swallowed hard. *The Successful Crusader always had a brilliant, guaranteed-to-succeed plan. Right?* "Well, uh, first, we need to make a list of people to contact on Rhys' behalf."

"Like Mr. Makepeace's daughter, the judge!" Della put in, the light of battle in her eyes.

"Exactly." Brina glanced toward the hall. "I'll get some paper—"

"I'll get it," Max said, already moving.

"While you're in there, play back Marina Danvers' message and write down her number," Brina called after him. "I'll give her an interview, all right—but only after she agrees to set up a press conference."

"Oh dear," Ernestine murmured. "Does that mean we'll have to fight our way through a sea of satellite trucks parked outside the inn?"

Brina laughed. "No, I think we'll arrange to speak to the press someplace with more emotional impact." She paused to consider. "Out at the freight depot, I think. With those monster trucks behind us." She sent an inquiring glance Della's way. "You could set it up, couldn't you?"

"Absolutely."

Ernie glanced from one to the other. "I think that's a wise choice. I read once where visuals are very important when one endeavors to sway public opinion."

"So far, the only visuals have been of Rhys being escorted into the courthouse with marshals on both sides," Lucy grated as Max handed Brina a yellow pad and a pen.

"Hank knows a lot of movers and shakers in Phoenix," Della said as Brina seated herself at the Scrabble table. "He could make some calls, generate some positive press, maybe even get some VIPs to express their confidence in Rhys' innocence publicly."

"Is that likely, though," Brina asked, "given the 'cover thine own ass' philosophy that's rampant in the country these days?"

"Ordinarily, I'd say no, but a lot of those VIPs got rich on North Star stock and it's a good bet their portfolios still contain those shares in significant enough numbers to make an impact on their net worth if the stock tanks."

"Ah, and isn't that the power and glory of a capitalistic system?" J. T. said with a twinkle.

"Damn straight it is," Della declared. "And Hank's just the man who can make it work in Rhys' favor. Max knows. He's seen Hank work a room."

"Best power player I've ever seen," Max amplified. "Better even than the boss when it comes to schmoozing the suits into or outta somethin' that's good for North Star." Max's sudden grin transformed his face. "Only man besides me who can go toe-to-toe with the boss and not end up flattened. Metaphorically speaking, of course."

Della chuckled. "Hank's beside himself, not being able to be here to support Rhys in person. Making calls would help his stress level, if nothing else."

"Then by all means, turn him loose," Brina told her with a grin.

"I've a mind to make a few calls myself," J. T. said. "Beginning with himself, the governor of this great state."

The room turned electric. All eyes swung his way. "You think he'll take your call?" Brina asked.

"He will indeed."

Brina and Della exchanged hopeful looks. "But will he do anything to help? That's the more important question," Brina said.

"When pigs fly," Lucy muttered.

"Ah, Lucy love, have you no faith in me, then?"

"I had faith once, and it nearly destroyed me. Now I require proof." Although Lucy spoke without venom, Brina caught the look of regret that crossed J. T.'s rugged features.

"If it's proof you're wanting, it's proof you'll get." His tone was lashed with determination—and something more.

"J. T., I'm sorry," Lucy said softly. "I shouldn't have said that."

He forgave her with a look. "Not to worry, love. We'll sort it all out later. Right now, we've a battle to wage and a war to win." Then, looking fiercer than Brina had ever seen, he unclipped his cell phone from his belt and flipped it open. Instead of dialing, however, he swept the others with a measuring glance before his gaze met Brina's head-on. "No one can predict how this will turn out, lass. Rhys might end up hating us all for interfering. Even if he walks out of court a free man, he might keep on walking and never look back the way he did once before." His eyes darkened. "Are you willing to risk losing him with no guarantee that what we do will save him?"

Brina felt a lump the size of a bowling ball jam in her throat. J. T. spoke from experience. His warning was also well-grounded. The media were as fickle as they were powerful. Let them get one whiff of calculated manipulation, and the backlash against Rhys would be horrific.

A sudden memory surfaced of the night she'd encountered Rhys and Marcy, sitting together on her bed.

What are you scared of, Uncle Rhys?

Small places with no windows.

Brina had heard the strain in his voice when he'd answered Marcy's innocent question. Just as she'd felt the tremors shaking his body when he'd awakened in a darkened room. Going back to prison had to be his worse nightmare.

"Make the call, J. T.," she said in a firm, clear voice. "Whatever happens, Rhys has to know we fought for him. If he's upset, so be it."

Rhys was livid.

Max had never seen such fury in another man's eyes.

"Why didn't you stop them?" Rhys demanded in a tightly controlled voice that had icy fingers squeezing Max's intestines.

"You ever try to stop a bunch of females on a mission?"

"I can't believe this, a damn press conference in my own facility."

The media blitz started on Monday evening. Keegan had been working the three-to-eleven shift and saw the six o'clock news on his dinner break. It seemed that Brina had gone one-on-one with that female piranha, Danvers. "Held her own and then some," Keegan had informed Rhys a few minutes later. Not that Rhys had any way of validating that information, since he hadn't seen the damned thing.

Max had been way too eager to fill in the blanks. "Started out pretty rocky for our side, but by the end Miz Sullivan was way ahead on points."

Things had snowballed from there. During the three days since then, requests from the media had jammed the switchboard so badly Hollister had issued strict orders for his people to hang up as soon as the caller so much as mentioned the name of Rhys Hazard.

From the other bits and pieces trickling in, Rhys was pretty sure his "side"—led by Brina, according to Max—had embarked on a full-on campaign to canonize him. Saint Rhys the Benevolent, he thought with a disgusted frown. He didn't even want to think about Kaplan's reaction. Probably pulling every string in the book to get himself assigned as trial judge. His belly spasmed at the thought.

"I'm not saying Ernie and Del and the others done right, you understand, but a lot of the media seemed impressed."

This time the words Rhys used came right off the loading dock. Even Max winced. "Doing others a good deed is something to be proud of," he said with total conviction, even though it might cost him his job.

"By the time the media get done with it, it'll sound like a smart con job, designed to take the attention away from my past," Rhys argued.

"I never thought of that," Max muttered, afraid the boss was right. "Guess they might think the same about the scholarship program for inmates' kids, too, huh?"

Nostrils flaring, Rhys leveled him with a look so hell born, Max actually took a step backward before he caught himself. "What other confidential information did my dear little sister give the sharks?"

"That's about it. It was Mrs. Sullivan who told 'em about you giving a job to two of the people who testified against you. She—"

"Sorry to interrupt, Mr. Hazard, but the chief wants to see you."

Max flicked Officer Keegan a look before saying, "I'll wait outside until you're done, boss."

Although Rhys did his best to keep up with Keegan's long strides, he couldn't quite manage. "My older brother nearly had his leg tore off by an artillery shell in Vietnam," Keegan said. "He walked with a cane, too—until it got so bad he ended up in a wheelchair. Killed himself a few years later. Left a note saying he'd rather be dead than live the rest of his life as a cripple."

Rhys shot him a look that had the young deputy's mouth snapping shut, and they walked in silence to the chief's office. Hollister was on the phone when he entered, and waved him to a chair. After a nod from the chief, Keegan took himself off.

"Yeah, I know you said twenty-four hours, but I got me a situation here, and I was hoping you could put a rush on it." He paused to listen, then nodded. "I appreciate it, thanks."

The satisfaction in his eyes as he hung up changed to speculation as he studied Rhys in silence. Then without saying a word, he swiveled around to fill a mug from the coffeepot.

"Thanks," Rhys said before taking a sip. "God, that's good," he muttered before he remembered he wasn't a guest, but a prisoner.

"This came in the mail," Hollister said, holding up a clear plastic sleeve containing a sheet of lined yellow paper. The top was sealed and had Hollister's initials scrawled in thick black letters across the seal. "It was addressed to me personally, so my assistant didn't open it. I had it dusted for prints and faxed the prints to the FBI. That was a tech I know in the lab, there on the phone just now. If the person who wrote this has ever applied for a government job, been in the service or been arrested, his—or her—prints will be on file."

"I take it there's a reason you're telling me this?"

"Might as well read it yourself."

Rhys took the sheet and held it at arm's length. He could tell the words were printed in what looked like block letters, but they were too blurry to make out. "I left my reading glasses in the cell," he admitted.

Hollister's mouth slanted. "Getting old's hell, isn't it?"

"Beats the alternative."

"Basically, it says that Sarge Stenner, Red Sturgess, and John Sullivan conspired to smuggle heroin from Canada across the border in one of your rigs. Heroin which the driver unknowingly delivered to a warehouse in Oakland."

Feeling as though he'd just been kicked in the balls, Rhys had trouble breathing. "That . . . miserable piece of shit," he enunciated slowly and distinctly. "I had a feeling that deal was wrong from the beginning."

"This letter could be a hoax," Hollister cautioned.

"But you don't think so," he guessed, watching Hollister's eyes.

"I don't think so. Too many details check out." He took reading glasses from his pocket and slipped them over his nose before picking up the letter again. "The informant states that the warehouse in Vancouver belonging to Pacific Rim Trading Post was to be torched after the dope was removed. A call to the local RCMP confirmed that in fact a fire occurred on that site two days after the shipment to Oakland. Ditto, the warehouse of Cascade Imports. Both fires were of suspicious origin."

Rhys' heart was pounding, and he had trouble regulating his breathing. "What happens next?"

"Hopefully the FBI gives us a name of our good citizen informant, and we talk him—or her—into testifying. From there, we take this to the DA." He glanced at Rhys over the glasses that had slid halfway down his nose. "I'm thinking it's a good bet your brother's the one who planted that kilo in your room at the inn. Brina admits he was on the premises the previous Sunday. She claims she heard him leave, but it's possible he only opened and closed the door to m-make those darn b-bells clang, then rushed upstairs." He narrowed his gaze. "Did you lock your door when you left?"

"No."

"So he had means, opportunity. Leaves us with motive."

"Money."

"For the smuggling, but why implicate you and risk implicating himself?"

Rhys took a slow breath. "His mother hated me and taught him well. He probably hates that I'm his boss."

"He's gonna hate it when the shit comes down on *him* this time instead of you."

Rhys nodded grimly. "I'll buy the department a new cruiser if you give me five minutes alone with him after his arrest."

"Damn, I wish I could, but that might compromise the case and—"

His phone rang, and he snatched it up. "Hollister."

He listened, his gaze flicking to the evidence envelope. Rhys' already racing heart speeded even more, and sweat pooled between his shoulder blades.

"Thanks, I owe you one," Hollister said before hanging up. His expression was both triumphant and grim. "God bless the FBI and modern science," he said as he slipped the evidence folder into his desk drawer and locked it. "It seems our informant is one Wayne Charles Makepeace."

"Call for you on line two, Mr. Sullivan."

John grinned at the note of adoration in his secretary's voice. Little more than a week after she'd started, he'd noticed she had a crush on him. Too bad he was shaking this burg. It might have been fun seeing what kind of tricks she had in bed. "Thanks, LuluBelle," he teased, and she giggled.

"My name's Luanne," she said before disconnecting.

Still grinning, he picked up the receiver and punched line two. "John Sullivan here."

"Hey, partner, how're they hangin'?" At the sound of Sarge's voice, John's blood ran cold.

"High and tight, how about you?"

"Can't complain." A cautious note crept into his voice. "Is this line safe?"

John nearly laughed in his face. God, what a gung ho *clown!* "Completely. My brother doesn't believe in invading the privacy of his employees."

"Seems like you invaded his privacy pretty good, planting that smack in his room."

John gave some thought to stonewalling, but he couldn't come up with a reason to deny it. "I thought the rabbit finding it was a nice touch."

Sarge chuckled. "Reason I called, me and Red got to talking and we figured that with Hazard cooling his heels behind bars, things might be a little loosey-goosey around there. Red thinks it would be safe to risk one more run. I wanted to get your take before I made the final decision."

John felt a jolt of excitement. "Hell, Sarge, you already know my take. I'm all for it."

"I figured as much, but with everything that's happened, I got to wondering if maybe you'd changed your mind."

"The DEA's still sniffing around, but they've been letting the runs go through. Might be a good idea to make one run across the border that's squeaky clean in case they want to do some 'interdicting,' as the head asshole calls it."

"Good idea," Sarge said with what sounded like genuine admiration in his voice. "I'll set it up for what—Thursday? Then if all goes well, we'll ship the smack the following week."

"Sounds like a plan, partner. I'll set things in motion here."

"Roger that," Sarge said. "By the way, some of the guys were wondering why you haven't been sitting in regular at the poker game. I'm thinking it might be a good idea if you sat in for a few hands now and then, just so no one gets suspicious."

Damn, he hadn't thought of that. "Truth is, I've been busy,

Sarge, but now that you mention it, I see your point. Maybe I'll stop by tonight for an hour or so after work. TGIF, you know?"

There was a brief silence. "How about coming later, then staying after closing so we can firm up some delivery dates. Save us both time that way."

John turned that over in his mind. It made sense. "I should be able to get away sometime after ten."

"Sounds like he went for it." Red took a final drag on his cigarette before leaning forward to stub it out in the tray on Sarge's desk.

"Like a bigmouth bass snapping at a worm." Sarge retrieved his cigar from the tray and took a puff, blowing the smoke upward.

Red dug another Marlboro from the pack in his shirt pocket and lit up with a Zippo.

"I been keeping track and Sullivan never drinks more'n two scotches while he's playing, so he won't even be close to drunk. I figure we'll all have a drink in here after closing, and while you distract him, I'll slip the knockout drops in his glass. Once he's out, I'll dump him in the Corvette and drive to the construction site on Highway 2 where they're still fixing the bridge. I checked it out this morning and there's a curve right before they got the bridge blocked off where a man who was driving drunk might easily skid off the road, if he was going too fast."

"Or get pushed," Sarge said with a grin.

"Good thing the 'Vette is fiberglass. Makes it easy to push." Red grinned. "Shatters real good, too."

"What about moonlight?" Sarge asked between puffs.

"Already checked. It's only a crescent this time of month." Red filled his lungs with smoke and felt the buzz in his head before exhaling. "I figure three a.m. might be a good time for Sullivan to die."

Chapter 29

John waited until lunchtime, when the loft was virtually deserted, before using his computer terminal to access the Pacific Rim file. Using his new cell phone, he punched in the telephone number listed in the file. Instead of reaching the company, he found himself listening to a familiar recording. Disconnected . . . no new number.

On the off chance the recording was a computer glitch, he called information for the number of the local police station. Pretending to be a salesman planning his itinerary, he asked if there was a reason why he couldn't get through to one of his potential customers.

Oh yeah, there was a reason, all right. *The frigging warehouse had burned to the ground.* Just like Sarge said it would, he thought as he leaped to his feet and paced to the window. The nagging suspicion that had led him to call in the first place exploded into full-blown terror. Sarge and Red were removing all the evidence against them. They were planning to kill him.

The last man who figured he could scam me took twelve hours to die. I made sure he was conscious the entire time.

John went jelly-legged, and his stomach threatened to empty. Somehow he made it back to his chair before he made a fool of himself. Now that he knew the score, he could finesse a way out. Sarge and Red were mean SOBs, but intelligencewise, they were no more than thickheaded goons. Brains and class would outwit muscle and gutter genes every time. Hadn't he proven that with Mick?

Calmer now, he pulled out a notepad and began jotting down the steps he needed to take to make good his escape without arousing suspicion. Money was the first on the list, and a grin broke across his face at the thought of all those lovely greenbacks in his attaché case. Next came a destination. Rio, he decided after running through a list of possibilities. Did Sherri have a passport? He would find some excuse to check it out tonight. If she didn't, he'd miss her, but not enough to risk his life staying in the States.

He would buy the tickets at the airport, even though he doubted Sarge would have the smarts to check out the local travel agencies. Before he made good his escape, he would need protection; one of the pistols from J. T.'s collection would do. The snub-nosed .38 would fit into the small of his back. Just like on frigging TV, he thought, grinning.

An hour later, his plan checked, revised and rechecked, he tore off the cheat sheet and tucked it into his wallet. Tomorrow was that silly graduation for his daughter, and Brina was giving a party afterward. After making sure everyone saw him there acting the loving daddy, he would slip out, drive back home, pick up the money and the bag he'd have already packed, along with his passport. Instead of leaving from Wenatchee, he'd drive to Seattle and catch a flight there. He would take the Lexus so that anyone who might be looking for him would see the 'Vette parked outside and figure he was upstairs taking a leak.

Of course, he wouldn't show up at Sarge's tonight. He'd call around nine, plead a family emergency and arrange the meeting for tomorrow night. By the time those two morons realized he was on to them, he'd be halfway to Brazil.

Feeling in control again, he sat back, stacked his hands behind his head and summoned up the delicious image of his asshole brother behind bars. His one regret was that he wouldn't be around to see the bastard reduced to the level of a sniveling, helpless animal.

Never call him Mick again? John snorted a laugh. Brains over muscle. Class over gutter genes.

God, revenge was fucking sweet.

"Family emergency, my butt hole," Red grated, drying the glass he'd just washed.

Seated in his favorite spot at the far end of the bar, Sarge took a furious drag on his cigarette and let the smoke dribble out through his nostrils. "Could be he's suspicious, although that seems remote. More like he really has a family thing tonight."

"Hey, Red, how about another round over here?" a biker from Moses Lake shouted over the din of a nearly packed house.

"Comin' right up, friend," the barkeep replied with a grin. "Frigging asshole thinks he shits gold bricks because he can buy his asshole buddies a few beers," he added in an undertone before heading down the bar to the taps.

It was a busy night and it was five minutes before Red could get back to Sarge's end of the bar. "Want I should just drive out to his place and take him out?"

Sarge took a sip of the fresh draft Red had brought him. "Might be the simplest plan all around." He took another sip. "Any chance you might have scoped out the terrain where he lives?"

"Does a bear shit in the woods?"

Sarge chuckled. "Might be best to make it look like robbery, the usual drill. House torn apart, electronic shit missing. Sullivan catches the guy in the act, gets blown away."

Red nodded. "Be tricky catching him alone, but it's doable. Damn but it feels good to be gearing up for action again."

Sarge lifted his glass. "Here's to you, buddy."

*   *   *

Rhys had just finished another tasteless lunch when Officer Keegan showed up with the keys to the cell.

"Afternoon, sir. Chief Hollister would like to see you in his office ASAP."

Surprised that Hollister would be working on Saturday, Rhys shoved back his chair and reached for his cane. "Did the chief say what he wanted?"

"No, sir, but I suspect it has something to do with the three suits who showed up about fifteen minutes ago."

"Any idea who those suits might be?"

"Not my place to say, Mr. Hazard." After stepping back, Keegan indicated that Rhys should lead the way.

Filled with foreboding, Rhys headed along the all-too-familiar corridor leading to the chief's glassed-in cubicle. Hollister sat behind his desk, his boots planted on the corner as usual, his hands steepled over his mouth as he listened to Mel Bailey. Also present was the assistant district attorney who had represented the state in his bail hearing. Reed thin, ADA Ryan McGinty had piercing green eyes, a prominent nose and close-cropped orange hair. The third man was lean, broad-shouldered and movie star handsome. His dark skin was tinged with bronze, suggesting Native American blood mixed in with his African heritage.

Hollister saw him first. "Afternoon, Mr. Hazard. Sorry to interrupt your lunch."

Conversation ceased, and all eyes turned his way. With so many bodies crammed into the room, it seemed to have shrunk. Panic shot adrenaline into his system, prodding him toward fight or flight. Since he was powerless to do either—at least for now—he covered his fear with a stony look.

"What's going on?" He directed his question to Hollister.

The chief grinned. "Seems you have some friends in high places who've let it be known they think you're being railroaded."

"There's no 'think' to it, Chief," Mel Bailey broke in.

"Makepeace's statement proves it." He shot a look at the African-American. "Isn't that right, Mr. Attorney General?"

"That's for the court to decide, Mr. Bailey." The man's tone was stern, but he smiled as he spoke.

Bailey caught Rhys' eye. "Meet Gabriel Jones, attorney general for the State of Washington."

Rhys and the other man exchanged nods. "Governor Luan sends his regards," Jones said, his expression impassive.

"Seems our esteemed governor received calls from both your father and Ms. Brina Sullivan, who, shall we say, waxed eloquent on your behalf," Bailey said. "He also found the recent press conference held at your new facility very, er, inspiring in terms of your character and your . . . reformation."

"As did His Honor, Judge Kaplan," McGinty added. "So much so that he issued an order releasing you on your own recognizance." His lips twitched. "I suspect the calls he received from the governors of both Washington *and* Arizona nudged him in that direction as well."

Rhys stared at him. "Governor Orozco called?"

The prosecutor nodded. "*He* received a call from Ms. Campbell-Browne, who reminded him in forceful terms of the revenue North Star contributes to the tax base. As well as the interest in Phoenix the North Star Tower has generated."

"Looks like I'm losing the pleasure of your company as of today," Hollister said with a smile.

Relief nearly sent Rhys to his knees. Or maybe it was surprise. Either way, he felt damned shaky.

"I've issued an arrest warrant for the three people mentioned in Mr. Makepeace's statement," McGinty continued. "To wit, Gunnar 'Sarge' Stenner, Philip 'Red' Sturgess, and John Sullivan."

Twenty minutes later, the three attorneys had departed, leaving Rhys alone with Brody Hollister. While the necessary paperwork to secure his release was being prepared, Rhys picked

up the phone to call Max, then changed his mind. Today was
Marcy's party and Max had volunteered to string up crepe
paper and blow up balloons. No doubt the celebration had already started.

He would call a taxi instead.

Suddenly a great weariness came over him. A week ago
he'd asked Brina to merge her life—and her future—with his.
Now he had no idea what his future held. Hell, for all he knew,
his board had voted him out as chairman.

"I sent Hingle with two other officers to Sarge's Place."
Hollister took a manila envelope from his desk and handed it
to Rhys. Inside was his wallet and other personal items.

"What about John?"

"He's mine." Hollister grinned. "Rank has its privileges."

"Are you sure he hasn't lit out?"

"I'm sure. Had a man watching his place since Makepeace's
letter arrived." The chief took his .45 from his bottom drawer
and clipped it to his belt.

"I figured I'd d-drop you at the inn, then head on out to
John's place." His grin took on a boyish cant. "I have a notion
to throw him in the same cell you just vacated. Poetic justice,
don't you think?"

Rhys tucked his wallet into his back pocket. "Have to
admit, Chief, before this moment I would have sworn there
was no such thing as justice on this planet. I'm beginning to
think I was wrong."

Hollister's expression turned serious. "You are *absolutely*
wrong, Rhys. The wheels grind slowly sometimes, but sooner
or later the bad guys get punished. And sometimes the good
guys get a much deserved second chance."

"Damn it, Lucille, Rhys should be here," J. T. growled in a
low tone as they stood near the gazebo, the laughter and conversation of the partygoers swirling around them.

"Shh, not so loud!" Lucy shot a quick glance toward the

grassy area where Brina was organizing a game of Pin the Tail on the Donkey. "Marcy is extremely upset because Rhys broke his promise to come to her party. Brina's done her best to explain why he isn't here, but the concept of bail is beyond a five-year-old."

J. T.'s gaze found his granddaughter. Although she was as bright as a daffodil in her new yellow dress, she stood apart from the other children, her expression solemn. Every now and then she cast a hopeful look toward the back door.

"By the saints, Lucy, Kaplan should be hung up by his—"

"Behave yourself, Sullivan!" Lucy punched him on the biceps, then, when her knuckles stung, wished she hadn't.

J. T. gave her an affronted look. "Suspenders, me darling. That's what I intended to say. The man should be hung up by his suspenders."

To hide the grin blossoming in her mind, she took a sip of the punch J. T. had spiked for the two of them. "I'm worried about Brina, J. T. On the one hand she really seemed to come into her own when she organized that press conference—"

"Did a bang-up job, she did. It's proud of her I am. As proud as if she were my own daughter."

Lucy nodded. "I agree, but . . . well, whenever anyone mentions Rhys' name, she changes the subject." She took another small sip. "She did the same thing when she was going through the divorce, remember?" She snorted. "Trust me, suffering in silence is a damn stupid way to live."

"Could be she's got her knickers in a twist because he's refusing to let her visit." He frowned. "Not that I blame the boy. A man has his pride, and having the woman he loves see him locked up is bound to dent it some."

Lucy's gaze sharpened. "You think he's in love with her?"

His blue eyes reflected surprise. "Have you gone daft, woman, or merely blind? The man's heart is in his eyes every time he looks at her."

"Then why—" She broke off suddenly as John and Sherri

approached. "Good Lord, J. T., if that skirt was any shorter, her butt would show," Lucy muttered, only to have J. T. choke on his drink.

"How's it going, Lucy?" John asked when he joined them, his party smile in place.

"You're sounding awfully cheery today," she replied after nodding to Sherri coolly.

Even J. T. had been livid when he'd seen John arrive with his fiancée in tow. For the sake of Brina and the children he'd kept his anger to himself, but Lucy knew the moment he and John were alone, his son would feel the father's wrath. Better late than never, she thought.

"Hey, my little girl just graduated from kindergarten," John said. "Why shouldn't I be in a good mood?"

Lucy just managed to keep from throwing her drink into his smug face. "For one thing your brother is in jail facing arraignment a week from Monday. One would think you would at least pretend to give a damn."

His grin disappeared while Sherri shot her a look of pure venom. "That's not fair, Lucy. John didn't have anything to do with that awful smuggling." She turned her practiced pout in his direction. "Tell her how upset you've been about this whole mess, honeybunch."

John shrugged. "What she said."

"Dad?" Jay stood a few feet away, a can of soda in his hand. "I finished the model of the depot. Wanna see?"

Lucy saw the refusal in John's eyes and couldn't stand it. "Of course, he would," she told the boy with a smile. "Wouldn't you, John?"

The inn's parking lot was full, so Hollister drove around to the rear. Rhys was surprised to see the 'Vette parked next to Lucy's rig.

"The g-g-good news is I won't have to drive all the way out to the orchard to arrest the SOB," Hollister said as he parked behind the Corvette, boxing it in. "The bad news is it's going to be tricky doing it without causing a scene." After killing the ignition, the chief keyed the radio and called for backup, ordering the female officer who responded to park in front of the inn, exit her vehicle and wait.

"Might be easier if you waited until he left the party and headed home," Rhys suggested.

"Maybe, but that would mean I'd have to hang around here until he left, and with all that's going down today that makes me real uneasy."

"John's an asshole, but he's also a coward. I doubt he'd have the balls to resist."

"You'd be surprised what people will do when they're trapped."

Rhys decided that was Hollister's worry, not his. Still, he couldn't help stiffening when he noticed Hollister unsnapping his holster in order to make his side arm easily accessible. "Brody, there are kids inside."

"You think I don't know that." Jaw tight, Hollister unlatched the gate and pushed it open. The scene that greeted them had both men swearing. The backyard party was in full swing.

"Plan B, we slip out and wait for him to return to his vehicle," Hollister said, but his decision came a second too late. Heads were already turning their way.

Standing with a group of women about her age, a plastic glass in hand, Brina went utterly still. In honor of the warm day, she wore a long flowing skirt splashed with pink and white flowers and a silky pink shirt. A floppy straw hat decorated with more pink flowers shaded her eyes. She looked adorable and sexy and brittle. Rhys' heart seemed to stop, then leap to a start again.

"Rhys!" After shoving her glass into the nearest pair of hands, she sprinted toward him. He just had time to shift his weight onto his good leg before she threw herself at him. She kissed him hard, then drew back to look up at him.

"You're *home!*" she exclaimed as a dozen conversations staggered to a stop.

"The judge changed his mind about bail." Conscious of the curious onlookers, Rhys kept his voice low.

"Nice party," Hollister said, glancing around the gaily decorated yard with a casual interest that Rhys knew was deceptive.

"You and Summer and the kids were invited," Brina said. "Summer promised to stop by later."

"Maybe I'll hang out here and wait for her." He shifted his gaze toward the house. "Is John around? There's something I wanted to ask him."

"Last I saw him he was upstairs with Jay looking at his science fair entry." Brina glanced around. "I don't see Marcy either. She probably went upstairs with her dad."

"Rhys, you're back!" The cry was Della's. She had just emerged from the back door with a bag of chips in her hand. Grinning, she rushed forward to give him a bear hug. She cried and laughed and generally made a fuss that had his face heating.

The dam broke then and he was suddenly surrounded by well-wishers, everyone talking at once, all wanting to know what had happened. When they heard the judge had changed his mind about bail, Rhys was subjected to a flurry of encouraging comments and congratulations.

J. T. slapped his back so hard he nearly ended up plowing up turf with his nose. Lucy hugged him so tightly his ribs nearly cracked. Del and Ernestine left lipstick kisses on his cheek. Max handed him a handkerchief to wipe them away.

"Judge finally see the error of his ways?" he asked in a low voice.

"Something like that," Rhys told him as he returned his

handkerchief. Max knew about the anonymous letter, but not who'd written it.

Deciding he'd taken all the good wishes he could handle, Rhys managed to excuse himself by pleading the need to make some phone calls. As he headed toward the back door, Hollister fell in step beside him.

The big house was quiet. "Which room is Jay's?" Brody asked when they reached the foyer.

"Third floor, first door on the right. You'll likely hear music."

Hollister nodded, but instead of heading up the stairs, he walked to the front door and looked out. The police cruiser was double-parked. A tall, lanky officer leaned against the front fender, her arms crossed, her face shaded by the brim of her cap.

Using the walkie-talkie clipped to his belt, Hollister ordered her to stop any male who exited through the front—and to use extreme caution. Knowing John, Rhys figured that was overkill, but he also knew how he would feel if someone tried to tell him how to run his business, so he kept his mouth shut.

Gritting his teeth against the pain he knew to expect after two weeks of little or no exercise, Rhys grabbed the railing and started the long climb. He'd only made it to the second step, however, when he heard voices from above. Seconds later John appeared on the landing where the stairs made a ninety-degree turn. Marcy was with him, but not Jay.

Marcy saw her uncle first and shot him a blazing smile. "Uncle Rhys, I knew you would come!" she shouted, racing down the steps to hurl herself into his arms. It took all his agility to catch her and keep his balance. As it was, he dropped his cane. As Hollister reached to retrieve it, Rhys noticed he didn't take his eyes off John.

"Hey, big brother, you got sprung!" John said, his grin almost real. Instead of continuing, he stopped a few risers down from the landing. Unlike the other guests, who were all dressed casually, he wore a tan blazer over dress slacks and a polo shirt.

After giving Marcy an extra squeeze, Rhys set her down carefully and took his cane back from Hollister, who gave him a warning look.

"See, Mommy, I told you Uncle Rhys wouldn't forget!" Marcy called as Brina walked into the foyer and looked up.

"You were absolutely right, sweetie," she said, smiling Rhys' way.

"Too bad about the 'Vette," Hollister said so convincingly that for a split second Rhys wondered if he'd missed spotting something as he'd exited the police cruiser. "Whoever hit you must have been going at a darn fast clip to do that amount of damage."

John shot the chief a startled look. "What are you talking about?"

"I can show you b-better than I c-can explain."

"Shit, I knew I shouldn't have parked in the alley!" Red-faced and fuming, John started down the steps. At the same time the front door opened to admit a pregnant mom and two little golden-haired girls, obviously twins. As soon as they caught sight of the chief, their faces lit.

"Hi, Daddy," the twins chorused.

"We saw one of your off'cers outside!" one declared.

"Only she said not to tell nobody she was there, 'cause it was a secret," the other added.

The twins' mother shot Hollister an apologetic look. "Girls, don't bother Daddy—"

"What kind of a scam are you running, Hollister?" John demanded.

Hollister stepped closer. "Why don't we step outside—"

"Why?"

The chief cast a pointed look at Marcy. "Trust me, John, you don't want to do this here."

"Fuck that!" John shouted, whipping a pistol from the small of his back and pulling Marcy to him.

"Daddy?" Marcy's voice quavered.

"Don't even think about it," John said as Brody's hand closed over the butt of his side arm. "Hands away from the weapon, or the kid dies."

Hollister immediately lifted both hands where John could see them, but the look in his eyes said that sooner or later John was going down. Rhys agreed. If Hollister didn't get the bastard, he would.

"Johnny, for heaven's sakes, what are you doing?" Brina cried.

She took several quick steps forward before John barked, "Stay where you are, Brina. All of you. First one so much as twitches, and I pull the trigger."

Although John's gaze was riveted on Hollister, the pistol was pointed at his own five-year-old daughter. Rhys had always known that he could hate, but deep in his soul, he'd doubted he could deliberately kill another human being. Now he knew he was wrong.

"Marcy, remember when I promised we'd go to Disneyland?" John said, descending slowly with her, one riser at a time. "Well, that's your graduation surprise. Only we have to go right away or we'll miss our plane."

Marcy looked up at him, her eyes full of confusion. "What about Jay?"

"He can't go this time, only you and me. Remember how it used to be, Daddy and his best girl?" John descended one more step.

Even as Rhys sensed Hollister's frustration and Brina's fear, he moved slightly, drawing John's quick glare. "Don't even think about it, bro," John warned, pausing in his descent. "Nothing I'd like better than to kill you where you stand."

Rhys held up one hand, palm out. "Hey, I'm no martyr, Junior."

"Just in case, why don't you let go of the cane?"

Rhys complied, only to sway unsteadily without the support. As he hoped, John's attention snapped his way. Praying Hollister was as quick-witted as Rhys thought he was, Rhys suddenly lunged, putting his body between John and the child. At the same time he sensed Hollister bracing himself.

"Run to Mommy, Marcy!" Rhys shouted an instant before hitting John's midsection with what had to be the clumsiest tackle in history. The two of them crashed backward. As he hit, he heard the blast of gunfire, felt a hot poker stab into his side, caught a glimpse of Jay on the step above him. Well, hell. Damn if he hadn't screwed up again, he thought as blackness crowded in. No, he couldn't die yet! He had to tell Brina . . . The blackness took him before he could complete the thought.

Static crackled from the eerily silent two-way radio as the souped-up police cruiser took the turn onto Old Orchard Road on two wheels. No doubt the cops had switched to walkie-talkies to communicate with one another, John thought, checking the mirror again. So far there'd been no sign of pursuit.

Even though he'd handcuffed Hollister and the lady cop to the banister, he knew it was only a matter of time before every cop in the area was after him. Keeping the gun all but embedded in Jay's back had kept the lady cop from shooting him when she'd come charging through the front door. Maybe he should have kept his wimp of a son with him as an insurance policy, he thought as he checked the mirror again, but the kid had turned stubborn all of a sudden, digging in his heels and calling him names. He'd come within a hair of smashing the little shit in the mouth with his gun butt. Would have served the kid right if he had. Brina, too. As for Mick, he hoped to hell the bastard was dead. True, he'd been a tad busy getting the hell out of there, but he'd seen enough to know the odds that his so-called brother would survive were slim to none.

He slowed for the turn into the lane, fishtailing wildly before the all-terrain tires found purchase. Gravel flew as he rocketed up the twisting track. Thank God he had planned for every contingency. Once he retrieved the money and the other things he'd readied, he would switch to the Lexus. Instead of heading to Seattle the way everyone would expect, he would go to Spokane and take a flight from there. He would have to change vehicles, of course, he realized as he braked to a stop near the back door of J. T.'s house.

His dad never bothered to lock the doors. Leaving the back one ajar, John hurried through the kitchen and dining room. He was jogging down the hall toward the stairs when he heard a stealthy footfall on the thick carpeting. He spun around, his hand fumbling for the .38 in his pocket.

His breath hissed out at the sight of Red standing in the middle of the hall, a sawed-off shotgun cradled in huge gloved hands. The last thing he heard was the all too familiar sound of a shell being racked. He didn't even have time to plead for mercy before his life ended.

The paramedics took Rhys to Osuma Community Hospital, where he went into surgery a few minutes before five o'clock. Word had spread through the valley. Someone had called the media, who, with microphones, cameras and minicams ready, milled restlessly around the corridor outside the double doors leading to the operating rooms. Brina considered them ghouls and glared at any one of them who crossed her path.

It was close to ten p.m. now and Rhys was still in the OR. The small waiting room in the surgical wing was filled nearly to capacity. At nine the blood bank had put out a call for more blood. Ironically, it had turned out that Rhys and J. T. had the same type, A-positive. J. T. had already given one pint and was willing to give more.

"Not a chance," Lucy told him.

J. T. glowered at her. His eyes were bloodshot, his face sallow.

Like hers, Brina suspected, leaning her head against the wall behind her chair and closing her eyes. The events of the last six hours were surreal.

After Rhys had been shot and John had leaped to his feet, his silk jacket covered with Rhys' blood, all hell had broken loose. To her shock, John had grabbed Jay by the scruff of the neck and dragged him toward the door, his pistol shoved in the terrified boy's back, effectively keeping everyone at bay.

Although details were hazed over by her frantic fears for Jay's safety and Rhys' survival, she remembered seeing Max and Emory laying Rhys on the checkerboard floor in order to perform CPR while someone else called 911 on a cell phone. While Rhys' blood spread over the black-and-white tile in a widening pool, Angela Morrison's nurse-practitioner mother fought to keep him from bleeding to death.

"Tastes lousy, but it's hot and black." Max stood in front of Brina, a Styrofoam cup in his hand. Ernestine stood at his elbow, her patrician features overlaid with concern.

"Thanks." Brina took a tiny sip.

"Summer called to tell you Marcy's asleep," Ernie said. "She was afraid you'd be worried."

"Thank God for Summer," she murmured, her voice catching. "If anyone knows how to help Marcy—and Jay, too—get over this, it's Summer."

"They'll both be fine," Max said. "Have their mom's moxie."

Somehow, she found a smile.

J. T. stood suddenly, his face ravaged. "I need some fresh air," he muttered as he strode toward the door. Lucy rose and followed him. As soon as they left the room, the media began barking for their attention.

"Poor J. T.," Ernestine murmured. "It must be horrendously painful to lose John in such a horrible fashion."

"He deserved it," Max ground out.

"Max," Ernie chided.

"Sorry, Brina," Max muttered. "Forgot Sullivan was your ex."

"After what he did, I have nothing but contempt for him."

"Surely they'll clear Rhys now." Della spoke up from the sofa, where she sat with Elena and Emory. The rest of Brina's Nightingale House family was there as well. Colonel Fitz seemed to have an endless supply of medicinal bourbon, which he poured liberally upon request.

"I just wish I knew what was taking so long," Brina cried, holding the half-empty cup of coffee against her breasts. She wore hospital scrubs, supplied by a sympathetic nurse after she'd arrived with the ambulance, her clothes covered with Rhys' blood. According to the ER doctor who'd talked with her and J. T. after Rhys had gone to surgery, he had very nearly bled out.

"The bullet did a lot of damage, dear," Miss Dottie soothed. "Then, too, there's his allergy to anesthetic to consider. Gray said they were going to try a brand-new epidural if he showed signs of regaining consciousness on the table, but—"

A sudden flurry in the corridor drew Brina's attention. A chorus of voices called Dr. Krebs' name, and minicam lights switched on. Brina sat up, her heart slamming. Gray Krebs appeared then, flanked by two burly hospital security guards. Still in scrubs, he cast a swift look around until his gaze locked on Brina's. "He's in recovery," he said in a tired but reassuring tone. "Once the staff has him settled and stabilized, you can look in on him."

Then, only then, did Brina start to sob.

He filled the hospital bed, all six feet four inches of him. He wore a hospital gown, and a pale yellow thermal blanket had been pulled to midchest. His arms were atop the covers, his big hands curled loosely. Even asleep, hooked up to electronic monitors and connected by plastic tubes to an IV and oxygen, he dominated the recovery room. A lanky nurse smiled as Brina tiptoed closer.

"Can I touch him?" Brina asked, her gaze riveted on the features she loved.

"Yes, but I doubt he'll feel it. Because of the problem with the anesthesia, they sedated him heavily and he's still sleepy." She adjusted one of the monitors. "I'll be at the desk for a few minutes if you need me." She indicated a workstation tucked into a corner of the room before stepping away.

Heart in her throat, Brina fumbled with the bed's railing until it slid down. Then stepping closer, she took his hand and kissed the scarred knuckles. He didn't react. The only sign that he was still alive was the rising and falling of his chest.

"While I was waiting for Gray Krebs to . . . to sew everything back in place, I must have run through a hundred speeches in my head. About how brave you were and how I can never thank you enough and how . . ." Her voice faltered.

"Brina?" His voice was faint and scratchy. Her gaze flew to his face, and her heart thudded. Although he lay unmoving, his eyes were open, dark as charcoal between golden lashes. His face was frighteningly pale, and yet there was a fierce strength etched into every line and carved plane.

"Welcome back. I missed you."

"You . . . okay?" It was clearly an effort for him to talk, but it seemed necessary.

"I'm fine." She felt his fingers twitch, and she tightened hers. She couldn't let him go.

"Marcy? Jay?"

"Shaken, but they're coping. They're staying with the Hollisters. Summer is helping them through this."

"John?" The single word was a mere thread of sound.

"He's dead, Rhys. After he shot you, he escaped in a police cruiser. He went home for some reason and surprised a man named Sturgess who was part of the smuggling scheme.

Sturgess shot John dead. One of Brody's men arrived in time to grab Sturgess as he was running from the house."

Rhys closed his eyes. Pain flickered across his face, settling in the knot between his sun-bleached eyebrows. "How's . . . Pop holding . . . up?"

"Other than wearing a groove in the floor of the waiting room outside with his pacing, he's doing okay." Leaning closer, she ever so carefully brushed his hair back from his forehead. "From now on you'll never be able to say you don't share the same blood." She smiled. "He gave at least a pint and would have established a direct line from his arm to yours if the doctors had allowed it."

His lashes flickered. "Doesn't matter. Love the stubborn SOB."

"Oh, Rhys."

His hand tightened around hers, surprising her with his strength. "Love *you,* too, wildcat."

Surprise shot through her, followed by a blinding joy and then, when memories crashed, a self-protective wariness. "You . . . do?" Her voice was little more than a whisper.

"Yeah." He wet his lips and cleared his throat. "Too . . . much, maybe. Turn me into a real . . . pussycat."

She choked out a laugh. "That's not possible."

He tugged her closer. "Marry me?"

The depth of longing in his eyes stunned her, but there was uncertainty there, too. It was, she realized, a negotiator's dream. She hid the giddy smile that wanted to break free behind a frown. "I might be willing to do that under certain conditions," she tossed out with just the right amount of reticence.

His mouth quirked. "Such as?"

She pretended to ponder. "A proper courtship when you're well enough."

"Define . . . proper."

"It might be nice to go on an actual date before the wedding."

"That's . . . doable." His eyes had lost their brooding darkness. "Next."

"A small, but perfect wedding in the parlor with something borrowed, something blue—and Marcy and Jay standing up with us."

"Agreed."

"Uh-uh, Hazard, not quite yet. There's an option clause." She felt her heart leap to her throat. "I'll want babies. Two preferably, but I'll settle for one."

He sucked in a harsh breath. His lashes flickered, then squeezed shut. When he opened them again, she saw love looking up at her beneath a shimmer of tears. "You drive a hard bargain, wildcat."

"Is it a deal?" she asked, her voice thick

"Ironclad with no escape clauses." His mouth relaxed into a peaceful smile as he drifted off to sleep.

Epilogue

"Bow ties are really dumb," Jay muttered, glaring at the ceiling while Del worked her magic beneath his chin.

"Stop fidgeting, sugar, and let Auntie Della make you gorgeous like your uncle Rhys."

Jay rolled his eyes in Rhys' direction. "Is she always this bossy?"

"As long as I've known her."

"Someone has to keep you men from returning to cavemen status," Della declared, unfazed. Her ankle-length bridesmaid dress was the color of moss. It had a high neck and long sleeves, nothing to arouse Rhys' protective instincts—until she turned around and flashed him what looked like an acre of bare back.

"How much longer?" Jay demanded, shifting from one foot to another. Rhys understood his impatience.

"All done." Grinning, Della gave the silk tie one last tweak before stepping back. "A perfect job, if I do say so myself."

Jay lowered his chin and made a beeline to the mirror over the dresser. "I look like a dweeb," he declared with disgust. "Everyone's going to laugh."

"You both look like gentlemen," Del said, flipping back her hair. "Brina is going to melt when she sees you."

Rhys went clammy inside. "I don't know why she changed her mind about a small wedding," he muttered, glaring at his watch. According to the timetable laid down by the Successful Innkeeper turned Wedding Planner, the groom and his best man—Jay—were due to leave for the church in exactly twenty-seven minutes.

"It was either change her mind or disappoint a whole passel of folks who wanted to show how much they cared about the two of you, brother dear."

Uncomfortable with his new status as local hero, Rhys shot her a frown. "So let 'em send a card," he muttered. "Max and Ernie had the right idea, eloping to Vegas." He glanced at his watch again. Twenty-four minutes. "Damn, I can't do this." He went to the door and jerked it open, ignoring Del's cry of alarm.

"Where are you going?" she demanded, following him.

"Upstairs to have a talk with the Wedding Planner," he said without breaking stride.

"Don't you dare. It's bad luck!" Del cried after him, her voice shrill with panic.

Ignoring her, he crossed the landing to the stairs leading to the third floor. Thanks to Gray Krebs—who, after discovering that he could tolerate the epidural, had agreed to perform hip replacement surgery—he could climb stairs without pain. Although he would never walk with complete ease and would always need a cane for balance, he had far more mobility now. He could even drive, although Max had made it clear he did not intend to retire.

On the third floor women in party finery were everywhere, laughing and chattering like a flock of bright birds. Marcy spotted him first and came skipping over, a pixie in a pale yellow dress and a lacy hat.

"Mommy's got hives," she said, reaching up to take his hand. She did that a lot, reached for a hand or folded herself into his arms for a hug, needing reassurance that she was loved. He knew the feeling, only Brina was the one he went to when he needed a hug.

"She does?"

"Uh-huh. She's itching something awful."

"Rhys Hazard, you turn your handsome self right around and scoot downstairs this instant," Lucy ordered, advancing on him like a militant angel in green-and-gold finery.

"Back off, Mama. I'm bigger than you."

She frowned, but he could see that she was touched. He'd started calling her that about five seconds after she and his dad were married last month. He'd said it to tease, but it had brought a lump to his throat and tears to her eyes. Pop's, too.

"Behave yourself, or I'll call your father," she threatened.

"What's going on—" Brina broke off at the sight of her soon-to-be husband going toe-to-toe with her soon-to-be mother-in-law. "Rhys, you shouldn't be here. It's bad luck."

His jaw flexed, then went granite hard. Over the past six months since his release from the hospital, Brina had come to recognize that as a bad sign. He'd gotten that same look right before he'd taken on his board of directors. After the dust had settled, he'd been firmly in control of his company, and a man named Sam Phillips had resigned. After the publicity surrounding his heroic save of Marcy's life—including the facts concerning his arrest and subsequent release—his stock had climbed to new highs and stayed there.

"We need to talk," he said when he reached Brina. "Privately."

A premonition shivered down her spine. *The Successful Wedding Planner keeps her cool, even in the face of pending calamity.*

"Marcy, why don't you and Lucy and the other ladies wait for me downstairs?"

"But, Mommy, Miss Dottie hasn't fixed your hair."

"Not to worry, dear heart," Dottie rallied with a jangle of bracelets. "Mommy and Uncle Rhys need some private time."

"Just for a few minutes, okay?" Marcy looked up at Rhys, who nodded. She didn't like it, but anything Uncle Rhys asked, she would do. "Okay, only Miss Dottie's gonna keep time, right, Miss Dottie?"

"Absolutely." Dottie made a big show of consulting her watch before leading Marcy toward the stairs. Lucy and the others followed.

"Inside," he said, jerking his head toward Brina's room.

She stepped back, careful not to tromp on her demitrain.

"Close the door," he ordered.

"That bad?" she muttered, but she did as he asked. "Okay, I'm ready," she said, bracing herself.

Instead of talking, he went to the dormer window and looked out. She folded her hands and let herself admire the long, lean length of him. He looked stunningly gorgeous in a tux, she thought. Almost as gorgeous as he looked without it.

"There are pom-poms attached to my Mercedes, for crissakes," he muttered. "*Pink* pom-poms."

"Is that why you came stomping upstairs like a bull? To tell me there are pom-poms on your car?"

"Hell, yes . . . no." He flexed his shoulders before setting them into a rigid line. "It didn't seem like such a big thing when we made this deal. Getting married, I mean. I figured you and me and the kids. Max and Del, Pop and Lucy, and Hank, but this . . . this circus thing." He stopped, drew a breath. "I feel like I'm on display."

Careful to keep from crushing the pale ivory satin, Brina lifted her skirt and went to him. "Rhys, if you're having second thoughts about marrying me—"

"Christ, no!" he declared, turning to face her. "You were mine the first time we made love. The ceremony just makes it legal."

Brina dropped her skirt in order to curl her hand over his rigid arm. "Then what's this really about?"

His jaw flexed, and his brows slammed together. "I figured I could handle making a fool of myself in front of people I knew, people I cared about, but I'll be damned if I make a fool of myself in front of the whole damned valley!"

Careful, she told herself. "I'm not exactly following you. How—exactly—would you make a fool of yourself?"

His eyes turned flinty, and a muscle ticked along his jawline. "Saying the words, standing there with you and the kids . . ." He jerked a shoulder. "Just thinking about it gets me worked up. Doing it . . . damn it, Brin, no way in *hell* am I going to get through that without bawling!"

A combination of relief and tenderness threatened to turn her knees to jelly. "Oh, Rhys, I do love you so!"

"Yeah, now, but how will you feel about me when I'm crying my eyes out in front of an audience?"

"Proud that you're mine," she murmured, arching up to kiss his jaw. He went rigid but didn't pull away. "Grateful you love me as much as I love you." This time she kissed his chin—and accidentally brushed his arm with her breasts. He jerked, but his gaze remained stony. "Deliriously happy." Going for a full-out assault, she flung her arms around his neck, pressed her breasts against that bulwark chest and kissed him hard on the mouth.

His arms came around her, steely bands holding her close. His body shuddered. "God, I love you, Brina Eiler. More than I'll ever be able to tell you. It scares me to think I might screw this up."

The light dawned then. He equated love with performance. Do well and you received love. Make a mistake and you're shunned. Or worse. And since everyone makes mistakes . . .

She drew back far enough to look up into gray eyes that were suddenly bleak with bad memories. "Oh no you don't, Hazard, you're not going to weasel out on this deal now."

He frowned. "What?"

"Ironclad, remember? No escape clauses." Her fingers ruffled his hair, which for once had been tamed into submission. "I intend to hold you to it, no matter what."

A look of caution crept into his stormy eyes. "I'm bound to piss you off. Even Del's been known to throw things at me—and nothing ruffles her."

"If I get annoyed—"

"I don't *annoy* people, Brin. I flat out piss them off. I think it's a mutant gene or something."

He sounded so disgruntled she nearly burst out laughing. "Okay, if I get *pissed* off, I'll just have to find a way to deal with it."

He didn't look convinced. "I can be thoughtless and selfish and a damned poor sport."

"I appreciate the advance warning, but none of those are deal breakers."

He was beginning to look a bit desperate. "I snore."

"And hog the covers, don't forget that." But he no longer had nightmares, and sometimes he even woke up with a smile on his face.

"Yeah, see what I mean? I'm a lousy risk."

His enormous need for reassurance both stunned and touched her. "Mmm, you could be right at that." She stepped back and eyed him sternly. "Do you cheat on your income tax?"

"Personal or corporate?" His tone was both wary and amused.

"Both."

"No."

She managed a straight face. "Will you cheat on me?"

His eyes flashed molten silver. "Never!"

"Lie to me?"

"No."

"Neglect our children? Walk out if I get sick or crippled or old and wrinkled?"

His face flushed. "Damn it, Brin, you know I won't."

It was the perfect opening and she pounced gleefully. "I won't do any of those things either, so I now pronounce us man and wife." She grinned. "You can bawl now."

His blank stare suddenly warmed, then turned tender. "Damn, but the next forty years are going to be interesting," he said in a thick voice. Right before he kissed his bride.